GAME OF LIARS

T J Hext

It was early. Far too early to be out and about, really. But Kieran had learnt to take the initiative on days like this. He'd never once convinced his dad he was too ill to go to school, even when he was coughing his guts up for real.

The fact was, he couldn't go to school today. Literally couldn't. If he did, his English teacher would demand the coursework that was already weeks overdue, and would remind him that several notes had already been sent home (each of which Kieran had intercepted). Worse, his form tutor would ask for proof that his two absences last week really were because his grandad had died, despite the fact that Kieran had already used that same excuse about five months ago, and anyway his grandad would still pick him up from after-school football practice on Tuesdays. To top it all off, Stu and his mates would be waiting for him at the school gates to collect the PlayStation 5 Kieran had said he'd give in exchange for not being smacked around the head each time they caught up with him. Kieran had never so much as played a PS5.

The lies were becoming too complex to track.

So here he was, wandering the headland at 6.30 in the morning, eating a Snickers even though his stomach was crying out for a proper breakfast.

Idly, he slunk past the static caravans of the holiday park. Every so often he rose onto his tiptoes to look inside one of them. Most were empty, as the season hadn't really begun yet. There probably wouldn't be any valuables, even in the caravans that were privately owned, but you never knew. Kieran fantasised about unlocked doors, videogame consoles, fridges full of Egg McMuffins.

He'd never resorted to actual theft. But maybe he was just putting off the inevitable.

Still, his feet took him past the row of caravans without him so much as trying a door handle. They took him down the hill and towards the cove and its little beach. That was where the best air was, and at this time in the morning it'd sting your lungs. His dad said that when the wind blew it went in one of Kieran's ears and out the other, and it was meant as a diss, but Kieran liked the idea. He liked imagining the wind would clear away all the crap as it passed through.

He squinted at something on the beach below him. A small boat was docking at the pier to one side of the cove. That wasn't unusual in itself, except it was rammed with people, all pushing and shoving.

The thought occurred to Kieran that his dad would be dead happy to have proof that immigrants really were washing up on the Northumbrian shore, just like he'd claimed would happen. But Kieran's phone was an ancient hand-me-down that could barely make calls, let alone take pictures.

So he crouched in the long grass and watched.

A group of about half a dozen people jostled with each other before streaming off the boat. Now Kieran could see they weren't immigrants but tourists, some wearing posh clothes. They could only have come from Red Cliffs Island. The mansion on the island a few miles offshore was occasionally hired out for events. These people were a strange-looking bunch, though, and they didn't give the impression they'd had a good time. The body language of one of the women made Kieran think she was crying. A couple seemed to be arguing as they left the pier and struggled to pull their wheelie suitcases across the sand to the boardwalk that led to the road.

Without warning, someone at the back of the group fell face-first into the sand. They rose again with difficulty, but then seemed to be struggling to walk: one side of their body was jerky and stiff, and it looked like they couldn't put much weight on their left leg. Kieran couldn't make out their face because a hood was pulled up over their head. After a few seconds, one of the others noticed and hurried back to help, then they supported the injured person, guiding them to and then along the boardwalk. The slope made the limp of the person in the hoodie even worse, and they kept having to rest.

There were still four people in the boat. When they stepped onto the pier, they did it carefully because they were carrying something between them. It must have been heavy, to need four of them, and it looked lumpy, and it was covered with a black tarpaulin.

Kieran gasped as something dropped out from beneath the black sheet to swing loosely. A hand, an arm. It kept swaying as the group hefted their load towards the path.

What the actual fuck?

There was a dead body under that tarpaulin. Kieran had always wanted to see a dead body.

Carefully, still crouching, he made his way down the slope. The sun was in his eyes, making the members of the little group just silhouettes. All he could tell was that two of them were tall and slim, two of them shorter.

Despite their load, they were making good progress. They'd already reached the wooden boardwalk. Between gusts of wind, Kieran strained his ears, but they weren't saying a word to each other.

He didn't dare follow the group too closely. If they spotted him, he'd end up getting involved, and the last thing he needed today was speaking to the police. So it was only when they were cresting the hill that he hurried in their wake. As he did so, he saw something drop from beneath the tarpaulin. It shone brightly, reflecting the sunlight.

None of the four noticed.

Whatever the object was, it was now gleaming between the slats of the boardwalk. Kieran knelt to prise it out, then cursed at himself because that meant his fingerprints were on its handle.

All the same, he whistled with pleasure at his find.

These things were illegal, weren't they?

He pulled at the arms, activating the mechanism, then gasped as the blade of the butterfly knife extended with a click.

Nobody would believe he'd seen a dead body. That he'd seen the corpse of somebody who'd been knifed and killed.

But this butterfly knife was real, and now it belonged to him. He could only imagine how impressed Stu's mates would be at seeing a weapon like this. It could boost his reputation.

Once he'd cleaned the dried blood from its blade, that was.

DAY 1

Four days earlier

Aura

When the island finally looms out of the mist, a communal "Ooh" comes from behind me, and to my surprise it sounds *real*. I turn around to look at the other contestants, wondering whether it's an act or whether they're really that easy to please. It's impossible to tell. They all look exactly the same, all wearing the same ugly yellow ponchos as me, all staring up at the island. Their faces are slick with rain. If they keep their mouths open like that, I swear they'll fill with water.

All six of us did our best not to appear horrified when we boarded, only to be told there's no downstairs area of the boat to shelter from the storm. The boat's driver (or is it captain? pilot?) said it was only a fifteen-minute journey to Red Cliffs Island, but fifteen minutes is a long time in lashing rain like this, plus there's the spray from the sea that shoots up with each lurch the boat makes. Most of the contestants have opted to stay close to the centre of the deck, where they're partially shielded from the rain by the cabin containing the wheel and controls. Me, I hoped that standing at the prow and watching the waves would help lessen the seasickness. Before today, the closest I've been to being at sea was aboard a pedalo in the park pond. But you know what? I feel fine. Chalk up one victory to Aura.

I consider joining the others, but I don't want to push my luck. Perhaps seasickness hits you quickly. The last thing I want to do is introduce myself by puking on someone's shoes.

So I stay at the prow, watching the growing red rocks of the island above a strip of flat shore, hoping I appear soulful rather than sulky. I pull the hood of my poncho further forward to protect my hair. It's going to need some serious attention once we arrive.

A thought occurs to me. They wouldn't dare set cameras rolling the moment we set foot on the island, would they?

I turn in response to a quiet little cough behind me. It's one of the other contestants, a mousy girl with mousy hair.

"I just *love* your look," she says, pointing at my purple highlights, which are all but hidden beneath the hood of my poncho. I try to hide my pleasure. These highlights cost more than the rest of my outfit put together.

"Yours too," I say. I don't elaborate. There's nothing about her appearance that I can conjure up a comment about. She's just *normal*.

"I'm Ruth," she says.

"Aura."

"Wow. Really?"

"Yes, really." I eye her suspiciously, but I see she's impressed rather than questioning my name.

It does have a nice ring to it, doesn't it? *Aura.* I'm still getting used to it myself.

"Are you nervous?" Ruth asks.

A bit too quickly, I say, "No. Why?"

She shrugs. "I'm nervous. Like, *really* nervous. What if everyone hates me? What if I make a tit of myself?"

"I guess those are possibilities we all face every day."

Ruth considers this for several seconds. "I'd never thought of it like that," she says. "My mum told me to imagine she's standing next to me, like *all the time.* So if I'm about to do something stupid, I'll think, *Oh, Mum's watching*, and then maybe I won't do it. Because she will

7

be watching, won't she? When this is on TV."

I nod, even though the idea of my mother witnessing my behaviour on a TV screen doesn't bear thinking about. I'm aware just how daft that is, how much doublethink is required. But I've come here to present myself to the entire world, not my mother. The last thing I need is to imagine her standing next to me, arms folded, lips quirked in that way they do before she delivers one of her classic put-downs.

The boat rocks violently, and I grab the rail with both hands, leaning over it. Spray shoots up before me, forcing me to pull away again and almost giving me whiplash.

"You all right?" Ruth asks.

I mutter something indistinct. My stomach's definitely getting more sensitive. Get a grip, Aura.

"There!" a deep voice says, coming from the huddle of contestants. I turn around. The guy who spoke is large but kind of pretty and clean-looking. What did he say his name was, back on the pier? Victor – that's it. "Home sweet *home*, brothers and sisters!" he says, spreading his arms wide like an old-time American preacher.

In my phone conversation with her, the director of the game show said it was in our interests to go *big*, to exaggerate our responses to everything. Victor's definitely doing that. I'll need to match him at least. Once I'm out of this rain and off this boat, that is.

I look where Victor's pointing. Sure enough, now there's a building visible, perched on a hill that rises directly from the red cliffs of the island.

"Ooh!" Ruth says beside me.

Grudgingly, I manage an "Ooh" of my own. It makes sense to go with the herd at this stage.

I *suppose* the building is a mansion, like I was told. It's large, sure. But the proportions seem wrong. Its tiny windows are like piggy little eyes in the large, black facade. Above the first-floor windows, the tall triangles of the roof eaves are like arched eyebrows. I swear the building is *leering* at me.

At the very least, it's more like a caricature of a haunted house than a swanky retreat. I shudder and pull my hood forward again.

As the boat chugs closer, it becomes clear that there's *literally* nothing on the island other than the house and a couple of outbuildings that look like they've seen better days.

"Hey," I say, nudging Ruth. "This isn't a survival show, is it?"

"What do you mean?" she asks.

I gesture up at the dark building. "It looks pretty bleak. Reckon it's even got electricity? Heating?"

Ruth shudders. "Hope so. I'm not very good at roughing it. I went camping one time and my boyfriend had this van? So I made him bring my favourite chair because it fit. In the van."

"Mm. Great story." It's already obvious I'm not going to get much sense out of her.

I remind myself of the mistake I made at school. *One* of the mistakes, that is, and far from the biggest one. In my early teens I spent too much effort trying to get in with the popular girls, copying their looks and their way of speaking, trying and failing to ingratiate myself. When I finally gave up, I realised all those people I'd previously shunned had become pally with one another. I'd missed the opportunity to find my *own* group, and I was left on my own.

Not this time. This is my opportunity for total reinvention. Maybe I should have plumped for the name Phoenix instead of Aura. Rising from the ashes, from my working-class background and from... the other thing.

I grin at Ruth. "You know what? Let's stick together," I say. "You seem really cool."

She beams, and I stifle an eye roll. Is it going to be that easy to lie to these people?

Ben

The double doors clatter open, and at first the interior of the mansion appears completely dark. Seconds later, several lights flicker on – fluorescent strip lights, like the ones in schools. We all gather in the centre of the entrance hall, dripping water onto the flagstones. The sulky man who piloted the boat comes and collects our ponchos, then ducks out of the doors again. During the crossing he told me he lives on the mainland and that he'll be coming over here daily to deliver supplies. Here's hoping he remembers to drop off our bags before he leaves the island.

When we all met up on the mainland pier it was already pouring, and the ponchos were handed out right away, so it's only now I really have the opportunity to observe my fellow contestants properly. There's one other man and three women. I remind myself that this isn't the entire group of contestants, though – apparently the other five have already arrived. The first thing that strikes me is that all these people have tried really hard with their outfits. The man, who introduced himself on the boat as Victor and who walks with a confident swagger, is wearing a pale blue suit. Two of the women are wearing strappy high heels. Didn't they get the instructions about arriving in practical clothing? Still, it bodes well for the game show itself. If these are their ideas of sensible outfits, my preparation for the tasks will be like an Olympian athlete in comparison.

"So… what now?" the fair-haired woman next to me says.

I glance around the entrance hall. "Perhaps it's a test," I say. "I'd definitely want to throw contestants into the deep end, if I was creating a TV show like this." The thought makes me shiver with pleasure. Running a game show would pretty much be my ideal job.

"You mean we could be being filmed already?" she says in a horrified tone.

Her loud comment makes everyone pay attention. It's not just the women who fiddle with their hair and their tops. Victor pays just as much attention to his appearance, smoothing his already creaseless jacket. I look down at my grey hoodie. Its front has patches of pale material where I picked off the North Face logo (because I was told that prominent brand logos weren't allowed on the show) and it's damp around the shoulders. So what?

There are closed doors on either side of the hall. The other contestants watch me as I check each door in turn. Both are locked.

"There must be some way of unlocking them remotely," I say.

Nobody says a word.

Finally, Victor says, "I reckon I could smash through them. They look kinda cheap."

"That's hardly in the right spirit," I say.

"What's the right spirit?"

"Thinking it through."

"Go on, then. Get thinking."

I turn on the spot. Then I approach a coat stand with three Barbour jackets hanging from its pegs – but a quick check reveals nothing in their pockets. Beside the rack is a tall Chinese vase containing a collection of pristine umbrellas, but they're equally uninteresting, even on their insides. On a counter beside one of the doors are three vases, decreasing in size from left to right. That could be something – maybe corresponding to a code – 3, 2, 1 – but seeing as I haven't found a lock with a numerical code or anything like that, what would I do with that information?

I hurry from side to side of the hall, conscious of

11

everyone's eyes on me. I've always been told that the trick when you're on TV is not to think about all the people watching, but I hadn't banked on literally being watched by other contestants while I'm trying to think.

I sigh. "I don't know. But I think it's something to do with the vases."

"Like what?" Victor asks.

I hesitate. "Maybe we should smash one and see what's inside?"

I can see Victor's about to crow in triumph at being right all along, but he doesn't get a chance to. We all turn as more lights flick on at the far end of the hall. At the head of a short series of steps is another door, which I didn't notice before in the darkness. It opens and a woman emerges.

"Is she the TV show host?" the fair-haired woman next to me whispers.

I recognise the newcomer. She's wearing a shapeless cardigan over black leggings, and her hair is a messy bun that's been pushed sideways by the headset she wears. The idea that she might be a TV show host is almost laughable.

"No, that's the director," I say. "She probably phoned you in the last few days? She's called Imogen."

I remember my own phone call from Imogen, how stiff and formal it was, and how short.

"Welcome!" Imogen says brightly. "Apologies for the slight delay."

Victor steps forward. "No problem at all, miss." He gestures with a thumb at me. "This very smart gentleman has spent the time well, solving the puzzle."

"What puzzle? There's no puzzle." Imogen glances at me, scowling faintly. I feel my cheeks heating up.

The dark-haired woman standing next to me raises her hand.

"Yes, ah... Mira?" the director says.

"Are we being filmed right now?" Mira asks.

"No."

Mira points at me. "He said we were."

This time, Imogen doesn't even look at me, but I notice a twitch at one corner of her lips. "Filming won't begin until after you're all settled."

"Can we see our rooms?" another of the women asks. She's working her purple-highlighted hair in her fingers as if she's trying to dry it out, strand by strand.

"In a moment. First things first. I've received all your signed disclaimers, and your bags were checked on the mainland, but I'd like to take this opportunity to reiterate some basic house rules. No drugs. No smoking, no naked flames. No sharp objects. Please be respectful of one another at all times."

Victor's hand shoots up. He turns to appraise the three female contestants as he says, "Define respectful."

"We'll let you know if any of you are out of line," Imogen says. "But remember this: a few months from now, after editing has been completed, every single member of your families will be observing your behaviour. Plus friends, coworkers... even talent agents!"

That shuts everybody up.

"One final thing," Imogen says. It's only as she raises it that I realise she's carrying a black canvas bag in her left hand. She descends the steps with it held open. "Please turn off your phones and put them in here, and I'll keep them safe for the duration of your stay."

Immediately, I pop my phone into the bag, not wanting anyone to see how old a model it is, or the fact that its screen is laced with hairline cracks. Imogen nods approvingly, without meeting my eye. Then I turn to the other contestants, who are staring in incomprehension at the bag. I'm not sure I've ever seen more appalled expressions than the ones on their faces right now.

Dez

"Can you repeat that?" the disembodied voice says.

"Which part?" I say.

"The whole thing. You were covering your mouth. It made your reply muffled."

I wrinkle my nose. "It's going to sound the opposite of spontaneous if I repeat it. Are you sure you want me to?"

There's no reply. Perhaps they're not used to being questioned, whoever they are.

"What did I even say?" I ask.

The voice remains silent for a few seconds. I watch the dark glass of the blank window. I can't see any hint of what's on the other side, only a reflection of myself slumped in this tartan-patterned armchair, both legs slung over one of its arms.

Finally, the voice says in its flattened, digitally processed tone, "You said: 'I'm doing this for my family. I'm doing this for the future. I'm doing it because it's important.'"

I nod a few times. "Yeah, yeah, okay." Then, after a moment's thought, "No. I don't want to say that again."

"Why not?"

"Because it's not true," I say.

"Then do you have another answer to the question? About your reasons for entering this contest?"

I look directly at the centre of the dark window, where I presume there's a camera lens. I lower my voice and say dramatically, "I'm doing this for *me*."

A few seconds pass. Then the voice says, "Great. Thank you."

I try to imagine how I'll come across, if that statement

is used in the TV broadcast as one of those short clips to introduce participants at the very beginning of a reality show. Will I appear confident, or callous? Or worse still, a total arse?

But it's true. I applied to take part in this show because I think I need it. Or rather, I need *something*, and given that I don't know what that something is, this might well be it. The most important thing is that here, I can't hide. I know it'll be tough – and by that I mean being among people 24/7, even before the consideration of being filmed by hidden cameras. Most people would expect it to be draining to put up a photogenic front all the front. Me, I've been putting up a front for most of my life. I suppose my hope is that being on display all day, every day, will force me to abandon the facade and present myself as just *me*. Warts and all.

Well… maybe not *every* wart. Everyone has secrets, don't they? That's only healthy.

"Any other questions?" I ask.

The voice says, "Does anything come to mind that you'd like to speak about while you're in here, alone?" The filter on the voice flattens the intonation, making it sound bored. Or maybe the person *is* bored.

I laugh. "Alone? You're here, aren't you? And there's a camera, too, which means millions of other people will watch, eventually. I'd hardly call that alone."

No reply. I decide the voice is being smart in not making this a proper two-way conversation. From the psychological experiments I conducted during my uni course, I know that allowing a subject to speak uninterrupted is valuable. Faced with silence, they reveal all sorts of things.

"When will this show be broadcast?" I ask.

"In around four months, I think."

I frown. "You don't know for sure? Shouldn't the

transmission date be locked down already?"

The voice doesn't reply.

I watch the black glass. My reflection has one eyebrow raised. I wonder if the expression will appear cool or passive-aggressive. I guess I'll find out in four months.

I decide to change tack.

"Can I ask who I'm speaking to?" I ask.

Quickly, the voice replies, "The study."

I look around at the room. It's small and wood-panelled, with ugly paintings on three of the walls. They're all old-fashioned scenes of farm workers, shooing pigs and prodding hay with forks, that sort of thing.

It's not just the paintings that are strange. I'd expected the mansion to feel like a film set – intentional, carefully arranged by a set designer. Instead, the whole place feels kind of shabby, like a holiday house where the owners have decided to leave their own possessions in full view, but only because they're basically worthless. A case in point: on a low table beside the only door is an array of knick-knacks, which look like the sort of thing my gran ordered from coupons on the back of the *Radio Times* in the eighties. Ceramic maidens wearing petticoats and holding parasols. Wooden foxes curled around one another in a foxy hug. One die-cast model of a red telephone box is small enough that it'd slip into my jeans pocket.

I look away, suddenly overwhelmed. I often get this way around clutter. Cluttered objects, and cluttered people. I remind myself of the many people outside this room. I'll have to speak to all of them. Explain myself to all of them.

I'm becoming breathless.

I pat the pocket of my jeans, feeling the reassuring snub shape of the lighter inside it. Instantly, I breathe more easily.

The strangest aspect of the room, obviously, is the big

dark glass panel a few feet in front of the only chair. It's like a giant widescreen TV, but one that can't be turned on. The wall it's embedded in is also odd. It looks solid enough, but instead of wood panelling it's just flat and grey. Conclusion: it's a false wall. I wonder how big the room actually is, and whether the owner of the voice has more or less space than me.

"Hello, then, 'Study'," I say. "Cute name. Tell me, are you sitting in an armchair like me?"

No reply.

"Can you tell me *anything* about yourself?" I ask.

Silence.

I laugh. "You know, I quite like the way your voice is treated, that weird filter that flattens it. Will your voice sound like that when you talk to each of the other contestants?"

"Yes, Dez. Why do you ask?"

"It's just that it's a classic technique, isn't it, for an interviewer to sound familiar to the subject. And I wondered whether the way you sound was some reflection of what you thought of me."

No response, and this time I'm grateful. I didn't mention my psychology degree in my video application, and I have no intention of telling other contestants about it either. I'm certain it'd raise suspicions. If I have any more random thoughts about psychological experiments, I'll keep them to myself.

Urk. Already, I'm burying parts of myself. Not a good sign.

I puff my cheeks and stand up. "It's been fun, Study, but I should get along."

At the threshold of the door, I turn to look at the black window. "Hey, just to be clear, if we're going to be spending time together, I'd like to get to know you just as well as you know me. That may be a one-way window, but

I'm going to make sure our relationship is two-way, okay?"

The cheesiness of my comment makes me snort with laughter. I really hope the camera wasn't filming that bit.

Dolly

When the door to the study opens again, the person who enters isn't who I requested. I'd put Victor's name up on the digital sign outside the contestants' door, a dot-matrix display like the kind you might see at a delicatessen counter in a supermarket. But this definitely isn't Victor, it's...

I tap at the keys of my computer keyboard, which is lit red by the single desk lamp with red cellophane over its bulb. The interface flicks back to the menu screen with its list of contestants, but then the screen freezes. What did I do wrong in a previous life to get lumbered with technology this ancient? And it's not just the freezing and glitches. Even the keyboard itself is dodgy. The space bar rocks every time I press it, looking like it might drop off at any moment, and the keyboard is missing a couple of its keys. Ironically, one of them is the Escape key.

I shuffle the stack of papers on the cramped area beneath the bolted-down camera stand, peering at them in the dim light from the red lamp. Printouts won't let me down. Printouts are my friends.

Each of the contestant descriptions features a black-and-white mug shot.

There she is.

"Hello, Ruth," I say into the microphone.

There's a buzzing sound whenever I speak. It took me a while to recognise that it's because my own voice is coming back to me through the hidden microphones in the main part of the study, after having been processed through the digital filter that ensures my anonymity. When I asked the director, Imogen, why my identity needs

19

protecting, she laughed and said she didn't give a *fig* about my identity, and that it's just to ensure that any of the production team can perform these one-to-one interviews in my place.

Ruth pokes around the study a bit, looking at the ugly paintings. Then she perches herself on the edge of the armchair. She's so tiny that it completely dwarfs her. I check the camera feed monitor, and sure enough she looks ridiculous, occupying only the bottom half of the screen. But it's not like I can do anything about it. Like all the cameras in the mansion, this one's fixed in place.

"Is it okay for me to be in here?" Ruth asks.

"Of course," I say. Then I can't help adding, "Even though your name wasn't displayed outside the door."

Ruth frowns. "There was no name outside the door. Just some speckly red lights. I thought it meant it was fine to come in. Like a sort of glittery welcome sign."

I groan. Another bit of tech broken already. It's going to be a long week.

"Sorry?" says Ruth.

Oops. I must have left the mic on. With the filter applied, my groan probably sounded like a robot suffering a meltdown.

"What would you like to talk about?" I ask.

Ruth hugs herself tightly. "I don't know. Is this being filmed?"

"Yes."

"Okay." She takes a deep breath, then grins. "I suppose I should begin with this. Hi, Mum!"

Instinctively, I want to say 'Hi' in response. How impressionable does that make me?

She goes on, "I just wanted to say how excited I am. How grateful I am to be here. I mean, this is *crazy*, isn't it?"

If I answered that question – which I won't – it'd take

a while. I wasn't even supposed to be here on this shoot. Only the day before yesterday, I was happily minding my own business, doing bog-standard admin at my production company's premises. Then Imogen calls me, telling-not-asking me to hurry on up to Northumbria on a train, and wasn't it true that I said my working patterns could be as flexible as necessary? I mean, sure, I have no hangers-on and no social life to speak of, but there's flexible and there's *flexible*. And spending a week on a rain-lashed island far further north of the Watford Gap than I'm comfortable straying, wrangling self-centred wannabes and wrestling with ancient tech, receiving not one single thank-you for my efforts... you'd have to be as flexible as a contortionist to be comfortable with all that.

"And have you *seen* the other contestants?" Ruth asks.

Yes, Ruth, I've seen them. That's literally my job.

"They're so *beautiful*," she says. "There's this girl who has this hair..." Her eyes roll upwards until her pupils disappear entirely.

This girl who has this hair. Really, Ruth? Is that the sort of material we'll be working with in the edit?

"And there's this boy. Victor." Ruth giggles. "He's beautiful too. Very strong, you know? Very manly."

She frowns and her head tilts. "Are you still there?"

I shake myself awake. "Yes, Ruth. What do you think of the other contestants you've met?"

"Oh, Mira's lovely. She's Asian, and I've never really known any Asian people before, but she's lovely. The girl with the great hair is Aura. I'm going to get highlights like that when I get home, if I can afford them." Her eyes widen. "Hey, maybe I'll win! How much money would I get?"

"The prize fund currently stands at two hundred and fifty thousand pounds."

"Two hundred and fifty thousand pounds," Ruth

repeats. "That's a lot of highlights." Then her expression clouds. "Hold on. Isn't it shared between *all* the winners?"

"Yes."

"Oh."

Is she actually disappointed? Even if all ten contestants ended up sharing the prize fund, that's *still* a lot of highlights.

"There was one other person in your cohort," I say, nudging her to ensure there'll be coverage for the edit. When Ruth's face scrunches up in confusion, I add, "You arrived with one other contestant."

"Did I?"

"Yes. Ben."

"Oh. I guess he's all right. Quite *clever*, though, you know?"

"Is that bad?"

"I don't think people much like clever people. People like people who are like them, don't they?"

"Would you describe yourself as clever?"

Ruth laughs. She keeps laughing. She can't stop laughing.

"No," she says. "I'm not clever. I'm just a nice person."

Like I said. It's going to be a long week.

Ben

I don't know what I expected of our accommodation here in the mansion, but it wasn't this. My room isn't particularly small, but the decor makes it *seem* small. There's clutter everywhere, old tat that you wouldn't even class as antique. The mantelpiece over a long-unused fireplace is crammed with ugly ornaments, candlesticks that have been made misshapen by dried wax, and a bowler hat balanced on a wooden stem. Next to the single narrow slit window is a tiny dressing table, its entire surface taken up by a glass case in which a bird of prey is awkwardly perched on a twisted branch. What little sunlight comes through the window illuminates the bird, and any change in the quality of the light makes it seem animated. I think about turning the case around, but on second thoughts I decide I'd rather see what it's up to.

But you know what's bugging me the most? It's the fact that even though this place is pretty crappy, it's actually far less crappy than my flat in Bristol. If their rooms are anything like mine, I can imagine the other contestants are spitting feathers right now. For me, though, this accommodation is positively luxurious.

Which is why I could use the prize money, obviously.

Somebody's left my bag in the centre of the room. As I lift it up and dump it on the bed, I notice the main zip is open. I guess there was some sort of security check? It doesn't bother me – there's nothing particularly personal in there. I put away my clothes in the dusty chest of drawers. It's just as well I don't own any shirts that would benefit from being hung up, because there's no wardrobe. Then I arrange my books on the bedside table. They're all non-fiction, mostly about game theory.

I lie on the bed. It's uncomfortable, but again, it's better than my own bed. I tell myself it's important to get some rest while I can. Partly, that's because I don't tend to sleep well at night – never have done, since I was a child trying to establish myself in any one of a series of foster homes. It's been even worse since the divorce. I have bad dreams most nights. But there's also another good reason to start this whole process feeling rested. Imogen said there'd be no tasks today, but on a show like this you have to assume the game has begun immediately.

My guess is that most of the contestants will take the whole experience at face value. Most of them probably just want to be on the telly, their eyes on the secondary prizes of sponsorship or becoming TikTok influencers, rather than winning the actual game show. They'll be surprised by every twist and turn that's thrown at us by the production team.

Me, I'll be ready. I was picked to be here for a reason, and I've prepped well – I know the gist of every logic puzzle going. Maybe, just maybe, I'll show Carla and the girls that being obsessed with puzzles isn't a waste of time. If I can win the prize money, surely they'll have to concede that I've done good, that I'm a provider.

It's a stretch, but Carla might even take me back.

My gaze moves around the cracks on the plaster ceiling. It occurs to me that all these signs of wear and tear might actually be faked, to achieve a certain effect. I jump to my feet and reach up to the ceiling. When I graze one of the cracks, plaster falls down, getting into my eyes. Not fake, then.

One corner of the plaster architrave is darker than the rest. I hop off the bed and drag the stool from the dressing table, then clamber onto it to examine the area.

Is that—

I inspect it from all angles.

It is.

It's a tiny fixed camera lens, smaller than a GoPro, embedded in the plaster. Presumably the bulky architrave hides the larger part of the kit.

I mean... *wow*. That's pretty unethical.

More than that. It's *completely* unethical. It's kind of sick.

I turn to align my view with the camera. If it's a fish-eye lens, its field of vision might easily encompass the entire room.

I try to remember the details of the disclaimer I signed, weeks ago. The document was so long, I can't recall if it mentioned private rooms being bugged.

I should probably complain. It's not that being watched matters a whole lot to me. My secrets are strictly in my own head, and I'm unlikely to do anything incriminating that's actually observable. But the other contestants may feel strongly about voyeurism in private spaces, and I'm pretty sure they won't think to check for cameras.

So I should tell them.

Except—

Except in a game like this, knowledge is power. I don't know how this piece of knowledge might benefit me, but giving it up freely will certainly do me no good.

"I'll keep it under my hat," I say aloud. I glance at the bowler hat on the mantelpiece, and I laugh. "I'll keep it under *that* hat."

Then I remember the camera, and I wince. Over the last few months I've found myself speaking my thoughts aloud more and more. I suppose it's a consequence of living alone after been used to the constant noise of a full house. I'll have to watch out for that while I'm here.

There's a knock on the door. I drop down to the floor – the floorboards groan ominously on impact – and put away the stool, then jog to open the door.

It's Victor.

"Ben, yeah?" he says.

I nod. At first I'm impressed he's remembered my name, but then out of the corner of my eye I notice the nameplate fixed to the door of my room.

"Be downstairs in three, yeah? And pass it on," Victor says. "It's time to meet the guv'nor."

Aura

It's a relief to find that the sitting room is actually fairly plush, unlike the low-rent conditions upstairs. My bedroom's really scruffy, with sun-bleached fabrics all over the place, which send up plumes of dust if you press down on them too hard. But it could be worse. You should see Ruth's room. She was almost in tears when she showed me how small it is. My guess is it was once a nursery, with room for a cot and not much else. I tried to calm her down by pointing out that at least she has an en-suite bathroom, whereas I'll have to scurry around the landing in my PJs whenever I need to pee. Then we investigated said bathroom, only to find it had *another* door, accessible from the next bedroom along. It turned out to be Victor's room, and he had the good grace to appear flustered when we burst in to find him half undressed. Ruth's cheeks actually turned crimson. Still, the experience seemed to placate her a bit.

Anyway, the sitting room is a whole other story. It's huge, for a start. There's a big U-shaped ring of sofas with comfy suede upholstery, and at each end of the room are huddles of wingback armchairs. It would be the ideal place to veg out with a group of friends on holiday, apart from the fact that there's no TV. That makes sense, I suppose – we're here to make a TV show, not watch one. Where a TV would naturally be placed is a free-standing bar. Lined up on it are an array of bottles. That makes sense too.

The lighting is atmospheric, but bright, presumably for the benefit of the cameras. That thought makes me spin to look around the room again – where *are* the cameras? There's a mirror above the fireplace, which could be hiding one, like in the study where we've all been conducting one-to-one interviews. I guess other cameras could be fixed in out-of-the-way places, but none are obvious at a glance. I make a mental note to hunt them out. If I'm going to be effective at controlling my image, I need to know where I should look when I want to deliver a dramatic performance. Everything I do here will comprise my audition tape for my future career.

The other contestants file into the room behind me. Some of them I met on the boat, but others are new to me. I summon all my extrovert energy to make a good first impression.

I lavish my attention on the women first, because it's crucial to get them on side. Sasha is a curvy mum type, and I immediately class her as someone not to worry about, although the fact she keeps giving me the side-eye is annoying. The other new woman is a supremely pretty blonde, with a French accent to die for – that's Cécile. I sense her sizing me up, her eyes lingering on my hair, my bare legs, my black satin cocktail dress. Her expression remains carefully neutral. Instantly, I decide she'll be tough to befriend, so the alternative is to keep her at arm's length for now.

The men all appear a bit hopeless. There's a shy-looking kid with wide eyes and glowing red cheeks – that's Ralphie – and a scruffy-looking short lad wearing a floppy hat who looks like he's at a music festival, who introduces himself as 'Doc Leaf'. When I ask him if that's his DJ name or something, he just sniggers. Then again, I'm going by the name Aura, and people in glass houses shouldn't throw stones, should they?

Finally, there's Dez, whose cropped hair is bleached ghost-white and who wears a serious, studied expression as they navigate introductions, clearly waiting for people to trip up over their pronouns and looking almost disappointed when nobody does.

So with the addition of my boat-buddies – Victor, Mira, Ruth and Ben – that's everyone. Quite a motley bunch, all in all.

Everyone whirls around as the door to the sitting room opens again, and a man wearing a *very* good suit and boasting a *very* nice haircut enters. He stands before the ring of sofas and gestures with a flourish for us all to sit. We do, each of us fussing with our outfits, suddenly hyper-aware that this is *it* and that cameras are *rolling*, baby.

"Good evening, friends!" the man says, revealing perfectly white teeth.

We all echo his greeting in bright voices. We're like the keenest primary-school class ever.

"Allow me to introduce myself," he says. "I'm Axel Griffin, proprietor of this humble abode."

From beside me, Victor says, "Do you really own it, mate?"

Axel's grin doesn't falter. Even from several metres away I can see that he's wearing a lot of foundation, which makes his face look a bit plasticky. He's probably beyond his mid-forties, and my guess is he's not taking it well. But he's movie-star handsome all the same. Why have I never heard of him before?

"Naturally I do," Axel says. He glances at the mirror above the fireplace, which pretty much confirms there's a camera behind it. His head tilts slightly, and I catch a glimpse of a hidden earpiece. He nods subtly, clears his throat, then spreads his arms and says, "And you fine people are not merely my guests! My sincere hope is that you will agree to help me access the missing two hundred and fifty thousand pounds… *at least*… that my ancestors stashed away."

Choruses of "Sure!" and "Yeah!" come from all around me.

Axel smiles indulgently. "It will not be easy... but perhaps I can make your challenge a smidgen more manageable. You will face a series of tasks, and the reward for each task will be twofold. Firstly, success in each task will result in additional amounts being added to the stockpile..."

This produces a ripple of excitement among the contestants. Nobody bothers to mention the fact that it doesn't make sense, within the tale Axel's spun. A long-missing store of money that can somehow increase due to our performance in random challenges? Sure, whatever.

Axel goes on, "...and those who are judged most successful will be awarded keys, which are the only means of actually *accessing* the money. And be warned: cooperation will be crucial. Only you ten guests can control who will open the vault, and therefore determine who will receive a share of the money."

Mira raises a hand. "So do you know where the money is?"

The movie-star grin remains in place. "In the family vault."

"Where's that?"

Axel looks up at the mirror again. He takes a deep breath. "You'll have to find it, won't you?" he says eventually. Then, with a sly smile, he adds, "I advise you to study your surroundings carefully."

"Did your ancestors set up the tasks too?"

"No?" There's a noticeable upturn at the end of the word. It seems Axel's been poorly briefed about the whole premise of the game show, which is admittedly quite flimsy. His hands are clasped together and with the index finger and thumb of his right hand he's turning a ring on his left hand constantly. (It's not on the wedding finger, I notice with satisfaction.) It's a small action, but it shows me he can't wait to get out of this room.

"Then couldn't you just give us the keys?" Mira asks brightly.

Axel's mouth opens but he doesn't manage to come up with a response.

I've taken the seat closest to him, and now I reach out to put my hand on his. It's surprisingly warm.

The others all appear amazed that I've had the nerve to actually touch our host. Despite his fish-out-of-water vibe and despite the fact he's not famous enough for me to recognise him, Axel exudes screen-star charisma. But I've never been one to be daunted by authority.

"I imagine you feel your ancestors are relying on you to make sure the money goes to a worthy winner," I say.

I squeeze Axel's hand, and wink at him. No doubt the cameras will be zooming in on me at this moment, which is ideal because my glitter eye shadow is well worth a close-up.

Axel blushes. Now *that's* a result.

Abruptly, my stomach lurches.

I tell myself that my mum isn't actually watching me. Yet.

Dez

Axel finally manages to bluster his way through the briefing. Here's the gist:

For each of the five days we're here, starting tomorrow, there'll be two tasks, one in the morning and one in the evening.

Winning a task will result in being awarded a key – just a single one, that is, even for team tasks.

The keys will open the vault containing the money.

We can choose to work together, or we can... not. I assume that'll make sense once we get started.

Now that he's got this far into the explanation, Axel has the look of a student about to stride triumphantly out of their final exam. He's eyeing the door constantly.

"And then," he says with an air of finality, "all you need to do is escape."

"Escape?" I echo. "Why?"

"Once you've stolen the loot, you will need to escape the island."

"Will that be with you?" I ask. "Aren't we finding the money on your behalf?"

"No." Axel shoots another glance at the door. I bet there'll be hell to pay when he gets his hands on Imogen, the director, who should have prepared him better for this ordeal. "No," he repeats. "Once you've acquired the money – whether it's one of you, or several of you sharing it – you need to escape the island on the rowing boat moored on the shore. Once somebody's done that," he concludes with relief, "then we have a winner. Or winners."

His back straightens and he flicks his cuffs, James Bond

style. It's clear he's returning to more comfortable – that is, entirely scripted – territory.

"And with that," he says in a plummy voice, "I bid you adieu. While I'd suggest you all get a good night's sleep in preparation for tomorrow's… ah, *trials*… you may like to spend the evening getting to know one another." He pauses, then lowers his voice to add, "And perhaps decide who you can trust."

Then he all but sprints to the door. I notice he's limping slightly, favouring his right leg. Within seconds, he's gone.

For a few seconds, all of us contestants stare at each other without saying a word.

It's Mira who breaks the silence. "Who even *is* he, anyway? I was hoping it'd be Vernon Kay."

Immediate laughter. There's nothing like relief – and a bizarre experience – to form bonds within a group.

Doc Leaf bounds to his feet and approaches the counter. "Now that's out of the way," he says, "let's get *fucked up*."

*

The evening is predictable enough. The alcohol flows, and so do the boastful claims, the posturing and the constant eyeing up of each other as ally material. That's how games like this work, don't they? You forge alliances, then you use those relationships as leverage.

The trouble is, I've never been one to work in that way. Anyone who earns my trust does it slowly. I keep people at arm's length. And that's a problem, because it's not just TV game shows that revolve around alliances. It's life in general.

In my first year at university, my accommodation was on campus, in a block housing eighty. Each kitchen-slash-living-room was shared by twelve students, and became

33

the default location for mingling, and pre-drinks before going out clubbing, then post-drinks afterwards. I was amazed at how easily people settled into their kitchen group in the first days after we all arrived. Even though they freely acknowledged it was just a quirk of fate that had thrown them together, they behaved as though their fellow kitchenites would be their friends for life. And in some cases, it was true. Social-media doomscrolling has shown me that two of the couples that got together during fresher's week are now married. Am I the asshole for being freaked out by that?

Me, I looked farther afield. I sought out the disenfranchised, the lurkers in the background. And this was before I even joined the societies that catered for *people like me*. As far as I'm concerned, there are no people like me. There's just me.

Tonight, I tell myself that history isn't repeating. This whole situation is false. I don't need these people to be my friends, because after this week I won't see them ever again.

Perhaps that's why I find myself actually having a good time.

First off, Mira is *excellent*. She's Manc, with an accent so strong that at times she might as well be speaking another language, and she takes no shit. The first thing that endears me to her is that as soon as the drinks start flowing, she takes off her boots and tosses them into the corner of the room – then spends the next ten minutes apologising to each contestant in turn for the stench of her feet, explaining that she sweats like mad when she's tense. What's tragic is that no scent in the world would overwhelm the reek of perfume and aftershave here in the sitting room. She's drawn attention to herself in the worst possible way, and she doesn't even seem to care. So I basically love her.

Sasha stands out, too. She must be in her late-forties, twice as old as some of the other contestants, and she's got a big bouncy fringe and she's wearing dungarees, like Felicity Kendall in that old sitcom. She reminds me of the mum of my childhood best friend. It takes all my willpower not to ask her to heat me up a Pop Tart.

Predictably, I'm drawn to the weirdos, the people who don't have a big persona at the ready, the ones who don't seem to be hiding behind a facade. Ben's clearly a massive nerd, and what's adorable is that he doesn't know it. He keeps telling people about the gaming evenings he runs at his local pub, where he teaches people how to play German board games with unpronounceable names. He seems put out when the other contestants react badly, as if he's appalled at the suggestion that board games aren't the natural way to engage with your fellow humans.

There's another guy, Ralphie, who's so quiet and timid that I want to pat him on the head and let him curl up on the carpet at my feet like a kitten.

Then there are the people at the other end of the extrovert spectrum:

Victor is full of adrenalin and spunk, and anyone might think he was real host of this party, refilling everyone's glasses and laughing too loudly at their crap jokes. He wants us to know he's *self-made*, and that he got where he is by *grafting* and *working from the ground up*, and that his first two businesses were nothing compared to his current one, which is… I don't know, I wasn't listening.

Aura has a perfect face and perfect hair and a gratingly outgoing manner, like a Barbie doll intent on social climbing. The disapproving glances that Sasha, the mum of the group, keeps shooting at her are really satisfying. There's another thing about Aura that unsettles me. The necklace she's wearing has a golden pendant shaped like a feather. It stirs all sorts of feelings in my stomach. The

35

wrong sorts of feelings. I push them away.

The last of the newcomers is Doc Leaf.

I know his type. I've clocked him watching me throughout the evening, but I'm practised at evasion and manage to go hours before he corners me. But he does, eventually. And of course he asks the question.

"So, uh, Dez… which are you, really?"

Sweat is beading on his pockmarked forehead, beneath the brim of his floppy hat.

I say, "I'm not sure I know what you mean."

He waves a hand up and down, gesturing at my whole body. "It's *weird*. I can't even *tell*."

Mira, who's standing next to me, groans. "Fella, take a moment to think it over. Then don't say anything, yeah?"

A grin forms slowly on Doc Leaf's face. He hasn't looked away from me for a second. "You're a bloke, right? But you got rid of it. Snipped it off."

Cue more groans from other people. All the same, I notice that several of them are watching me closely. They all want to know the answer.

"*They* and *their* and *them*," Doc Leaf drawls. "I bet it's fun tripping everyone up about all that. But it's easier for you, isn't it? You still think of yourself as 'I', no matter what."

This final comment strikes me as surprisingly profound, coming from pond scum like him.

"I was assigned female at birth," I say calmly. "That label didn't work for me."

Silence. I sense everyone assessing my body, looking for corroborating evidence.

"Happy now?" Mira says, shoving Doc Leaf in the ribs.

He chews his lip. "Yeah, yeah. I see it now," he says. "Is there *anything* down there? Or are you, uh, antisexual?"

"They don't owe you any explanations," Mira says

36

defensively.

Doc Leaf nods thoughtfully. He gestures at me offhand and says to Mira, "My guess is no sexy time at all. No one's going to want that, are they? Or I should say: no one's going to want *they*."

"I have a partner," I say hurriedly, even though Mira's right that I don't owe him any explanations. I can feel my cheeks glowing. Why am I offering this idiot anything of myself? All the same, I add, "A girlfriend."

His face contorts as he performs immensely complex calculations. "So then you're…"

"I'm nonbinary. So, no."

"Yeah, but… You're not straight, clearly. Not *normal*."

Mira emits a low growl. She takes me by the arm, trying to guide me away. But I tell myself I'm not fazed by any of this. Doc Leaf's a foot shorter than me. I can hold my own in a fight, if it comes to it. Then again, he'd probably be delighted if I took him on, as it'd no doubt support at least one of his many prejudices.

His expression brightens. "Dez. Dez. Can I have a go at guessing your real name?"

For some reason, this is what breaks me. What is this obsession with what's real? On the set of a TV show, of all places. As if all these other people aren't hiding behind facades of their own, which they don't even have the courage to acknowledge.

"How about you?" I snap. "What's Doc short for? Doctor? Docklington? Hickory Dockery Dick? And what have you come to this party as? I'm guessing your costume is… let's see… underage farm labourer having a mare on his first ecstasy pill at Reading Festival 1995, finally discovered by his parents in the first-aid tent wearing no pants and with dried sick on his tie-dyed T-shirt."

I hear titters of nervous laughter. Doc Leaf just stares at me, not even looking like he's trying to formulate a comeback.

"Or is there a cuter reason?" I continue, even though I'm willing myself to just walk away. "How about… when you were a kid you always wore shorts, and got so many nettle stings that Mummy always had a dock leaf to hand?"

There's something odd in his eyes now. A dangerous glint.

"It's just a name," he says in a low voice.

I fold my arms slowly, focusing on slowing my breathing down.

"There you go, then," I say.

*

Now I'm standing outside the double front doors of the mansion, sheltering from the rain under the projecting roof of a surprisingly rickety wooden porch. In the past I'd have come outside to smoke or vape, but I made a promise to Priya that I'd quit. So now I do what I've taken to doing in these sorts of situations. I dig out from the pocket of my jeans the lighter I got from Priya a few years back. Even though I've given up smoking, I'll never give up this lighter. I don't give a toss about the housekeeping rules the director of the game show insisted on. There's no lighter fluid in it anyway. On the side of the lighter, inscribed in Gothic script, are the words *Fuck 'em*. It nestles in my palm, and its familiarity transports me to Priya in an instant, which feels good and bad at the same time. I flip open the lid, flick the spark wheel a few times, producing no flame.

Breathe. Breathe.

"You all right out here?" a voice says behind me.

I turn to see Mira in the doorway.

"All good," I say quickly.

"I meant what I said. You don't owe anyone any

explanations."

I nod. "I guess I've learned to be cagey. I'd hoped that while I'm here I might have more confidence in myself. I see it as a sort of test."

"You did good, Dez. You stood your ground."

"No. I got riled up, and with cameras trained on me."

She shakes her head. "Getting riled up is the least that prick deserves. The viewing public will agree with me, I promise. TV shows like this are how most of the general public encounter new ideas."

"And I'm a new idea?"

"Hey, don't get defensive. You're a threat to the way some people think. And that's wrong. But one day they won't think that way, and you're leading the charge."

She says all this like it's no big deal. I try to laugh it all off, but it comes out more like a shuddery sigh.

I wipe my eyes with my free hand, even though I haven't shed a single tear.

"Come on, then," I say. "Let's head back into battle."

She laughs and puts her arm around my shoulder. Then her eyes flick downwards to look at the lighter, before I pocket it.

Dolly

The very same moment I push at the swing door, which leads from my study cubbyhole to the main production suite, someone pushes it from the other side. The sheaf of notes slips out of my grasp and paper flutters everywhere, and I drop to the floor to pick it all up.

"Sorry about that," I say.

Imogen crouches down to my level. She doesn't help me gather my notes, though.

"Why are you apologising?" she asks. "I was the one who knocked them out of your hand."

I smile nervously. "I don't know. Sorry."

Imogen rocks back onto the heels of her expensive-looking boots. She gestures at the mass of paper in my hand and says, "What is all this, Dotty?"

"It's Dolly," I murmur.

But if Imogen wants to call me Dotty, who am I to argue? She can make or break my career. I'm a mere production assistant, whereas she's a hotshot director with a twenty-year career and a collection of awards that'd demolish any coffee table under their sheer weight.

I clear my throat. "They're just some notes I made during the one-to-one interviews. I thought they might be useful."

Imogen raises an eyebrow. She stands and offers a hand to help me up. Her palm is smooth and cool, in contrast to my hot little paw.

I rifle through the papers, then pull one of them out. "For example, here's a list of timestamps from this particular contestant's interview, where they said something that I thought revealed their character. You know, a reference to something or someone at home, or a hint of their world view."

Imogen's eyebrow is still raised.

I press on. "I've also made notes about what sort of approach to take in future interviews, to draw information out. The contestants are all a little different in terms of how they respond to direct questions, or suggestion, or silence."

"They are, are they?" Imogen says.

"I'm sure you've noticed the same thing," I add hurriedly. "These are really just for my own purposes. Seeing as I'll be conducting a fair amount of the interviews?" I wince. My intonation accidentally turned that comment into a question. But it's not as though I've been briefed clearly about my responsibilities, and I really could do with some explanation about my precise role.

"You'll be conducting *all* of the interviews," Imogen says. "I've no interest in sitting in that box-room listening to these bottom-feeders opine about their failed relationships or their split hairs."

I nod. "Great," I say, though I'm not sure why.

Imogen plucks a sheet of paper from the top of the pile. "What about this one?" she asks.

I look down and grimace. Dotted amongst my scrawled notes are childish doodles: spiders, a skull and crossbones, a dagger dripping blood. Pretty unprofessional, Dolly.

"That's another collection of notes for my own purposes," I say weakly. "It's... just some thoughts about which contestants might present a challenge. In terms of being interviewed on camera, I mean."

Imogen turns the sheet around to examine it. She traces a finger across the area of the paper where my biro went through when I was writing, because I was pressing so hard. Alongside it is a caricature of somebody being hanged, the rope taut and their tongue sticking out of one side of their mouth.

"It looks as though Doc Leaf has attracted your attention," Imogen says.

I hesitate. "I think he might be a bit of a handful."

"He might be great TV, too."

That shuts me up. Honestly, I hadn't even thought of it in those terms. Only the pain in the arse that he's likely to cause me. Throughout his first interview he made it clear that he considers being offensively crass his particular *thing*.

"Good point, Miss Dorrien-Stewart," I say.

Imogen laughs. "Did head office tell you to call me that?"

"No. Sorry. Should I call you Imogen?"

She clucks her tongue as she considers. "No. Stick with formal. I like it. Makes me feel important."

"You're the director. Who's more important than the director, during filming?"

She snorts. "Oh, child, you're so sweet. So naive. Haven't you looked around yet?"

I'm not blind. I have an excellent eye for detail. It says so on my CV.

I look around, like she told me to. The production suite is a mess of open boxes, as if somebody's abandoned them in the midst of unpacking. In the centre is a table cluttered with empty styrofoam coffee cups and crisp packets, plus two laptops with closed lids. The only evidence of actual TV production is the bank of video screens at one side of the room, which is comprised of maybe sixty individual monitors stacked on top of one another. Each of the monitors displays a feed from one of the cameras hidden in the various rooms of the mansion.

Imogen saunters over to the monitors. The monitors in the top-left corner must all be feeds from cameras in the sitting room, as they're the only ones that currently contain any people. Even without sound, it's clear the evening social event is in full swing. Victor and Aura are dancing seductively in the centre of the ring of sofas, and a few other contestants are clapping along as they watch. On one of the other screens I can see Mira and Dez talking earnestly in a corner of the room. On another, Ben, Ruth and Ralphie are sitting on the carpet at Sasha's feet, their drinks spilling as they laugh riotously at whatever story she's telling them.

"What do you notice?" Imogen asks.

"Just the contestants," I say blankly.

"Remember which side of the wall you're on," Imogen says. It must be obvious that I have no idea what she means, because she adds, "You're a member of the production team. Not a contestant, and not a viewer."

I stare at the screens again, thinking in terms of TV production. The framing's neat enough. Each time Victor and Aura perform a turn in their dance, the camera adjusts to focus clearly on the face that becomes visible. When Sasha pauses her story to sip her drink, Ben begins speaking and the camera zooms in on him subtly.

My eyes move down. Normally I'd expect to see a console beneath a bank of monitors like this, with complicated dials and sliders. But there's nothing at all.

"There are no camera controls," I say.

"Bingo. The cameras are automatic, zeroing in on movements, changes of expression, heat register…" Imogen puffs her cheeks out. "Probably much more besides. When the producer explained it all, I could barely hear him after a certain point. The sound of the bell tolling drowned it out."

I frown. "I'm sorry. What bell?"

"A death knell. Foretelling the end of my career."

"Oh." I pause, unsure how to respond to a statement like that. "I suppose with a show like *Escapism*, the skill is in the edit. You can craft a narrative based on the raw footage that's recorded."

It's immediately clear I've said the wrong thing. Imogen's hands curl like talons.

"The edit's due to take place in Sweden, overseen by the producer," she hisses. "A producer, let me add, who hasn't even felt the need to be present here during filming. The only footage stored on site are your one-to-one interviews in the study. Everything else only exists up there." She points upwards, and instinctively I look at the ceiling. Imogen tuts and says, "I mean in the *cloud*, silly child."

Before I can think better of it, I blurt out, "Then what's the need for a director at all?"

Do I detect Imogen's eyes welling up? It's hard to tell, in the dim green light from the monitors.

"Beats me," she says. "It's been made clear to me that after this week my services won't be required on this project. If they think they can stick my name on the credits, they can think again." She points at my sheaf of papers. "Maybe you can earn yourself some brownie points by shipping all of that to Stockholm. It's of no use to me."

On the monitors, I see that Doc Leaf is now standing on the bartop in the sitting room, a bottle raised above his head so that its contents fall into his mouth, though a lot of it is streaming down his shirt.

In a tone of supreme weariness, Imogen says, "So what I said earlier about being on this side of the wall? All you and I can do is watch passively while the monkeys throw their shit at it."

Six months later

Rhea

An email pops up while I'm watching my inbox, as if it's a direct response to me willing job offers to show up. But the email isn't from the cash and carry, or the shoe repair shop, or even the local museum about the voluntary explainer role. In the 'sender' field is simply the word *INSIDER*. The subject line: *SUBJECT FOR INVESTIGATION.*

I don't know why I click on the email. Probably it's because when I was a kid I was fixated on Diamond Brothers and Sherlock Holmes stories, and this is exactly the sort of thing I imagined would happen to me. A note slipped under the door with a coded message on it. A map found rolled in a Pringles can. Adventures have to begin somewhere, and I've always been primed for adventure. Throughout my teens, I was determined to learn every skill going, in preparation for the grand undertaking that I told myself would *definitely* begin, any day now. Sleight of hand from magic guides. The art of persuasion. Tough Mudder and zombie runs, so that I'd be limber and cool under pressure. Krav Maga, in case things turned nasty. During my short-lived journalism course at uni I began horse-riding lessons, so I'd be ready for a chase across the plains of some distant country.

It was the horse riding that ended that chapter of my life. Or rather, it was the *fall* from my horse – embarrassingly, from a stationary position and when we were just outside the stables, as opposed to hotfooting it across the plains or anything exciting like that.

After the fall, the headaches began. And when I say headaches, I mean a sensation like the clashing of continental plates, like avalanches of disintegrating brain matter, like the end of the world. They lasted for days at a time. Now my most adventurous experiences involve undergoing treatment courtesy of exciting new pieces of bulky medical kit, during frequent visits to Leeds General Hospital.

The specialists say I should cut down on my screen time, because flickering lights can trigger episodes. But I'm on my computer more and more. There's still a world out there, waiting to be explored, and nowadays my computer is the only way I know to access it.

So yep, I click on the email.

It says:

Ms Hildred,
I'm an admirer of your podcast.

That gets my attention. iTunes tells me that the first episode of my podcast – which is about the experience of being on disability benefits in broken Britain – has had only 146 listeners, most of whom couldn't have been as impressed as INSIDER was, seeing as the second episode has had only 85. Six weeks on, I haven't got around to recording the third episode yet.

Back to the email.

I have a suggestion for another subject you may like to investigate. Please see the attached.

And that's it. No sign-off, no explanation.

There are two attachments, both of them video files.

You don't open attachments to emails like that, do you? Of course you don't.

But INSIDER knew my name. That's something. And they mentioned my podcast, though I suppose that's public knowledge, and they didn't refer to it by name. (It's a good name: *Rhea View*, reflecting its broad scope and... Ugh. No. It's kind of crappy.)

All the same, this sort of message must get sent occasionally, and must sometimes be legit, like when whistleblowers tip off media outlets.

Sod it. All my data's backed up, and this computer's getting old. If it comes to it, I'll divert some of my Employment and Support Allowance to buy a new one. Living on toast for a week isn't so bad. I've done it before.

Clickety-click.

The first file, named *PretitleReelDemo.avi*, opens in my media player.

It's disappointing, is what it is. The video compression makes the quality pretty low, but it's immediately clear that it's a flashy intro to some primetime TV show. It begins with a sped-up drone shot of a large house on a rocky island, accompanied by a foghorn noise like a Hans Zimmer soundtrack to a blockbuster film.

A caption flashes up in white text: *10 CONTESTANTS*. Then there's a handful of dizzying clips that threaten to trigger my condition – seriously, I can't afford to spend the next few days in bed with the curtains drawn and the lights out! In the moments before I clamp my eyes shut, I see beautiful twentysomethings laughing, beautiful twentysomethings pointing accusing fingers at one another... that sort of thing. The soundtrack's a gabble of unintelligible voices. When I open my eyes there's a new caption: *£250,000 AND RISING*. Then another drone shot, zooming away from the mansion and down the cliff to the coast of the island, where a rowing boat is tethered to a rickety jetty. *ONE MEANS OF ESCAPE*, says the caption.

Next, there's another montage. It begins with an underwater shot of one of the beautiful twenty-somethings wearing a teeny bikini, looking panicked at something off-camera. Then it cuts to four contestants standing in a line, performing a dance – the Macarena, perhaps? Then a blurry night-vision shot of some young guy going totally *Blair Witch*, his eyes wide in the dark.

THE CHALLENGE OF A LIFETIME, the caption says.

More foghorns. The progress bar of the media player indicates the title sequence is coming to an end, thank God.

The title flashes up, a single word in scrawled but stylish handwriting.

ESCAPISM

Clever. I bet the programme makers were pretty chuffed with the title. Bonuses all round.

This is all well and good, INSIDER, but why send it to me? Perhaps they've mistaken me for a TV reviewer. Maybe I *should* be a TV reviewer. I watch enough of it. In fact, there are worse names for a TV-review podcast than *Rhea View...*

I'm getting distracted.

At least one thing is clear: the attachment didn't kill my computer. The second attachment has an even less illuminating filename than the first one: *Cec16.avi*

I click on the file, willing INSIDER to come up with the goods. Deliver me from my boredom.

This video's far less likely to trigger a migraine. It's higher-resolution, and the camera's fixed. It shows a young woman sitting on an armchair in a wood-panelled study with paintings on the wall.

She looks in a bad way. Her blonde hair is mussed. Tears have formed black mascara streaks below her left eye, and the right side of her face is blackened as though from soot. And there's another dark smear on her forehead. It glistens, reflecting the light from nearby angled lamps.

It looks like blood.

She's staring up at the ceiling, breathing heavily, her hands clutching each other.

I turn up the volume. I can hear her uneven breathing. Is she injured?

I yelp as an abrupt, echoing click comes from the speakers.

The woman's eyes flick down so that she's staring directly at the camera. Directly at me. She's very beautiful, despite the state she's in. Now that she's lowered her head, the blood begins to drip down from her forehead and into her left eye, but she doesn't seem to notice.

"Are you there?" she asks. She has an accent, European. French, maybe. "Are you there?" she says again.

I shudder. It really feels like she's speaking directly to me, as if this is a live webcam rather than a recorded video.

There's another click.

"You have to get us away from here," the woman says. She takes a long, ragged breath. "You must get us all off this island right away."

No response.

Her face crumples. "What will it take to convince you?" she asks in a pleading tone. "First a serious injury. Then a building on fire. And now... you understand that someone's been killed, don't you?" Her breath hitches. "They're actually *dead*."

Her eyes dart. I wonder what she's looking at.

"Talk to me!" she demands.

The only response is another echoing click.

She rubs her left eye, smearing blood into her eye

socket. Then she looks at her stained hand, grimacing, her nostrils flaring.

Abruptly, she pushes herself off the armchair to come closer – closer to *me* – so that her face fills the screen, so close that I can see the pores in her nose. The blood appears crimson now.

She shields her eyes as if peering into darkness. When she speaks again, her tone is harder, her French accent more pronounced.

"Get me off this island now," she says, "or I'll break this fucking glass and I'll drag you out of there kicking and screaming. Do you hear me?"

Then her resolve seems to fail. She slumps back onto the chair, a puppet with cut strings.

In a much quieter voice – a tone of defeat – she says again, "Do you hear me?"

DAY 2

Six months earlier

Aura

As the other contestants troop into the dining room, gazing around at the nicotine-yellow flock wallpaper and the framed portraits of old-fashioned military types, I imagine they're taking part in a bizarre fashion show. The range of outfits on display is hilarious. There's Ben, for example, wearing corduroy trousers that are worn at the knees and a fleece that has bobbles on its bobbles. And there's Doc Leaf, who's opted for a scuzzy camo gilet over a Stone Roses T-shirt. At the other end of the spectrum are Victor, in the same pale blue suit he was wearing yesterday, somehow still lacking any creases, and Cécile, whose crimson pencil dress and stiletto heels match her lipstick in both colour and severity.

And me? This morning I'm wearing a shiny black backless catsuit, an outfit that not only shows that I'm badass, but also emphasises the purple of my hair. I call the look *cyberpunk ninja*. Paying attention to my appearance is the easiest way to make sure viewers will notice me. And I can't help but think further ahead. After *Escapism* is broadcast, I'll appear on *Saturday Kitchen*, chat shows… basically everywhere.

I was first into the dining room, so I've been able to watch the disappointment on each face as the other contestants enter and see what's on offer to eat. Let's see… there's a stack of toast with crumbs littered around the serving rack. Croissants so dry that a fingernail can't

52

penetrate their flaky shells. Boxes of cereal with white paper wrapped around them so the packaging isn't visible, but applied so badly that I can see they're cheap supermarket-own brands. A bowl of fruit that at first glance I jokingly told myself looked like plastic, and you know what? They actually are.

We all take our seats, without too much jostling for position. I suppose we're all still getting the measure of each other, and haven't settled into cliques yet. A lot of the contestants look a bit worse for wear, having drunk most of the beers and spirits in the bar yesterday evening. I called it a night just after midnight, kissing everyone I met as I weaved my way to the door of the sitting room, telling them I loved them. The truth is, I wasn't at all drunk. But the character I've chosen to play is *party girl*, and I have to live up to it.

Sasha is sitting at the head of the table, as if she's decided she's the mum of the group. When she glances at me, I look away. What is it with her and her judgy looks?

"Mate, I so need this," Victor says, downing his black coffee in a single gulp. Then he drops the cup to the table with a clatter, wincing and sticking out his tongue. "What the actual fuck is that supposed to be?"

Others sip their drinks too. Their noses all wrinkle.

I try my drink. I swear it tastes like Marmite mixed with salty tears.

Ralphie appears close to tears himself. "But I *love* coffee," he says mournfully. "I really need it, every morning. It sets me up for the day."

"I'm guessing we all feel that way," Dez says in a dry tone. "Maybe it's intentional. Maybe the idea is to make us desperate before we even start the games."

This prompts murmurs around the table. Sasha and Cécile giggle about what they'd do with their share of two hundred and fifty thousand pounds. Victor interrupts them, insisting that investment is the only way to go, and he could double any amount of money in just a few months if they entrusted it to him.

"But honestly, I don't know what I'll do without coffee," Ralphie says, still behaving as if he's the only person in the world who's discovered the stimulant effects of caffeine. Then his eyes light up, and he reaches for a huge teapot in the centre of the table. He pours his rejected coffee into a nearby cereal bowl, then refills it with tea. It's the colour of rainwater. Ralphie plops the pot down, opens the lid and peers inside. "There's only one teabag in there!" he complains.

Ben tugs at the white paper masking one of the cereal packets. "There's no ingredients lists for most of these things. No allergy information. That's not just inconsiderate, it's downright reckless."

People start helping themselves to food, but quite slowly, as though they still hold out hope that somebody will walk through the door pushing a trolley laden with *proper* breakfast items. I don't have much sympathy for them. I was brought up on this sort of food, this sort of disappointment, at every meal. I might not like it, but it doesn't faze me.

"I tell you what," I say brightly, nibbling a hard corner of croissant, "when our Tripadvisor reviews go up, this place is done for."

Dez laughs. "I'm composing it in my head already."

"No, no, please don't talk of it," Cécile says. There's a playful, melodic quality to her heavily French-accented voice. "You make me think of my poor phone, trapped in that dark sack!"

There are groans from all around the table.

"I miss my phone so much," Dez says.

"Last night, when I went to bed, I was looking for it for like twenty minutes," Ruth says. Then she blushes and adds, "I *was* quite drunk. But then I did the same thing again this morning."

"It's weird, isn't it?" I say. "When Axel showed up yesterday, the first thing I thought was: Who's he? And the second thing was: I'd better Google him and find out. Does anybody recognise him?"

Everyone shakes their heads.

"He's quite the silver fox, though," Ruth says, and her cheeks glow even more fiercely.

"And he knows it," Dez adds. "Have you seen how often he looks in the mirror?"

Then Victor says sharply, "Mate, you okay?" He's speaking to Doc Leaf, who's slumped so far down in his seat that his eyes are level with the surface of the table. This morning he's not wearing a hat, and I realise he's older than I first assumed, his hair thinning at the crown.

When Doc Leaf doesn't respond, Victor puts a hand on his shoulder and jostles him roughly. "Big night last night, mate. Maybe should have gone easy on day one."

Even though I'm halfway along the table, with three other people between us, I jolt when Doc Leaf pushes himself up abruptly, roaring, "Fuck yeah! Let's do this thing!"

People all glance at one another. I can't imagine anybody wants this particular type of livewire in the group.

"Do what thing, mate?" Victor asks.

Suddenly, Doc Leaf is on his feet. He knocks over his chair. "Let's get this show on the road, people!"

The silence is deafening.

It's Ben who finally speaks up. "We haven't actually been told what we'll be doing this morning."

"We'll be raising hell, am I right?" Doc Leaf says. Spittle sprays from his lips, some of it raining onto Cécile's plate. Without a word, she pops her croissant back on to the serving plate.

Victor rises to his feet and approaches Doc Leaf slowly, as if he's a wild horse. Victor's shoulder muscles are visible through the fabric of his shirt. The sight strikes me as delicious. I'll compliment him on it later and see where that leads.

But he doesn't get a chance to tame Doc Leaf. When the door bursts open, everybody's immediately distracted.

"Have you seen it?" Mira says breathlessly as she barges in.

The only response is a bunch of Scooby Doo "Huh?" noises.

"Come and see!" she says, and then she's gone again.

Immediately, we're all up and out of our seats. We follow Mira to the study and all go inside, ignoring the LED sign with the name *Ben* just about legible amongst its flickering pixels.

The study's far too small for all of us, and people start huffing and complaining right away. In fact, there's even less space than there was yesterday. The area behind the armchair is now taken up by a large, freestanding safe.

"I came in to chat to the robot voice before brekkie," Mira says. "But fuck that. Look at this thing!" She jabs a finger at the safe and grins. "My money's being kept in there, you know."

This prompts a load of posturing from other contestants, like they can just argue their case to win the cash, instead of competing in tasks.

I shove my way closer to examine the safe. Ben's already walking around it, studying it like it's a sculpture in an art gallery.

"The back and sides are completely blank," he says. Then he drops to his hands and knees to look at the base, which is supported by stubby metal legs. "Nothing down here either. Seems like it's opened the usual way."

But it's not usual at all. I reach out to touch the door of

the safe. Its join barely registers under my fingertips, it's so well fitting. The door is blank, with no instructions or maker's mark. There's no wheel mechanism like in old heist films, and no keypad either. The only things that break up the flat surface are four keyholes, one in each corner of the door.

"Can't believe I'm gonna have to win four tasks before I can get my cash," Mira says. She reaches out to grab Dez's wrist. "Or two tasks each, if you fancy going sharesies?"

Dez grins and nods. I stifle a grimace at seeing the first alliance being established so quickly and so easily.

"It's true that our host told us to work together," Victor says thoughtfully. Then he lunges forward and flings his arms around the safe. "So let's just chuck this bastard off the cliff and smash it open!"

Everyone else just watches on. It's not only that Victor's plan won't work. If it *did* work, it'd mean sharing the prize money between all ten of us... or fighting for the spoils.

To my relief, the safe doesn't budge an inch.

Doc Leaf pushes through the group and starts kicking the safe. I mean, what the hell?

Even Victor seems horrified.

"Mate, I was only joking," he says. "You need to calm down."

"Calm is for old people," Doc Leaf replies. He swings around to point at Sasha. "Like her!"

There's a chorus of defensive "Hey" sounds, but nothing more than that.

Then the robotic voice of the study comes from hidden speakers: "Please return to the dining room for your briefing."

"And what if we don't?" Doc Leaf shouts.

Victor clamps his hand on Doc Leaf's shoulder. "Good

idea. Maybe take yourself away, get your head together. Yeah?"

Doc Leaf sizes Victor up. Then he says quietly, "Yeah." He turns to the rest of us and shouts, "Got to get my head in the *game*, people!"

With that, he stumbles towards the door and he's gone.

We all let out the breaths we've been holding in.

I go to Victor, putting my hand on his muscly arm. "Thank you," I say.

He grins. In a mock-American accent, he says, "No trouble at all, ma'am."

But Doc Leaf *is* trouble, and we all know it.

Dez

When Axel reappears after breakfast, he seems a bit more prepared than he was yesterday. He's wearing a black polo neck shirt, as if he's deliberately attempted to match Aura's slinky catsuit. It occurs to me that might actually be possible: he could have been watching us all via hidden cameras since we came down to breakfast. It's funny how quickly you forget you're being filmed.

"I trust you've all had a pleasant night's sleep, and a hearty breakfast?" Axel begins.

A few people start to speak, but he cuts them off. He glances down at the piss-poor food we've been fed, then looks away. "Good. Now that you've got settled in, I propose that we set to work. What say you?"

There are murmurs of approval. I don't say anything, but my stomach rumbles audibly. If this was a psychological study of some sort, there might be good reason for providing inadequate food. It'd make subjects compliant, more needy.

"Personally, I like to keep the mind active while I enjoy my morning coffee," Axel says. He pulls out his phone from his pocket, and I notice the people sitting near me lean forward as if drawn to the forbidden technology. Axel mimes tapping on the phone screen. "Puzzles are all the rage, aren't they? Like everyone else, I can't get enough of them. Who here enjoys word games?"

There are half-hearted murmurs and a single whoop, which comes from Ben, of course. No hint of irony from him.

"And who's more a fan of spacial puzzles?"

Fewer cheers this time. Probably, some people aren't

certain what 'spacial' means. It doesn't help that Axel's pronouncement of the word is slightly unusual, as if he's sounding it out himself. For the first time, I wonder if he's not actually English.

"And who enjoys both equally?" Axel asks.

No response.

Axel's face falls, but it's an exaggerated pantomime of an expression. "Oh dear. Then you may not relish the task I've prepared for you this morning."

He brightens. "Without further ado, then, how about we make our way to the hall where we will find our first task? It's a place I like to call…" he pauses, milking the silence for effect, "*the hall of tasks.*"

Almost everyone groans, but it's good-natured. Axel has managed to get everyone on side.

As the contestants troop out of the room, following our host, I turn to look at the table and my stomach rumbles again. There's nothing here I can bear to eat. Instead, I take one of the silver teaspoons and stick it in my pocket.

*

The door labelled *Hall* is on the opposite side of the entrance lobby, next to a room with a sign reading *Billiard Room*, even though it actually contains a pool table rather than a big billiard table. The door to the hall of tasks has been locked before now – I know, because I checked it.

The hall is big enough for our voices to echo, and it has tall ceilings and mock-Greek pillars along the length of each wall, and a parquet wooden floor, like a village hall. Its ceiling is painted with roses and thorns, which doesn't match the tone of the rest of the room at all. It might once have been a ballroom, or perhaps a banqueting hall, something like that. The fact that our group doesn't eat here but in the much smaller dining room makes me wonder in turn where the production team eat. Since Imogen welcomed us to the mansion, the only non-contestant we've seen is Axel. How many people are involved in the running of this show? How many are watching us at this moment?

Lined up in the centre of the hall are four collections of blocks each as tall as a person, which look like they might be made of plywood or fibreglass. The blocks in each group are a uniform colour: yellow on the left, then blue, then red, then green on the right.

Axel dances towards the blocks. "Do come closer," he purrs. "I can assure you there's no danger." Then, with a wicked grin, he adds, "On this occasion."

As we approach, I see that I was wrong about the blocks in each group all being the same. One block in each collection is different – it's actually a cage. Inside each cage hangs the sort of rubbery full-size skeleton you might see in a shop window at Hallowe'en.

Ruth squeals when she sees them. Is she for real? I have an unnerving suspicion that she is.

"Of course, it's too late for these poor chaps," Axel says, gesturing at the skeletons. "Try as they might, they failed to escape. But that doesn't mean that my family wouldn't prefer their ancestors to be freed. And let's face it, you can use all the practice in escapism that you can get."

Like so much of this show already, his explanation barely makes sense. But fair enough, a puzzle's a puzzle. Getting a cage out from the middle of some blocks shouldn't be too hard.

At the far end of the room is a short balcony with wrought-iron steps leading up to it. I can imagine it's where a quartet of musicians might have played, or where someone might deliver a speech to the occupants of the hall.

Axel moves to the nearest puzzle. "Each long block can be slid back and forth, but not sideways. And the aim, of course, is to release the central block."

Now I see there's a small wall around each collection of blocks, and a gap on one side.

Axel surveys us all thoughtfully. "I can see that several of you have gleaned the aim of the task. You must release my unlucky ancestors by rearranging the blocks and then delivering their cage to me."

Ralphie raises his hand. He's probably been out of school for little enough time that the action comes naturally to him. "Then do we have to get the cage open to get them out?"

For a moment Axel looks flummoxed. Then he says, "No, I'll keep them in their cages. In my bedroom."

Nice one, Axel. It might have been a desperate ad lib, but his comment is bizarre enough that it prevents any further questions.

"You will work in four teams," he continues. "Whichever team frees one of my ancestors first will be presented with a key. One member of each team will move the blocks, and the remainder of the team will be up there—" he points to the balcony "—providing assistance from a bird's eye view."

It's only now that I realise that the blocks are so tall that whoever's sliding them won't have visibility of the overall puzzle.

"But!" Axel says. "That's not all! Those sliding puzzles are child's play, and you're not children. You've had your coffee and now you must do your daily word puzzle."

He gestures for us to follow him as he moves closer to the balcony at the rear of the room. Hanging below it are four signs covered with black cloth. "When I remove these coverings, whoever has been chosen to move the blocks will see a word puzzle – a word with missing letters.

Whenever the klaxon sounds, that player must shout a word that completes the puzzle. Shall we hear the klaxon, for reference? Yes, we shall."

He pauses, looking up expectantly.

The wait lasts so long that the rest of us look around, too. As well as huge lamps dotted between the Greek columns, there are heavy-duty speakers on metal poles.

"The klaxon, please!" Axel shouts. His expression becomes more pained the longer he's made to wait.

Finally, a sharp siren sound comes from the speakers. It's loud enough to make a few of the contestants clamp their hands over their ears.

"If you fail to provide a suitable word within ten seconds of the klaxon, you must halt all work for *another* ten seconds," Axel says. "And I should mention that giving the word puzzle your full attention will pay off – literally. Five thousand pounds will be added to the prize money for each correct word solution, across all teams. Now, is everything perfectly clear?"

We contestants look at each other. No, Axel, *clear* is not the word that springs to mind. But the mention of more money is enough to keep everyone sweet.

"Good," Axel says, oblivious. "Now please arrange yourselves into four teams!"

Suddenly, everyone hurries to form themselves into groups, each of us desperate not to end up shackled to one of the hopeless cases.

Dolly

"Shit," I mutter. "Shitting shitbags."

The production suite is empty. Imogen was here when I settled down in front of the monitors to watch the contestants eat breakfast and then troop to the hall, but now she's nowhere to be seen.

I rush to the door and stick my head out into the servants' corridor that allows us to move around the building without being seen by the contestants. I sprint along it to reach Imogen's bedroom, then knock on it, hard.

"Imogen!" I hiss. I remember that all of the contestants are in the hall, and can't possibly hear me. I raise my voice to a shout. "Imogen!"

No answer.

There's no time to lose. I run along the hall, past my own bedroom, and another than isn't in use, to reach the door to Lonnie's room. Lonnie is the 'everything guy' – his job is to take care of anything physical involved in setting up the tasks. That means we have to place a lot of trust in him, though it's now clear to me that we definitely shouldn't.

"Lonnie!" I call, hammering on his door.

I hear a murmur from inside the room, which continues even when I knock again. What's he up to in there?

I grunt in annoyance and scurry back along the corridor to the production suite.

In a last-ditch attempt to find someone who can help me, I push the swing door leading to the mini studio where I conduct the one-to-one interviews. My area is empty, lit as always with a single red desk lamp – but to my surprise, the study beyond the one-way glass *isn't* empty. Doc Leaf is sprawled in the armchair, somehow taking up loads of room despite being really short. I'd forgotten about him after he blundered out of the dining room.

I haven't got time to speak to him. I hit the mic button and snap, "You need to go to the hall of tasks!"

Doc Leaf's body spasms and he lets out a muffled "Wha—"

"Go to the entrance lobby, then first door on your right," I say. "Go *now*."

He's moving. I have to believe he'll do as I say. I *really* don't have time for this.

I duck back into the production suite to check the monitors. To my relief, the contestants are still haggling over who's in which team.

On the desk beneath the bank of monitors are the objects that made me panic in the first place: the four signs containing word puzzles, which should at this moment be placed beneath the black cloths on the hanging placards. In the hall of tasks.

I'll kill Lonnie when I get my hands on him.

Later. Right now, there's only me to save the day.

I snatch up the four word puzzles and hug them to my chest as I push through the door. There are corridors all around the mansion, and my key will get me past any of the locks installed by the team that prepped the place long before we arrived. Even so, it surprises me how easily I'm able to navigate to a door that leads to the balcony in the hall of tasks.

I push open the door a crack. The contestants are at the other end of the hall, more or less arranged into four groups now. Axel is cajoling them playfully – he seems to be getting into the swing of things after his less than impressive start yesterday. He's as handsome as ever, to the point of distraction.

I take a breath and creep onto the balcony. Like the hall floor, its surface is made of wooden parquet blocks. They're slightly uneven and each of them makes a faint click as I put my weight on it.

At times I've worried I might be agoraphobic – even the idea of being in open countryside leaves me unable to breathe normally. The sensation I'm feeling now is something like that panic. I feel totally exposed. The idea of any of the contestants turning to look up at me fills me with horror.

Of course, I'm already being watched, by the cameras fixed to the edges of the balcony railings. I have to believe I'll be left out of the edit.

Concentrate, Dolly.

I lower myself to the surface of the balcony, the puzzle boards hugged to my chest, and I reach through the metal railings. It's a bit of a fumble, but I manage to snag the first of the black cloths from beneath the overhang, then shift along to repeat the action three more times. The railings are a filigree of wrought-iron and fiddly to negotiate, and the thorns of metal roses dig into the flesh of my arms.

That was the easy bit.

A loud sound makes me look up. Axel has clapped his hands together. It looks like the four teams have been agreed upon: three teams of two and one team of three. Any second now, Axel will direct everyone's attention to the task. And when that happens, everyone in the room will see me, squished against the floor of the balcony, grinning in panic.

My hands are shaking as I feed the first of the puzzle boards through the railing and struggle to place it in the housing of the placard beneath the balcony. But it's done. This is doable. I can do this.

Puzzle board number two. Pull it from under my body,

ease it through the gap, feel around for the housing, slip it in.

I'm *amazing*. I'm so good under pressure that I should be one of the contestants.

"It took a while, but we got there eventually!" Axel says.

No, no, no. Not yet, Axel. Ten more seconds. Maybe twenty.

Board number three. Shuffle sideways, board out from under the body, through the gap, feel for the housing, into the—

Shit.

The puzzle board slips from my fingers, which are damp with sweat.

My hand shoots out. My left cheek pushes painfully against the metal thorns of the iron railing as I extend my arm as far as it will go.

It's not possible—

And yet I catch it. Somehow, I catch it.

I push the board into the housing. Retract my arm. I'm shaking like a leaf.

"Now, let's get started!" Axel calls.

I hear a flurry of cheers, then the sound of feet shifting on the creaking parquet floor.

I could weep right now. I squeeze my eyes shut, as if I won't be seen if I can't see the contestants.

Then I hear a loud thud.

"Sorry," a husky voice says.

My first thought is that it's Lonnie come to help me, but then I realise the voice came from the far end of the hall, behind the contestants.

I open my eyes.

Doc Leaf is standing in the doorway, leaning heavily on the frame.

Everybody turns to look at him. Axel doesn't seem to

know what to say.

It takes me a few seconds to recognise that the last thing I should be doing right now is just *watching*.

Board number four, out from under the body, through the gap, feel for the housing, into the frame.

I did it.

I *did* it.

"No problem at all!" Axel says to Doc Leaf. His avuncular tone sounds even more forced than usual. "Your teammates will explain what's required of you." He points at Ben and Sasha, who exchange uneasy glances.

I back away. The balcony flooring creaks, but I don't slow down.

After I make it through the door I drop to my hands and knees, gasping with relief.

Ben

This is exactly my sort of thing. That's what I keep telling myself. But the moment the task begins, I experience a sinking feeling that I can't shake.

The other teams seem to be making good progress. Each of their block puzzles are beginning to clear, leaving the cage block free to slide little by little towards the gap in the frame. Up here on the balcony there's a cacophony of voices, making our advice for our block-pushers hard for them to make out. It doesn't help that our team has been assigned the red puzzle, which is one of the middle ones. Contestants keep shoving me on either side, and even Sasha, who's on my team, keeps jogging my arm and breaking my concentration.

It doesn't help that Doc Leaf insisted he'd be the one to push the blocks. I'm not even sure he understood the aim of the task. He keeps losing his grip on the blocks and slipping to the floor, giggling. Several times, he tried to slide them sideways instead of forwards or backwards, earning a scolding from Axel.

I lean over the railings and gesticulate like crazy, trying to get Doc Leaf's attention. "That one in the corner!" I shout. "Bring it towards me! No, not that way – towards *me*!"

It's hopeless. Doc Leaf doesn't even raise his eyes to look at Sasha and me on the balcony. He just keeps pushing at random blocks, sniggering to himself.

Abruptly, the klaxon rings out. Three of the four contestants below us stop pushing the blocks. Doc Leaf carries on stumbling around, as if he didn't hear a thing.

Victor pauses only for a moment to look up at the

placard bearing the clue for the yellow team, then shouts, "Horse!"

"Youth!" Mira calls out from the next puzzle along.

"Yellow and blue, your answers are accepted," Axel says. "Carry on!"

Ruth turns and stares at Axel. Both her hands are waving madly, as if that might help her think of a word that fits her puzzle clue.

Finally, she says weakly, "Horse?"

"No," Axel says. "Green and red teams, you have five seconds to offer an appropriate word."

Ruth's mouth opens and closes, but she doesn't offer another answer. Doc Leaf still doesn't seem to understand what's happening.

"Doc Leaf – the sign!" I shout at him.

To my surprise, he looks up. He sees me pointing downwards, and his eyes drop to the sign hanging directly below my feet, which I can't see. His nose wrinkles and his head tilts. What on earth is he doing?

"Time's up, green and red!" Axel shouts. "Please stand away from your blocks."

Ruth does as she's told, but Doc Leaf keeps shoving at the blocks.

"Stand *back*, please," Axel says. He puts his hand on Doc Leaf's shoulder, then jerks back when Doc Leaf whirls around to leer at him.

From beside me, Sasha shouts down from the balcony, "Hey, Axel? Can we swap out? Doc Leaf's getting nowhere."

Axel's face is white. "Certainly," he says in a quiet voice.

Sasha moves towards the balcony steps. But we're so far behind in our puzzle that we haven't got time to make mistakes or be democratic about who gets to have the next try. It has to be me.

I bound past Sasha and hurry down the steps. I shoot her an apologetic look as I reach the floor, and she responds with a raised-eyebrow expression that means *I'm not angry, I'm just disappointed.*

"Sorry, Doc," I say. "We have to swap places if you don't solve the word puzzle."

It's not true, but it's plausible enough. Doc Leaf gives the nearest block a kick, then lumbers away, dropping to his haunches directly beside Axel, who edges away from him.

Axel taps his watch. "Red and green teams, you may recommence the puzzle!"

I set to work. The thing is, when I was up on the balcony, I had a clear idea of which blocks needed to be moved to free the cage, but down here my mental image of the layout of the puzzle is immediately muddled. I spend valuable time pushing blocks to and fro, before it occurs to me to move to the opposite side of the frame so that my orientation is the same as when I was looking from above. Even then, I have no real idea what I'm doing.

I realise that Sasha's been calling down to me. I look up at her, lip-reading rather than hearing her voice due to the shouts of the other teams. I squint as I track her gestures to understand which blocks she's referring to.

With Sasha's help, I think I'm beginning to get somewhere.

So of course that's when the klaxon sounds again.

I'd forgotten about the word puzzle. I thought I was prepared for this sort of task, but it turns out I'm as clueless as anyone, under pressure.

I look up. On each of the signs hanging beneath the balcony is written two letters, with three blanks that need to be filled.

"Retro!" Mira calls out. I glance up at her sign, which reads R□T□□.

Axel hesitates. He touches his ear. "I think that's not a proper word," he says uncertainly.

"Retry!" Mira shouts instantly.

Axel nods, and Mira sets to work again.

I look at my sign – and now I understand why Doc Leaf tilted his head earlier. The sign is upside down. The others are all as they should be. What have we done to deserve this extra challenge?

It's not difficult to read a single word upside down, is it? But for some reason this unexpected change throws me completely. For a couple of seconds I can't even force my brain to recognise the letters.

I take a deep breath and say out loud: "A, blank, blank, blank, E."

Again, not difficult at all.

A□□□E

But my mind is as blank as the middle of that word.

"What are the letters?" Sasha shouts from the balcony.

I just shake my head. I need to think.

From somewhere behind me, Doc Leaf calls out, "Arse!" But that's only four letters.

"Chimp!" Ruth shouts.

I actually growl at her for putting me off.

"Yes!" Axel says. "Carry on!"

I turn to look at him. "Chimp's an abbreviation, just like 'retro'," I say.

Axel shrugs.

"Ignore the others!" Sasha shouts at me from above.

She's right. I need to focus. I need to wake up.

"Two seconds, red and yellow teams," Axel warns.

Wake up, Ben.

I bellow, "Awake!"

"Carry on, red team," Axel says. "Yellow team, stand back for ten seconds."

I shoot a glance at Victor, who's staring at our host with

undisguised loathing. For a moment it looks like he might disobey, but then he steps away.

My heartbeat almost blocks out the sound of voices as I set to work again. This time, I face the balcony, and my eyes are on Sasha as much as the blocks themselves. I have to trust she knows what she's doing. I push and shove, no longer thinking, just carrying out her directions.

The klaxon sounds again.

"Arise!" I shout.

Then I look up at the sign. It's still upside down, but the letters have changed.

D □ □ □ T

I stare at it.

I keep staring. I call up to Sasha, "D something something something T."

"Conga!" Mira shouts.

"Punch!" Victor cries.

"Laugh?" Ruth says. "Lamp… no, lamps?" Then, bafflingly, "Horse?"

I shake my head, willing everyone to shut up.

"Carry on, blue, yellow and green teams," Axel says.

Sasha's shouting at me. What's she saying? I squint up at her, trying to watch her lips. Is she saying *dig it*? But that's two words.

Even when I hear her say "digit" it doesn't register as a real word.

It turns out I can't do this.

Then:

"Doubt!" I roar. "Doubt!"

"Very good," Axel says. "Carry on, red team."

Now that I'm paying full attention, Sasha's instructions are crystal clear. I can see that she's solved the puzzle even before the cage comes free and drops down from the gap in the frame.

"The red team wins!" Axel announces.

73

"All *right*!" Doc Leaf says, lurching to his feet and making an obnoxious klaxon sound to rival the one from the speakers.

"Very good work, teams," Axel says. "Now, please gather around and I will present the red team with their prize."

The contestants file down from the balcony, looking dejected. Sasha comes to stand at my side. She has that judgemental look on her face again.

"I'm sorry," I whisper. "I really thought I'd be good at it."

She puts her arm around me. "It worked out in the end, didn't it? No sweat."

I realise that I *am* sweating. Not only was I terrible at the task, I'll look a disgrace on the TV to boot.

When we're all gathered in a horseshoe shape, Axel says, "First, a minor administrative matter. I'm happy to tell you that eight word puzzles were solved, which will result in forty thousand pounds being added to the prize money."

Everyone goes nuts. I mean, not me, obviously – I'm too self-conscious for that. And I'm struggling to take it in: £40,000, for that dreadful performance? The starting prize pot of £250,000 was already more money than I can actually imagine. After ten tasks, the total might easily sail over half a million. Suddenly, the idea of sharing the money doesn't seem so bad.

Axel draws a white envelope from his pocket with a flourish.

"Red team, please nominate one of your number to receive your prize," he says.

Me and Sasha look at each other. Doc Leaf seems to have forgotten he was on our team, which suits me fine. Sasha raises an eyebrow in an echo of her earlier disappointed expression. I get the message, and gesture for her to move forward.

As I watch her take the envelope and turn her back on the rest of us to peer into it, I can't shake the feeling I've made another mistake.

Winning this game is going to be much harder than I expected.

Six months later

Rhea

The second the door opens, I use my walking cane to hoist myself from my seat in the corridor, and then I push through the throng of students leaving the lecture hall. Even though they're only a few years younger than me, I imagine myself as an old hack, doling out advice to these kids: *You want to be a sound engineer? Ah, it's a young person's game.*

Ted's standing behind his desk, chatting cheerfully to a male student with a ponytail, but when he glances up and catches sight of me, his expression glazes.

I wait for a few seconds to give the student time to finish up. When he doesn't, I reach out to tap the table with my cane, then say, "We had that appointment, Ted?"

The student turns, clocks me and begins to apologise.

"Don't mind her," Ted says. "We don't actually have an appointment."

"It's a sort of open appointment," I explain. I give the student a friendly nudge. "And don't you have another class to get to?"

"This is my last lecture of the day," he replies. "And I really would like to ask Mr Monhegan about a couple of aspects that—"

"Off you pop home, then," I say, my tone oozing warmth. "The sooner you get to bed, the brighter you'll be tomorrow morning. Ted and I need to discuss something… and just maybe it relates to your grades."

The student begins to speak, decides against it, then shuffles away looking bewildered.

"Nice boy," I say.

"I'd appreciate it if you didn't come in here and scare my students," Ted says. "My *actual* students, as opposed to whatever you consider yourself to be."

"An alumnus," I say.

"But you came to only a few lectures, and you weren't even supposed to be here in the first place. You were escorted off the campus, Rhea. Frankly, I'm amazed you've managed to get back in here without being spotted. Are you going to tell me you've enrolled on the Music Production BA legitimately?"

"Don't need to. You're an amazing tutor, Ted – the speed you can get information across! You should be proud of yourself. Hey, do you really get them all to call you Mr Monhegan?"

He shrugs. "I'm not sure I specified either way."

"Sure, Ted. Sure."

"Maybe it's because I'm a visiting lecturer. It does confer a level of respect—"

"I suppose the truth is that your *actual* audio engineering career has stalled, which is why you've ended up here at Leeds Beckett, teaching wastrels who think they have a chance of becoming the next Mark Ronson or something."

"My module's actually specific to TV and film, so that's not…"

He trails off as the final few students make their way outside, chatting about, I don't know, hair or vodka or something.

"*This* is my career, for now," he says quietly, "and I take it very seriously."

"We both do."

He sighs. "Remind me, what is your career?"

"Journalist. Adventuress. Podcaster extraordinaire. Did you listen to my podcast?"

He hesitates, weighing up his answer. "The first episode, yes."

"And?"

"It was… passionately delivered."

"Have some sense of decorum, Mr Monhegan! I'm one of your *students*!"

"I mean it was clear that you care about your subject."

I can see he's being as honest as he can be. But I can read between the lines.

"You thought it was crap, didn't you?" Before he can answer, I add, "In terms of sound engineering and all that."

He rubs his nose, which is his tic whenever he's embarrassed. Before I was caught sneaking into lectures a couple of months ago, I'd keep out of sight at the back of the hall, and more often than not, my notes consisted of doodled caricatures of Ted. I actually used it as my line of defence: how could I be accused of stealing an education if I'd learned precisely nothing?

"I thought it needed a fair amount of work, in terms of production," Ted says.

"Everything I know, I learnt from you."

"If you'd come to more of my lectures…"

"They wouldn't let me. But I *did* come and bother you in your free time, didn't I?"

"You did indeed," Ted replies wearily. "I suppose that does demonstrate enthusiasm, at least."

"And it filled up some of your lonely hours. Not having a family, and all that."

"Neither do you, Rhea."

"But I'm twenty-seven. You're… what? Sixty?"

"Fifty-one. Do I look sixty?"

His hair is white at the sides, and so's his scruffy beard. His glasses are huge, the lenses shaped like teardrops, a style that was maybe fashionable in the 1980s. He wears a brown cardigan. Ugh, just those two words next to each other: Brown. Cardigan.

"No," I say decisively, even though he definitely does look sixty. "Anyway. I'm just saying I might be able to introduce something to your life that you're missing."

He rubs his nose again. "How about you get to the point, Rhea?"

"I'm starting a new podcast. A proper one. And it needs to sound like the real thing."

"Is it the same subject? Because I'm not sure it's really appropriate—"

"No. It's a big story. Seriously."

Ted eyes the door again. Then he seems to admit defeat. He sits down behind his desk and I scrape a chair noisily to sit opposite him, staring into his eyes.

"*Escapism*," I say.

"Like Harry Houdini?"

"No. The TV game show."

"I've never heard of it."

"That's because it was never broadcast."

"You mean you have an *idea* for a TV show?"

I shake my head. "It was filmed, six months ago, up in Northumberland – or rather, an island off the Northumbrian coast. And it all went south." I see his immediate confusion. "I mean the filming went wrong. And I mean *wrong* wrong. Badly wrong."

"How badly?"

"Someone was killed. Utter panic. Blood everywhere. And then it was all covered up."

"Where did you learn about this?"

"The internet."

Ted pats the table twice, as if to say he's done here. "It's not really a cover-up if you read about it online, is it?"

I reach out and clasp his hands. They're dry. He really is old.

"There are witnesses," I say. "Someone who lives on the coast say they saw a bunch of people panicking as they hurried off a boat that came from the island – and one of them was badly injured and they were carrying a body with a knife sticking out of its back. And I've been sent video files. From an insider. They literally call themselves INSIDER. One of the clips showed this really pretty woman talking to camera. She said someone was killed. And she was in a bad way herself. Bloody."

Ted's eyes are wide now.

"But why were you sent this?" he asks. "Why you?"

I wave a hand airily. "Because I'm full of obvious potential. A better question is, why should *you* be involved?"

"Because you're a terrible sound engineer, and you need a good sound engineer."

I point a pistol-finger at him. "It's like we can read each other's minds."

Ted's quiet for more than ten seconds. Then he glances at my walking cane. "You're sure you're up to it, in terms of your health?"

I tap on my forehead with my knuckles. "I'm steady as an oak." In truth, the forehead-knocking hurt quite a lot, and now I'm dizzy. Since my accident all those years ago, I've always imagined each extra bonk on the head destroys another bit of my brain, wipes another memory, and I've already lost enough. I can barely remember my childhood.

"There must be real information about it," Ted says thoughtfully. "From a source we can trust." His head tilts back and his eyes dart.

Then they flick back to me. "You'll take heed of my advice?" he says. "You'll let me do my thing in terms of editing, as well as recording? Because true crime has its particular conventions that you need to get right."

"*Take heed?*" I repeat. "Yes, old-timer, I'll *take heed*. You can have carte blank."

"I think you mean carte blanche. Or a blank cheque."

I nod. "Yeah, good point. You might need to spend a bit up front."

"And I'll want to see those videos."

"How about now?"

"You have them on your phone?"

I roll my eyes. "Us young folk have *everything* on our phones." I pull my phone from the pocket of my vintage bomber jacket, then stick out my tongue, which for some reason is the only expression the facial recognition accepts as proving I'm me. Then I say, "Oh!"

"Oh?" Ted repeats.

I tap at the screen. "Perfect timing, huh? I've been sent another one."

I open the email from INSIDER, then shift to Ted's side of the table before I open the attachment.

The setting is the same wood-panelled room as in the previous video, but the person sitting in the chair is different. It's a bloke, maybe in his mid-to-late thirties, pretty nondescript, with one of those sorts of faces that makes someone seem immediately familiar. His face is pale, suggesting he's the sort of indoor person who plays lots of computer games or D&D, and even if it wasn't for the paleness, his complexion isn't great. He's wearing a grey hoodie with a ghost of the North Face logo on it. It has wet patches on both shoulders.

He's leaning toward the camera, squinting as though he's looking into darkness.

"Before we get started," he says, "I just want to know it's you in there."

I don't hear any reply. It seems he doesn't hear anything either. He sits back, looking deflated.

He continues, "Because I thought maybe we'd... I don't know. Compare notes or something. I'm nervous about saying something wrong. Doing something wrong."

Still no reply. I can hear Ted's breathing in my ear. He's as hooked as I am, even though neither of us have any idea what's going on.

Finally, a voice speaks. It's grating and metallic, like a robot.

"Yes, Ben," it says slowly. "It's me."

Six months earlier

Aura

Axel herds us all into the sitting room, but when I turn around he's disappeared as if by magic. I swear this mansion must have secret corridors everywhere.

People flop onto the couches and armchairs. They seem to have forgotten that in a game show like this, there's no let-up. Just because we've finished with a stressful task doesn't mean we can take time out. We're being filmed *right now*.

"Amazing work, guys!" I call out, scampering over to high-five first Ben, then Sasha. "That puzzle was like, *so* difficult." Then I raise my voice for everyone to hear. "And forty thousand added to the prize money – go us!"

It pains me to behave in such a simpering manner. But that's how TV presenters behave, and that's my long game, isn't it? If I can continue behaving larger than life, I might be spotted by an agent or talent scout or whatever, and then I'll be able to make something of myself. That's my escape route.

Ben clears his throat and glances sideways at Sasha. "Yep," he says. "It was tough."

Luckily, I don't have to high-five the other member of their team. Doc Leaf is slouching over to the door leading to the bathroom, looking very hungover.

"What's with him?" I say.

Ben shrugs.

"It's amazing he got through the application process,"

Sasha adds.

Suddenly, Ben can't seem to look either of us in the eyes. He examines the wallpaper as if he finds it fascinating.

"I suppose we all have our secrets," Sasha says. "Don't we?"

I actually take a step back. The look she's giving me isn't just judgemental, like it was earlier. It's somehow familiar.

"Sasha," I say, "do I know—"

I'm cut off by Cécile, who calls out, "Everybody! There is a message here for us!"

She picks up from the coffee table an old-fashioned scroll of paper, and tugs at its red ribbon to unroll it. Her eyes scan down to the bottom.

"It's from Axel," she says with a grin. "He is shy, sending a note instead of speaking to us!"

Or he's working to rule, I suppose. He's done the first task and now he needs a breather.

Cécile continues, "It says: 'Escapism takes many forms. After this morning's arduous activities, I find myself in need of relief.'"

Sniggers come from all around. Sure. Relief, I get it.

Without meaning to, I picture Axel in his room – wherever that is – stripped to the waist, sprawled on his bed. I bet his muscles still have good definition, despite his age.

I shake my head. It's not okay to think like that about people in positions of authority. It was never okay.

Cécile waits for the laughter to die down. "There's more," she says. Then she continues reading from the scroll. "'Friends, I ask you to provide me with escapism of my own. In pairs, decide on an entertainment that you will perform. At seven this evening I will be in the sitting room to enjoy your three-minute performances, hoping that they will raise my pulse. My heart will be the judge.'"

Mira tuts. "Who wrote this stuff? 'My heart will be the judge' – seriously?"

Ralphie's been looking more and more worried. "Is he talking about tying ourselves up and then escaping? Because I've never done that before." He looks around as if trying to determine whether any of us might have had the opportunity to learn those sorts of skills. He's probably only five years younger than me, but honestly, he's like a wide-eyed school kid.

Not that I'm what you'd call worldly wise myself. Last night was the first time I slept in any bed other than my own for… let's see… eight years, maybe? I barely leave the village, and my parents keep me busy with duties at the farm shop.

Mira says, "No, mate. He's talking about escapism, as in distracting yourself from everyday life. Basically, he wants us to put on a talent show tonight."

"I have a *lot* of talents," Cécile says. What's annoying is that her French accent is so appealing and she has such natural confidence that it doesn't even sound like a boast. "In Paris I've appeared in many plays. Who will be my acting partner?"

Hands shoot up all over the place. Cécile takes her time before approaching Ruth. I'd never have guessed mousey Ruth would be such a hot property. I notice Victor watching them carefully.

I take my time to choose a partner. This isn't about picking a friend, it's about assessing who's the best match, and who's most likely to entertain Axel. What sort of performance would he like to see? And what would make me stand out the most?

Then again, I don't have any obvious skills myself. I'm good with people, sure. I charm the customers at the farm shop. I scrub up well, for rare social events. But other than that...

People are moving around me, giving me sideways glances while I stand here like a lemon. Nobody's approaching me. It's just like school, all over again.

I glance at Sasha, but for once she's not looking at me. She's standing near the mantelpiece, chatting to Ben, whose cheeks are flushed. Dez and Mira are laughing as they tramp around with their arms held out, playacting at being monsters or zombies or something. They're having fun already. Why aren't I having any fun?

I zero in on Victor, who's sitting on the sofa, watching everyone else with an amused expression on his face. Last night he clearly took a shine to me, asking me to dance again and again. I bet he can be pretty entertaining. If nothing else, it's worth continuing to make an impression on the alpha male of the group.

"Victor?" I say, introducing a cute note of shyness to my tone. "Would you like to work together?"

Victor folds his arms over his chest, his head drawn back as he appraises me. His eyes move around my face, then dart down. I can't remember the last time I felt so conscious of my appearance.

"Nah," he says. "Nah, I don't think so."

I'm frozen, utterly stunned. Victor leaps up and catches hold of Ralphie's arm as he passes. "How about me and you?" he says.

Ralphie freezes, just like me. But his expression is one of total gratitude.

"Sure!" he gasps. "Yeah. Ralphie and Victor for the win, am I right?"

Victor snorts softly. "We'll see. Come on, let's go put our heads together."

I'm left alone again. I move to the bar counter, even though a drink is the last thing I want, my stomach is churning so badly. I gaze around the room, at the pairs of contestants.

Everyone is in a pair. How can that be?

Oh.

Oh no.

There's someone else I've forgotten about.

I turn to look at the toilet door, from which comes a series of faint sounds: a flush, then a retch, then the unmistakable impact sound of a dollop of spit.

Dolly

I've always struggled with distractions in public places. In any bar, the noise levels always seem that bit too loud, the conversations of people at nearby tables easier to tune into than the voices of whoever I'm with. Sports bars are the worst, with their screens everywhere. I'll catch myself watching them over people's shoulders, totally engrossed in the football or the rugby, even though I know precisely zero about any sport.

So it's no surprise, really, that during our production meeting my eyes keep straying over Lonnie's head to the bank of monitors. Now that the contestants have realised nobody actually insisted they stay in the sitting room, they've spread out around the building and grounds in pairs, chattering about their plans for this evening's talent show. I wonder which of them will come up with anything worthwhile. Mira and Dez seem as thick as thieves, so I bet they'll work well together. Cécile might have had my vote, though I still can't understand why she picked Ruth, who strikes me as pretty untalented. Then there's Sasha and Ben, who are perhaps the brainiest contestants. There's no telling what they might conjure up.

I blink, trying to clear my thoughts. I've zoned out again.

"For the last time," Lonnie is saying, "it was an honest mistake. And nobody mentioned those word puzzles this morning – only that the signs themselves had to be covered up. How am I supposed to know what you want, if you don't actually tell me?"

His tone is matter-of-fact, but somehow he still seems aggressive. Maybe it's the bad tattoos lining his arms, which make him look like some sort of drug dealer. From the moment I met him, he's conveyed an attitude of being above everything, even though he's technically the lowest-ranking member of the production team. He's in his thirties, I think, and always wears horrendously bright T-shirts – neon orange, mucus green – as if to prove he's too important to hide away like the rest of the team, dressed in black. His chin is dotted with spikes of coarse black hair that don't add up to a beard but are too long to be described as stubble.

Imogen sighs. "We should all be mindful of communication, yes. I accept there was an oversight, and we were lucky that Dolly caught it and resolved the issue. But my question, Lonnie, is where were you when we needed you?"

Lonnie glares at her sullenly. "Performing other duties."

When he doesn't continue, Imogen prompts, "What duties, Lonnie?"

He gestures at his toolbox, which seems to be permanently installed in the production suite. It's overflowing with hammers and saws and screwdrivers. Another health and safety nightmare. "Setup of task four's causing trouble. Needed attention."

"Then you were in the barn?"

"Yeah."

But he wasn't. He was in his bedroom, muttering.

Imogen seems to accept his answer. "In future, I'd like to inform at least one other member of the team when you leave the main building." She looks at me. "Everyone should ensure others know where you are."

I so want to call Imogen out. Where was *she* while I was charging around, trying to fix Task 1 before the contestants got started? But Imogen has a particular aura, a sense of entitlement that means rules don't apply to her.

"Can I ask a question?" I say.

Imogen nods curtly.

"Wasn't there supposed to be a psychologist in the team? And a doctor?"

"Mobeen Baig is performing both roles."

"Okay." I think of the production-team bedroom that's currently empty. "But where is he?"

"He was unable to be here as planned," Imogen says. "Indisposed. Ill, I suppose, or at least too ill to be stuck out on an island. But I'll be in touch with him each day."

"And is that enough?"

"Enough for what?"

"To be sure that contestants are safe."

"Of course. The Helmedia team have been over this place with a fine-toothed comb. All that's required of us is to follow their instructions. There's no safety issue." She glares at me, an instruction to stop pushing.

But I can't help asking, "And is that Mobeen's assessment? How does he feel the contestants are taking to the situation so far?"

"Very well, in his opinion."

Imogen's gaze strays to the bank of monitors. Instinctively, I scan them for any sign of Doc Leaf. It takes me a while to find him. He and Aura are still in the sitting room. She's sitting at one end of the horseshoe sofa, her hands placed on the cushions to either side of her as if she's preparing to jump up. Doc Leaf is slumped on one of the armchairs. It looks like he's asleep. Even so, I don't feel comfortable at anybody being alone with someone as unpredictable as him, especially a young woman. If something happened, even if we saw it on the camera feed, how long would it take one of us to race to the sitting room to intervene?

And there's something else: Imogen already told me that we don't even have access to the footage being recorded. My guess is that our supposed health expert has no oversight of the contestants at all.

I say, "But Doc Leaf—"

She cuts me off. "He's a live wire, sure. But that's what a show like this needs."

Then she just stares at me, daring me to speak up again.

I need this job. I need to continue working here in the mansion, because if not, then nothing else I need in life will happen. So I'm amazed when I actually challenge the great Imogen Dorrien-Stewart. "So can you assure me that he's been assessed thoroughly?"

"All the contestants have been assessed," Imogen says.

Given her anger at her own situation and her tense relationship with our absent producer, it's clear that she's phoning it in. It's the same with Lonnie.

Which means the safe running of *Escapism* is basically all down to me.

The door opens again, so hard it smacks into the wall.

"Fuck!" Lonnie shouts, clasping his heart in a pantomime of shock. For such a tough-looking guy, he's kind of a wimp.

I turn in my seat. It's Axel.

Instantly, the production suite feels smaller. There's something about 'talent' that does that – as if we all need to be on our best behaviour. As Axel pushes his way into the room to stand at the head of the table littered with mugs and papers, he seems to take up way more space than he should.

I knew he was handsome. I've studied pictures of him online. Like, *really* studied them. But he's even more striking in the flesh.

I feel too warm, suddenly.

"Imogen, I won't stand for it!" Axel says.

Imogen stands up. Her natural confidence is no match for Axel's power.

91

"What's the problem?" she asks. "We can sort it out, whatever it is."

My mind races, trying to anticipate Axel's grievance. He's already made clear how unhappy he is with his script, and he made a huge deal about the fact he felt obliged to rewrite his introduction to the first task. If it's not that, then perhaps it's something outside my sphere of influence – his fee, for example.

"My *room* is the problem!" he snaps. He twists to show us his shoulder. "Look!"

"I'm looking at your shirt," Imogen says in a neutral tone, as though she's addressing a child throwing a tantrum. "Is that what you want me to see?"

"There's *water* on the collar of my shirt," Axel says through gritted teeth. "And do you know where that water came from?"

"A tap?"

"From the ceiling of my bedroom." He holds up a hand to prevent Imogen from responding. "My bedroom, which was already intolerable. It's cold, and it's small. I mean, it's *tiny*. I bet it's no bigger than any of *your* rooms."

He's right, actually. All the rooms near to the production suite are exactly the same size, and none are anything like as fancy as the bedrooms upstairs. I know this because I nipped into each of them before they were allocated, just out of curiosity. What's making my cheeks flush at this moment is the fact that I saw the damp patch on the ceiling of the room Axel was given, and when I prodded at it I accidentally made a teeny hole. I think I'll keep that information to myself.

"Right. Okay. Your bedroom has a leaking ceiling," Imogen says.

"My tiny, cold bedroom—" Axel begins.

"Understood. I'm sure one of us would be happy to swap with you…"

92

She glances at me. I shake my head subtly. That won't solve the problem. I was so cold last night that I slept in my clothes.

Perhaps I should suggest me and Axel sharing a bed? That'd keep us cosy. I feel quite warm now, just thinking about it.

Imogen falls silent. Lonnie hasn't made eye contact with anyone since Axel entered the room.

"I think I may have a solution," I say quietly.

Everyone turns to me. My cheeks flush as I'm examined by Axel. My guess is that before this moment he hadn't even registered I was here.

"The groundskeeper's cottage," I say quietly.

"What cottage?" Imogen says.

"It's behind the mansion."

When I first arrived on Red Cliffs Island I wasn't comfortable at the idea of being isolated, so I strode around, getting my bearings, walking the periphery and investigating the buildings scattered around the mansion. Charting a new place helps reduce my anxiety.

"Describe it to me," Axel demands.

I take a breath. "It's quite sweet, actually. The decor is sort of homely, but newish."

"How many rooms?"

"Living area, bedroom, bathroom. There's no mess, and the bed's even been made up already."

"The owners didn't mention it," Imogen says warily.

"Could be it's usually reserved for private use," I say. "But don't worry. I can speak to them about it."

This time, Imogen's raised eyebrow somehow suggests she values having me around. I'm pretty sure I deserve more recognition than that, though. A salary bump would be nice, for a start.

"I can take you there right now, if you like?" I say to Axel.

All of his anger seems to have leaked from him. He nods.

I will him to flash his movie-star smile at me, but he doesn't. But it's nice to have been noticed at all.

As I pass Lonnie, I put a hand on his shoulder and say firmly, "Would you bring Mr Griffin's belongings from his old room to the groundskeeper's cottage, please?"

Then I hold the door open for the talent.

Dez

"Do you know any jokes?" Mira asks.

I turn to look at her as we walk. "What do you call a cat wearing a policeman's hat?"

"Dunno. What?"

"Officer."

Mira nods and manages a weak smile.

"You forgot to laugh," I say.

"Yeah. Sorry. Maybe it's the delivery." Abruptly, she stops walking and grips my shoulder. In an urgent tone she says, "Hey! What do you call a Brussels sprout wearing a policeman's hat?"

"I dunno."

"Officer!" Mira bellows.

She snorts with laughter, and soon enough I'm laughing too.

"Okay," I say. "Maybe it *is* the delivery."

"We can pull this off," Mira says. "But I'll deliver the punchlines, yeah? You can be my straight man."

I laugh again. "That's all I've ever wanted, really."

As we cross the courtyard we pass Victor and Ralphie, who are standing on a yellowing patch of lawn that looks out of place in the centre of the mostly paved area. Victor is speaking earnestly and Ralphie's nodding.

"What do you reckon they'll come up with for the talent show?" I ask Mira.

"Vandalism, maybe? Petty theft?"

"*Mira*. Ralphie seems really sweet. He wouldn't do that."

"What about Victor?"

Victor is waving his hands, pulling poses that wouldn't

look out of place in a Mr Universe contest. His arm muscles are huge. As we watch, he lashes out at Ralphie, whose head snaps back.

I gasp and make to run towards them, but Mira puts her hand on my arm to stop me. She juts her chin, telling me to look again.

Ralphie's fine. He's flailing his arms now, windmilling them as if to prevent himself from falling backwards, but it's a pantomime – he's grinning. Victor sweeps his extended right leg, catching Ralphie from behind, but instead of Ralphie dropping to the grass, Victor eases him down slowly with one strong hand supporting his back. Then Ralphie lies prone, and Victor raises his foot and mimes stomping on the boy's head. Ralphie lets out a squeal, then uses one of his hands, fingers splayed, to suggest blood spraying from his nose.

"Boys," Mira says dismissively, rolling her eyes.

"Could be Axel's impressed by that sort of thing," I say doubtfully.

We keep walking, exiting the courtyard. The wind picks up, billowing my jacket. Mira's long hair is thrown about all over the place. She gestures to a series of enormous boulders on the slope to the shore, which look like snapshots of a single tumbling rock. The second we huddle among them the wind becomes quieter, shooting over our heads in our hiding place.

Mira settles into an arrangement of lichen-covered rocks that has a dip more or less the size of her bum. "Hey, it's a throne!" she says, delighted.

I perch on a stone opposite her.

"So what do you make of Axel?" I ask.

"Fancies himself. You?"

I trace a finger over a nearby stone that has been worn smooth. "Polished," I say. "At least, he's somebody who's used to being polished. He's out of his depth here. Can you place his accent?"

Mira tips her head. "I thought it was just boarding-school posh?"

"No. There's a hint of something. Or maybe it's that his accent is more American than British – a sort of international hodge-podge, the way that English-language learners pick up enunciation from Hollywood films."

"I'm no good at identifying accents. If I think about it, I know my Manc accent's pretty strong, but to me it's more like all of you guys sound the same, like you're not even trying to sound different."

I nod, but I'm not really listening. "I wonder how Axel landed this gig. It's possible this isn't even a British show. I never thought to ask."

"Sod Axel. It's the other contestants we need to worry about."

"You mean Doc Leaf?"

She shakes her head. "He's a shitshow, everyone can see that. He might be a problem in a basic sense, but not in terms of the game. I'm talking about who's a threat to getting our hands on the money. In games like this, you have to form alliances, don't you? Like ours." When I don't respond, she says forcefully, "Dez, this is the point when you say 'I've got your back, Mira'."

"I've got your back, Mira." I point down the slope to the jetty, where the rowing boat is bobbing up and down. "A few days from now, you and me are going to be heading to the mainland on that little boat, laden down with cash."

She nods, satisfied. "So who's on your radar? Who's gonna go far?"

I take time to consider the question. "Ben, I suppose. He lives for this sort of challenge."

"Maybe, but he properly went to pieces during the first task. Whereas Sasha's a cool customer. Smart and too old for this shit, in the best possible way. She won't get rattled easily."

It's true, Sasha is calm in a way that's unlike any other contestant. Maybe it's her age, or maybe she's just the type to observe and not get embroiled. She's unlikely to lose sight of the fact that everything we're asked to do here on the island is absolute nonsense. If I'm honest, that's how I'd have expected myself to behave too. But during the first task I found myself screaming from the balcony at Mira below me. I got caught up. I haven't decided yet what that says about me.

"Have you seen the way Sasha looks at Aura?" I ask.

Mira snorts. "Like she's going to take off her jacket and throw it over her shoulders, saying, 'Young missy, when we get home we're going to have a talk about the way you present yourself to others.'"

"It's not like Aura's that bad, either. I mean, she's flaunting her assets, but it could be way more extreme. And I get the sense it's mainly for show, that she wouldn't follow through."

"You've thought about this a fair amount, then?"

I cluck my tongue

"Course not," Mira says. "You already said you're attached, didn't you? What's their name?

"Her. Priya."

"Got a picture of her?"

"Didn't think to bring one," I say hoarsely. Almost unconsciously, my hand strays to my jeans pocket and I pull out Priya's lighter. It's the only memento of her I need.

Mira's looking at the lighter too, but she doesn't say anything about it breaking the rules.

I realise we've stopped talking. I can't speak.

I came here because being watched by cameras wouldn't allow me to hide. Yet I've been doing nothing *but* hiding.

I groan.

"It's a lie," I say.

"What is?"

"I don't have a girlfriend."

"Oh. Right. So you made this Priya up?"

"She's real. We split up. Months ago."

"That sucks. Want to talk about it?"

I shake my head. "It was my fault. That's the start and end of it."

"There'll be other people, I promise. If you want."

I look up at her. She's over my confession already. No repercussions. I squeeze the lighter tightly, then put it away.

I rub my eyes, and Mira notices. She leans forward to hug me. Without really thinking about it, I slip one hand into the pocket of her jacket. My fingers close around something small and solid.

I pull back, making an ugly sniffling sound.

"What about you?" I manage to say.

Mira makes a gurning expression. "Single. Maybe forever? It's too obvious to say that men are dickheads, and let's be honest, so's everyone."

I fall silent, thinking of Priya again.

"Should I have said 'present company excepted'?" Mira asks.

I shake my head. "Nah. I'm a dickhead like the rest."

Ben

"What would be really helpful, Ben, is for you to restate the rules of the task. But please do it as if you're hearing it for the first time."

I nod rapidly. "I get it. And then you'll edit my explanation into Axel's briefing, or into footage of us contestants getting ready. Is that right?"

"That's right," the robotic voice says.

"Sure, sure," I say.

I take a breath, arching my spine in the armchair.

"Here goes." I lean forward. "So... Axel asked us to entertain him – we need to provide him with figurative escapism, that is."

"No," the voice says. "Please imagine you've been told the task only seconds ago."

I blink, then nod. "Present tense, yep. So... we wander into the sitting room, and there's this scroll on the table, and we're all like *okay... this is new*." I pause. "How's that for a start?"

"Excellent, Ben. Please continue."

"It turns out it's a talent show. At least, that's how the others seem to take it. But I was listening carefully. Sorry – I mean, I'm listening carefully. Present tense. In the note Axel puts emphasis on the heart. Something like 'My heart will be the judge'. And there's a mention of his pulse rate, too. So I'm thinking whatever we come up with needs to be *viscerally* exciting."

The voice doesn't speak for a while. I go over my words in my mind, trying to decide whether I've given them what they need for the edit.

"You've partnered with Sasha," the voice says finally.

"What sort of performance are you planning, Ben?"

"Like I say, it needs to be visceral. So we've decided to try and shock Axel. That's why we've both been wandering the building, looking for ideas, which is when I saw the sign outside the study flashing. Anyway, I'm on the lookout for fake blood, basically. But I can't find the kitchen. Any chance you could point me in the right direction?"

"I'm sorry, Ben. Contestants don't have access to the kitchen."

"Sure. But this is me we're talking about."

No reply.

I squint at the black surface of the window. Whatever it is that causes the one-way visibility, it's incredibly effective. I can't see any hint of anything beyond the window, only my reflection, an armchair, the vault behind it and half a dozen paintings of haystacks.

"I can't accept that you and I need to be secretive in here," I say. "It's not like this show is broadcast live. You control everything that'll be shown in the final programme. So why can't we talk freely, when it's just the two of us?"

The voice still doesn't speak.

"Imogen!" I say.

"Yes?" she replies in her flattened robotic voice.

"You're the one who said you needed me for this show. But you never explained why."

"You know why."

"Because I'm good at game shows?"

"Because you're good at game shows. Yes."

"Then I'm just a normal contestant, now that I'm here. Is that it?"

There's a pause. Then, "Did I give you any cause to think otherwise?"

I feel my cheeks heating up. "No. I suppose not. I just

supposed—" I shake my head.

What a fool I've been. When Imogen contacted me, there seemed a suggestion that I'd be an important part of *Escapism*. I imagined double-crossing the contestants, working with the production team to confound them, maybe even being responsible for dreaming up some of the challenges they'd face. In my wildest moments, I pictured myself in the longer term, rising up the ranks behind the scenes of TV game shows, then becoming the next Richard Osman.

I'd been reading into the message far more than was actually there. Imogen just needed another body. All I've got going for me is that I've proved I don't freeze on camera. I didn't even win the two TV quiz shows I took part in last year.

"Bollocks," I say. "Sorry, Imogen."

I hear a dull pop, which I've come to interpret as the sound the microphone makes before Imogen speaks. Several seconds pass before she says, "Give me two minutes."

Two and half minutes later, the metallic voice says, "You can leave the room now."

I rise from the armchair and push open the door. On the carpet directly outside is a squeezy bottle of ketchup.

*

I find Sasha outside the doorway of the sitting room, standing to one side as if she doesn't want to be seen through the half-open door. When she notices me, she puts a finger to her lips. I move to stand beside her.

Inside the room is only Aura. No, that's not right – Doc Leaf is also in there, but his body is just a lump in one of the armchairs. Aura is bending and twisting in the centre of the horseshoe of sofas, and after a few seconds my eyes adjust enough to make out the red strands of wool that are stretched across the space, through which she's ducking and weaving. Paired with her skintight black suit, she looks every bit the action-movie spy.

Abruptly, Aura stops her elaborate routine and glances in our direction. Sasha pulls my arm and yanks me away from the doorway and along the corridor.

"Why were you watching—" I begin.

Even though we're now far from the doorway, Sasha shakes her head quickly. It seems to mean, *Don't ask.*

"I actually wanted to talk to you," she says, and I get the sense that she's saying anything that she thinks will get my attention. "About the key we won. I want you to have it."

She holds out her hand. I stare at the large, silver key.

"What?" I say stupidly.

"I trust you. And I want you to trust me. So I'd like you to look after it. But you understand what this means, don't you? It means I expect you to work with me."

She presses the key into my hand. I don't know how to respond. A hug? Instead, I initiate a high five. Our hands miss each other slightly. Pretty awkward.

But Sasha looks as calm as ever, clearly content that she's done the right thing, the smart thing. I almost feel guilty about her naivety.

Almost.

Aura

After dinner – cheap microwaved pizza that's barely digestible – we end up in the sitting room again. Axel is there already, wearing a tux and bow tie. He's sitting in a chair fixed to a large wheeled platform. It must have been pushed in here by the production team while we were looking the other way.

"Urgh, what *is* that?" Ruth says next to me. She's pointing at the equipment on a stand next to Axel.

The main piece of equipment is a bulky device with a green screen. There's a horizontal line, and a blip that waves up and down as it crosses the screen. I've seen that sort of thing before, when I visited my gran in hospital before she died.

"It's a heart-rate monitor," I say. I track the wire that leads from the monitor, which ends at Axel's right hand – or, rather, the index finger of his right hand, which has a plastic cap covering its end.

We all find positions on the horseshoe sofa. On the coffee table are a bunch of bowls filled with crisps. People dig into the snacks immediately.

"Of course," Ben groans as he munches on a crisp. I can just picture him snacking for hours at a time during the gaming sessions he keeps going on about. "The note said 'My heart will be the judge'."

No shit, Sherlock. Is he just stating that so the cameras record him coming up with it, or has it really taken him this long to cotton on?

"Is Axel ill?" Ruth whispers. When I shake my head, she wipes imaginary sweat from her forehead and mouths *phew*.

"My dear friends," Axel says, "I thank you for coming

here, and for agreeing to help me. As you can see from my current get-up, I take escapism very seriously. You may consider it an affectation, but I like to know exactly how much my heart rate rises when I'm having fun." He laughs, then seems offended when nobody else joins in. In a more sober tone, he continues, "The rules are simple. Entertain me, and my heart rate – as recorded by this equipment – will be judge of your efforts. Significant increases of my heart rate will result in five thousand pounds being added to the prize money. And, of course, the team that wins will receive a precious key."

With that out of the way, we crack on. There's a bit of argument about which order the teams will perform, but I hold my ground. In a talent show it's always best to be near to the end – that's a trick I learned from watching every Eurovision Song Contest since I was nine.

Mira and Dez's willingness to go first shows how little they care about winning, and their dry 'comedy' routine is the opposite of heart-racing. Mira's funny, sure, but Dez appears constantly edgy, as if they hate being the butt of the joke. All they can do is prompt Mira's punchlines without contributing much themself.

Cécile and Ruth are another story – or at least Cécile is. I was as puzzled as anyone when Cécile picked Ruth over everyone else, but as soon as they begin, her reasoning is crystal clear. They perform a snippet of a play – Cécile's been up front that she's an actress, and it's clear she's a damn good one. Ruth's playing her older sister, who basically just listens as Cécile pleads for her freedom, real tears streaming down her cheeks. How does she do that on demand? For her part, all Ruth needs to do is pretend to do household chores, and she has only two or three lines in total. When Cécile reaches a crescendo and marches out of the room, slamming the door behind her, I glance at the heart-rate monitor. The blip goes pretty high, and Axel's blinking rapidly – it's clear he was emotionally invested in the little scene.

Victor whoops and jumps up to hug Ruth, shouting, "All *right*! That's my *girl*!" And then he kisses her. No shame at all – he just kisses her.

I glance around so see a few raised eyebrows. Now that he's calmed down, Victor looks really awkward as he backs away from Ruth. For her part, Ruth is gazing wide-eyed at Victor, like he's the only person in the entire universe. I wouldn't say she seems happy about the kiss, though, which is annoying in itself. He's the life and soul of this place, and she's... almost nothing at all.

So my hackles are already up when Ben and Sasha begin their piece. I concentrate on Ben, not wanting Sasha to catch me looking at her. For some reason, this sparks an odd sense of déjà vu. No – it's more specific than that. It sparks a memory of not wanting *Sasha* to notice me.

Because I *know* her.

Oh shit. It's been lurking at the back of my mind all day, and now it's suddenly obvious. Of *course* I know her. Despite the fact I haven't seen her for years, despite her new longer hairstyle and her fringe that almost covers her eyes. How could I possibly have failed to recognise her immediately?

I can't believe she's here. Surely it can't be a coincidence.

I watch, stunned, as Ben and Sasha perform their routine. It's pitiful. Ben fusses with the marigold gloves he's inexplicably wearing, then makes an announcement that they're going to teach the group a new, complicated handshake (because that sounds *totally* natural, guys, nice one), and then in a twist that surprises precisely no one, Sasha somehow contrives to yank one of Ben's hands so hard it comes free of his arm, or at least his yellow marigold glove does. Ketchup sprays out from the stump, which Ben thoughtfully points towards himself so that it's only his own fleece that gets stained, and not the carpet. The blip on Axel's heart monitor barely even registers that anything's happened, and Axel manages only a tight grimace.

Ben flops onto the sofa and immediately begins shoving more crisps into his mouth. His face looks puffy, like he's upset.

Like everybody else, I saw Victor and Ralphie practising their fight sequence in the courtyard, so there's hardly any reaction when they start to scrap. But in fairness, it's quite convincing, and once or twice I wince as Victor throws realistic-looking punches and his opponent reels backwards against the mantelpiece. They've managed to introduce the barest hint of a story to the scene, too: after taking more punches than any human ought to be able to take, Ralphie manages to rise to his feet a final time. His right arm swings in an exaggerated undercut, and I figure he'll be the victor over Victor after all.

But while Ralphie's still in mid-swing, something appears to his right, rising from the huddle of armchairs. I wince at the sight of my own partner, Doc Leaf. I'd hoped he'd stay unconscious for the duration of the contest.

"*Yeah!*" Doc Leaf shouts, applauding loudly. "Get that motherfucker, man!"

Immediately, Ralphie's attention is shot. His neck twists so he's facing Doc Leaf.

That's when his fist connects with Victor's nose.

Victor staggers back, clutching his face.

Doc Leaf applauds even louder, whooping with delight.

Ruth leaps up and rushes to Victor. When he removes his hands from his face, I see that blood – real blood – is streaming from his nose. Ruth looks around, then shrugs off her cream-coloured bolero top, which she uses to dab at Victor's face, the blood soaking into the fabric immediately and turning it red.

Ralphie stares at Victor in horror, his hands pressed to his own face as if he's been hit too.

For several seconds Victor glares at him, his head tilted backwards to stem the flow of blood. Then his eyes flick to Ruth and all his anger seems to drain away. He darts forward to take Ralphie's hand, then turns so that they're both facing Axel with their clasped hands aloft. Then he pulls Ralphie's hand down in a dual bow. Unfortunately, that makes the blood flow all the stronger, and he drops to sit on the carpet, still pressing Ruth's top to his face. His eyes follow Doc Leaf as he sidles out of the room.

Axel's completely mute. How do you respond to something like that? On the monitor his heart-rate is blipping up and down like crazy.

It'll be a hard act to follow, thanks to my so-called partner.

I fish out the ball of red wool from the sofa, ready to perform my spy laser routine. My hands are trembling as I try to find the end. Everybody's watching me.

Sasha is watching me.

She always was judgemental. That glowering look she's been giving me since we arrived yesterday is the same expression of dismay she'd always make when she'd visit my family home, all those years ago. I remember actually punching the air when Mum told me that Sasha, her once-upon-a-time best friend Sasha, would be moving away from the village. That was six or seven years ago. But I'm amazed I could have forgotten her sour face even for an instant.

Sasha was always the one whispering in Mum's ear, telling Mum just how outraged she ought to be at my behaviour. So when Sasha gives me one of her baleful looks, it's Mum's voice I hear in my mind. *I don't know how we'll ever get over this, as a family,* she says. *I don't think you realise how much you've spoiled things for yourself.* And then, *Me and your dad have been discussing it, and there's no question of letting you head off to uni now. You'll stay here, where we can keep an eye on you.*

And she was true to her word. My parents have kept an eye on me for the best part of a decade. When I applied to take part in *Escapism* I was warned about the psychological effects of having cameras trained on me the whole time, and you know what? I laughed. Being watched all the time is nothing new. It's actually a nice change that it's cameras instead of my parents.

Something inside me snaps. If everyone's going to watch me, they might as well see something truly impressive. And I'll win this talent show in the process.

I chuck the ball of wool into the corner of the room.

And I begin to dance.

At first it's mild stuff, the same shapes I'd pull at 'club nights' at the village hall. But the moves segue into the kind of routine I sometimes do in my bedroom at home, when nobody's watching.

I can feel Sasha's eyes on me as I approach Axel. I turn slowly, letting him gaze at my body in its catsuit that leaves little to the imagination.

I can hear a hum of disapproval from the other contestants. I don't care. I see the deep lines in Axel's face that are filled with concealer. The fear in his eyes as he tries not to stare at me but can't look away. The monitor behind his head, its green blip almost off the scale. He's gripping the arms of his chair tightly and he seems to have forgotten how to blink.

Then I hear a choking sound from behind me.

"Oh shit!" one of the women calls out. "He can't breathe!"

I whirl around. Ben's toppled to one side on the sofa.

He's clutching his throat.

"Give him water!" someone yells.

"Give him space!" says someone else.

The other contestants all ignore that instruction, huddling around him. Ben's trying to speak, but his voice is scratchy and small. His lips are swollen and red.

"Pen," he says.

"Oh God," Ruth wails. "He wants to write his last words!"

Ben shakes his head with difficulty. "Epi. Pen."

"I think he's having an allergic reaction," Sasha says.

"The crisps – it must be the crisps," Ralphie says. "Nobody eat the crisps."

I've seen this before. My cousin's allergic to peanuts, and he once reacted like this in a cinema. Ben needs a shot of adrenaline, and quick.

"Ben," I say, bending to him, "do you have your EpiPen on you?"

He shakes his head and coughs.

"Is it in your room?"

I take his judder to be a nod.

It feels weird to put my hand in someone else's pocket, but I brace myself and pull out the contents. Alongside his room key is a creased rectangle of card – from the design on the back I'm guessing it's a playing card, which is totally on brand for Ben. I chuck the card to one side, and the moment I do, Dez darts forward and scoops it up quickly. Weird.

With Ben's room key in hand, I race from the room and kick off my heels before running up the stairs. I try a couple of doors before I find Ben's room.

He's clearly a neatness freak. There's nothing personal on display other than a line of boring-looking books. There's no en-suite, and the small bag of toiletries only contains the usual: toothbrush, toothpaste, deodorant. I pull open drawers and try to ignore the horror of rummaging through his underwear. Finding nothing of use, I reach under the bed and pull out a small suitcase. Nothing, even in the side pockets.

Shit.

I stand in the centre of the room, clueless what to do next. I've exhausted everything I can think of.

I spin around at a knock on the door.

"Ben?" I say, even though that'd make no sense at all.

I open the door to find Doc Leaf, of all people. His expression is unreadable.

He holds something out to me, a slim cardboard box. On its side is written the word *EpiPen*.

"Is this yours?" I ask.

He shakes his head. "I didn't know what it was."

I stare at him. What's he telling me right now?

But there's no time. I grab the box from him and rush downstairs.

The contestants are all still clustered around Ben on the floor. Axel is hanging back, still connected to his stupid heart rate monitor. Where are the production team right now, during this emergency?

"I've got it," I gasp, ripping the box open clumsily. "Anyone know how to use this?"

Sasha nods and takes the EpiPen from me. I watch as she bends to Ben and injects him. He groans and manages a weak thumbs up sign.

"He'll be all right," Sasha says, and for once I'm grateful for her mumsy confidence. Then she turns to look up at me. "Good job, Amie."

I guess now I'm a hero. But a hero that feels like puking up on the carpet.

Six months later

Rhea

The more I find out about *Escapism*, the more excited I get. The corkboard above my desk is covered with Post-it notes and pages ripped out of my Hufflepuff notebook.

The show could have been a massive hit. In fact, it *was* a hit, in Sweden, where it was first broadcast. *Eskapism*, with a 'k', was the one of the most-watched programmes on Swedish TV, three years running. Then it was licensed for production in other countries, the first being the UK.

In practice, the only commonalities between the two versions were the producer, known in the industry only by the self-important name 'Helm', and the host of the show, Axel Griffin.

Since the filming of the UK edition halted six months ago, a bunch of Swedish media outlets asked Helmedia – the production company operated by Helm – about the fate of the show. No answers, no response of any sort. The show appears to be dead, in both countries, without explanation.

And we all know what happens on the internet when there's a lack of information. What's the phrase? Nature abhors a vacuum. Internet forums even more so.

Most of the forum posts are sheer speculation, most users just echoing other users' posts, creating a spiralling breadcrumb trail that leads precisely nowhere. But every so often new information is injected into the discussion. Someone with the username Key posted: *I live on the mainland near Red Cliffs,* one post reads. *Saw the rescue boat with my own 2 eyes. One person had a fucked leg or summat. Four people carrying a body with a big F-off nife stickin out its back.* Another post, by user 60PlusNProud, reads: *My friend lost her kid to that show. No justice.* I've sent messages to each user, but both accounts have been deactivated.

The most useful post I've seen was put up by the ominously named TheyreHere a month or so ago. I only came across it yesterday. Their only post is a jpg, a photo of a crumpled A4 printout of an Excel spreadsheet. Eleven rows of the table are populated with typed names, and the next column contains a tick against every name, under the column heading *Disclaimer signed.* The printout has pride of place on my corkboard, and by now I know the list off by heart.

The names under the subheading *Contestants* are:

Ruth Bastable
Cécile Guillaume
Rádhulbh Ó Cárthaigh
Victor Okojie
Amie Osborn
Ben Parrish
Mira Qureshi
Sasha Shiel
Dez Votel

Against two of the names are biroed notes. An arrow leads from the name Rádhulbh to a note reading *Ralphie,* which I suppose is the name he goes by. Brackets have been drawn around the name Amie Osborn, and in capital letters is written *Aura: no surname,* which suggests Amie might be a stripper or a stage magician.

There's one more contestant name that's been written

113

by hand below the typed list. At least I assume it's a name. It just says *Doc Leaf*. There's no explanatory note, and no tick to show a disclaimer was signed.

Below the list of contestants is a handwritten list, each with a tick in the *Disclaimer signed* box. It includes, with no surnames:

Imogen
Dolly
Mobeen
Lonnie

I'm guessing these must be members of the production team, though it's a surprise that there are so few of them.

The doorbell of my flat rings. I stand up too fast and my head whirls. I should know better: any sudden movement can trigger my headaches. When I answer the door, Ted gasps and says, "Are you okay, Rhea? You look like death warmed up."

I compose myself. "Come on through into the studio."

He follows me for a few paces, then looks around at the unmade bed, the blink-and-you'll-miss-it kitchenette, the desk groaning under the weight of my ancient desktop PC.

"Oh," he says. "*This* is your studio."

"Or 'creative hub'. I can't decide which term I prefer."

Ted wanders around, glancing at the few scruffy items of furniture. He pats the walls and the fireproof curtains. "Oddly enough, it's quite good in audio recording terms. Small rooms are best for sound quality." His gaze travels to the corkboard above the desk, where I've begun pinning scrawled notes. "You've been working hard, then?"

"You know me," I say. "I'm a grafter."

He stifles a laugh. "I watched the video files. That one with the girl talking to camera is..." He puffs his cheeks. "Well, it's..."

114

"An excellent inciting incident to use as a jumping-off point for a true-crime podcast?"

"Exactly. D'you think you can do it justice, describing the visuals to give it full impact?"

"Course."

I haven't actually prepared a script. I haven't given it any thought at all. Like so many things, I've basically assumed I'll be able to step up when the time comes. (Spoiler: I always do.)

Ted notices the printout of the list from the forum. His expression changes as he studies it, and he fumbles with his bulging satchel.

"You need to see this," he says, pulling out a folded photocopy.

At first I don't know what I'm looking at. After years of completing paperwork for medication and treatment, I'm sort of blind to anything bureaucratic. This just looks like a tax form or something. It's dated six months ago.

Ted taps his finger on the logo in the top-left corner: a star topped with a crown, and the words *Northumbria Police* circling an image of a castle turret. "I went to college with a guy who made it high up in the police force. I called in a favour."

A phrase on the form jumps out at me. *Cause of death.* It's followed by *Suicide.* Lower down, the location states *Red Cliffs Island,* then the out-of-place term *Workplace.*

My eyes dart up to the top.

Name: Lawrence Bunce

"Who's—" I begin.

Then we both turn to look at my corkboard list.

"Lonnie?" I say.

Ted shrugs. He gestures at the second list. "If these are staff rather than contestants, it matches the reference to it being a workplace death."

I rub my forehead.

"Look, I don't want to come across as callous…" I begin.

"You're wondering whether him being a member of staff makes the situation less mysterious."

"Yeah. Then again, not many suicides involve stabbing yourself in the back with a knife, so I suppose we can take the details on this form with a handful of salt."

"And there's still the fact that it was hushed up." Ted goes to my PC and brings up the Google search page. He types *Lawrence Bunce death.*

None of the search results are about a Lawrence Bunce who died on Red Cliffs six months ago. There's a few links to local tradesmen, plus an investor report and some sort of tech blog all referring to people of that name, but nothing about anyone who worked on a TV game show.

"What about your pal?" I ask. "If he sent you that report, it's hardly a cover-up."

"That's just the thing. Half an hour after he sent it, he rang and begged me to delete it. He sounded quite desperate."

"And still you brought it to me. You're a good egg, Ted."

He responds with an awkward smile. "I never liked him anyway." He points at the list again. "So, have you tracked anyone down yet?"

"Some of them."

The real answer is none. I've spent most of today on the phone to my broadband provider, shouting at them for briefly cutting off my internet. I mean, I was just *about* to pay my bill, if they'd only be a bit more patient.

"But we're not going to start with the contestants, or even poor dead Mr Bunce," I say. "We start with *Escapism* itself, which means starting with the Swedish show. The link between the two versions is the host. And guess what? Axel Griffin has gone AWOL since filming was halted."

Ted absorbs this new information. "You mean he hasn't worked on any other project in the six months since then?"

"He's disappeared off the face of the earth. One day he's super ambitious, determined to use his success in his home country to leapfrog into UK prime-time TV, then he's involved in a clusterfuck of a production which results in..."

Ted interrupts me. "A serious injury, a fire, a death – that's what the girl in the video said."

"That's Cécile Guillaume. And immediately after filming fell apart... *poof!* Axel disappears."

Ted's nodding rapidly. He knows I'm right to be excited. There's a mystery here to be unravelled. More than one mystery. A mansion full of them.

"I've got some ideas about how to incorporate the audio from the promo reel footage," he says. "It could be really effective. I can see it in my mind's eye."

"You can see audio in your mind's eye?"

"It's a figure of speech, but..." He adopts a faraway look. "Actually, yes. I can see audio. I can't even explain what I mean by that."

I squeeze his shoulder. "This is why I need you on the team, Ted." I point at the satchel that's still slung over his shoulder. "Now, you unpack your kit and I'll make us two cups of almost undrinkably strong tea. Then let's make us an inaugural episode of a hit podcast."

Six months earlier

Dolly

I can see the groundskeeper's cottage from my bedroom window, but only if I stand on tiptoes on the bed, because the window's so high up. These rooms really are like cells – it's no wonder Axel wanted out. I wonder how he's getting on in the cottage. I wish I had the nerve to pay him a visit. There are lamps on, making the curtains glow faintly, even though it's past two o'clock in the morning. Either he can't sleep, like me, or he's intent on enjoying the creature comforts his new accommodation provides... or perhaps he just tends to leave the lights on when he sleeps. Perhaps he's afraid of the dark.

Me, I like the dark. I find it soothing, and the knowledge that everyone else is tucked up in bed calms me even more. My shared house is chock-full of women, so the middle of the night is the best time to roam the place, cook in peace, choose which TV shows to watch. I always was a night owl, even during childhood – until my parents found out and put a stop to it. They always were good at removing any glimmers of fun from my life.

The downside is that I can't exactly nap during the day to make up for the lost hours of sleep. I have to work, don't I? So it's no wonder that I often feel like I'm sleepwalking through daylight hours. The fact that I still get loads done amazes me. I'm basically a superhero: *Survives-on-three-hours-of-sleep-woman!*

I sigh and hop down from the bed. Sleep isn't coming

my way any time soon.

My stomach rumbles. It's asking for cheese on toast. Cheese gives you bad dreams, but I figure that any sort of dream would be welcome, because dreams mean sleep.

The flagstones in the corridor are like ice against the soles of my bare feet. I yelp, then clamp my hand over my mouth, because I'm standing directly outside Lonnie's room. He's been a pussycat so far, but there's always a glint in his eyes that makes me wary of upsetting him, like he'd be capable of snapping.

For some reason, my feet take me to the production suite instead of the canteen. During our meeting, nobody raised the question of whether any of us should be watching the monitors at night. I know the footage is all being recorded ready for the edit in Sweden, but what use is that if there's an emergency? The safety of the contestants – both physically and mentally – is supposed to be Mobeen's responsibility, and he's not here.

The safety of the contestants. The idea that they're safe seems absurd now, after what happened today. When Ben collapsed, me and Imogen ran around madly, first struggling to locate and then scrambling to forage in the first-aid supply. We ended up watching helplessly as Aura and Sasha saved the day.

Then came the recriminations. Who'd put out the crisps? Me, of course, because who else was going to do it? Who ordered the crisps? Me, back at the production office last week.

There's nothing about Ben's peanut allergy in his file. I couldn't have been expected to know. And who on earth would predict the invention of peanut-flavoured crisps? Unless someone drenched the snacks in nut oil or something. I've no idea where the packets are now. It's Lonnie's job to take out the rubbish.

It doesn't bear thinking about. It certainly won't help

me sleep.

The production suite is washed with green light from the bank of monitors. It's strangely soothing. I sit before the monitor bank and let my eyes drift from screen to screen. The rooms of the mansion are all empty. At least, all the rooms containing cameras are empty. The contestants must all be in bed. Perhaps the Helmedia prep team ought to have installed cameras in the bedrooms too – you know, for the contestants' own safety. I laugh softly. Who am I kidding? That thought only entered my mind because I want to watch something on TV, and there's no actual TV here.

Abruptly, several of the screens flicker. One near the bottom-right corner blinks off entirely.

That's not good.

Another task to add to Lonnie's to-do list in the morning, then. It's just as well I didn't wake him up.

I see movement out of the corner of my eye.

Other than the blank one, the monitors look fine. But there's that change again, something moving within one of the otherwise static images. At first I can't pin down which screen it was on.

There it is: the central upstairs corridor that leads to the bedrooms in the west wing of the mansion. Somebody's walking casually along it. I can't make out their face, because at night the overhead lights are dimmed. Whoever it is, they're wearing a puffy dark jacket. Images flick through my mind of each of the contestants and their outfits, but I draw a blank. What if it's not a contestant?

The person stops in front of one of the doors. I fumble around for the ring binder on the table and leaf through its contents to find the floor plan of the building. It's Victor's room.

And now I can see the face of the person pushing the door open.

It's… Victor.

I shake my head, scolding myself. I'm always so quick to leap to conclusions. My mind does everything it can to make the world appear more exciting and dangerous than it really is. It's a bad habit.

I slump, watching the unmoving images on the screens. Then Victor's door opens again.

He comes out, still wearing his puffy jacket. Then he's followed by another person, much smaller than him.

I lean forward sharply. Now *this* is something worth watching.

From screen to screen, I track their progress along the corridor, then down the stairs. I curse the dim lighting that prevents me from identifying the second person. Then, in a flash of inspiration, I grab the folder again. Of course! The floor plan contains the answer. There are two shared en-suite bathrooms on the first floor, one of which is shared by Victor and Ruth – which means there's a way to get from one bedroom to the other without the cameras spotting it. It's another example of lax supervision on the part of the production team. There's no way that arrangement is safe.

Now I see that Ruth is clinging on to Victor's arm. That's weird in itself. When Victor kissed Ruth after her performance in the second task, she barely seemed to react.

They creep through the entrance lobby. Where are they going? They reach the front door and let themselves out. The doors of the building aren't locked even at night. Being on an island is more effective security than any number of locks, and anyway there's literally no one else here.

My first impulse is to rush out of the room and follow them, but I tell myself not to. The first rule of Fight Club is: Don't reveal yourself to the contestants. Anyway, I have a better chance of tracking them on the monitors.

There aren't nearly so many cameras fixed on the exterior of the building, but the prep team anticipated that contestants would head to the courtyard or beyond, to conduct furtive discussions about backstabbing other players, or to declare undying love for one another, that sort of thing. I see Victor and Ruth move along the edge of the paved courtyard before taking a left at the corner of the hall of tasks. For several seconds I lose them, but I spot them again when they emerge at the garden at the rear of the main building. I flick through the pages of the folder to find the map of the whole island. They pass the blunt, modern concrete building that contains the swimming pool, and for a moment I'm afraid they're approaching Axel's cottage – but no. They walk straight past it.

What are they up to?

For more than a minute, they're gone. My stupid mind conjures an image of them hurling themselves into the sea. I sigh with relief when they show up again, outside a barn that's a couple of hundred metres from the mansion.

The six screens in the bottom-right corner are dedicated to the barn, with only one on its exterior. So far, all the footage recorded must either have been completely static, or else showing Lonnie setting up Task 4, which is due to take place in the barn tomorrow afternoon. No, I remind myself: *this* afternoon. I really should get some sleep.

But how can I sleep when two contestants are prowling around, getting up to who knows what?

I'm not a prude, honestly. But the fact is that Victor and Ruth have adjoining rooms, which means a choice of two beds to cavort on. So poking around outside is definitely suspicious.

The barn's exterior camera shows them approaching its door. It should be locked. And yet Victor spends a few seconds fumbling with the door catch, and then they're inside.

I'm not great at cursing. The word that comes out of my mouth is a mix of 'shit' and 'bollocks'.

This situation really is total *shollocks*.

I lean forward, staring at the screens in the bottom right of the bank of monitors.

I can't see them any more. The screen that's gone blank must be the feed from the entrance area. The other barn feeds show a series of pale stripes in criss-crossing formations, the overhead view of Task 4.

Where are Ruth and Victor?

Finally, I glimpse them as they move further into the building.

Then the screens in the bottom right-hand corner of the bank of monitors flicker and go blank, one by one.

DAY 3

Ben

The breakfast table is littered with little signs made out of folded card. Somebody from the production team has taken it upon themselves to flag any possible allergen advice imaginable. None of the contestants says a word about the change. They're all preoccupied with arguing about the results of the second task. From what I gather, Axel shocked everyone by announcing Ralphie and Victor's fight as the winning performance. Apparently Aura then challenged Axel directly, pointing out that the heart-rate monitor had shown she'd had by far the greatest effect on him, and our host had to plead his case that her absurdly sexy dance somehow didn't count. The fact that three of the performances, including Aura's, added to the prize pot to the tune of £15,000 hasn't seemed to soothe Aura, and she's uncharacteristically quiet this morning.

"How are you doing, Ben?" Sasha asks me.

"So-so." I trace a circle around my face. When I woke I looked in the mirror and was surprised to see my lips are back to normal. I look a bit beaten up, but that's usual enough.

"Shouldn't we get you to a hospital?"

I shake my head. "I don't think it was a bad attack."

Maybe I didn't even need the EpiPen, I don't know. I haven't suffered anaphylaxis since I was a kid, when I scared the life out of my foster parents after eating a slice of my own birthday cake. It's hard to know what's a mild reaction and what it'd actually feel like to be facing the end of your measly life.

When I was curled up on the floor, my life didn't exactly pass before my eyes. But the faces of Bethany and

Jill and my ex-wife, Carla, did. But you know what? They weren't even looking at me. They were looking away, occupied with something else that I couldn't see.

I mean, that's tragic, isn't it? My mind can't even summon tenderness from an imaginary version of my family.

I treated them badly over the years, I suppose. I just wasn't around. Even when I was physically present, my mind wasn't. I was fired from job after job for the same reason. Anybody would tire of somebody dreaming their way through life instead of participating in it. I don't blame them, really.

But what they never understood is that games and puzzles are a part of me. It's almost a physical thing. When I was a kid, I was lonely and I was empty. After having been passed from place to place, the foster parents I spent most of my childhood with were kind, but I knew they were performing a service, and that I was only a visitor rather than real family. I kept to myself rather than embarrass them by demanding their time, attention and love, I suppose. I filled up the empty hours, and the empty part of my mind, with puzzles. Later, when a few kids at school actually offered to play board games with me, I leapt at the chance. It was how I communicated with people. Before long, games became the *only* way I knew to communicate.

The girls and Carla, they've never been gamers. They like real things: chatting, exploring outdoors, crafts. None of them has a competitive streak in their body.

I can't change who I am, even if doing that might win my family back.

But I *can* prove myself. I can prove that puzzles can be worthwhile.

I can win this stupid contest and return to my family with a sack of cash and my pride reinstated.

I realise there are tears in my eyes. Sasha reaches out and takes my hands in hers.

"Thank you," I say. My throat is so tight it feels almost like another attack.

She offers the most maternal smile imaginable. Having no memory of my own biological mother, the shock of all that warmth directed at me is almost painful.

"I only stuck the pen in you," she says. "It's Aura you should thank for finding it."

I follow her gaze to look at Aura, who's sitting at the other end of the table. Aura glances at me, then at Sasha, but then her cheeks redden and she just stares at her empty plate.

Aura

After breakfast we all gather in the entrance hall. Axel hands out umbrellas from the stand in the lobby, then leads us outside and through the grounds to the rear of the mansion, heading towards an ugly, low concrete building. As he descends the slope, careful not to slip on the wet grass, I notice he's struggling with a slight limp, though he seems to be doing everything he can to disguise it.

Somehow, he manages to maintain his lord-of-the-manner bearing as he throws open the rusting metal door of the ugly building. The smell of chlorine hits me immediately.

"Why didn't you tell us there's a pool?" I ask him. I've been walking alongside him the whole way, refusing to let him put me out of mind after his outrageous judging of Task 2. "I *love* swimming."

As we venture into the building, my question's answered for me. The place is an absolute dump. The paint on the walls is patchy, revealing bare plaster, and lots of the tiles are cracked. Not for the first time, I wonder how all these interiors are going to look onscreen, when this show is broadcast.

The other contestants seem too preoccupied to care much about the crappy decor. Their attention is fixed on the pool itself. The water appears clean enough, but it's what's at the bottom of the pool that's unnerving.

There are three barred cages arranged in a row. They look like the ones that we pushed around during Task 1, which makes me shudder at the thought of skeletons hanging inside them.

There are other shapes in the pool, too, scattered around

on the bottom: little rocks.

"My dear friends," Axel begins, and we all gather around him automatically. "We have reached our third task, which will be the most demanding yet. Whereas the first was a test of intellect, and the second a test of, um, entertainment…"

I notice he can't help glancing at me. Seems that my little dance really had an effect on him, no matter who he announced as the winner.

He concludes, "This task will be one of physical ability… and of endurance."

"All right!" Victor says.

"Think of the money," Sasha says to herself, then repeats it like a mantra. "Just think of the money."

Mira raises her hand. "Axel? I just wanted to say, fella, I can't swim."

Axel frowns. "What?"

"I don't know how to put it any other way," Mira says. "I. Can't. Swim. It's my bad, I know. I'm owning it. But I'm not going in that pool, okay?"

Axel's abandoned his host persona now. "But it was in the disclaimer. You all agreed that tasks could involve swimming, didn't you?"

There's a chorus of *No*s.

Axel glances up, and I follow his line of vision. The cameras in here aren't even hidden. I wonder how the director is responding to this bombshell. Is she whispering in Axel's earpiece right at this moment?

"We'll figure this out," Axel says after a few seconds. "For now, I'll describe the task, okay?"

Mira gives a grudging nod.

Adopting his ringmaster tone again, Axel says, "First, I would ask you to arrange yourself into three teams."

We all look at each other, trying to figure out who's likely to be the most physically able.

130

"But what will we be doing?" Cécile asks.

"I don't even have my cossie on," Ruth says. She turns to me, pointing at my yellow sundress. "Are you wearing yours under that?"

It's just as well I don't have a chance to answer, because if I told her what I was actually wearing under this dress, she'd only get flustered.

Axel ignores the interruption. "The teams are as follows: Victor, Aura and Ruth."

It's a surprise that we don't get to pick our team mates this time. And my pleasure at being matched with strong Victor is completely undermined by the meaningful glances exchanged by him and scrawny Ruth.

Axel goes on, "The second team will comprise Cécile, Ralphie, Dez and Sasha."

That seems a strong team, even without considering the fact it contains four people instead of three. I see other contestants peering around, calculating who's left to make up the final team.

"And that, of course, means that Doc Leaf, Ben and Mira will make up the third team."

I watch as the three of them shuffle to stand together. My mum would describe them as a motley bunch, Doc Leaf scowling, Ben with his still slightly puffy lips, Mira clearly horrified.

"Excellent!" Axel booms, his voice echoing from the tiled walls. "I suggest you pick your strongest swimmers to search for keys beneath the rocks at the bottom of the pool, with your other team member relegated to the locked underwater cage." He seems to be doing everything he can not to look at Mira. "All successful rescues will contribute to the prize fund, with one thousand pounds added for every ten seconds below the three-minute mark."

I look down at the cages with their thick metal bars. I'm definitely not volunteering to get stuck in there.

"I swam for my uni in a national contest," I say to my team. It's not true, of course – I didn't actually go to uni, and I've never joined a swim team, let alone compete. But I really am a good swimmer.

"You're not going in the cage, then," Victor says, and me and Ruth both nod. We seem to have accepted him as the leader of our group. "And not me either," he adds.

Ruth is glaring at Victor.

"Sorry," Victor says. "But don't you worry, girl. I'll rescue you."

Finally, Ruth nods. I scowl, even though they're hardly sharing a tender moment, then I remember the cameras and force a placid smile onto my face and say, "We'll have you out of there in no time at all, Ruth!"

Sasha has peeled away from her group to peer down at the cages. I guess that means she's accepted the role of captive. I feel a flush of satisfaction. If I get really lucky, she'll drown.

It's clear the third team is having a much tougher time picking who'll go in the cage. Doc Leaf's arms are folded and he says firmly, "It's not going to be me, all right? I'm a fucking brilliant underwater swimmer."

"Not me either," Mira says. "Seriously. I just can't."

Seriously, the setup of these teams is a joke. It's obvious that Doc Leaf's never going to volunteer for any meaningful role in tasks, and Mira's afraid of the water. So it has to be Ben in the cage, even if nobody can be relied upon to rescue him.

Ben looks utterly miserable. "I really don't think I can do it," he says. "I can't be down there, either in the cage or swimming. I still feel really ropey this morning." He turns to Axel. "I'm sorry, but I think I'm going to have to sit this one out."

Axel hesitates. He puts a hand to his ear – my guess is he's listening to instructions through his earpiece.

"I'm sorry… we do need you to play the game," he begins. Then he bites his lip, maybe deliberating over what he's been instructed to say. Watching Ben almost drop dead last night must be playing on his conscience.

He clears his throat. "Actually, no, it's fine. Ben can opt out, which neatly leaves three teams of three."

I hear a tinny raised voice through his earpiece. Is he being shouted at? Axel reaches up and pulls it out to dangle freely. He's gone rogue.

But he seems to have forgotten about Mira.

Dez strides forward. "I'll take Ben's place, to even the teams up." It's clear Dez is determined to take the heat off Mira, but in doing so they've basically thrown away all chance of winning this task.

More shouts come from Axel's earpiece. He ignores the voice, his eyes darting as he performs rapid calculations. "Yes. That seems fair."

As Dez moves over to their new team, Doc Leaf asks them, "You a good swimmer then?"

"The best," Dez snaps. Then they shake their head sharply as if they wish they could take back their reply.

Doc Leaf smirks. "Me too. So there's only one answer, isn't there?" He jabs a finger at Mira. "If she can't swim, she has to go in the cage."

Mira shakes her head. "I already told you. I'm not even going in the pool."

"You want us to lose this task, do you?" Doc Leaf accuses her.

"What do you even care?" Mira snaps. "This is literally the first time you've shown any interest in a task. You fucking *slept* through the last one! As far as I can see, you just get off on making people uncomfortable – which you do bloody well just by walking into a room, I might add – and you've clocked this as a way to make me suffer."

Doc Leaf just watches her, still smirking. Nobody else

speaks. It's obvious everyone thinks Mira's accusation is spot on.

Then Doc Leaf turns to Axel. "You agree with me, don't you?"

Axel looks like he's trying to disguise his panic. He scrabbles for his earpiece, but it slips below the line of his collar. Without it, he's stranded.

Finally, he says uncertainly, "I did say that you should choose your strongest swimmers for the rescue team."

Mira shakes her head. There are tears in her eyes now.

"Have you all lost your actual minds?" Dez shouts. "Don't you dare stick Mira down there. She's told you she can't swim. Obviously that means she's not going to be able to hold her breath underwater."

"Ah!" Axel says in relief. "There's no need to worry on that score. Those of you in the cages will have oxygen tanks."

We all go quiet, each of us considering whether this affects our opinion about the level of cruelty involved. Ben looks particularly sheepish. It should be him down there in his team's cage. Allergic reaction or no allergic reaction, all he'd have to do is sit in a cage and breathe. The stern voice in Axel's ear seemed to feel the same way.

Doc Leaf pipes up first. "You don't want people at home to think you're a coward, do you?" He gestures up at the cameras, and Mira looks up, too. Her eyes are glistening with tears.

I swear, Doc Leaf is the actual devil.

But his tactic seems to have worked.

Mira's shoulders slump.

"I fucking hate you all," she says quietly.

*

The swimming costumes that have been left for us in the

134

changing rooms are all identical bright orange so that we look like rejects from a *Baywatch* casting call, or a prison swim team. Once we've changed, the victims are shown the oxygen masks they'll be wearing in the cages, and the tanks that'll be strapped onto their backs.

But Axel hasn't quite finished with them yet. He holds up a finger and says, "Ah, I forgot to mention one little detail." He cups his hands over his mouth and calls, "Lonnie!"

We all flinch as a stranger appears from a side room. And when I say 'stranger' I mean *really* strange. He's wearing cargo shorts and a lime-green T-shirt, and both of his arms are covered in lurid sleeve tattoos. He has lank black hair and tufts of stubble on his chin. There's no way he'll appear onscreen when this is broadcast, surely. Which makes Axel's theatrical reveal sort of pointless.

The man's carrying a bundle of beige fabric. He pulls one of the items out of the pile and holds it up. At first it looks like a shapeless sack, but then I make out long arms. *Very* long arms, as it it's designed to be worn by an ape rather than a human. It's covered with straps and buckles.

"That's right – you'll also be wearing straitjackets," Axel says.

We all look at Mira, whose only response is a low groan.

Dez

It's hard to concentrate when you're as furious as I am right now. When Axel says "Go", we all cannonball into the pool, but I'm not concentrating on the rocks on the floor. Mira is barely moving in her cage, and her body's sort of spasming. Her spine is twisted so that her face is directly upwards, as though she believes she might catch a breath of air if she only tries hard enough. During her test with the oxygen mask I spent the whole time afraid she'd hyperventilate.

I can't imagine how she feels right now. If that was me in the cage I know I'd be freaking out, and I've tried scuba diving a few times, on a trip to the Canary Islands when I was a teenager.

What's worse is that I can see Doc Leaf in my peripheral vision, doing backstroke on the surface of the pool, his thighs sickly pale. He doesn't give a monkey's about winning the task. It was supposed to be Ben in the cage, but after he bailed out the obvious choice was Doc Leaf, who's good for nothing else.

Orange-suited bodies zip around me, heading down to the bottom of the pool. The other contestants pick up rocks, scrabble to remove the keys from them, then come up for air, then dive back down to try each key in the lock of their cage door.

I take a gulp of air, then plunge downwards. I scoop up a rock. It's fake, and underneath it must be a magnet, which is what holds the key to it.

I don't come up for air. I swim straight to Mira's cage and stick the key in the lock.

It doesn't turn.

I need to come up for air, but before I do I reach through the bars to squeeze Mira's arm. She doesn't respond at all. This whole thing is literally insane.

Up I go, deep breath, down again. I dive straight down to the floor again. I've always had strong lungs. Air is for weaklings.

Grab a rock, back to the lock. Cécile is trying to unlock Sasha's cage, but she gives up immediately and bobs away as I approach Mira's.

Key in. Twist.

Yes! It turns. The door is open.

I remind myself this is only the first stage. One of the straps of Mira's straitjacket is wound around one of the bars of the cage, and the buckle is fixed with another padlock.

I shout at Mira, trying to tell her that she'll be free soon, but all that comes out of my mouth is a stream of bubbles. I don't think she'd have paid attention to me anyway. Her eyes are squeezed shut and her head is shuddering like crazy.

Up for air. Straight back down. Ariel the mermaid has nothing on me.

Rock after rock after rock. Key after key after key. I swear I've tried them all now. If it wasn't for the fact that the blokes' swimming trunks don't have pockets, I'd suspect one of them of hiding keys they've already tried and discarded.

The door to Ruth's cage is open now. Sasha's is still locked.

Rock, key, twist, air. Rock, key, twist, air.

I see that Sasha's door is open, finally.

Then I spot Victor reaching into the other cage and pulling Ruth out. They whoosh to the surface like superheroes.

So they've won. But the task doesn't just end there,

does it? Not while people are still trapped.

More rocks, more keys. Cécile's still attempting to free Sasha, but Ralphie stops and bobs, watching me work on Mira's lock. His body twists and he brings his key to Mira's cage instead of Sasha's.

Me and Ralphie each try another key each on the straitjacket padlock. Mira's spine is even more arched now, and her whole body is juddering uncontrollably. Is there a problem with the oxygen tank?

Ralphie gets my attention and shakes his head, then points upwards. Seconds later, we're up and out of the pool. Ruth's team has gathered around her, congratulating her. I whirl around as more people rise to the surface of the water – it's Cécile and Sasha. Sasha pulls away her oxygen mask, gasping.

I stride over to Axel.

"Mira's trapped," I say. "None of the keys unlock the padlock on her straitjacket. Tell me there's a master key or something?"

He shakes his head mutely.

"Then I need something sharp. I'll cut her free." When he doesn't move, I say sharply, "Right now!"

He doesn't move an inch.

I spin around as someone puts their hand on my arm. To my disgust, I see it's Doc Leaf.

"Gimme a sec," he says. Then he runs into the changing room. When he comes back only a few seconds later, he's holding a shining silver object in his palm. A butterfly knife.

I don't have time to get angry about him breaking the rules, or the fact that butterfly knives are illegal, or my shock that the only truly dangerous person in the group has been carrying a knife this whole time. I snatch it from him and throw myself into the pool.

When I reach the open cage, I panic immediately.

Mira's not shaking any more. She's not moving at all.

I fumble to unfold the knife, then begin sawing at the fabric strap of the straitjacket. It's thick, and tough. After a while my lungs are burning. I gasp in frustration, which makes me lose my remaining air. I rise to the surface, then allow myself three seconds of breathing, then I go back down.

It's slow work, but I'm getting there. I make another trip to the surface after I reach the halfway point through the strap. In the moment I'm up there, I glimpse the other contestants watching on, not a single one of them brave or smart enough to come and help me. Ralphie's face is pale and he's retching without bringing anything up.

It doesn't matter. I'm not about to ask for anyone's help now. They'd only get in the way, mess things up even more.

I'm determined I'll cut through the strap on this dive. I saw like mad, holding the strap away from Mira's unmoving body as I work.

Nearly. Nearly.

The strap is down to its last threads.

And that's when Mira wakes up.

Her entire body lurches, shoving me backwards out of the cramped cage. She contorts herself to look at me. Her eyes are completely wild, like she doesn't even recognise me. I raise both my hands, trying to calm her. Mira's eyes go to the knife in my right hand. Her eyes bulge and her eyelids squeeze shut and her mouth opens, sending a flurry of bubbles either side of the oxygen tube. I think she might be hyperventilating.

I don't have time to try to make her understand. I grab the bars of the cage with my left hand, pulling myself forward. I ease the knife behind the remaining threads of the straitjacket strap.

But Mira's having none of it. Her body convulses,

preventing me from completing the cut. Her chin somehow smacks me in the eye socket, making my vision flash with bright light. My mouth opens in response to the pain, and all the air leaves my lungs.

I'm not going up without her. I reach into the cage again, finding the strap and yanking it with my fingers.

I see blood wisp in the water. I don't know whether it's mine or Mira's.

Finally, the strap rips off. She's free.

She doesn't seem to realise it, though. I put my arm around her waist and force her upwards. She fights me the whole way.

When we reach the surface, my gasp for air is like the roar of a wild beast. I drag Mira to the edge of the pool and – somehow – heave her upwards until Victor rushes over to drag her the rest of the way.

I'm weeping and all my strength has left me. Ben lifts me up from under my armpits to hoik me out, then I bat him away weakly and slump to the floor.

I roll over to look at Mira.

My stomach flips. I choke and spit on the tiles.

Mira's unconscious. Her head is turned towards me and her dark hair is plastered over her face. But that's not what's really scary.

Somebody's pulled off her straitjacket, or at least half of it, freeing her right arm.

And her forearm is covered in deep lacerations that are bleeding freely, making crimson puddles on the tiles.

I'm dimly aware of people staring at me.

I look down at the knife I'm still holding in my hand.

Dolly

"How is she?" I ask as Lonnie and Imogen enter the production suite together.

"She's sleeping in Axel's old room," Imogen says, as if that's enough, as if Mira really only needed a good long nap.

"We've managed to apply a dressing," Lonnie adds. "We spoke to Mobeen, and he thinks something called the brachial artery is damaged, but not severed. If it had been, she might be—" He breaks off, putting his hand to his mouth.

Yesterday, after Lonnie messed up the preparation of Task 1, I asked Imogen whether she still had faith in him. She replied vaguely that she felt he deserved a second chance. Afterwards I replayed her reply in my mind, and I became convinced that she wasn't referring to a second chance on *Escapism*, but something more general. What's the deal with Lonnie, really?

I turn to look at Imogen. She doesn't speak.

"This situation is pretty bad," I say.

Imogen sits at the table, twisting a piece of string around a biro, tighter and tighter. For the time since filming began, she's not wearing her headset.

"Miss Dorrien-Stewart," I say. The formality seems absurd in these circumstances, so I say, "Imogen. What are we going to do?"

Finally, she looks up. "You heard Mobeen's assessment. Mira is going to be fine."

I stare at her. "Firstly, are we sure we can take him at his word? A medical assessment via Zoom is hardly…" I trail off. "And even if Mira is physically okay, she's had a huge shock. There's no telling the repercussions her experience might have."

Imogen glowers at me. She's probably telling herself I'm only a lowly production assistant, and do I even *know* who the great Imogen Dorrien-Stewart is? But after a few seconds her hard exterior cracks. Her eyelids flutter and she looks down at the pen she's gripping, pulling the string even tighter around it.

"Mira needs to leave," I say. "She needs to be taken to the mainland, seen by a professional—" Imogen looks up, and I can see she's about to interrupt me, so I add quickly, "A professional who's actually present in the room with her."

Imogen sighs. "There's nothing I can do about that in the short term. There won't be another supply boat until dawn."

"We could call the authorities. An air ambulance, or the coastguard could come and get her."

"No!" Imogen says sharply. She blinks rapidly as if her own tone has surprised her. "Look. We'll wait until Mira's awake, and then we'll assess the situation. If she's genuinely okay, it would be wrong to alert the authorities and waste their resources. But I promise that if she shows any signs of continuing distress, or if she'd simply like to leave the island right away, I'll call 999. All right?"

Deep down, I know it's badly wrong that none of us called 999 the moment we heard about the accident. Every minute we delay will make us look worse, if Mira turns out to be in real trouble. But I don't want boats and helicopters arriving at Red Cliffs Island any more than Imogen does.

I will the memories not to come, but of course they do. I remember being numb with shock, all those years ago. The sound of approaching sirens mingling with the almost deafening ringing in my ears.

142

I shake my head to clear it. I look at Lonnie, who shrugs.

"All right, we won't call for an ambulance yet," I say. My skin crawls with self-loathing. "But we should talk about some of the other issues." I gesture at the bank of monitors. The feeds from the underwater cameras are completely blank. That technical problem is the reason we didn't know anything about Mira's accident until one of the external camera feeds showed Lonnie and a bunch of contestants hauling her unconscious body across the grounds to the mansion, slipping and sliding on the rain-sodden grass.

"I don't have training in fixing the cameras," Lonnie says quickly.

Imogen obviously senses that my next question will be directed at her. "I've been in touch with Helm, our esteemed producer. His reply amounts to the same thing. If there are any technical issues with the cameras, we just need to work around them. In this case, we're lucky – we have no need of the poolhouse now that Task 3 is complete."

Except it wasn't just one camera in the swimming pool that failed, it was a whole bunch of them. The ones in the barn are back on, but they might easily blip off again. I imagine it as a disease spreading, infecting the cameras one by one.

Imogen stands up wearily. But I'm not ready to let her off the hook just yet.

"What about Doc Leaf?" I ask.

She stiffens. "What about him?"

"He's a liability."

"It was Dez who injured Mira."

"Mira was only in that cage because Doc Leaf insisted on it. That's what the other contestants said in their interviews."

There's also the fact that it was originally supposed to be Ben down there in the cage, of course. But Ben's just a sap, whereas Doc Leaf's refusal was sheer bloody-mindedness.

"I suspect the situation was more nuanced than that."

I puff out my cheeks. "Maybe. But Imogen, you've seen what I've seen on those feeds. Doc Leaf is a destructive force. There's no telling what he might do next."

Imogen watches me silently for several seconds. Then she says, "Helm is aware of that situation too."

"And?"

"And he insists that Doc Leaf stays. It's clear you're acutely averse to conflict, Dolly. But let me remind you that TV programmes like this thrive on it. Without conflict, there's no show. We need him."

I clench my fists so hard that my fingernails dig into my palms. "What about the other contestants? Do they need him? Are serious accidents the sort of thing that great TV is made of?" I laugh abruptly. "We don't even know if the task was recorded, whether the cameras captured any footage, or whether all we've got is TV static.

"Helm is perfectly content. Everything is in hand. We just need to carry on."

The calmer she becomes, the more enraged I get. When my hand stings, I hold it up, force my clawed fingers open, and see that my nails have dug in so far that I've drawn blood. I stare at it, thinking of Mira, feeling sick.

"You're needed," Imogen says.

"What?" I say weakly, still staring at the blood.

Imogen points at the door to the study. "You have an interviewee."

I tell you, my diligence is a curse. Obedient as ever, I stumble over to the door.

*

Dez looks an absolute wreck. Their shirt is crumpled and only half tucked in, and their eyes are red and raw. They're staring at the ceiling, their chest rising and falling irregularly.

I try to compose myself before I press the mic button.

"Hello, Dez," I say.

They lurch forward immediately. "Is she all right?"

"Mira has been assessed and treated by the medical team," I say. "She'll be absolutely fine."

Dez exhales raggedly. "Fuck. Thank God for that. Fuck."

They pull their arms tight around their body, shivering. I wish I could open the door and give them a hug. From what I've seen on the feeds, Mira is their closest friend here.

After a minute, I ask, "What happened, Dez?"

I'm not sure if I'm asking the question in order to get useful footage, or in order to gather details to pass on to the police, if it comes to it… or whether I'm just indulging my own morbid curiosity.

Dez's head hangs. "She was trapped. She wasn't moving. I— I couldn't tell if she was even breathing. I had to get her out."

"It sounds like you were very brave."

They shake their head. "I was scared. I think—" Another long, ragged breath. "I think maybe she was fine. The oxygen tank hadn't failed – it was just my paranoia telling me it had. I could have just searched harder for the key, got her out that way."

They look up. "Has she said anything about me? Does she hate me for what I did?"

"Mira is resting at the moment," I say.

Dez stares at me, or rather at the black window that

145

separates us. I can see they're processing the implications. Mira needing to rest could be a good or a bad sign.

"It doesn't even matter," they say, and now they seem to be speaking to themself, not to me. "I hate myself enough for the both of us. What kind of friend slices up a friend's arm?"

I freeze. Nobody in the production team actually explained how Mira was injured. When I saw her briefly when she was carried inside, all I could focus on was the blood rather than the wound itself. I'd assumed that she was cut on the edge of the metal cage, that their shoddy construction was another act of negligence that could levelled at the prep team.

"What actually injured Mira's arm?" I ask.

"A knife." Dez mumbles the words, like they're speaking in their sleep.

"What knife?" There are no knives allowed. Of *course* there are no knives allowed.

"Doc Leaf gave it to me."

For several seconds, I can't speak. Doc Leaf has been carrying a knife. What's terrifying is how unsurprising that is. Even more terrifying is that I know that when I tell Imogen, she'll somehow manage to brush it off, reassuring me that everything's fine.

Another realisation makes my stomach lurch: I already know I won't call the police myself.

"Where is the knife now?"

My hoarse voice must be impossible to understand, after going through the filter that flattens it. Dez just frowns and looks up at the speaker above my window.

I say again, "Where is the knife now?"

Dez's back arches as they push their hand into a pocket of their jeans. They fumble around for several seconds.

"It's gone," they say in horror.

"Did you give it to anyone?"

"No. Shit. Shit."

I lean forward, and when I speak again my voice is more echoey and strange because I'm so close to the microphone. "This is very important, Dez. Do you have any idea who might have the knife now?"

Dez blinks and looks up. "What?"

"I need to know where the knife is."

They just stare. "The knife? I don't know. It must still be in the poolhouse."

I don't know how to respond. Dez panicked and said "It's gone." What were they talking about having lost, if not the knife?

Dez jumps to their feet, rechecking their jeans pockets and searching in the pockets of their shirt. They drop to their hands and knees to look around beneath the armchair, then beneath the bulky safe.

"What are you looking for, Dez?" I ask.

They straighten up and look directly at me.

"Nothing," they say stiffly. "I was just confused for a sec."

But the expression in their eyes is… what's the word? Haunted.

Six months later

Rhea

Today's all about the contestants.

I've been making notes on a second copy of the Excel table that's also pinned to the corkboard. I've taken to performing a little celebration each time I find a snippet of information about any of the contestants: I ring a little bell on the desk next to me. It's an old-fashioned one like you might find in a hotel reception, except it's bright blue and on its curved side is written *Ring for tea.*

I'm also drinking a lot of tea.

Despite my celebrations and my very full bladder, I'd be hard pushed to claim it's going well. There are stubborn blanks next to the names of four of the contestants: Ralphie, Victor, Sasha and Dez. Several of the others are hardly much further along. Mira Qureshi and Ben Parrish appear to be on Facebook, but their accounts are set to private and neither have responded to my friend requests.

The thing that's most important about Cécile Guillaume is that she ended the week of filming covered in blood and threatening the programme-makers. Not that I can ask her about it, though. She isn't on social media – I'm guessing she sees herself as being above all that. Her name has plenty of Google hits, though, because her stage plays have been reviewed in French publications. Running the articles through an online translator leaves me with the impression that she's recently become a big deal in her home country.

For a while, I'd assumed Ruth would be an easy catch. She accepted my friend request only minutes after I sent it, so now I can see her posts and photos. *Ding ding ding* on the little bell! But she hasn't replied to my messages. Strangely, none of her posts refer to *Escapism* at all.

Screw all that. Rhea Hildred always looks ahead, never back. (No jokes about *Rhea View*, please. That particular podcast is officially on hiatus.)

I do have leads to follow. Amie Osborn was my first catch, and was easy enough to find so long as I used her real name rather than her ridiculous nickname, Aura. The website she operates appears to have been set up in the last month or so, judging by the number of pages containing only the words *Coming soon!* accompanied by a gif of a hedgehog tapping on a laptop computer. The site is basically a self-important blog about organic food, like something from the nineties, though I suppose health and wellness is all the rage right now. Its search ranking is high and there are dozens of comments on every post, plus intrusive ads that are probably raking in cash.

She replied quickly to my contact-form message, saying she's prepared to talk to me. In, like, ten minutes! I'm properly nervous, as if this is a job interview.

It feels good to be nervous. To be doing something exciting, after months of essentially nothing.

An email pops up in my inbox. To my relief, it's not Amie cancelling our Zoom call. It's a notification of a LinkedIn message. I click the link.

What is this regarding? it says.

The sender is Victor Okojie. As in Victor from *Escapism*.

My hands hover over the keyboard. *I'm a researcher for a mainstream outlet*, I type.

A few seconds pass. Then he replies: *Media? Not interested. Insta-block.*

Shit. Shit.

Not media, I type hurriedly. *Sorry for confusion.*

What would impress a guy like him? I click on his profile image and enlarge it. Immaculate blue suit, smugness oozing from every pore. City guy, thinks he's the centre of the universe.

Insurance, I type.

On behalf of Helmedia?

That's confirmed he's the right Victor Okojie, at least.

Yes. I type it before I have time to question whether I'm doing the right thing. What's the technical definition of internet fraud?

Go on.

We're initiating an investigation, I type. I'm impressed at myself – that sounds genuinely professional. Now for the hook. *Which may result in payouts.*

After a long pause, Victor responds, *More than before?*

Interesting. *Do you mean the initial fee?*

No. The value attached to the NDA.

I'm pretty sure I know what NDA stands for, but I Google it anyway. Non-disclosure agreement. The fact that it was signed after filming was halted is more proof that something serious happened during the filming of *Escapism.*

Potentially more, I type. Then, pushing my luck, *My records for each cast member aren't to hand. What value did you receive?*

I watch the flashing cursor. Come on, Victor. Think of the extra money. The imaginary extra money.

20k.

I stare at his reply, unable to make the combination of numbers and letters make sense.

Twenty thousand. As in, twenty thousand pounds.

It takes a while for me to do the calculation. If all ten contestants were paid that amount after filming was halted, it would add up to £240,000, almost as much as the prize money itself.

Are you still there? Victor types.

My brain's turned to mush. I don't know what to say next.

Again, my records are incomplete, I type eventually. *Would you be so good as to remind me of the terms of the NDA? What is it Helmedia asked you not to speak about?*

I wince. No, no, no. Why isn't there an undo button?

Victor doesn't respond. I can picture him at his computer, frowning and shaking his head.

Finally, another message appears.

I'm going to need to see some sort of identification.

Bollocks. But I deserve it, for being so clumsy.

No problem at all, I type. *I'll send it through momentarily, then let's talk.*

My hand is shaking as I log off.

So that's one contestant I can never contact ever again.

*

The whole thing with Victor has left me numb by the time I receive the Zoom call alert. I click on the link before I'm fully prepared.

The screen is bathed in light. On the bare red-brick wall behind Amie Osborn is the word *NAMASTE in* cursive script, and through a huge sloped window I can see more neon signs in a busy city street viewed from above. Amie must live in a high-up apartment, maybe a penthouse, given the size of the window and the presence of blindingly bright sunlight. And she's glowing with good health. Her hair is perfect, falling to her shoulders in waves, and it's so blonde it seems luminescent.

She puckers her lips as she peers at me.

I half-turn, ashamed at what the background to my own

video must look like. I did make my bed this morning, but it's cluttered with soft toys and graphic novels. I change the settings quickly so that everything behind me is blurred.

"You're Rhea?" Amie asks.

"Yes, indeed, that is I," I say. My nervousness is making me sound like a lunatic. "I'm working from home today. Apologies for the mess. This is, uh, my daughter's room."

Amie smiles, seeming to accept my answer.

"It must be hard, finding time to work when you've got kids," she says. "But it's a blessing to spend time with family."

I know this sort of girl. They always consider themselves 'blessed', as if every aspect of their own lives is by definition optimal.

"Do you have kids," I begin, then, to maintain my lie, I add, "too?"

She laughs and shakes her head, making her lovely hair dance. Is it okay that I kind of hate her already? She couldn't be more complacent if she tried.

"My path is not to have a family of my own," she says. "I was thinking more of my parents."

"Do you see them often?"

"They visit regularly. They're very proud of me."

"I understand you used to work for them."

"I worked *with* them for eight years, until I set out on this new venture."

"That's sweet," I say. "Most people wouldn't be so keen on that setup."

"You wouldn't work with your parents? Or your daughter?"

I ignore the second part of her question. "My parents are retired now, but I suppose you could say I was involved with their business my whole childhood. They were full-time foster carers, though I'm their biological child, and I get the impression that me showing up was a bit of a surprise. Anyway, a stream of children came through our house, some staying for only a few days, some for months or even years. I always had a playmate, I'm told."

Amie's head tilts. "Why do you say that? Why do you say 'I'm told'?"

Why are we talking about me, all of a sudden? This isn't good interviewing technique.

I wave a hand vaguely. "I don't remember much of my early years. I got a bump on the head a while back, and it knocked some memories out. It's fine. I tell myself it means I'm free of childhood hangups."

I clear my throat and rifle through pieces of paper on my desk, hoping to look like the busy media type I'm pretending to be. "So. We should talk about the piece I'm working on."

"It sounds wonderful. Despite being a fledgling startup, I have a lot of—"

I hold up a hand. "I should make clear that I'm aware of the NDAs each of the contestants signed."

She freezes. "This is about *Escapism*?"

"That's how I came across your profile."

I watch her beautiful face crease with thought. She's weighing up the conditions of the NDA with her desire to self-promote.

"You needn't worry, though," I say. "I'm less interested in *Escapism* than I am in you, having seen the footage."

"You've seen the footage?"

"Some of it. Auditions, mainly."

She nods slowly. "And you thought I was good?"

"Very good. Perfect for this article."

"Which is about what, exactly?"

Damn. I've failed to think this far ahead. Time to

153

improvise.

"It's about reality TV shows that have never been seen," I say. "While our readers are perfectly familiar with reality-TV stars, I think there's something interesting to be written about the contestants who never had the chance to become known to the public. Their initial expectations, then the sharp return to their old life, that sort of thing."

Amie frowns. "I didn't do that, exactly. My time filming *Escapism* allowed me... the opportunity to think. When it was over, my path didn't lead back to the village where my parents live. I set out on a new course. That might be of interest to your readers? A success story."

I glance at the hints of her beautiful urban apartment. Even an NDA payment of £20,000 could get eaten up quickly in a place like that. Perhaps Amie's parents are really wealthy, and are happy to spoil their child.

I nod. "I like it. A young go-getter who first tries for fame, then finds something that they can truly dedicate themselves to, which earns them big money."

For a second Amie's smug smile falters. Her wealth definitely wasn't generated by her website, then. "I consider myself very lucky," she says. "I'm also very proactive, which is a lesson in itself, isn't it? I'd be delighted to take part, so long as we can plug my site alongside the article."

"Not a problem. And, like I say, we wouldn't need to refer in detail to *Escapism*. But I should warn you, the NDA may represent a stumbling block. Can you reassure me it wouldn't cause legal issues for my publication, down the line? We have a huge readership, so we can't afford to take risks."

Amie's response is weird. The definition of her bare arms has changed, the tendons standing out. She's gripping the table, hard.

"Nothing that relates to me personally," she says

vaguely.

I nod. "That's good. But I do need to press you for a little more information than that. Otherwise, I'm afraid I may decide to find a safer bet, if you see what I mean." I laugh. "You should see our legal team – some of them are right old dragons."

Now Amie's biting a manicured thumbnail.

"I can see you're uncertain," I say, "and the last thing I want is for you to be uncomfortable. I think I'd better look elsewhere after all. Thanks so much for your time." I lean forward, as if I'm about to end the call.

"No!" Amie cries out.

I settle back in my chair.

"Things went wrong," Amie says slowly. "It was all quite… unfortunate."

"Such as what?"

She's still chewing her thumbnail.

I ask, "Was it something to do with one of the other contestants?"

"Yeah," she says quietly.

"Was somebody hurt?"

She nods, her eyes lowered. "Two people. Quite seriously."

"Did anything worse than that occur?"

She looks up and her pupils dart from side to side. She's thinking about the money and the career boost I might represent, versus the payment she received when she signed the NDA, which might easily be taken away from her.

My excitement gets the better of me. "Amie… how did Lawrence Bunce die?"

Amie's hand darts up.

The screen goes blank.

Six months earlier

Dez

It's like I'm still underwater. Each time I take a step, the ground doesn't feel solid. There's still water in my ears, too, making the chatter of the other contestants a constant drone. The beating of my heart is louder than they are.

They wouldn't let me see Mira. By 'they' I mean Study, who I presume is really Imogen. There's nobody else to speak to, even though there was mention of a health professional somewhere behind the scenes.

I have to believe that Mira's okay, at least in a physical sense. But that doesn't mean I haven't fucked things up between us. She trusted me, and look what I did to her.

And look what it's done to me.

My hands are shaking constantly. Each time someone approaches me, they back away again – I must be doing that face I do when I'm totally strung out. Priya called it a defence mechanism, but it's not me that should be prepared to defend themselves. It's everyone else. It's the entire world.

We're all trooping out of the entrance hall with our umbrellas being battered by the rain, meekly following our Pied Piper, Axel Griffin. As we pass the concrete building that contains the swimming pool, a few people turn and look at it, as if there might be some evidence of the awful thing that happened in there, as if blood might be seeping out from under the door.

I already know there's no blood. There's none on the

tiles inside the building, either. I know this because I went back into the building an hour ago, holding my breath for fear of seeing evidence of Mira's injury. The tiles had already been mopped clean.

I wasn't looking for the Doc Leaf's knife, though. I was looking for Priya's lighter. I can't believe I've lost it. It's just one more example of how badly I'm fucking things up today.

I hit myself on the forehead with a fist, then look around to make sure nobody noticed. It's a bad habit from my childhood. A good whack on the forehead is enough to stop you noticing that you're still yourself, just for a second or two.

I hurry to catch up with our host as he strides ahead of the chattering contestants.

"Hey, Axel," I say, raising my voice to be heard over the rain. "Have you seen Mira?"

"Mira?" he repeats. "Ah. Yes. She's asleep, I think."

"But did you see her?"

His expression softens when he realises I'm being weak and needy, rather than accusing him of anything.

"Mobeen says she'll be fine."

"Mobeen. Is he the doctor?"

"Yes. He's very capable. Mira is in good hands."

"Yeah? You promise?"

He stops walking, leans the stem of his umbrella against his shoulder, and takes my right hand in both of his. My hands are still shaking, my fingers twitching.

"I promise," he says in a sincere tone that he must have learned at TV presenters' school. It works. I want to believe him, and right now I *do* believe him.

I nod and I keep clinging to his hand, my fingers still trembling. He looks more and more on edge as the seconds pass.

"Try to put it all out of your mind," he says. The

warmth in his voice seems more forced now. "Enjoy the task. The game is supposed to be fun."

Fun is the last thing I'm interested in, but I nod again. Finally, I release his hands. He turns and continues walking.

I hang back. I look down at the small object nestled in the palm of my right hand. It's one of Axel's gold cufflinks, which is in the shape of a crown.

Ben

"Here we are, friends!" Axel announces, throwing open the double doors of the barn. We shake off our umbrellas and follow him in.

I have less and less faith in him as time goes on. When we were waiting in the entrance hall for the other contestants, I asked Axel a simple question: Who won the third task? He was evasive, but eventually his TV-star persona just flicked off, and with an expression of total guilt he replied that *Mira* had won. Not Mira's team that also contained Ralphie and Dez. Just Mira. Apparently Axel told her about her triumph after she was taken indoors, and he gave her the key.

I'm as sorry as anyone that Mira was injured, especially as it really should have been me in that cage instead of her. But giving her the key... that's just nuts. After the awful experience she's had, I bet she doesn't care at all about competing in *Escapism*.

But it works well for me, I suppose. I've got one key, and either Ralphie or Ruth have the second. Four are needed to unlock the vault. Despite having to duck out of the third task, I'm still in contention to get a share of the prize money, which has risen by £8,000 due to the other contestants' efforts in the last task. If I can get even one more key, I'll have leverage to demand half of the total cash.

I turn my attention to what's inside the barn. Blocking our access is a large white plywood fence with a single open doorway. Through it I can see a plain corridor that ends at a blank wall – a junction with passages that lead left and right. If I stand on tiptoes to look above the plywood wall, I can see steps leading to a raised platform against the rear wall of the barn. Blindingly bright lamps shine down from the wooden beams of the roofspace. There are other odd objects up there alongside the lamps: bulky cuboids that give no clue to their purpose.

Axel takes our umbrellas and put them in a metal locker. Then he says, "This task will be a new challenge. On this occasion, you will be required to work alone."

A few of us exchange glances. It's not as if Mira benefitted from having teammates, is it?

Axel continues, "The aim is simple. Reach the raised dais at the other side of the barn. That is to say, at the other end of the maze."

Groans come from all around me. Seriously, do these people experience no joy at the prospect of a puzzle? Why are they even here?

I love a maze. A couple of years ago I made a blog with entries on all my favourite mazes around the UK: Hampton Court, Blenheim Palace, the Minotaur maze at Kielder Castle. Carla and the girls weren't nearly so enthusiastic, though. Our trip to Hever Castle in Kent was our last family holiday. The girls squealed when jets of water sprayed them – and not the fun kind of squeals – and afterwards Carla scolded me, pointing out that a freezing mid-October morning was hardly the time to be getting young kids soaking wet. They all retreated to the hotel while I navigated the maze again and again, shivering with cold but not caring.

I pushed my family away, consistently, either for the sake of a blog that nobody read, or for the sake of games weekends with nerdy friends, or to attend auditions for TV game shows. That is, for nothing important at all. Nowadays I see Jill and Bethany only once a week, and I glimpse Carla only over their shoulders at the doorstep of their house, which used to be *our* house.

I still have all my hobbies, my passions, but what use

are they? I live in a tiny one-bedroom flat, and I've allowed games to consume my life entirely, for fear that without them I have no life at all.

I realise that Axel has been speaking while I've been dwelling in my misery.

"That's right," he says. "I can assure you there's no need to be coy – you can simply put them on over your clothes." He assesses each contestant in turn, rifling through a collection of white outfits hanging within the metal locker before handing them over.

"I don't think you understand how women's clothing works," Cécile says. In one hand she's holding up the entirely white boiler suit she's been given. With her other hand she's pointing at the absurdly narrow grey pencil skirt she's wearing.

Axel has the decency to blush. "I'm afraid you *will* each need to wear a suit."

Eventually, Ralphie, Victor and Dez offer to stand side by side to form a human wall, facing away from Cécile and Aura to give them privacy as they shrug off their skirts and put on their boiler suits. Ruth is wearing a dress too, but she just ruffles the loose fabric above the legs of the boiler suit as she pulls it up. Victor watches her the whole time, which is a bit creepy.

The rest of us just pull on the suits over our clothes. Even though they're roomy, like biohazard suits in a post-apocalyptic film, I overheat immediately. I get even more claustrophobic when I pull on the chunky goggles Axel hands me. After a few seconds I have to pull them back to sit on top of my head, the elastic tangling in my curly hair.

"Are you going to tell us what these are for?" Cécile asks, patting her suit. Somehow, she doesn't look absurd in the bulky outfit. Some people look good in anything.

I'm surprised she's the one to challenge Axel. Usually it's Victor speaking up. I glance at him, but he's not even looking at Axel. He's staring along the blank corridor that leads to the maze, his head bobbing left and right, as if he's trying to memorise a sequence of directions.

"I'm so very glad you've asked," Axel says. He points to the steps, far beyond the entrance corridor. "Reaching the end of the maze is only part of the achievement." He adopts a mock-serious expression. "I'm quite particular about the sartorial appearance of my guests, you see. I'd very much prefer that these beautiful white suits you're wearing remain pristine. So let me simplify the rules: you will only contribute to the prize fund – and be in contention to win the key – if you reach the end of the maze *without* spoiling your suit."

There's confusion among the contestants – why would our boiler suits get mucky, just by walking through a maze? But I know better than to assume we've been told everything.

Axel turns and waves a hand at the corridor. "One final thing. I'm as particular about security as I am about cleanliness." He raises his voice to call out, "Initiate the security system, please!"

Nothing happens. After five or six seconds, Axel's fixed grin begins to falter.

Finally, a series of clunks sounds as the overhead lights are extinguished.

A few feet along the corridor leading into the maze is a thin line of red light at ankle level. Just before the junction, there's another one passing from one wall to the other, this time at eye level.

Laser beams. Neat.

I look up at the boxy shapes among the roof beams. Sure enough, the first two are above the red beams of light. Whatever's in the boxes is what will stain our suits, no doubt.

"Now," says Axel, "there is only the matter about who

will go first!"

We all look at each other, trying to work out whether allowing other people to go first will give some sort of advantage.

Ralphie puts his hand up. "I'll go."

"Then the best of British to you," Axel says – and perhaps it's the oddly specific phrase, but for the first time I notice that he has a slight accent that definitely *isn't* British.

Ralphie bunny-hops over the first light beam, then ducks beneath the next. At the junction he hesitates, looking in each direction, then heads left.

I raise myself onto my tiptoes again. I can't see Ralphie at all. But within thirty seconds or so, it's obvious where he is. The snub end of one of the boxes above the maze opens, and a pale blue puff comes from it. Immediately, a shout comes from within the depths of the maze: "Ah, crap!"

Paint. I think back to a charity run Bethany once took part in, in her final year of primary school. It was a mile and a half run on the school field, and all the kids that participated had powder paint flung at them by teachers and younger children. Most of the runners wore white T-shirts for maximum effect, and afterwards not only Bethany's clothes were ruined, but her face was covered in blotches of carnival colours. I'd forbidden her from going in the bath, telling her we'd have to hose her off in the back garden, but Carla overruled me. She and Bethany bathed together, spreading rather than washing off the coloured paint. The faint blue stain never quite left the tide line of the bath. At the time it had seemed to matter.

I shake my head. More distractions.

It occurs to me that with every new contestant that tries and fails, I'll be provided with more evidence about a safe route… but there'll also be more paint distributed around

163

the maze. By the end, it'll be difficult to avoid the paint on the walls even if I don't trip any of the light beams.

Ralphie appears in the distance, clambering up the steps to the podium. He whoops and raises his arms. One of them is bright blue.

"I'll go next," I say, lowering my goggles as I push my way to the entrance of the maze.

"Go forth," Axel says.

And I'm in.

The first two beams are easy to avoid. At the junction I turn right, moving slowly now that I'm in unknown territory.

It's *really* dark. It's difficult to see the end of each stretch of corridor. The crinkly fabric of the suit makes me so bulky it's almost impossible to avoid brushing against one wall or the other. I was right to head into the maze early – the final contestants are going to have their work cut out.

The next light beam is at waist height. I drop to the floor and commando-crawl underneath it.

I turn the corner, scanning ahead. I see a light beam, but then I realise it's a glimpse into another corridor through a long horizontal slot in the wall. There's no light beam in this corridor, and it's too dark to see if there are paint containers above. But halfway along the passage there's an odd square patch that's lit by an overhead lamp. I approach it carefully, and make out a slightly raised area and a strip of beige duct tape leading to the base of the wall. It must be a makeshift pressure plate. I press myself against the wall to edge past. My heart is racing. I tell myself I'm enjoying this, because I love this sort of thing, don't I?

Slowly but surely, I make my way deeper into the maze. I move over a light beam, then under the next. I avoid the pressure plates, only some of which are lit from above.

Then the steps leading up to the podium are visible through a horizontal slot in the right wall. It looks like the exit might be just around the next corner.

The trouble is, there's not one but two light beams, directly before the corner. One of them is at ankle height, the other at shoulder height. The only way through is to hop between them with head bowed.

I look up to see the black shadow of a paint container hanging above the light beams.

Don't overthink it.

I swing back and forth, rehearsing the movement.

The second I push myself from the floor, I know my approach is all wrong. I feel like I'm in slow motion, conscious enough to try to yank my shins closer to my bum and to duck my head lower. And it might have been enough, if I'd also managed enough forward motion. But even as I'm sailing into the air I know I'm going to come down directly on the lower beam.

I try to abort the attempt, throwing out my arms to either side, hoping to brace myself and drop to the floor before I hit the beams.

I spin, out of control.

When I hit the floor, my bent knees jab into my chin, and all the breath leaves my body.

I hear a click.

I try to scramble forwards. But I'd forgotten about the turn in the corridor, and my head smacks into the wall, dazing me even more. We should definitely have been given helmets.

I drop to one side, then twist my neck to look up... just in time to see a cloud of pink powder falling. I let out a wordless shout as the paint falls onto my shoulders and arms and then enters my mouth, silencing me.

Aura

I swear, if it wasn't for this stupid boiler suit, I'd have aced this task.

As it is, I hit two light beams and one pressure plate, and when I climb onto the raised platform I'm coughing because of the coloured powder I've inhaled. Ben clumsily tries to give me a high-five but I duck away – one of his arms is bright red and the other yellow, and my guess is he's trying to spread his paint to as many people as possible.

Then I look down and sigh in dismay. I can't see a single square centimetre of my suit that *isn't* covered with paint.

The other contestants on the podium are Ben, Sasha, Cécile, Ruth and Doc Leaf. I'm relieved to see that none of them have come through the maze untainted. Doc Leaf looks like he must have triggered the release of purple powder and then rolled around in it like a dog. He seems delighted with himself.

From this vantage point on the podium I can make out the white lines of the tops of the walls. The maze is far smaller than it seemed when I was in it, but there are more junctions than I realised too.

"What *is* that?" Sasha says.

I follow her pointing finger. Towards the centre of the maze, I see something bright red moving along a passage.

We all watch as the domed shape bobs to the end of the passage, then moves around the corner. It stops for a few seconds, then continues.

Suddenly, one of the black boxes overhead opens, releasing a plume of green paint. The red dome doesn't move, and within seconds it's marked with blotches of green. Then I realise what we're looking at.

"It's an umbrella!" I say.

"That's not fair," Ben complains. "Where did they get that?"

"Who even is it?" Sasha asks.

I look at the other contestants on the podium. Doc Leaf is sitting on the floor, swiping on his phone. It takes me a second to register how wrong that is, because the action seems so normal. Phones aren't allowed here. How did he manage to keep hold of his after we all handed ours in?

But any thought of accusing him goes out of my mind when I see Ruth. She's watching the umbrella in the maze too. Her expression isn't one of confusion or annoyance. Her neck cranes as she tracks the umbrella's progress, and her eyes are gleaming.

"You know who it is, don't you?" I say to her. Before she can reply, the answer occurs to me. "Is it Victor?"

She shrugs, but it's a bad attempt at playing innocent.

"I saw how he was behaving during Axel's introduction," I say. "He was muttering to himself, staring at the maze. And he was standing really stiffly. Did he have an umbrella hidden in his trouser leg?"

I take Ruth's silence as a yes.

Ben and Sasha have turned to look at Ruth too. "How did he know he'd need it?" Ben demands.

Now Ruth's cheeks are as red as the paint staining the left arm of her boiler suit. She looks like she wishes she could just disappear.

The answer is obvious to me. Last night I knocked on Ruth's door before turning in. I figured a girly heart-to-heart – or at least a pretence of one – would help keep her on side, in case I needed an ally later in the contest. But she didn't answer, even though she'd only gone into her room fifteen minutes before.

"You and Victor came here last night," I say. "Didn't you?"

Ruth's expression hardens, suggesting the sort of resolve I didn't realise she had in her.

"He learnt the route of the maze last night?" Sasha asks.

Ruth is saved from having to reply.

"Fuck's sake!" a voice shouts.

We all turn to look at the maze.

The umbrella isn't red any longer – it's a mishmash of yellow, green and pink. It's hard to imagine any of the paint has got onto Victor, though – the umbrella is large enough to protect him. I see it move back in the direction it came from, then bob, then turn back again. It's not paint that's causing Victor trouble. He's lost.

After another roar of annoyance, the umbrella disappears from view. Why would Victor abandon it now?

My question is answered a moment later. Victor's close-cropped head appears, shining under a spotlight.

He's climbing the wall. He must be using one of the horizontal slots for purchase.

Within seconds he's balanced above the maze. His raises his head to look over at us standing on the podium… No, just at Ruth. He grins.

"Don't, Vic!" Ruth calls out. So he's *Vic* now, is he?

He doesn't listen. He must be thinking that if he stays above the passages of the maze, he can't trigger any of the light beams or pressure sensors.

Except he's a big lad. Heavy.

He lowers himself to a crouch, reaching down. When he rises again, he's holding the umbrella.

To my amazement, he navigates the length of the top of the first wall pretty well, arms wide and using the umbrella for balance, like a tightrope walker. It looks like there are actually only two more walls he needs to walk across, then he'll drop down at the foot of the podium. His suit is still spotless. He might actually get away with this.

"Vic, don't!" Ruth calls again. "You'll fall!"

He shakes his head. He's having fun.

When he reaches the end of the next wall, we all gasp as he makes the jump, landing with only a slight wobble on top of the final one.

"Ha *ha*!" he shouts. "I *got* this!"

He's really doing it. He's kind of incredible.

Then the smile disappears from his face. It takes me a couple of seconds to understand why.

The wall's moving. It's tilting away from the podium.

Victor's arms flail madly, then he drops to his haunches, scrabbling to grip the narrow wall even as it topples towards the centre of the maze.

The wall strikes the next one along, then there's another thud as that one hits another. The domino effect would probably be quite satisfying to watch, but none of us see it, because that's when all the boxes overhead open at the same time, releasing a torrent of coloured paint that drifts down over the entire maze like pesticide from a crop duster.

Dolly

None of us say a word. For *ages*. We just stare at the bank of monitors, watching as the clouds of powder paint settle to reveal the full extent of what's happened. Victor's sprawled on a heap of fallen plywood panels, lying on his back, his goggles and his entire face caked in paint. His stupid umbrella ended up flying off somewhere as he fell.

I look over at Imogen. Her eyes are fixed on the screens. Less than a minute ago, she assured me that Victor's cheating wasn't a problem. She said that Helm had anticipated that some of the contestants might figure out workarounds to the tasks, and that it was all part of the format. She doesn't seem quite so sure of herself now.

Imogen whirls around. Her eyes rest on me for a second or two, but then she obviously decides I'm not the right fall guy. She points at Lonnie.

"You were responsible for the integrity of that maze!" she hisses.

Lonnie just gazes blankly at her. Maybe he doesn't know what 'integrity' means.

"Did you check it this morning?" Imogen demands.

"Sure I did," Lonnie replies. "It was fine this morning. Safe as houses."

Imogen's eyes bulge. She and I both look at the monitors again.

"Maybe *condemned* houses," Lonnie adds with a chuckle. "Cos that Victor bloke really chucked a demolition ball at them, didn't he?"

I move closer to the monitor bank to watch Victor rise to his feet. At first his movements are jerky and tentative. Then, with a wince that cracks the paint caking his face, he lifts both his arms. I'm glad I can't hear the idiotic whoop that I'm certain he's making right now.

My eyes dart around, assessing the damage. Victor took down around a quarter of the maze. The plywood walls in each corner appear more or less intact, but the centre is a wasteland.

The contestants on the podium haven't moved a muscle. No – that's not true. Ruth is scurrying back into the maze, triggering paint drops as she goes. Then a couple of the contestants that were waiting at the entrance do the same, barging along the still-intact first corridor to find out what's going on. More powder spills from above.

Axel's only visible on one of the monitors. He's looking up, directly at the camera, his finger pressed to his ear. He's mouthing words. Now I register a buzzing sound from nearby. It's his voice, speaking through Imogen's headset.

"You need to make a call," I say.

"I'm thinking." But Imogen doesn't look like she's thinking. She looks like she's just turned off entirely.

"We need to get Victor seen by Mobeen," I say.

"We've gotta get those people away from the barn," Lonnie adds, surprising me. "The rest of that maze is bound to fall down any minute. With these idiots running around like headless chickens, who knows who it'll land on."

"I need to call Sweden," Imogen murmurs. "Helm needs to make a call about what we do next."

I can't bear her indecision. In a single quick movement I yank the spindly headset off her head and direct the microphone towards my own mouth.

"Axel?" I say. "End the task. Get everyone out of there."

His voice buzzes again. Dodging Imogen's flailing hand, I push the headset onto my head. Now that the earpiece is in place, I can hear Axel properly.

"—who's the winner, though?" he says.

My eyes flick up. None of the contestants who completed the maze came out of it without paint on their suits. We can't assume any of those who were yet to attempt it would do any better.

"There's no winner," I say. "No prizes. Now, *please*, just get everyone out of there."

Six months later

Rhea

Somebody had to be accountable for the death of Lawrence Bunce, and whatever other disasters occurred during filming of *Escapism*. My research tells me that even though Helmedia retained production responsibility for the UK version, they employed the services of a British company to run the game show: Kestrel Productions, based in Hammersmith. The person I spoke to on the phone at Kestrel eventually clammed up – and hung up – but I was able to sweet-talk a nugget of information out of him before that point. Only two of their in-house staff were present on Red Cliffs Island during filming: a director named Imogen Dorrien-Stewart and a production assistant called Dolly Nyman. He mentioned there were a couple of other staff on the production team, but they were freelance hires, and I wasn't able to get their names. But from the list I found online, they must be Mobeen and Lonnie – that is, Lawrence Bunce himself.

It turns out that Imogen Dorrien-Stewart is pretty well-known – or at least she was once, when she directed Brian Cox in *Hamlet* at the RSC back in the late nineties. The come-down of taking on a reality game show must have stung.

Not that *Escapism* appears on her IMDb page. There's no record of it anywhere.

Online, I can't find any record of Imogen having worked recently. The only reference is to her leaving

Kestrel, almost six months ago – that is, directly after the shit hit the fan at Red Cliffs. I can't think of any way to get her contact details, now that I've hit a brick wall at Kestrel.

I've already tried and failed to find out anything about Lonnie/Lawrence, and the name Mobeen isn't enough to go on, so Dolly's next up. She's easy enough to locate on Instagram. Her feed is full of pictures of camera equipment and script pages with the titles coyly blanked out, so it's definitely her. Her bio states she's freelance, so she must have left Kestrel too, perhaps at the same time as Imogen. I click like on a few of the posts, then send Dolly a message: *Hey! Am I right in thinking you did some work for Kestrel? I've got an interview and I'd kill for some inside info.*

That's that, then. While I wait, I turn my attention to Helmedia. Most of the information I find online is written in Swedish, and running the text through translator sites gives patchy results. From what I can make out, the company hadn't actually produced any TV show of any sort until it came up with *Eskapism*, four years ago, and since then it's dedicated all of its attention to that single format. I note down a few names of people attached to the Swedish version of the show, but it doesn't feel like a lead.

I'm starting to go cross-eyed, staring at the garbled Swedish-to-English translation. There are bright flickers at the edges of my vision.

Ah, shit.

I scrunch my eyes closed. It's the only thing that can head off one of my migraines. I stagger over to my bed and flop onto my front, pressing my face into the duvet.

In the darkness I see shapes: people with spindly arms waving, like those inflatable men outside of petrol stations, except not fun. Not fun at all. They're in agony.

The fact that during my episodes I see visions of tortured people is probably significant. I'd be the first to admit that. It probably raises a lot of questions about my fundamental character.

I don't normally hear anything. But this time they're calling out, and their limbs are drumming on the walls.

Hold on.

I roll over. Even through my eyelids, the overhead light is blinding. I put my arms over my face, then wait, listening.

"Rhea?" a voice calls.

Then another knock.

It's Ted.

"Come in," I manage to say.

The door rattles, then Ted says, "It's locked."

"Key's under the mat."

More sounds of fumbling.

"Oh. Are you okay?" Ted asks. His unmuffled tone tells me he's in my flat now.

I keep one arm clamped over my eyes. "Migraine."

"I'm sorry to hear that. I'll come back tomorrow?"

"No. Turn off the big light, then sit down, over there." I point, *probably* at my desk chair.

I hear Ted plod a few steps, and the blazing light lessens, then there's a sigh like a deflating bouncy castle as he drops into the chair.

"Is there anything I can do for you?" he asks.

"You can speak in a quieter voice."

He does. "You're in no shape to record another episode."

"You're in no shape to run a marathon, Ted, but you don't hear me going on about it."

"My point is you need to rest."

"I'll rest when I'm dead." I don't know why I said that. I'm hardly the James Dean type.

I hear a shuffle of papers, then the click of a mouse button. Cheeky Ted.

"You're investigating Helmedia, then?" he says. "They don't sound very prolific. And it's weird about their boss."

"What?"

Click click. "There's nothing listed on their upcoming projects slate."

"No. The other thing. What's weird about the boss?"

"Oh. The first article in your search results mentions he left the media business, without explanation. Six months ago."

"It must be catching," I say.

"I'm sorry?"

"You quit the business around then, too, didn't you? Then you got the gig as guest lecturer at Leeds Beckett Uni."

Ted hesitates. "I didn't so much quit as fail to secure work."

Excuses, excuses.

Hold on a sec.

I sit up sharply. White-hot pain lances into my brain, making me squeal.

"Hey, how can you read the search results?" I ask.

"I know a little Swedish. I visited the country once or twice. A long while back."

"Why didn't you tell me?" I say. "All morning I've been trying to get sense out of those search results, and now it turns out I needn't have bothered. That's what gave me this stupid headache, Ted."

"Sorry," Ted says meekly.

"So what else does it say? About the Swedish producer?"

"What Swedish producer?"

"Helm!" I say, and the sharpness of my own voice makes me feel sick.

"Oh. You confused me," he says, "because he's not Swedish. It says here that Helm is British, though it's

176

peculiar that his real name isn't given – he must be a very private guy. He's been based in Stockholm for more than a decade, and made a fortune in trading before he founded Helmedia – he's one of those dot-com millionaires you hear about, so it seems. He had tons of investments in tech companies. That's about all I can glean about him."

I drop back onto the bed, not even caring about the black ghosts that flood into my vision again. All I want to do now is sleep.

"What's this?" Ted says. His voice comes from a thousand miles away.

I grunt. I'm sinking into the mattress, into the void.

"A message just popped up," Ted says. His voice echoes like he's speaking from inside a cave. "It's from someone named Dolly."

Six months earlier

Dez

We all troop from the barn in silence. Everyone seems pretty stunned. Axel walks far ahead of the rest of us, and when we reach the entrance he doesn't even enter the lobby. Instead, he just waves us in through the wooden porch, like he's a teacher overseeing a school trip. Then he hotfoots it in the other direction.

We stand in the lobby, looking at each other, and mostly at Victor. He looks like a multicoloured effigy of a person. Every time he moves, paint wafts onto the flagstones.

Abruptly, Doc Leaf lunges at Victor, who's too blinded by paint to see him coming.

To my surprise, it's not an attack.

"My *man*!" Doc Leaf shouts. "You completely fucked that place up! It was fucking *glorious*!"

Somehow, Victor manages to free himself from Doc Leaf's bear hug. He staggers back and wipes his goggles, then pushes them on top of his head, revealing two patches of unpainted skin that make him look like the most colourful panda bear in the world.

"Yeah," he says gruffly. "Yeah, I did."

While we were walking back to the mansion, I saw Victor pressing his hands to his lower back – he must have really smacked his tailbone when he fell.

"Look, guys," he says to the group at large, "I'm sorry, yeah? I didn't think that'd happen."

"What did you expect?" Cécile demands.

Victor shrugs. "I thought the maze would be, you know, more solid."

"Climbing on top of it would still have been cheating," Sasha points out.

Doc Leaf whirls around to face the group. "It wasn't cheating," he insists. "He literally thought outside the box! *That's* how we win this game. *That's* what people want to see on the telly!"

Everybody just stares at him. I wonder if they're beginning to suspect that Doc Leaf may actually be right.

"I need a drink," Victor says in a hoarse voice.

He moves in the direction of the sitting room, but Sasha blocks his way.

"No you don't," she says sternly. "Not a single one of us who went through the maze is going into that room until they've washed the paint off and changed their clothes. Off you trot upstairs, Victor, and all you other colourful clowns too."

Nobody protests. Mum's said her piece, and nobody wants to see her mad. The painted contestants head upstairs, heads bowed, even Doc Leaf. Ruth guides Victor by the waist to prevent him from toppling over the banister for another painful fall.

*

Me and the other contestants who didn't attempt the maze wander into the sitting room, muttering about drinks. I take the opportunity to head to the study. There's no name on the sign, and when I push open the door it's dark inside. So much for Study's assurances that they're always available to speak to.

I flick on the light, then say, "Hello?"

There's no reply.

I sit in the armchair. I wait.

I rise and tap on the dark window.

"Study? Is anyone there?"

No reply, so I guess not.

I look at the paintings of peasant haymakers. I run my hand over the blank face of the safe. I fiddle with the ornaments on the sideboard, and think about pocketing one or two of them. I remember that even though Study's absent, there are cameras trained on me at all times.

I leave the room. Instead of turning right towards the sitting room, I turn left. The door marked *PRODUCTION PERSONNEL ONLY* has been taunting me from day one.

There's a swipe card reader next to the door, which looks newly installed. I tell myself the door will be locked, but when I glance down I see it's not even fully closed. Even though the bolt is sticking out, it's not holding the door at all.

I push it gently.

The sense of entering a forbidden area is intoxicating. Not for the first time, I tell myself to have a good long think about why breaking the rules is so appealing to me. A psychologist would say it was something to do with my upbringing – the long years of confusion about who I really was, and therefore where I belonged. My rule-breaking goes all the way back to my pre-teens. When I was first brought home in a police car, twelve-year-old me wasn't able to explain to my shocked middle-class parents why I stole a platinum credit card from the purse of a well-dressed banker type on the Tube. I kept insisting I knew I couldn't actually use it, as if that was any defence. Yep, a psychologist would have a field day with me.

I remind myself that I *am* a psychologist.

The first wooden door on the left has the words *PRODUCTION SUITE* printed on a temporary laminated sign. Greenish light shines from beneath it. There's another card reader alongside it, and the door's fully closed. Even if it had been ajar I wouldn't have ventured in there, because I'd be sure to be caught.

It occurs to me that, for the first time in three days, I'm not being filmed. The realisation makes me want to do something – what? Perform an embarrassing dance? Graffiti a cock and balls on the wall?

The next door along is wide open, revealing a large room containing a square U-shape of sofas echoing the arrangement of the sofas in the sitting room. But these ones are bright red, and the cushions are boxy foam – it's the sort of seating you'd expect to see in a dentist's waiting room, designed to withstand hundreds of bums and yet offer no actual comfort.

Beyond the sofas I see a galley kitchen: a microwave, a double fridge, a sink. It's reassuring to see that the living quarters of the production team are even worse than ours.

Speaking of which, where *are* the production team? Shouldn't there be dozens of people scurrying around here, like in the backstage area of a theatre? This place is a ghost town.

All this time, I've felt self-conscious about being watched. Now the idea of us being left to our own devices, *not* being watched, seems even more daunting.

There are five identical doors on the right-hand side of the corridor, like the doors to identical hotel rooms. I guess these are the production team's rooms. Only five, though?

There are names on more laminated signs. Imogen. Lonnie. Mobeen. Dolly. Axel.

I hear a strange swishing sound. Then a low voice.

I place my hand on each door in turn. When I was a kid my favourite game was hide and seek. On playdates, and at birthday parties and during the week-long holidays my parents organised with their old uni friends and their families, I was always the one to suggest playing it. I could

181

hide for hours, long after the other players had given up, far beyond the point when anyone was still curious about where I might be. Although I was less keen on being the seeker, I was equally good at it. I reckoned I could tell whether someone was within a room or a box or a cupboard just by putting my hand on the door and sort of *sensing* them.

I move along the row of doors.

Whoever's making those swishing sounds, they're in Axel's room.

Maybe it's—

I rattle the door handle. To my amazement, the door opens.

Mira's lying on the bed. She's clutching the bedsheets tightly, wrenching them back and forth, making the swishing sound I heard from outside.

She's asleep, breathing in fits and starts. She's muttering, too. Beneath her eyelids I see constant movement, and each time her eyes dart her head seems to follow suit. Perhaps she's dreaming of being trapped in that cage underwater, searching for a way out.

Any psychologist would tell you she'll probably dream about it for years to come. And like I say, I *am* a psychologist.

I know better than to wake her. I drop to my haunches beside the bed, watching her. Her arms keep writhing about, bundling the sheets. After a minute or so, I guess something really alarming happens in her dream – her whole body jerks, and her arms lift, and now I can see the inner side of her right forearm.

A mixture of revulsion and relief swells up inside me. I feel like I might puke.

It's not as bad as I'd feared — that's my first response.

But while the skin around the three lacerations has been cleaned up, showing the damage is quite localised, the streaks are dark and raw, more black than red. Mira might easily end up with permanent scars. And whenever anyone glimpses them, when Mira wears a short-sleeved top, when she's getting dressed, when she goes to the swimming pool (no, I remind myself, she'll never go near a swimming pool ever again), they'll think *Oh shit,* and then they'll think, *I wonder if she still cuts herself.*

That idea almost seems worse than the injuries. Mira is the least self-conscious person I've ever met, but now I've given her a reason to feel self-conscious. She'll have to correct people's assumptions, again and again and again. Having been in that position my whole life, I wouldn't wish it on anyone, certainly not on somebody I love.

That's what I tell myself.

But my psychologist-brain is working overtime, analysing my actions and the unconscious intentions behind them.

And that prick of a psychologist is suggesting, in an oh-so-professional, prissily neutral tone, *Is it possible, on some level, that you did this on purpose?*

Ben

Something's changed.

I think maybe it began with Victor's doomed attempt to cheat at the maze. I can't be the only one to have mixed feelings about what he did. Climbing on top of the maze was daft, but the earlier part, the sneaking around, gaining insights into the next day's tasks – that's another matter.

What's worth noting is that there have been no comebacks, no repercussions. When Mira was injured she was whisked away to recover, but *Escapism* just continued. If Victor hadn't actually destroyed the maze, my guess is that Axel wouldn't have said a thing about the umbrella.

So what's stopping the rest of us from trying to get ahead?

Until now, there's been very little discussion about the keys that unlock the vault containing the prize money. Now it's all anyone wants to talk about. When Sasha revealed that she'd given me the key to look after, I could sense everyone's attitude to both of us changing. They see Sasha as a fool, and me as even more of a threat than I was already.

"I mean, why *him*?" Victor asks Sasha, pointing at me. "Just because he was on your team in the first task. It's nuts."

"I'm trustworthy," I say, but my tone doesn't even convince me.

"Anyway, you can hardly talk, Victor, seeing as you already have a key," Aura snaps. She cocks her head at Ralphie. "I'm guessing you weren't trusting enough to let *your* teammate so much as touch it."

Ralphie's face is blank and he keeps looking at each of them in turn, like a cat watching tennis.

"You gotta pick your people right," Victor says. "And I'm saying Ben here isn't the sort of guy you can trust not to stab you in the back. We've all heard him talk. He loves *games*, man."

I don't at all like his emphasis on that word. What's so bad about loving games? At least games have rules, not like conversations like this, brimming with anger and danger.

For some reason I can't even begin to understand, Aura seems to have decided she's my defender. She steps forward and places her hand on Victor's chest. Despite the gentleness, almost seductiveness of the gesture, it strikes me as invasive.

"It seems you've made firm decisions about who your *people* are," she says. Then she narrows her eyes and adds, "*Vic.*"

That shuts Victor up. No idea why.

Aura turns to Ruth and announces, "Victor and Ruth knew each other before coming to Red Cliffs Island."

Gasps from all around.

Aura's not finished. "In fact, they're a couple."

Now we're *all* cats watching tennis. We look at Ruth, then Victor, then Ruth, then Victor.

"Is this true?" Cécile asks.

Ruth's and Victor's eyes meet. I see minute expressions flickering across their faces.

"Fuck it," Ruth says. "Yeah, we're together."

I'm surrounding by sounds like a whole room of party balloons being deflated at once. In the centre of the group of contestants on the verge of asphyxiation is Aura, arms folded across her chest, relishing her moment of being dead right.

"Why?" I ask.

"Why? Because my man there is *hot*," Ruth replies. Now that her secret's out, she seems nothing like the meek girl she's appeared to be before now.

Victor points at Ruth. "She reckoned we wouldn't both be let on the show if anyone knew."

I shake my head. "No, I mean, what's the benefit, in terms of the game?" But then it's suddenly obvious to me, and I answer my own question. "Of course. You've made sure you're on different teams each time, except in Task 3 when the teams were picked for us. Your idea is to cover your bases in terms of earning keys, then pool them to take the prize money. An alliance that you can both actually trust."

In response, Victor shoots Ruth a goofy grin. She makes a little beckoning gesture, and he trots over to her and she nuzzles into his arms.

*

When contestants begin leaving the sitting room in little groups, drinks in hand and muttering, I approach Ralphie as he's helping himself to an alcopop at the bar counter.

"Hey, mate," I say cheerfully.

Ralphie freezes. In a guarded tone, he replies, "What's up?"

"I just wanted to say hi."

"Okay."

I was never any good at small talk, or any conversation that doesn't have a clear agenda. That's partly why I like board games so much: there's plenty of chat, but everyone's clear what the *point* of the conversation is.

In a lower voice, I say, "Actually, I wanted to talk to you about *keys*."

Like Aura, my assumption is that after they won the second task, Victor snatched the key for himself. Any other outcome is almost impossible to imagine.

Ralphie looks around. The only other people in the room are Cécile and Sasha, sitting in the armchairs before the fireplace, chatting. You might easily think they'd been friends forever.

"I forgot you'd won a task too," Ralphie says. "So then you know."

I hesitate. "Know what?"

Ralphie just stares at me. "You said... I mean, you put emphasis on the word 'keys'."

I blink in confusion. Is he deliberately acting dim? Keys are what this game is all about.

Then I realise what he's going on about.

"Plural," I say. "Keys, plural."

Ralphie nods.

Carefully, I say, "You were given two keys?"

"Yeah. Like you and Sasha were. Right?"

"Right."

Victor and Ralphie should never have won Task 2. And they definitely shouldn't have been rewarded with twice the number of keys to unlock the vault. It's insane that they're already halfway to sharing the prize fund between them. And they're friendly with a bunch of other contestants, who'll no doubt happy contribute their keys if they win them.

I can't look Ralphie in the eye any more. I slink away, unable to put the thought of out of my mind that I've already lost the game.

Dolly

The contestants are crawling all over the building. This must be how security guards feel when they're monitoring CCTV in a shopping centre. I have this growing certainty that *something* will happen at some point. Shit will hit the fan, and my job is to spot it soon enough that a full-scale disaster can be averted.

It's frustrating that I can't hear what any of them are saying. But it was easy to identify the moment when the tone morphed into... what's the word? Mutiny. After they got cleaned up and then ate the sticky pasta that Lonnie cooked for them, they all huddled on the sitting-room sofas for a while, necking drinks like there was no tomorrow. I could see that their expressions had changed. They were all speaking urgently, using their hands for emphasis, like a gathering of conspiracy theorists. I'm pretty sure I can guess the topics of conversation. First up, the shoddy running of the game show, and the threat to their safety as well as the pretty basic living conditions. Then, to a lesser extent, the conclusion that Task 4 having no winner makes progress far harder. Also, the additions to the prize pot have only been going down after a promising start. The first task saw £40,000 added, then £15,000 for Task 2, but then only £8,000 for the third task and nothing at all for the fourth.

After a while, the group broke up. The people that remained in the sitting room began inspecting the walls, the mirrors, the dado rails. They didn't find all of the cameras, but once or twice they nailed it, freaking me out as their faces filled one of the screens in the monitor stack.

I can understand the impulse to find the cameras, even

though it won't help them win the prize money. They just want a degree of control.

Victor and Ralphie went straight to the study, trying their single key in each of the four locks in turn, then conferring in a serious manner. I watched them through the one-way window for a while, but I left when they started trying to rock the safe from side to side. If it falls on one of them, I don't want to be held responsible.

Doc Leaf has been moving from group to group. From his gestures it seems he's goading the other contestants on, encouraging them to disobey the rules. From what I've seen of Doc Leaf so far, his outlook can be summed up in a single word: *anarchy*. Now, when he speaks, everyone else nods along. After a while I lose sight of him, which puts me even more on edge.

Other people make their way upstairs. I watch them move along the upstairs hallway, but of course I lose them whenever they enter one of the bedrooms.

After Victor and Ralphie give up on the safe, Ruth leads Victor into her room. Sasha and Cécile spend ages in Cécile's room, which is puzzling. Until that point they'd been on the hunt for cameras, Sasha noting down locations on a map hand-drawn on the back of a folded-out cereal box. But the bedrooms are a dead end in that respect. There are no cameras in any of them.

"Any of them getting any warmer?" a voice says behind me.

I turn around fast. I'd actually forgotten I wasn't alone here in the production suite.

Lonnie is in the process of laying all the tools from his toolbox on the table, as if he's sorting them or looking for something in particular. Beside him, Imogen is frowning at the screen of her laptop, which bathes her face in blue light.

"As far as I know," I reply, "the only way to get the

money is to win keys. And they're not hidden."

"You don't know for sure? It's the blind leading the blind," Lonnie says. Then he guffaws and prods a finger in the direction of the silent monitors. "Or the *deaf* leading the blind."

Abruptly, he literally jumps out of his chair in response to a sharp *clack*. The second he's on his feet his body lowers into a hunched defensive stance. But the sound was only Imogen slamming the lid of her laptop shut.

"I need to go for a walk," Imogen says, seeming not to have noticed the effect she's had on Lonnie. She rises and slopes out of the room.

When she's gone, I say to Lonnie, "You okay?"

"Yeah." His throat seems clogged. He clears it and says again, "Yeah. Fine."

"I've seen you get startled like that before," I say, thinking of Lonnie clutching his heart in shock when Axel entered the production suite yesterday.

Lonnie watches me warily. "I just don't like surprises, that's all," he says. "Never did, even as a nipper."

It's not like we have common ground there, then. When I was a kid, I craved surprises. Anything to break the monotony of my parents' strict routine. Anything to distract me from the harsh reality of my life.

Lonnie turns back to the tools laid out on the table. Hammers and screwdrivers and drills. Potential weapons, all of them.

And he's muttering to himself, but I can't make out the words. It reminds me of the muttering I heard from outside his room, during the night.

I push the thoughts away. You have to place your trust in people sometimes.

"I tell you, I gotta get off this island," Lonnie says slowly.

"We'll be out of here soon," I say. "Only two more

days. Though I can't promise there'll be no more surprises."

Lonnie huffs – I *think* it's a sort of laugh – then waves at the bank of monitors. "Tension's cranking up, though, innit?"

I don't look at the monitors. My attention is taken by Imogen's computer. Without a word, I lift the lid.

There's no password screen, no login. For whatever reason, it's unlocked.

"That's Imogen's personal laptop," Lonnie warns.

"She won't engage me in a serious discussion about what's been happening," I say. "Do me a favour, would you? Look the other way for a sec."

Lonnie weighs this up, then nods.

I sit in Imogen's chair. The internet browser of her laptop is open, displaying results for package-deal holidays – hiking breaks for single women in Tenerife and Crete. From day one, Imogen's mind has been far from Red Cliffs.

There's another application open on the taskbar. I click on it. It's an instant-message app I've never heard of before.

The conversation is between two people: Imogen and Helm.

Helm. Our mysterious absent producer.

I scroll upwards. The conversation is really short, and the timestamps shows that all the messages were sent in the last half-hour. If there were previous conversations between the pair, they must have been stored elsewhere, or wiped – but it's immediately clear that it's a continuation of an earlier discussion.

IMOGEN: You have to fill me in. Seriously.
IMOGEN: I don't know what the parameters are here, in terms of deviation from the production notes.

IMOGEN: Have you been watching the feed?

IMOGEN: Helm. Come on. There's only an hour's time difference between here and Sweden. You can't pretend you're asleep. I know you're watching.

HELM: yep yep yep I'm watching

IMOGEN: And?

HELM: it's all gold baby

IMOGEN: ?

IMOGEN: But you saw that Task 4 got canned? And we've already talked about what happened to Mira.

HELM: you said shes ok

IMOGEN: She will be. Though who the hell knows what repercussions there'll be in legal terms.

IMOGEN: Fuck's sake. If nothing else, what about Escapism? Now two keys have effectively vanished. Assuming Mira hasn't had a chance to pass hers on while on the verge of *bleeding to death*.

IMOGEN: Helm. Answer me.

IMOGEN: Helm. We're drowning here. I don't know what to do. You need to take control.

HELM: nah

HELM: i'm liking what I'm seeing

HELM: control is for cowards

Aura

I'm sick of them all. I'm sick of conversations about escape rooms and games. That stuff is for kids.

I know there's money at stake, and God knows I could use it. I could finally get away from the farm, from my parents. And if I manage to establish myself as a TV personality at the same time, all the better.

Earlier this evening, Victor and Ruth disappeared upstairs for ages. Afterwards Ruth homed in on me, saying that now that we all knew her secret she wanted to start again, to get to know me and let me get to know her, the real Ruth. As if. I'm pretty sure she just wanted to rub my nose in it. *Look, Aura, I got the guy, not you. Plain old Ruth wins.*

What do I care? Victor's a lout. Sure, he's more attractive than the hopeless types at Young Farmers events in the village, but that's not saying much.

I realise it's somehow past eleven o'clock. I'm holding a drink that someone pressed into my hands at some point. I don't know how many others I've had, but it's a fair few.

Everyone else is chatting around me. I've been quiet for ages.

This isn't right. I'm supposed to be at the centre of things. Noticed.

It occurs to me that I *am* being noticed. By cameras. Earlier, Ben said he estimated there were six cameras in this room alone.

When this show is broadcast, how much footage will be broadcast of me sitting here, getting drunk and feeling sorry for myself?

There are two possible answers. Either this footage will

be chucked out immediately, or it'll be featured in full, sped up as time-lapse to show the other contestants bobbing around me while I sink into a stupor. There'll be a soundtrack overlaid to emphasise my loneliness. Sad piano music, or the opening bars of 'The Sound of Silence'.

It's unacceptable. I came here to create a new persona and control my image. I came here to become a star.

I jump up from the sofa, wobbling slightly. I hear the micro-movements of the cameras all around me. Possibly.

"Fuck off," I say.

Everyone turns to look at me. Big bland faces, all gawping. By far the worst is Sasha bloody Shiel.

I point at her, my hand wavering unsteadily.

Sasha seems to understand. She always was perceptive.

"Just you," I say. "Fuck off, Sasha."

Sasha shakes her head subtly. "How about we go somewhere for a quiet chat, in private?"

I hoot with laughter. "There are cameras everywhere, duh."

The other contestants watch with great interest as Sasha approaches me.

"It's hard being watched all the time, isn't it?" she says softly.

I just glare at her.

"It's hard being watched by *you*," I say.

"I'm sorry."

"For what?"

"I'm sorry if it's intimidating, having me here."

"Ha!" I squawk. "You're the last person to indimitate anyone." I know the word's come out wrong in my drunkenness, but I also know it's not going to improve if I try again.

Victor scratches his head and blurts out, "Anyone else have a clue what's going on right now?" but he's quickly shushed by several other people at once.

"I really would like to have that chat," Sasha says. "Somewhere else."

"No," I snap. I came on this show to be in the limelight, didn't I? So I say, "Now. Here."

Sasha's soft maternal face creases. "You're sure?"

I feel like I'm sure of nothing and everything at the same time. "I'd prefer not to speak to you, Sasha. Ever. I never wanted to back then, and I certainly don't want to now."

"I can't exactly leave. That's why I want to make peace with you."

God, she sounds so reasonable. It's absolutely infuriating.

"This is *exactly* how you behaved all those years ago!" I blurt out. "I could always tell when it was you at the front door, with your feeble little tappity-tap. And you'd always bring a gift of bloody biscuits – anything to get into our house. And your simpering attitude. You know me and Mum used to laugh at you behind your back?"

Sasha blinks. "No. I didn't know that. I always considered Maddy a close friend. But Amie, we don't need to talk about any of that right now. Remember that—"

"I don't care!" I shout. "And it's not Amie, it's *Aura*."

"Nobody's called Aura, Amie."

Her tone is so matter-of-fact that it seems true. But anyone can be called anything, can't they? And I can decide who I am, rather some prissy village gossipmonger.

For several seconds we stare at each other in silence.

"I'm a bit worried for you, that's all," Sasha says.

"Why?" It's a genuine question. What have I done wrong?

Sasha winces. "The cameras, Amie. The microphones. All these people in this room. I don't want you to—"

"Just fucking spit it out."

Sasha's posture slackens. I've seen this before. When she'd spill the beans to Mum about my exploits, Sasha always performed this sort of *it-pains-me-to-say-this-but* routine. Like she wasn't pissing her pants in excitement about chucking a bomb into the centre of our family.

"The way you've been behaving here," she says finally. "The way you're dressed. I worry about history repeating."

I look down at myself. My clothes got covered in paint during the last task, so I changed into my evening outfit earlier than usual. A dress like this wasn't intended to be worn for hours on end, and the pale pink silk is creased and it's ridden up over my thighs. I glance in the mirror (which is probably also a camera) and I'm shocked to that my hairstyle's like it'd be when I'm staggering out of a club after a long night.

But that's not what she meant about history repeating.

I try not to think about Axel. Earlier Doc Leaf blurted out that Axel's staying in a cottage in the grounds of the mansion, and I filed away the tidbit of information in case I ever feel like visiting Axel, for whatever reason. And now here's Sasha, predicting just that.

"You think I'm a slut," I say.

Gasps come from around us, but it's like the spotlight's on me and Sasha, and I can't see anyone else.

"I would never say that," Sasha says.

I laugh bitterly. No, she would never say that out loud. Instead she'd insinuate it to anyone who'll listen.

"Did you tell her?" I say.

Sasha frowns. "I haven't spoken to anyone here about your past." She looks around at our audience as if seeking backup.

"I don't mean here. Was it you who told my parents?"

Sasha watches me for a while. I focus on not swaying. I'm determined not to look like what she thinks I am.

"You know I was only there to help out at the school

disco," she says finally. "I wasn't watching out for you, particularly. But I couldn't help noticing."

I squeeze my eyes shut. I'm back there, in the big assembly hall, twin disco balls making feeble colourful patterns across the displays of sixth-formers' art on the walls. I'm laughing with my mates, I'm drinking, I'm having fun.

But the whole time, my real focus is on *him*.

Once, after school hours, he'd laughed when I called him Mr Berry. He said he'd never been comfortable with that sort of formality even in the classroom, though he wasn't any less uncomfortable when I called him Evan. All the same, he opened up to me, saying he wasn't even sure he'd seek another teaching role beyond this temporary placement, despite the year he'd dedicated to his PGCE. Maybe he wasn't cut out to be a teacher after all.

That night of the school disco, he couldn't stop glancing at me from up on the stage where he was overseeing the event. And that was understandable, because I was *gorgeous*. I kept thinking how much like children the rest of the girls in my year seemed, like they were just dressing in their mum's clothes.

Not me. I was adult already.

Eventually, I approached Mr Berry. Evan. By that point, the evening had fragmented, the smuggled-in bottles of vodka had been emptied. Everything seemed dimmer but also more sparkling and beautiful. Evan was tidying up, lugging stacks of chairs, and I followed him through a door into the room where musical instruments and theatre props were stored.

When the door opened again, the room was flooded with bright light. I've no idea whether the main lights in the hall were turned on early, whether the whole event was stopped, or whether me and Evan were in there for ages.

But it's not like we *did* anything. Even though I tried to

make it happen.

Evan pleaded with the headmaster, but Mr Finch was having none of it. Evan was made to disappear – instantly, that night, and I never saw him again – and the headmaster watched me in silence while we waited for my parents to arrive. And when they did, my life ended.

"Yes," Sasha says. "It was me."

I rush at her, throwing out my hands, hoping to scratch her face and tear away her placid expression.

Sasha steps back smartly into the ring of watching contestants. "Me and your mum were already fretting over you. And people were already talking, Amie."

"So what?" I shout. "Is that what it was all about? People *talking*? And it wasn't Evan's fault. You didn't have to destroy his life."

That's what it comes down to, I suppose. I ended up trapped, and I hate my life. But I'd thrown myself at Mr Berry, and to an extent I deserved what happened. It's the guilt that's eaten me up, all these years.

I realise I'm sobbing. I look in the mirror. Yep, there goes the mascara.

"He was only like four years older than me," I manage to say.

"Is that what he told you? He wasn't twenty, Amie. He wasn't even *in* his twenties." Then, before I have a chance to take that in, she adds, "And he'd done it before, what he did with you. At another school."

I stare at her in horror. Her words refuse to sink in.

"He…" I begin, but then can't complete the thought.

"He took advantage of you, Amie. Whatever he had planned for you, it was nothing good."

What he had planned for *me*? What's she talking about?

Suddenly, it's like I can see another version of that same event, glimpsed like a garden seen through the slats of a fence. Evan stroking my hair, talking about our future.

I'd always told myself I'd invented those parts, that they were just instances of my wishful thinking.

If those things happened, then I was... what? Innocent? Certainly less to blame than I've always told myself.

It's too much to process. What does it even matter? What happened to me afterwards was a whole other thing.

"What you did..." I begin, but then I have to take a big gulp of air to stop myself from hyperventilating. "What you did got me trapped. For eight years. No freedom, no prospects. Absolute fucking suffocation."

"I didn't—"

"You didn't what? You didn't mean to blab? You didn't mean to ruin my life?"

"I didn't enjoy exposing you. It was for your own good."

I stare at her. The loose hair tickling my cheeks pisses me off suddenly. I push it back, but it won't stay. I throw my head back and shout at the ceiling, a sort of animal howl of frustration.

The other contestants shuffle and fret, but I know they're not going to intervene. Right now they're just the audience. In a few months, there'll be a far bigger audience watching my meltdown.

"Amie—" Sasha says, moving closer.

"Don't you touch me," I shout, pushing her away. "Don't come near me. I won't let you ruin things for me again."

I stagger towards the doorway. Then it occurs to me that I haven't made my point clearly enough, and that the spotlight is still on me.

I move back to stand directly in front of Sasha.

I slap her, hard.

Then I get the fuck out of there.

Six months later

Rhea

When the call comes through, I answer it before the first chime has ended. The woman who appears on the screen blinks in surprise.

"Hi?" she says uncertainly. "Is that Rhea?"

"Yes," I say. I summon all the investigative-reporter energy I can muster. "I appreciate you agreeing to speak with me."

"It's just that you look like a mouse."

At first I have no idea what she means – it's not an insult that's been levelled at me before – but then I glance at the screen-within-a-screen that shows my own video feed. Sure enough, instead of my face there's the head of a purple cartoon mouse.

"Shit." I go into the settings and flick off the filter.

Dolly grins. "I thought maybe it was to maintain anonymity."

"No. I mean yes, it is, but not because I'm talking to you."

"Have you been speaking to someone more dangerous, then?"

I shake my head. "Just a… guy."

"Ah. And you didn't want him to recognise you? I suppose he's a valuable source of information, something like that. What do they call them in films? A mole." She chuckles. "A mole chatting to a mouse. Cute."

I laugh despite my embarrassment. The 'guy' wasn't anything to do with my investigation – he was some rando

200

I met on *Fortnite* and who convinced me to let him call me. It wasn't a long conversation.

Speaking of cute, though, Dolly's certainly that. I know from her Facebook profile that she's 28, but she appears at least five years younger. Her nose and cheeks are littered with freckles and her fair hair is tied back in two bunches. She's wearing corduroy dungarees. Somehow, the overall effect isn't childish, just... I don't know. Fun.

Dolly points at me. "Hey. Turn your head to the left?"

I do, without a thought.

"Oh. No, to the right, then. For a second there I was thinking of you as a mirror image."

I turn my head to the right.

"There it is," Dolly says delightedly. "Oh man, I love your piercings!"

I reach up to touch the series of small hoops on my earlobe, then the three chunky half-cylinders fixed to the cartilage above.

"They're not all piercings," I say. "Most are cuffs, snapped on. And they're daft, because they hurt if I forget to take them off and then sleep on that side. I don't know why I put them in each morning, actually, because I hardly ever go out."

Dolly just smiles.

"Sorry," I say. "I'm over-sharing. I don't normally do that."

"It happens," she says. Then she adds, quietly, "To me."

We're both silent for a while.

Then Dolly says, "It's funny. Just talking to you like this, on camera, is a flashback to being back *there*. On Red Cliffs."

I nod. "Are you happy to talk about it?"

"I shouldn't. Not in detail."

"Because of a non-disclosure agreement."

201

"Yeah."

"Others have mentioned it too. I can see that it'd be a big motivator, being given a big payment like that."

Dolly freezes. For a moment I wonder if the video's frozen. Then she says, "Sorry, what?"

"The payment associated with the NDA."

Dolly blinks. She puffs out her cheeks, and her body slumps, which changes the camera angle – she must have her computer on her lap. She's reclining on a single bed, her back resting against a plain beige wall.

"How big?" she asks. Then, immediately, "No. Don't tell me. It'll chew me up even more."

"Why did you sign an NDA *without* a payment?" I ask.

"Because I want to keep working in this industry. Because I'm too junior to stand up for myself. Because I was *told* to sign it, basically."

I wait, hoping that she'll connect the dots. If there's no money attached, then what repercussion could there be if she breaks the agreement?

It's as if she reads my thoughts. "But I still can't talk about it. They've sewn my mouth up good and proper. But I wanted you to know – I think I can say this – that I'm glad you're doing this. I'm glad you're poking around into what happened."

"Because something really bad happened during the filming of *Escapism*?"

Dolly presses her lips tight together, then performs a mimed gestured in front of them, her hand weaving. Lips sewn shut.

Then she holds up a hand: *wait*. She mimes unpicking the thread from her lips, which makes me laugh even though it's kind of gross.

"You do the talking," she says. "And I'll just happen to examine… um… these knick-knacks." She leans out of sight, and when she reappears she's holding two gift-shop souvenirs: a red telephone box and a snowglobe containing a family of green trolls. "Look," she says, holding each of them up in turn. "This one's very *red*, and this one's full of *green* things." She pauses, eyebrows raised.

I give a thumbs-up sign.

Dolly says, "Red means stop, or no, and green means go, or yes."

"Yeah, I got that."

"You're smart. You'll go far. All right, Ms Rhea Hildred. Shoot."

What sort of tack should I take? Dolly seems way more approachable than anyone else I've spoken to, and as a member of the production team she's bound to have insights that none of the contestants have. But I might easily scare her off if I jump straight to the big-ticket questions.

"Let's start with your role," I say. "You were involved as a production assistant. Would you say your involvement with the setup of the show was in-depth?"

Dolly holds up the red telephone box, peering at it as if she's only examining it.

Okay. That's a no.

"During the filming, was it you conducting the interviews?"

Dolly raises the snowglobe full of trolls.

"Was that always the case?"

The snowglobe remains visible, the telephone box out of shot. It's a yes.

"At one point," I say, "Cécile Guillaume appeared on camera with blood on her face. Was she badly hurt?"

Dolly frowns. She lowers the snowglobe. But there's no telephone box either.

"Do you know what I'm referring to?" I ask.

Telephone box. No.

I don't think her conflicting responses make her a liar.

Someone else could have been conducting interviews as well as her. She might not have known about it.

Her confused response means I don't need to ask the question I was going to ask next: *Did you send me the video files?* Because she couldn't have, if she doesn't know about Cécile.

I work through a mental list of leads. I think of the later video I was sent, which showed that Ben knew who he was talking to in the study.

"Did you know Ben Parrish before filming began?"

Telephone box.

"Did anyone else in the production team know him?"

Dolly lowers the ornament so that neither it or the snowglobe are visible. Her forehead creases, a pantomimed expression of confusion.

"How about Lonnie?"

She blinks rapidly and then squints at me. She holds up the telephone box.

"Did Lonnie appear to have made any enemies while you were on the island?"

The telephone box waggles impatiently. I get the sense Dolly's telling me I'm on the wrong lines entirely.

"What actually happened during filming?"

It just slipped out. I know she can't answer it with a yes or no.

"Was somebody seriously injured?"

Snowglobe. Green. Yes.

"More than one person?"

Snowglobe.

My heart rate keeps increasing all the time.

"And Lonnie died out there on Red Cliffs Island."

The snowglobe lowers. Telephone box. No.

What?

"But I've seen the police report. Lawrence Bunce died on the island. And I thought the body came back on the boat ferrying the contestants."

There's the snowglobe again. What's Dolly up to?

Suddenly, I realise my mistake. I groan.

"Lawrence Bunce... he isn't Lonnie, is he?"

Telephone box.

Carefully, Dolly says, "I can tell you the freelance technician I worked alongside at Red Cliffs is named Lonnie Hall."

"Then who is Lawrence Bunce?" I growl, annoyed at myself. How can I turn that into a yes/no question?

But suddenly it's obvious to me.

"Lawrence Bunce. Is he... I mean *was* he... Doc Leaf?"

Instant snowglobe.

Fuck.

So one of the contestants was killed after all. This is *huge*.

"And was it suicide, Dolly? That's what the police report said. Or was he killed?"

Stupid, stupid. That's not a yes/no question either.

Dolly's looking really edgy now. Her eyes flick up to look somewhere above her camera. I hear a muffled voice, and she nods sharply.

"I've got to go," she says to me.

She lifts the laptop, giving me glimpses of more beige walls, ratty curtains, a condensation-covered window with green stickers on the frame, and then a person standing silhouetted in a doorway with their hands on their hips.

Dolly says, "Sorry to cut you off. I'd say it's been fun, but... you know. Memories resurfacing and all that." She puts the laptop down, and I see her hand reach up. She's going to end the call.

"Wait!" I say quickly. "I have more questions!"

She hesitates. "Another time? But maybe not online. I'll be in touch."

Then she's gone.

DAY 4

Six months earlier

Dolly

The glare of the rising sun makes me squint. The flagstones are glossy with rainwater. If I'm not careful, I'll slip and break my neck.

I turn to look up at the first-floor windows of the mansion. I can't see any lights. I have to believe that all the contestants are still asleep. It's only five-thirty in the morning, after all.

I hear voices, and I head towards them, skidding down the rocky slope that leads to the shore of the island.

The sea is calm and flat and grey. The supply boat is docked at the pier, bobbing gently beside the tiny rowing boat intended for use by the eventual winners of *Escapism*. Three people are standing on the jetty. Noah, the boat owner, is holding a bulky, plastic-covered pallet. Standing before him are Imogen and Mira.

It's a relief to see Mira. When I found the door to Axel's old room wide open and the bed empty, my first thought was that she died, that her body had been taken during the night. Then I wondered if she'd just stumbled out of the building, confused and afraid, in which case she might easily have slipped into the sea.

They all turn as I approach.

"What's going on?" I ask.

"I'm leaving," Mira says, pointing at the supply boat with her left arm, then returning it to a position supporting her injured one.

I nod. "Okay." I turn to Noah. "If that's okay with you?"

Noah's shrug is jerky because he's still holding the pallet of supplies. "Whatever." Then he says to Mira, "But lass, you're not my responsibility when we reach the mainland. I get you there, then you do your own thing. You hear me?"

Imogen makes a face at me over Mira's shoulder. She juts her chin in Mira's direction. I understand what it means: *Help me talk her out of it.*

"How do you feel?" I ask Mira.

"Like I'm fucking done here."

"And your arm…"

"Stings. But I don't think I'll need it amputated. Unless you're a doctor, and you know better?"

I remind myself that Mira's never seen me before, even though I've been watching her for days.

"No," I say. "I'm just a production assistant. You're sure you want to leave? You don't want to carry on?" I glance at Imogen, hoping I'm not about to say something daft. "You could skip the tasks, just hang out with the other contestants. You could still be in with a shot at getting a share of the money."

Behind Mira, Imogen nods vigorously.

"Nope," Mira says simply. "No interest in any of that. I don't reckon there's any money anyway. This whole setup reeks."

Imogen starts to protest, and when Mira makes a move she tries to block her from reaching the boat.

"What the fuck?" Mira says, stepping back.

Imogen stares at her wild-eyed. I'm not sure she knows what she's doing. This is the first time I've seen her display any interest in *Escapism* being completed.

It occurs to me that Mira might easily sue Helmedia, despite the fact that Imogen keeps reporting that Helm is still supremely unbothered by the disasters that have occurred. Then again, he's a multi-millionaire, so he can afford to be casual about money. But if Mira sues, Imogen might easily become embroiled. Me too, come to think of it.

"There may be some paperwork we need you to sign," I say to Mira calmly. "But we could send it to you at your home address, rather than hold you back this morning?"

Mira's stance becomes a touch less defensive. "I'm not going to lawyer up or anything. Is that what you're afraid of?"

I weigh up my responses. Without looking at Imogen, I say, "Basically, yes. That's what we're afraid of."

Mira studies me for a while, then nods, accepting my answer. Sometimes honesty is the only way.

"What happened was an accident," she says. "And it wasn't you who did this to me. It was Dez."

Imogen and I exchange glances. It's like I can hear her thought processes. She's thinking: *This is good for us. This gets her off our backs.*

But I've watched Mira and Dez become close. I've envied their friendship. And like I say, sometimes honesty is the only way.

"I didn't see what happened," I say, "but I've heard about it from the other contestants."

Mira's eyebrows raise. She's made the connection: I'm the voice she's been confiding in during visits to the study.

I go on, "I want you to know that Dez was only trying to help you. They were desperate to get you out of there. Other people should have helped too. More than that, *we* shouldn't have put you – any of you – in that situation."

I register Imogen's silent, desperate appeals to shut up.

I could go on. I could draw attention to the fact that Doc Leaf somehow brought a knife into the mansion, and that nobody knows where that knife is now. But an admission like that has lawsuit written all over it.

So I finish up by saying, "I want you to know that Dez hates themself for what they did to you."

At first, Mira doesn't respond. There's a glassy sheen in her eyes. She nods sharply.

"Tell them they're forgiven, yeah?" she says. "But tell them maybe I won't be seeing them again."

I don't even realise what I'm about to do. I move forward and put my arms around Mira's shoulders, careful not to stray too low and graze her injuries. Her body remains hard, until it doesn't. Her head drops to rest in the hollow of my neck.

"Thank you," she whispers.

Then she backs away, hopping onto the boat and ducking to enter the central cabin.

Imogen groans behind me. I turn.

"Thanks for nothing, Dolly," she says.

Imogen can't read people the way I can. I give her a tight smile.

"This is the end of it," I say. "We won't hear from Mira Qureshi again."

Imogen seems about to say something, but Noah interrupts her.

"If you don't mind," he says, "could one of you take this pallet off me? It's doing my back in, and there are two more that need unloading, if you want any meals today."

I take the plastic-wrapped box. It's filled with tins and boxes, but it's not as heavy as he makes out.

Then a thought occurs to me, and I freeze.

"Noah," I say, "Have you only brought supplies?" When he looks at me in confusion, I add, "Where's the guy who was supposed to come with you today?"

"What guy?"

"The man from the acting agency. The stuntman."

Noah chuckles. "Planning to go all *Mission: Impossible*

211

around here, are you? Wish I could stay and watch." Then he registers my serious expression. "No, sorry. There was no man, and nobody told me to hang around and wait for one."

I rub the bridge of my nose. "We need him, Noah. For the next task."

Imogen moves forward and says to Noah, "What you're going to do is go back to the mainland, drop off Mira, then check around for a man named Jim, uh…"

"McLeod," I say. Imogen's really not on top of any of this.

"Tell me you'll do that," Imogen says to Noah.

He nods vaguely. "Yeah. And if I don't find him, I'll see you tomorrow, same time, same place, okay?"

"You *have* to find him. I was in touch with the agency first thing this morning. He'll be there, somewhere, waiting."

"Got it."

Imogen seems placated, but like I say, she can't read people. It's clear to me that we'll have to manage without our stuntman.

Six months later

Rhea

My computer *ding*s. It's a Facebook notification. Friend request accepted. I'm breathless as I flick through the dozens of tabs that are open in my browser.

It's Mira.

I tell myself that just because she's accepted my request doesn't mean she'll talk. But then there's another *ding*, this time signifying a direct message.

Who's this? Mira asks.

My hands are shaky as I type, *Rhea Hildred.* Then I hesitate, not wanting to make a wrong move and scare her off.

She replies before I can figure out what to write next.

Think I know what you're after.

I wait. Let her lead the conversation if she's willing.

Sure enough, she adds another message: *This is about Escapism isnt it.*

Yes, I reply.

Looked you up. Saw you're a podcaster.

I wince. I keep forgetting that I have my own breadcrumb trail on the internet. Every time I've imagined I'm undercover, I've been fooling myself.

That's right, I type. *I'm interested in the show.*

Meaning what happened.

Yes. But I know you may not be able to talk freely.

Several seconds pass. Then: *Whys that.*

I don't know how to respond. If she's not going to

mention an NDA, I'm not going to bring it up.

Again, Mira writes before I have a chance to dig myself into a hole.

Cant tell you much. Seeing as I didnt make it to the end. Left the island 4 days in.

This is new. And if Mira wasn't made to sign an NDA, it suggests that the *really* bad stuff occurred after she'd left.

I didn't realise it was the kind of show people got voted off from, I type.

Lol. Voted off? Lol. More like getting slashed to bits with a knife then bleeding on the deck of the boat on the way back.

I stare at the blinking cursor. What?

I type, *Tell me what happened.*

And just like that, she tells me.

Six months earlier

Aura

I groan and press a palm to my forehead. My skin feels clammy and my ears are ringing.

With my eyelids squeezed tight shut to stop the sunlight leaking through them, I roll over. My ankles get caught in the twisted bedsheet, which I must have kicked away during the night – bad dreams, I suppose. Goosebumps have formed on my thighs and upper arms. With a start I realise I'm naked. I grope to pull the sheet up, but something's weighing it down.

I roll away from the bright sunlight, and open my eyes carefully.

At first my muddled brain can't identify what I'm looking at. A smooth cream-coloured hill. It's only when it moves, and lets out a soft sigh, that I cotton on. It's a big, broad set of shoulders. A man.

This wasn't what I intended. Was it?

At this moment, I've no idea. Whoever I was last night – under the influence of however many drinks and after that standoff with Sasha – I think she knew what she was doing.

I tell myself that was Aura, not me.

It was Aura who stumbled out of the mansion and tottered past the swimming pool to reach the groundskeeper's cottage. It was Aura who knocked on its door and who somehow said the correct sequence of words to be allowed to come inside. It was Aura who laughed prettily and invented all the right reassurances as she slipped her dress over her head.

It's cruel that my hangover's doing nothing to block out those memories. Because the woman lying in bed now is far more the old Amie than the new Aura.

Axel stirs. He makes an ugly low sound, like one of the cows in our farmyard might make when they're shuffling into position to be milked.

He turns slowly, making the bed creak. Naked, he appears bulkier than when he's dressed in one of his smart suits. His chest must be waxed, but instead of making him more attractive it draws attention to the wrinkles. What might once have been pecs are just flaccid flesh. My eyes are drawn to a criss-crossed network of scars on his left thigh, which must be connected to his slight limp I've noticed in the past.

He's twice my age. Once the thought lodges in my mind, I can't shake it.

I've done it again.

Or rather, Amie once attempted to do this. Now Aura has risen from the ashes, and she's followed through.

Sasha will find out. So will my parents. So will every contestant. So will every member of the TV audience of *Escapism*.

Which is basically the whole country.

Bile stings my throat.

I yank the sheet up to cover myself. Then I shake Axel's shoulder. He grunts.

"We can't let anybody know about this," I say.

His eyes open.

"Hi… uh…" he says groggily.

"Aura. My name's Aura."

"Yes. Of course." He grimaces. "Last night, did we—"

"Seems like it."

Actually, I remember the sex perfectly well. My first in

216

many months, perhaps even a year. It was… fine.

Axel rubs his eyes. "What time is it?"

"Nine."

"*Attans*. Damn. I've missed my chance."

I frown. "Your chance to do what?"

"Leave. I told the director I'd be leaving today. She tried to talk me out of it, and I let her believe she had. But I was going to get on that boat all the same."

"What? You can't leave." Without Axel, there's no game show, surely.

He shakes his head, but the action is made awkward because he's lying on his side. He winces again, and I remember how unsteady he was last night. His hangover might easily be worse than mine.

"I can't stay," he says. "This whole thing is insane."

"You mean *Escapism*?"

"Yes. And me being here. Here in the UK. I don't know what I'm doing…" He gazes at my face with a searching expression.

"Aura."

"Yes. Aura. But that is not your real name?"

I say firmly, "Yes. It is."

He grunts again, and it becomes a cough. I back away, as much as I can.

Again, the thought passes through my mind: *Without Axel, there's no game show.* I wince at the memory of my outburst last night, watched by all the other contestants. Do I really want that broadcast on TV? Because it will be, obviously. Whereas if Axel leaves…

On the other hand, if the filming of *Escapism* is cancelled, that means no prize money and it means no fame. I'll be trapped with my parents, like before.

I've no idea which outcome I'd prefer. My head really hurts.

"What's your problem?" I ask in a husky voice.

Axel watches me warily, interpreting my question as aggressive.

I shake my head, then wince again at the pain. "Sorry. I meant to ask why you feel that you shouldn't be here in the UK, filming *Escapism*."

Axel hesitates, as though he's not used to speaking about himself, his emotions.

"I came here for my career," he says. "Helm convinced me that I was being held back in Sweden. The original series, *Eskapism*-with-a-K, it was a success. But Helm – he's the producer of the show – he told me I could have more."

"Sounds like pretty sensible advice."

Axel shrugs. "I would still have stayed in Sweden if I could."

"If you could? What stopped you from staying? Nobody's forced you to try and be famous in the UK."

Axel's head hangs. "There are people in Sweden who would have liked me to stay. They loaned me money, and they want it returned."

Ah. It's like that, is it? So it's not fame Axel wants so much as a bigger pay packet, and even then the money's already allocated to freeing himself from his past. Our situations are similar in that sense.

Axel's head keeps bobbing gently. It takes me a few seconds to realise he's sobbing silently. I shuffle closer to him and put my arms around his bare shoulders, grimacing slightly at the feel of his dry skin.

"It's okay," I say. "You've got a plan. You'll earn the money back. Then you can go back to Sweden and everything will be back to normal.

Suddenly, the sobs are audible. Clearly I've said the wrong thing.

"Things will never be normal," Axel mumbles.

"I think maybe your hangover is making things seem

worse than they are," I suggest.

"My hangover won't bring my mother back."

He pushes me away, wiping his eyes with his forearm. There's not a trace of his usual movie-star appearance. He's all mucus and tears.

"She was the reason I stayed in Sweden as long as I did," he says. "She lived in an... *ålderdomshem*. What's the word in English? A rest home. But she was healthy, and she was happy. Then suddenly—" His hand slices horizontally through the air.

"How old was she?"

"Seventy-eight. She should have lived another ten years. I still don't know what happened. The staff at the home were as shocked as I was."

"That's awful," I say, meaning it. "I'm so sorry, Axel."

He clasps my right hand in both of his.

"What do you think you'll do?" I ask.

"Escape."

"But your debts..."

He stares at me, but his eyes are unfocused. We *are* in the same position. There are no good outcomes.

"I can't leave, not today," Axel says finally. "The supply boat has been and gone. But if Imogen thinks I will participate in any more of this... this charade. Then she'll—"

"You're sure you shouldn't play along, just for now? While you're stuck here?"

Axel blinks several times, but he doesn't respond.

I don't need him to respond. That advice was really aimed at myself. While I'm stuck here, I should play along. Whatever happens, the moment I leave the island the mistakes I've made in the past will crash down on me, maybe crush me. But my original plan is still the best one. Doing everything I can to win a share of the prize money is secondary, really. The most important thing is getting myself noticed, making myself famous.

There's another thought worming at the back of my mind, too. It's ugly.

I created Aura because I understood I'd have to behave larger than life. If I end up becoming known as a man-eater, so be it. Being notorious means chat shows and tabloid articles. Paparazzi and flings. It's still a way out of a dead-end.

Sleeping with Axel would be one way to ensure that... except there are no cameras here. Perhaps I could seduce him all over again, when we're being recorded. Failing that, I can just tell all to the media at a later date... so long as Axel becomes famous in the UK, which again relies on *Escapism* being completed and broadcast.

"So we're agreed, then?" I say, already hating myself for what I'm prepared to do to get ahead. "We'll both play ball. It's for the best."

Axel wrinkles his nose in confusion. I don't know whether it's my use of the idiom 'play ball' that's foxed him, or the realisation that I've been having doubts of my own.

"I will play ball," he says. "Now will you let me sleep?"

He just grunts and rolls over to face the wall. Within moments his breathing deepens, suggesting he really has fallen asleep.

I slip out of bed and pull on my pink silk dress. Thinking of the walk of shame back to the mansion, I open a wardrobe and pick out one of Axel's jackets, which covers my dress entirely.

It's only as I stride back towards the mansion that I put my hands in the jacket pockets, and my fingers close around an envelope, tracing the outline of a key.

Dolly

I'm a production assistant, not a runner. And yet here I am, literally running across the grounds of the mansion, the only person on the staff who actually seems to care whether this show gets made.

I rap on the door of the groundskeeper's cottage so hard my knuckles hurt.

No answer.

I knock again, blow on my sore knuckles, then more knocking.

"Axel!" I shout.

I can't see into the cottage from the steps that lead to the front door, or even from the ground because the whole building is slightly raised and I'm too short to jump and look through the windows. But eventually I sense that Axel's up and about. There are little tremors as he plods to the door.

When the door opens, I let out a little sigh. It's partly dismay, because he looks *awful*. His hair's sticking up at one side and his eyes are red. He's wearing a silk dressing gown, left untied so I can see that he's wearing nothing but white boxer shorts underneath. But my sigh's partly something else too. I won't deny I have a real thing for Axel, and here he is, standing before me half naked. It's a heady moment, all told.

"You should already be in the hall of tasks," I say.

In a thick voice, Axel says, "I'll be there momentarily."

My eyes move up and down his body again. "Do you need some... help?"

I sort of hate myself for offering. It definitely isn't in my job description. At the same time, the thought of just me and Axel in his little cottage, stripping him bare, then tenderly preparing him for the day… it's not the worst idea I've ever had.

"No," Axel says sharply.

Talk about popping a bubble. Of course Axel doesn't want to invite me in. I'm nobody to him.

I'm distracted by the faint overlapping lines on his left thigh. I can't help myself. I point at it and say, "Is that your injury from your car crash?"

Axel freezes. "What do you know about that?"

"I read about it online," I say. Then I add hurriedly, "Being a production assistant involves doing research on everybody involved in the show."

He doesn't seem to have spotted my outright lie. I just like looking at pictures of Axel Griffin, that's all.

"It was a long time ago." His voice is strained.

"Does it still cause you pain?"

He studies me carefully. Perhaps he's wondering if I'm referring to his injury, or the memory of the car crash. The Swedish press reported that he was driving at ninety-five miles an hour on a country road, and the family car he hit was almost stationary, turning out of a junction.

"A little," Axel says stiffly.

I realise I'm still staring. I blink hard.

"I must get ready," Axel says.

After a while, I nod. It's only then that I realise I'm staring at a door that was closed several seconds ago.

Ben

By the time Axel finally shows up at the hall of tasks, we've pretty much figured out what this morning's task is. There are ten mannequins lined up in the centre of the hall, each sporting a chunky headband with a white strip that looks like something a bicyclist might wear in the dark, with armbands to match, plus a sort of chest holster with a pale disc on the front and back.

As Axel enters the room, I notice he's limping slightly. Has he hurt himself, or is it an existing injury he normally hides? Either way, he doesn't look great this morning. There are dark shadows beneath his eyes, and his usually immaculate hair is sticking up at one side. He's wearing the same suit as he was yesterday.

"All right," Axel says, then clears his throat. "Good morning, everyone."

"Good morning," we all chime, like kids at a school assembly.

"I trust you all had pleasant evenings?"

There are a few *yes*es, but not particularly wholehearted.

I see Axel's eyes flick left. I turn to see Aura, who also arrived late, a few minutes before Axel. Unlike him, she appears calm and as immaculately presented as always. She even smiled at Sasha, as if she's determined not to acknowledge the embarrassing display they both put on last night.

"Hunting is a tradition that dates back many hundreds of years," Axel begins. His heart doesn't seem in it. "And my ancestors have always been devotees of the sport. You might say my family is *rabidly* enthusiastic. So, to honour their memory I have arranged that this morning's task will be—"

"Laser tag!" Victor shouts. He leaps forward, shoulders hunched and both hands curled as though he's holding a machine gun. "Say hello to my little friend! Hasta la vista, baby!"

Axel winces. He's definitely suffering from a hangover.

"Very good," he says with a forced smile. "Now—"

"Will we put these on?" Cécile asks, pointing at the items on the mannequins.

Axel nods and waves an arm at the mannequins, then slopes off to one side of the hall.

We all pick a mannequin and start pulling the holsters on. Why does it make me feel oddly empowered? The pale disc reminds me of something. Ah, I know: Iron Man. I decide not to say anything, because I don't want people branding me as a geek.

"Hey, I look like Iron Man!" Ralphie says, and everybody laughs.

I sigh inwardly.

Soon enough we're kitted up. We look like the worst battalion imaginable. Cécile's wearing a cocktail dress, and Aura's wearing a tartan skirt that barely covers her bum. Victor's holster and headband are stretched to breaking point, and Doc Leaf's holster strap has caught on his basketball vest at one side, pulling it taut and revealing a pale moob.

Ruth asks Axel, "Where are our guns?"

"There are no guns," Axel says, pushing himself away from the wall wearily. Then he adds, "We're all pacifists here," and grins goofily. He turns to an upper corner of the hall, where I presume a hidden camera is fixed, and he gives a thumbs-up sign.

Seriously, what's up with him today?

"Then how can we play laser tag?" Ruth asks.

Axel exhales loudly. "All right, all right. There *is* a gun. Just one. You see, my ancestors…" He stifles a belch, and when he recovers he seems to have changed tack entirely. "You're not going to be hunters. You're the prey."

"Then who's the hunter?" Victor asks.

"And where will they start from?" Dez asks.

"And can we make weapons of our own?" Doc Leaf adds.

Axel seems to come to life suddenly. "The hunter is the ghost of my great-great-uncle, who was a crack shot, and a big game hunter, and the president of the local hunting group, and a bad father, and…" It's clear he's winging it, and that doesn't have much experience of improvisation. "And who died clutching his rifle, which he took with him to the afterlife."

"But it's a *laser* rifle," Ralphie says.

Axel points to a door at the top of the balcony.

"The hunter will emerge from that door presently. And no other weapons are allowed. Just concealment. You have stay inside the building."

"So it's more like hide and seek, then?" Ruth says.

Axel rubs his clammy forehead. He's done with this whole thing.

Out of the corner of my eye I notice the strip of light beneath the hall door disappear. Somebody's turned off the lights in the lobby.

"One hit and you're out," Axel says. "Last person standing wins. Everyone hiding for more than five minutes will add five thousand pounds to the prize fund. You have three minutes to hide. Then the hunt will begin."

Dez

It's like this task was made for me. Dez, the hide-and-seek champion. Dez, the kid whose disappearance once marshalled all the neighbours in the cul-de-sac to search wheelie bins and sheds for a whole hour.

But the timing's lousy.

Maybe I should just stay here in the hall of tasks. Tell Axel and his great-great-whatever that I can't be arsed to scamper around the mansion. Since Mira left, everything seems pointless.

But then all the other contestants scurry through the doorway, squealing in excitement, and I realise the lights in the lobby have been turned off… and it's like a switch has been flicked inside me. I shrug off my bomber jacket and drape it over a mannequin, then salute to Axel and dive out of the room.

In the lobby, I instantly spot a leg clad in skinny jeans beneath the sideboard. My guess is it's Ralphie, and he doesn't realise that his lower half is in the direct line of sight of anybody coming this way.

I suppose that's one down, ten to go.

I bet a couple of other people will have similar impulses to Ralphie – that is, they'll stay close to the door to the hall of tasks, thinking the hunter will stride past them, buying them time. That means someone's probably in the dining room, huffing and puffing as they try to squeeze into one of the low cupboards filled with boxes of cereal.

I move on, keeping to the middle of the lobby to avoid stumbling in the dark. The next door on the left leads to the billiard room. There's bound to be someone under the pool table already, and I don't remember noticing any other likely hiding places in there.

I laugh at the realisation that that's what I *do*, still. Some anxious types scan for exits when they enter an unfamiliar or threatening space. Me, I look for somewhere to hide.

I pause at the door to the sitting room. It's big, and there's loads of seating with loose, puffy cushions that might easily be pulled up to hide beneath. In the dark, that could be pretty effective. Then there's the drinks counter, and another door that leads to the toilets.

But if the hunter headed that way, I'd be totally trapped. No thank you.

At the foot of the stairs are several corridors. One leads to the main set of toilets and the other goes to the study, where the only furniture is a single armchair and a metal safe.

I rush up the stairs, blundering in the dim light.

It's another mistake. The doors of the contestants' bedrooms are all locked. I curse as I realise something even more annoying: I can't even enter my *own* room. The key's in my bomber jacket, which is at this moment being worn by a shop dummy in the hall of tasks.

I dash back to the staircase. Then I freeze.

There's a bulky figure lumbering around downstairs. They're wearing dark clothes and holding a laser rifle trained into the shadows every so often, but more often than not it hangs loosely at their side. Even from here, I can hear their laboured breathing. They're definitely out of shape.

They shuffle along, then stop, turning sharply to press their body heavily against the sideboard, the one Ralphie's hiding underneath. Are they trying look over the top of it?

No. They're just stopping. Resting, perhaps, even though they've barely moved from the hall of tasks where they began. They're wearing bulky clothes, all black, including a black balaclava over their head, which has eye holes but no mouth, like something worn by a bank robber in a cartoon.

The hunter stays there, leaning over and huffing. Are they ill?

Finally, they begin to move again. They pause at the door of the billiard room, muttering.

They move inside.

This is my chance.

I tiptoe down the stairs, wincing whenever the boards creak.

Now I've seen the hunter in action, the hiding places in the sitting room seem way more attractive. Whoever they are, they're shit at hide and seek. I could even push my luck and run straight past the door to the billiard room to reach the hall of tasks, find my bomber jacket and my keys, increase my options...

But then the hunter reappears in the passage, blocking my way.

They put both hands up to their head. The rifle knocks against their forehead, and they mutter again. It sounds like a curse.

This isn't right. They don't seem in control at all.

Perhaps I should go down there, hands in the air. Tell them I just want to check they're okay.

One of the stairs under my feet creaks again, and the black-hooded figure whirls around, rifle in hand, pointing directly at me.

I turn and run.

Dolly

"What are you doing in here?" I snap.

I'm already at the door of the production suite when Lonnie enters, because I saw him heading this way on the camera feed.

Lonnie pushes past me and yanks off his balaclava. His forehead is sweaty and his doughy cheeks are pale, almost green.

"Fuck," he gasps. Then he seems not to be able to speak at all. He flops into a chair and his head hangs back, his tongue lolling.

"You're okay," I say, willing it to be true. "It's just a game of hide and seek."

He shakes his head slowly. "It's dark out there. I don't like the dark."

"You're a grown man."

His shoulders slump. "A tough guy. Right?"

I don't answer.

"I was a tough guy," he says. "Once. And then…" He shakes his head.

I think about his earlier jumpiness, and I hazard a guess. "Were you in the army? Is it PTSD?"

"I wish. That sounds nice and honourable, doesn't it? Coming back from who knows where, fucked up but having done your duty." He sighs deeply. "Nah. No pride for me. Got in a pub fight over… I can't even remember what it was about. Then six years inside."

I nod and smile, trying to perform those little actions that add up to an appearance of sympathy. But we don't have time for any of this.

"I'm a different bloke now," Lonnie says. "I've worked

hard on getting myself in order. I meditate. I stick my headphones on, and I repeat my mantra. And it works, Dolly, it really works."

Of course. The repeated muttering I heard from outside his room. It was a mantra, nothing more sinister than that.

"Those years inside beat the toughness out of me," Lonnie says. "They left me jittery. Some of the things that happened in the dark when I was in prison... they'd make you think twice about wandering around with the lights out."

I look around at the empty production suite. Where's Imogen right now? She's always missing when she's actually needed.

"What are you saying?" I ask.

Lonnie throws the balaclava onto the table. "I'm not doing it. Screw *Escapism*. Whole thing's fucked anyway."

I gaze at Lonnie in silence for a few seconds, processing the situation. Then my eyes flick to the balaclava.

*

I pause to let my eyes adjust to the darkness. With my hand that's not holding the rifle I push up the sleeve of the black sweatshirt, which is like a tent on me. I'm just glad I was already wearing black jeans, because if I'd put on Lonnie's combat pants I'd have had to turn them up two or three times to make them fit.

The balaclava is the worst, though. It's not just that the eyeholes are spaced too far apart, letting me see through one or the other, but not both. It's the fact that Lonnie's sweat seems to have impregnated the fabric, and I feel like I'm being smothered by a damp dishcloth that also happens to smell like utter panic. The mouth area is the worse, because there *is* no mouth area, just a patch of

230

fabric that's damper and more fetid than the rest.

I need to get this whole thing over and done, as soon as possible.

I do have one advantage over Lonnie, though. I was watching the camera screens when the contestants fled in all directions from the hall of tasks, and I saw most of them as they burrowed their way behind sofas and pressed themselves behind doors. Some of them will be a breeze to catch.

At the foot of the stairs I turn on the spot, considering my options. I make my way unsteadily along the dark passage to the door of the billiard room.

The moment I open the door, I glimpse a bare arm beneath the pool table. That's Ruth, who nobody would expect to be any good at this game.

There's a better hiding place in here. Beside the pool table is a small table with a chess set on it. A tablecloth droops down on all sides. I know for a fact that Ben's under there.

I turn away from the chess set and crouch to look under the pool table. Ruth stares back at me.

I raise the rifle and shoot her in the forehead. Red lights flash on her holster, and there's a tinny sound of an explosion.

My heart rate's skyrocketing. I hear a scuffling sound behind me, and I know that Ben's making a run for the door. But he won't get far.

"I knew I'd be bad at this," Ruth says, rolling out from her hiding place. "What do I do now?"

"Return to the hall of tasks," I say, trying to keep my voice low. I'm not sure why. The contestants have only ever heard my voice through a digital filter that disguises it anyway.

Ruth says brightly, "Okay!" and scurries out of the room.

The contestants hiding in the sitting room are sitting ducks. Aura's behind the long curtains that cover one of the bay windows. Cécile has managed to squish herself between the seat and back sofa cushions. Each of them comes out of their hiding place grumbling. I direct them back to the hall of tasks in a gruff voice, then move away.

I'm enjoying the sense of power. I'm anonymous, and all of these people are afraid of me. It's not a situation I've ever found myself in before.

I head to the dining room. I could have sworn I saw somebody go in there, when I was watching from the production suite. But after a sweep of the cupboards, curtains, and behind the huge yucca plants in pots, I convince myself the room's empty. Then I pause on the threshold of the room, listening. I hear a faint sound – a sigh, maybe, or just weight shifting.

I scan under the table with my rifle held out. There's nobody there.

I stand up and pull the chairs from beneath the table, one by one, expecting to find somebody lying across the seats.

I curse under my breath.

My gut instinct told me they'd be under the table. I can see the entirety of the carpet beneath it, and it's clear. But—

I drop to my hands and knees and twist my neck to look up.

I see limbs emerging from swathes of dark cloth, but their arrangement doesn't seem to make sense. Where there should be a head is only a black void.

My heart is thumping.

"I've found you," I whisper.

"Ah, crap."

The voice is female. There's a grunt, and legs drop down, and finally I can see a headless figure crouching before me. The fingers draw back the darkness, and I realise it's only dark hair that's been hanging in front of her face.

"Back off a sec, would you?" Sasha says. "I could really use straightening out my spine right now." She pats her tummy. "I'm a bit past it these days, but when I was a teen I was something of a gymnast. Not sure my teachers would have recommended holding that position for *quite* so long, mind you."

I can bear to interact with these people in the study with its one-way glass barrier, but standing face to face with any of the contestants makes my stomach churn. I wonder why that is.

"Please return to the hall of tasks," I say.

I shoot her in the chest.

Ben

It's an absolute gift. How is it that until now I had no idea that there was even a door beneath the stairs?

I don't have time to debate whether it's a good idea to go through the door. I was amazed I managed to sneak past the seeker when they came into the billiard room. When they came out again they turned slowly to look around the lobby, and I was forced to edge back into the shadows in the corner, and that's when I discovered the door hanging slightly ajar.

I go through the door and ease it closed behind me. The latch snicks.

The space is pitch black and confined – I can't stand up fully. But that hardly matters. It's a terrific hiding place, even if it's only a cupboard. I'm in with a shot of getting a second key to the vault.

My breathing is loud in my ears. But there's an odd quality to the sound, an odd echo. It suggests this isn't a small cupboard after all.

If only I had a torch.

The best thing to do would be to open the door, just for a second or two, letting in enough light to make out my surroundings.

Carefully, I push at the door.

It doesn't budge.

I feel around. I can't find a handle. There's just a big hole where the handle *should* be.

Okay. So I'm trapped.

I force myself to remain calm. I could bang on the door and shout through the hole, and somebody would come. But I'm not going to do that. I'll wait until it's clear I've won, and *then* I'll shout for help.

Deep breaths, Ben.

Dolly

I'm tired of this whole game. I hate the fact that my role here on the island keeps changing day by day, and there's nothing I can do about it. I came here for one reason and one reason only. All I want is to keep my head down and get on with it.

I hear a whimper. I turn to look at the sideboard. Ralphie's done a decent job of hiding his face and upper body, but his fashionable trainers are bright white and shine like tiny suns.

"Found you," I say.

Out of the corner of my eye I see movement near to the door that leads outside.

Ralphie rolls out from under the sideboard.

"Go back into the hall of tasks with the others," I say distractedly.

I pull the heavy curtain away from the front door. The lock is on the latch. Somebody's gone outside.

Axel's script should have made it clear that nobody was allowed to leave the building. As long as he told the contestants that, anybody who's gone outside can be disqualified.

The rifle rattles against the surface of the door as I pull it open. The light stings my eyes – it's so dark inside the mansion that I'd forgotten it's daytime outside.

Whoever came out here, they know they're cheating. And yet I'm going to have to traipse around the grounds, more exposed than ever. I didn't sign up for this. Imogen – and the missing stuntman, and Lonnie, and particularly our absent dickhead of a producer, Helm – shouldn't have let this happen.

And it's raining. Just perfect.

Standing beneath the roof of the rickety wooden porch, I scan in all directions. If somebody was cheeky enough to come outside, they might easily have decided to hide behind one of the external buildings: the pool or Axel's cottage. They could even have headed to the barn or down the rocky slope to the shore, where the rowing boat is moored.

None of this should be my problem. I'm done here.

The second I turn to go back into the mansion, I see a flash of movement. Victor was hiding just behind the door, and now he's making a run for it.

"Hey!" I cry out.

A thick arm lashes out, pushing me away roughly. I'm pretty sure it's just part of Victor's attempt to escape, rather than him actually attacking me, but that hardly matters when you're toppling over, does it?

I slip on the wet flagstone, then hit something, hard, and pain sparks up my left leg.

Dez

I can't decide what to do. I curse myself again for leaving my room key downstairs.

Perhaps that's where everyone else is: in their own bedrooms. Axel didn't tell us not to go into them, and if we did, I've no idea whether the hunter could follow – that is, I don't know if they'd have a key, and whether ethics would allow them to enter anyway.

I laugh silently. Ethics? This game show has been a shambles from the start. Look at what happened to Mira. It was my fault, obviously, but it shouldn't have been able to happen either.

A thought occurs to me.

This morning at breakfast, a note had been left for us on the table. It read simply: *Mira has chosen to leave the game.* I was pissed off at the cowardice of telling us like that. Axel didn't even show up while we were eating breakfast, he must have been so scared of the questions that would come his way.

I shot out of the dining room and ran to the locked door to the production area, hammering on it. Then I stormed into the study and demanded to know where Mira was, only to be told by that stupid robot voice that she'd already left the island.

What does it say about me that I didn't believe it?

I sprinted upstairs to Mira's room, next to mine. The door was unlocked, and a quick glance inside showed me that all her possessions were gone.

But the important thing is that the door was *unlocked*.

Mine and Mira's rooms are at the rear of the building. That means heading away from the staircase, which is good, but it also means being exposed in the corridor for longer than I'd like.

I set off in a sort of crouched run, keeping close to the wall. Several times, I hear distant sounds – perhaps from downstairs – and each time I freeze, then tell myself that freezing is exactly what I *shouldn't* do.

Here's a funny thing, though. I feel an odd flush of excitement as I run. I always loved hide and seek. Playing this game feels more like being *me* than anything I've done for ages.

I open the door to Mira's room and throw myself inside. I lie on the carpet, panting, feeling weirdly elated.

Where should I hide? Beneath the bed? It's a bit obvious.

The something catches my attention: the door to the bathroom.

Hang on.

Mira's bathroom is *my* bathroom. We share an en suite. It's another failure of health and safety, though that thought didn't cross my mind earlier because me and Mira sharing things seemed so natural.

The point is, I can get into my bedroom after all, even without my key.

I pass through the shared bathroom. But the second I put my hand on the handle of the adjoining door, the door to my bedroom, my spider-senses are tingling.

There's someone in there.

Dolly

"Shit. Oh shit," Victor says. "You okay, mate?"

I try to speak, but the pain in my leg is too much.

I'm sitting on the ground. I'm outside the mansion, and something's digging into my back. It's one of the struts of the porch canopy. Sharp-looking bolts poke out from the wood. I look down at my thigh. My jeans are torn, revealing a dark smear of blood. When Victor pushed me, I must have scraped against one of the exposed bolts.

The injury is on my right thigh. Like a mirror image of Axel's scars.

"Don't move, pal," Victor says. Then he adds doubtfully, "I could fetch help?"

"There's nobody who can help," I say.

It's true. Nobody on Red Cliffs Island cares about anybody else. A sudden certainty pops into my head: *Someone will die here.*

"Oh fuck. You're a girl, ain'tcha?"

I wince as the balaclava is pulled over my head carefully, almost tenderly.

"My name's Victor," he says.

I don't reply, as if I might still remain anonymous if I'm only quiet.

Victor crouches, looking deep into one eye and then the other. He shuffles to look at the back of my head. "There's no obvious damage back here. So it's just the leg. You should see a doctor pronto."

I push him away and fumble for the laser rifle where it's fallen on the ground. Then I struggle to my feet, wincing at the pain in my thigh and gripping the porch strut for stability.

I hold out my hand. At first Victor doesn't understand, but then he looks down at the balaclava in his hands. He gives it to me and I pull it on.

"You lose," I say as I shoot him in the chest. "Back to the hall with you."

I stagger back into the building.

Dez

The air in my bedroom is thick with smoke. Even before I see him, it's pretty obvious who's at the centre of the cloud.

"What the fuck are you doing in here?" I hiss.

Doc Leaf is sitting cross-legged on my bed. He looks up at the ceiling and lets out a plume of smoke.

"Hiding," he says simply.

"You can't come in here."

My eyes flick to the little shelf above the radiator. I think I'm going to be sick.

Doc Leaf laughs. "There's a lot of things people *can't* do, but they do them anyway."

"Get out."

Doc Leaf rubs his sweaty face. "Or what? Are you going to tell on me?"

Is he actually dangerous, or does he just enjoy making people uncomfortable?

"What do you want?" I say. My throat is so tight that my voice is hardly audible.

He laughs again. It's much calmer than his usual manic bark. "Are you trying to bargain with me?"

I stop myself from looking at the little shelf again. I can't risk drawing his attention to the items lined up there, if he hasn't already clocked them.

"I just want you out of here," I say, trying to keep my voice level. "You make me very nervous. If it's just that you want to win this task, I'll go out there now, give myself up. I'm pretty sure we're the last people still playing."

Doc Leaf chuckles. "Oh. The task. The game."

He stretches both arms lazily. In his right hand he's holding his spliff. His left hand reaches out to tap on the radiator shelf.

So he's seen my collection after all.

I change tack immediately. "We can work together. I'll find out who's got the keys, and where they're keeping them. I'm good at getting secrets out of people." I wince at my use of the word 'secrets'. "I'll give the keys to you, and you can have the prize money. You can walk away from this place two hundred and fifty thousand pounds richer."

I don't know whether I mean any of it. I'm panicking. Here in this room there are no cameras. But if Doc Leaf leaves this room and shoots his mouth off, broadcasting my secret to the whole world, then that's it. Game over.

He leers at me. "You don't want to share the prize money?"

"I don't care about it."

"Why did you come here, then?"

I'm being completely honest when I say, "To escape the past."

Doc Leaf watches me with his piggy eyes. Then he shakes his head.

"I don't give a shit about the money either," he says. "But I do like the idea of having a partner in crime."

He shuffles off the bed to stand before me. Then he frowns at his spliff, which has gone out. Still frowning, he taps his pockets in an oddly theatrical manner.

"Ah, here it is," he says in an exaggerated tone of delight.

From his back pocket he pulls out a lighter, and sets to relighting his spliff.

I stare open-mouthed.

Doc Leaf notices my expression.

"Ah, yes," he says, waving the lighter before my face.

243

"This is yours, isn't it?"

My eyes follow the glint of metal. I can see the words *Fuck 'em* in Gothic script. That lighter is my most prized object.

My voice is tiny as I say, "Give it back."

Doc Leaf lets out smoke in a long exhalation, then coughs. "Give it back? You gonna give *them* back?"

We both look at the radiator shelf. The seven objects in a neat line.

Bile rises in my throat.

Doc Leaf moves closer to the shelf. "I'm gonna guess who they belong to."

I don't reply.

He points at the leftmost object. "This is from the mumsy one, Sasha. Am I right?"

The hair clip is like nothing I'd ever have worn myself, even during one of my rare femme phases. Attached to its centre is a white satin daisy.

I nod silently.

Doc Leaf moves on to the tiny stud earring that shines even though it's not in direct sunlight. The amount of times I've turned it over in my hands, admiring its gleam...

"Victor?" Doc Leaf says. "He's enough of a poser for it."

I nod again. "It's not a real diamond, though."

He points at the next item, a slim wristwatch with jewels set around the face. "The French lass?"

"Cécile. That's right."

"Worth a bit, that one. Does it make you feel any guiltier than the others?"

I consider the question. It doesn't often occur to me to estimate the monetary value of the things I take. But the watch is almost certainly the most expensive item in this collection.

"She has more than one," I say. "The one she's wearing now looks more expensive."

"A very good deflection, Desdemona." Doc Leaf picks up the next item, a crumpled piece of card. He unfolds it to reveal a creased playing card, a jack of spades. Pasted over both of the jack's faces are scribbly smiley faces.

"Is this Ben's?" Doc Leaf asks.

"Yes."

From the way Doc Leaf tosses the playing card down, I can see he thinks nothing of it. But the card is perhaps my favourite item of all. The fact that it's so creased, and that it was taken from the tiny coin pocket of Ben's jeans, shows it's precious to him. And that makes it precious to me too.

Doc Leaf picks up a gold cufflink. "I'd have said this belonged to Victor too. But something tells me you only take one thing from each person."

I scowl. I hate being easy to read. "It's actually Axel's."

Doc Leaf's eyebrows raise. "Really? Nice one."

He looks at the final item, a tiny plastic puppy with its paws raised in a begging position. "Looks like a prize from a cereal packet."

"I'm guessing it is."

"But someone here cares about it?"

"Yes."

"Who?"

I hesitate, but there's no point trying to fob him off. "Mira."

"Did she tell you why she had it?"

"She thinks it's lucky."

Doc Leaf takes a drag from his spliff, watching me thoughtfully. "When did you steal it?"

"I don't remember," I lie.

"Yeah you do. Was it before or after you slashed her arm up?"

245

This is the very thing I've been telling myself not to dwell on. Taking the puppy was bad enough, given that Mira was my friend, but the repercussions were far worse.

"The day before," I say.

Doc Leaf's eyes flash dangerously. "You stole her lucky charm. And the next day was the worst day of her life, ending with you knifing her."

He roars with laughter.

"Shut up," I snap. "They'll hear you."

He keeps laughing. He splutters, "You still care about hide and seek?"

No, I don't care about hide and seek. I don't care about *Escapism*. I just want my secret to remain a secret. I want the people in my life not to know that I've stolen from them, compulsively. Every single one of them.

Finally, Doc Leaf manages to compose himself. He gestures with a thumb towards my collection. "I was hoping to find my knife here. Any idea where it went?"

I wince. I've been bothered about its disappearance, too.

"I don't know who took it," I say.

Doc Leaf studies me carefully. He nods, accepting my answer.

"What about this?" he asks, holding up the lighter. It occurs to me that in order to use it he's filled it with lighter fluid, somehow.

I haven't the energy to attempt to lie to him. What would be the point, when he already has such a hold over me?

"It belongs to my ex-girlfriend, Priya," I say.

"Interesting use of the word 'belongs'. 'Cos you've got it, not her. But she didn't give it to you, did she?"

He's playing with me.

"No," I say. "I took it from her, a few weeks after we first met. She doesn't know I've got it. If she did—"

"If she knew you had it, it wouldn't hold the same magic for you. Am I right?"

I'm done with lies. "I was going to say she'd see it as proof to support her suspicions of all the other times I stole from her. That I wouldn't have a hope in hell of ever winning her back. But yes, what you said is also true. What are you going to do, now that you know all this?"

An awful leering smile creeps over his face.

"Don't know," he says. "But I'm going to have fun deciding."

He tosses the lighter from hand to hand, watching me the whole time, enjoying my agony.

Then he presses it into my hand. I'm shocked at the warmth of the metal. I squeeze it tight. Waves of something like pleasure rush through me. I've got it back.

"Keep it safe this time, yeah?" he says.

He rummages in a pocket of his cargo shorts. Then he places something else in my open palm: a crumpled but unsmoked cigarette.

He stubs out his spliff directly on the radiator shelf, leaving it at the end of the row of objects as if it's intended to be an addition to my collection. Then he goes to my bedroom door, unlocks and opens it, and strides into the corridor.

Ben

I can't tell what's going on out there. A couple of minutes ago I heard the stairs creak above me, which suggests the seeker has gone upstairs. It's been quiet since then.

I crouch at the little hole where there should be a door handle. I can't really see anything, just vague shapes.

But then I can see even *less*, and I realise that's because somebody's standing directly in front of the door.

I clamp my hand over my mouth and shuffle sideways.

The door rattles. Can it even be opened, or would it need to be smashed to set me free?

I keep sidestepping in the pitch black. This is *definitely* not a cupboard, it's a corridor.

The door rattles again, then clicks, then opens.

"Is someone in here?" a male voice whispers.

I freeze. Maybe they'll go away again?

But no, they're coming in. I hear the snick of the door as it closes. Great, so now we're both trapped.

All I can hope to do is put off the inevitable. Or maybe this corridor will lead to a room with places to hide.

I keep shuffling.

Then I gasp as my foot drops further than I expected, lower than floor level.

Get a grip, Ben. It's only a step. It makes sense that this corridor leads to a basement or a cellar.

"I can hear you," the voice says.

The tone seems wrong. There's no threat in it.

Now I understand. They're hiding, not seeking.

"Who are you?" I whisper.

"Ralphie. I was found, but the seeker forgot to shoot my sensors. So I thought I'd hide again, just in case it didn't count."

I breathe a sigh of relief. My body slumps against the wall, and in doing so I put more weight on the wooden step. It creaks loudly.

"Is that Ben?" Ralphie whispers.

"Yes. Listen, we should talk about the key," I say. "If we're joint last to be found by the seeker, then—"

Suddenly, I'm falling. The iron taste of blood fills my mouth even though I haven't hit anything yet, my body responding physically to the danger.

I shout for help but it comes out as a wordless shriek. Something scrapes along the side of my torso and then my arm, then my whole body swings to one side and my forehead hits hard brick. Then my chin hits my forearm and I bite my tongue, and then there's blood in my mouth for real, as if the earlier taste of it was a premonition.

"Ben!" Ralphie calls out.

I can't answer. I've bit my tongue and there's blood in my mouth.

And my legs have gone weird.

"Where are you?" Ralphie asks.

"Don't know," I say, spitting blood.

I can't see anything. I can barely tell up from down. It seems crazy, to be in such danger and not to be able to visualise what's happened.

What's going on with my legs?

Then I figure it out. They feel strange because they're hanging freely. Dangling beneath me.

Because I'm holding myself up. I'm supporting the weight of my body with my crossed arms.

Suddenly, I can picture it all. One of the wooden steps splintered under my weight, and I dropped through it. One false move, and I might drop all the way.

"I'm going to fall," I say thickly.

"Fall where?"

It seems a stupid question. Who cares?

I count to three, then try to heave myself up.

Not for the first time, I realise I'm badly out of shape. It's like my stupid doughy body wants to succumb to gravity and fall to its death.

"Help," I say.

I yelp as a hand brushes against my arm, then grips it tight.

"I've got you," Ralphie says. I hear scuffling sounds – I'm guessing he's feeling around, trying to determine what we we're dealing with.

"On three, okay?" Ralphie says. "One. Two. Three."

He hauls on my arm, and I use my other one to pull myself almost up my belly button. I grunt with triumph, but it becomes a squeal of dismay when I hear wood splintering again, and the board I've been supporting myself on groans and threatens to snap.

Shit. Shit.

"Again," Ralphie says. "One. Two."

I don't wait for three. My limbs are flailing like mad, grasping at the steps, at the bricks of the wall, at Ralphie's arms. I'm no longer Ben Parrish, I'm a scrabbling octopus of panic. My actions are like a mad dance choreographed to the thud of bits of wood hitting a surface far, far below me, and shattering into a hundred million pieces, just like my bones will, any second.

I hear Ralphie grunt. There's a flurry of movement, and now I can't tell if he's pulling or I'm pushing, and up and down have got mixed up again. I wince at the sound of a heavy thud, and for a second I think I've fallen and hit the ground far below.

But—

I'm up. I'm out of the hole.

I'm safe.

My breathing is so laboured that I barely manage to say,

"Thank you."

Ralphie doesn't reply.

"Ralphie?" I whisper.

No reply.

Still crouching, I edge my fingers along to where the floor ends in splinters. Beyond it there's nothing at all. The entire wooden staircase must have collapsed under my weight.

And if Ralphie's not up here with me…

Dolly

I'm in the corridor upstairs. A muffled crashing sound comes from somewhere downstairs, but I ignore it. The waves of pain from my injured leg have reduced my focus to just finishing this stupid game.

I've checked the whole downstairs of the building now, and I'm pretty sure I've found all the contestants except two: Doc Leaf and Dez.

I hear the click of a door.

"Hello hello," Doc Leaf says. "How many you caught so far?"

"Seven!" I say proudly. The pain is making me giddy.

"Make that eight. I'm giving myself up."

"Oh." I wince at another shooting pain from my thigh. "That's nice."

Doc Leaf takes the rifle from the floor and manipulates it carefully to shoot himself in the head.

Doc Leaf points back the way he came. He doesn't seem his usual clownish self at all.

"Last door on the left," he says. "They're in there."

We move away in opposite directions. I push open the final door. Then I gasp as a shape looms before me.

But it's only Dez, standing in the doorway as if they're trying to block my view of the room.

At first I don't know what to say. Then I remember my role. When I pull up my oversized sweatshirt, Dez frowns in confusion. I take a plain envelope from the breast pocket of my shirt.

"You win," I say as I hand it over.

Dez takes the envelope without a word, and toss it into their bedroom. Then they edge into the corridor and close

252

the door behind them quickly.

The pain's returned in force. I think I might throw up.

But what's upsetting me right now is that Dez's reaction is so disappointing. They won the game, didn't they?

"I'm proud of you," I say.

Dez frowns again. "What did you say?"

When I don't reply, they say, "Hey, are you okay?"

The pain is unbelievable. It takes all my strength to raise my hands and form two thumbs ups.

"Really, really good," I say.

I can't decide whether it's the weakness in my body, or a lingering sense that Dez deserves proper congratulations, but I fall forward into a fumbly, clingy hug.

Six months later

Rhea

As I walk through the doorway of the imposing building, my cane clacking loudly on the tiled floor, I worry I won't recognise Dolly. But it turns out there are no other visitors, only a single member of staff behind the counter and another half-heartedly pushing a broom around the circular lobby. Dolly's waiting to the left of the counter, leaning against a sign covered with sketches of Victorian ladies.

I pay the entrance fee, then approach Dolly. She's a fair bit shorter than me, and her hair is a nice mix of blonde and ginger. She's wearing oversized round granny glasses and a brown dress that's so shapeless that her body could be any size at all underneath it. Her look is probably fashionable down in London, I assume. I feel self-conscious about my leggings and cardigan, even though on the face of it I'm more smartly turned out than she is.

"Rhea Hildred, as I live and breathe," Dolly says with a smile.

"Hello, Dolly," I say.

Dolly rolls her eyes. "Do you know, I've never seen it?" It must be clear I don't know what she's talking about, because she adds, "I mean the film: *Hello, Dolly!* For a while I worked in a retirement home, and the residents would bring up the title of the film every time I showed up." She adopts a faraway look. "Nice job, though. I pretended the old folk were my real parents. They gave me sweets."

I laugh. I don't know why. I guess I'm nervous.

"I've never done this before," I say.

"What is 'this'?"

"Meeting a source, face to face."

Dolly smiles. "I like the idea of being a source. Makes me feel important. But prepare yourself for disappointment, Rhea. I don't know that I've got much to offer. Hey, shall we head in? That teenager behind the counter keeps looking our way." She lowers her voice to add, "Either he fancies you, or he's a government mole."

I shake my head. I think I might be blushing.

As we enter the first exhibition, I sense Dolly's eyes on me, on my walking cane. I do my best not to lean on it heavily, despite the bright fluorescent lights that are knackering up my balance.

We pass through a dark passage into a space that's barely any lighter. There are stone cobbles on the floor and the walls around us are filthy brick. When my eyes adjust, I see that we're in a Victorian slum. A waxwork boy drains joints of meat, dripping its blood into a tub. A father carries the slumped body of a barefoot young girl. A man in a dirty coat sells pies beside a tall heap of shit.

"Why here?" I ask.

Dolly shrugs. "It's near your place, isn't it? I was trying to do you a favour."

"The Corn Exchange has some quite nice cafés."

She studies me. "I told you, I need to be certain of my anonymity."

"Fair enough. There's nobody here. I guess Tuesday morning isn't the obvious time for people to come and witness Victorian hell."

Dolly chuckles and looks around. "I suppose it is grim. Funny, I hadn't thought of it like that. There's actually another reason I wanted to come here. I visited it once before – a school trip – and it made an impression."

"I bet," I say with a shudder. "Bringing school kids to a medical museum seems a sure-fire way to ensure lifelong nightmares."

I hurry through another grotesque chamber. When we reach a wider area that's obviously designed for school groups to gather in, we sit on a bench.

"How much are you prepared to tell me?" I ask.

"I haven't decided yet," Dolly says thoughtfully. As I reach into my satchel and pull out my tiny handheld recording device, she says quickly, "I don't want to be recorded."

I suppose I'd expected her to say that, but it's still a blow.

"You do know I'm making a podcast, right?" I say.

"I just need to know I trust you first. When I decide that I do... we'll see. Maybe then I'll go on record."

"Deal. Okay. Where shall we begin?"

Dolly puts her hands on her lap, an oddly prim gesture. "Once there was a young girl named Dolly..."

"Perhaps skip forward a tiny bit?"

"If you say so."

*

The gist is this:

Dolly had worked for Kestrel Productions in Hammersmith for only nine months before filming began on *Escapism*. Before that point she'd worked as a runner on two light-entertainment shows – meaning she was the dogsbody, making tea and carrying out errands – and then as a production assistant on a kid's show about a magical cat, which didn't get beyond its pilot episode. When Kestrel got the gig to produce a British version of the Swedish hit *Eskapism*, Dolly was initially overlooked as a member of the production team. Whoever was originally intended to be on duty as production assistant was an outside hire, and Dolly doesn't remember her name. When that person didn't show up at the mainland dock near Red Cliffs Island, two days before filming was due to begin, Dolly got the call at the Hammersmith office and was told to hotfoot it up north.

In fact, none of the production team involved in filming knew anything much about the island or the mansion. The Swedish production company, Helmedia, had been responsible for setting up all the cameras and the tasks to be played by contestants during the week. According to Dolly, this was the main issue at first: she and the other production team members had to trust that everything had been prepared correctly, and hope that nothing would go wrong. Lonnie Hall had the role of technician, but Dolly didn't rate him at all. The director, Imogen Dorrien-Stewart, felt the whole thing was beneath her and did as little work as possible. Most damning of all, the psychologist-slash-doctor, Mobeen Baig, didn't even make it to the island due to contracting a virus. The contestants had no idea they had so little support from the production team, because they never came into contact with its members during filming. The only other person who appeared occasionally on the island was Noah Milne, a local who delivered food supplies via his private boat each morning, and who was essentially the group's only means of returning to the mainland.

As for Axel Griffin, Dolly's opinion is that he was partway through a midlife crisis. He was erratic throughout filming, fluffing his lines, failing to hide his secret drinking. Dolly suspects he slept with one of the contestants, Aura. When I think of the Amie Osborn I spoke to, her glow of good health, it's hard to imagine her behaving in such a tawdry manner. This new knowledge

257

about her seedier past is oddly reassuring, though that makes me feel cross with myself.

Dolly heard Helm mentioned plenty of times, but she was never in touch with the absent producer, and even Imogen only communicated with him via instant messages. To this day, she knows nothing about Helm at all. He retained all control over the end product that would have been *Escapism*, if it had been completed.

Dolly was the voice the contestants spoke to in the interview room, though the study was used less and less as the week went on, when things began to fall apart.

*

"Was the camera in the study filming the whole time?" I ask.

"No. It was the only one that was manually operated. If you can call turning it on and off operating it."

"Then you can't have performed all the interviews."

Dolly blinks in surprise. "What?"

"During our call you said you didn't know anything about Cécile Guillaume being injured. But I've seen a clip where she's talking to the camera, and there's blood on her face. There's no voice replying to her questions... but there's a click every so often, and if the camera needed to be turned on, then somebody must have been there."

After a few seconds thinking about this, Dolly says, "It can only have been—"

A family of four enter the large cobbled space, then lean over a railing to look at one of the waxwork dioramas. The parents are presumably explaining all the intricate details of Victorian laundry, in German. I think of my own parents. I may not have many memories of my childhood since my accident, but I've read the diaries I kept back then. They're full of love for my parents, and it's clear how patient they always were with me, and with the foster kids they looked after over the years.

I sense Dolly tensing beside me.

"Let's head upstairs," I say.

*

The gruesome visions of Victorian Leeds are nothing compared to the sterile chrome machines on the upper floor, or the jars containing who knows what bobbing in murky liquid.

"Are you okay?" Dolly asks.

I nod, even though I'm not.

I'm afraid of medical instruments, which is stupid, because I don't even *remember* the surgery. I was knocked out by the fall from the horse, then knocked out again by a cocktail of drugs while the doctors pieced me back together. In the brief periods of almost-lucidity during that time, I'm told that I insisted on referring to the medical staff as either 'king's horses' or 'king's men'. Since then, my experience of the NHS has been mainly therapy rooms.

Partly in an attempt to distract myself, I say, "I think you were about to say that Imogen must have conducted some of the interviews."

Dolly's been examining an X-ray machine built in the 1920s, which was used in shoe shops to examine customers' feet. I wonder what effect it had on the salespeople. I suppose they got ill and never knew why. She sounds distracted as she says, "Yep. She's the only one who could have, other than me."

She turns. "I already told you that Ben Parrish knew somebody on the team, didn't I?"

"Meaning Imogen?"

"He kept asking for her, in the study. That is, he kept asking me if I was her, because my voice was disguised and he couldn't tell either way."

"Do you know what their relationship was?"

"All I know is that Ben seemed to expect special treatment. And…" She trails off, deep in thought. "Now that I think of it, his file was different to the other contestants."

"What file?"

"I wasn't due to work on filming of *Escapism*, and I wasn't present during any of the casting calls, but I was still expected to do more than my share of admin. Imogen's a dinosaur, and always insists that everything's on paper. I printed out and collated all the files for each contestant, and at the time I noticed that there was nothing in Ben's file relating to his original application."

"Then it was Imogen who arranged for him to take part."

"Seems that way. I don't know what that means."

I'm getting close to something, I can feel it in my bones. Dolly moves into another hall of the museum, and I hurry to catch up with her, my walking cane clacking noisily.

"Did any of the other contestants have information missing from their files?" I ask.

Dolly wanders towards a display of artificial limbs. I try not to look at them.

"Not exactly," she replies.

I'm getting frustrated at her vagueness. What's worse is that she doesn't seem particularly obstructive, just distracted.

"What do you mean?" I ask.

"One file was missing entirely. There was none at all for—"

At the same time, we both say, "Doc Leaf."

"Who *was* he?" I murmur. "Who was Lawrence Bunce?"

My eyes drift to the display in front of us, but I'm so zoned out I barely register the metal joints or the harnesses or the pins.

I weigh up whether to tell Dolly what I've found out about Doc Leaf. If I can't trust her, who can I trust?

"I was sent another video," I say. "Just this morning."

Dolly turns sharply. "Who's sending these videos to you?"

"No idea," I say. "This one came with a note, saying that the interview files are all encrypted, and that recovering them is taking time. I don't know whether that's true."

Dolly shrugs. "Can't help you there. I'm crap with computers."

"This new one just showed Doc Leaf, slumped in the armchair. Cigarette hanging out from the side of his mouth. He looked wasted, but more like somebody playing the part of somebody who's wasted, you know? And he was singing."

I watch her face for any sign of recognition. Her puzzlement appears genuine. She wasn't in the study for that interview either.

I go on, "He was singing what sounded like a soul song, or maybe it was just made up. The words went something like: 'If they only knew, the sort of man I am...'" I scrunch up my face, trying to remember. "'They'd run, they'd flee, 'cos I'm the boogeyman.'"

Dolly just stares at me. In a tiny voice she says, "Fuck."

"That's not all," I say. My throat's gone tight. "He carries on singing that same thing a few times, slurring more and more. Then he's cut off."

"By Imogen?" Dolly asks.

"By the interviewer, yes," I say carefully. "The voice says, 'Stop it!' No, actually, it's more schoolteachery than that: 'Stop that, this instant!' Then the voice says, 'You'll spoil everything. Helm will be very disappointed.'"

"I don't understand," Dolly says. "I hope you believe me, Rhea. I wanted to help you, but this... I don't know what any of it means."

She seems genuinely shaken. I put my hand on her arm. Inside the sleeve of her baggy dress, her arm feels insanely thin. Dolly looks down at my hand, and I see colour come back into her cheeks. Then she coughs and edges away. She drifts over to a display case in the centre of the room.

"Wow, this is it," she says. "This is what haunted my dreams. When I fell asleep on the plane I saw it coming at me, clanking its way down the aisle."

At first I think the object in the display cabinet is a suit of armour, before I realise it would be hopeless as protection in battle. Between the steel plates of the figure are large gaps, and the belly of the wearer would be completely exposed. I check the label beneath the case, which states it's from the late seventeenth century, and that it's a frame for correcting deformities. The whole suit wouldn't have been worn at once, only whichever piece was required for correction. That explains why the legs are different lengths to one another.

I'm suddenly self-conscious of my own posture, my weight placed on my walking cane, making me as lopsided as the eerie figure in front of us.

I hate it.

"I love it," Dolly says in a faraway voice.

"You said it haunted your dreams."

"What can I tell you? I like horror films too. The gorier the better." She pauses. "When I was a teenager I was involved in a car crash, and in the few seconds before I knew I was okay an image of this contraption came into my mind. The thought of me wearing something like this for the rest of my life."

Suddenly, all I want is to get out of this place. But I

can't shake the feeling that once we leave this bubble, Dolly will clam up. I can't miss this opportunity to get every morsel of information out of her.

"What happened to Lawrence Bunce?" I ask.

Dolly doesn't look away from the corrective frame gleaming under the neon lights. I can't look at it. I need to get out.

"He fell from the cliffs. The Red Cliffs."

"Suicide?"

"That's what we were told. I don't know anything about that. All of my questions were brushed off by Imogen, and later by Kestrel lawyers, and Helmedia wouldn't answer my calls."

"Except he died with a knife in his back."

Dolly flinches. "A knife?"

"There are rumours online, dating from when the body was brought back to shore."

"Oh, cool. *Internet rumours*. That proves it, then."

I'm can tell I'm losing her. Soon, she won't cooperate at all.

"But you have to agree that too much went wrong during filming for it all to be sheer bad luck," I say. Immediately, I'm certain it's the wrong tack to take, that it just sounds like an accusation.

Dolly exhales and stares at the floor. "Let's see. Mira Qureshi was injured – a knife wound. Dez Votel did it." She holds up a hand to stop me from interrupting. "But it was definitely an accident, even if it was ultimately due to negligence on the part of the production team. Ralphie Ó Cárthaigh had a really bad fall, trying to help Ben Parrish – another accident, which only happened because they strayed into a part of the mansion that wasn't health and safety checked. And I got a bit banged up during a task, and Victor Okojie did in another one, but that was totally his fault. I don't know anything about Cécile Guillaume being injured, and I don't see how she *could* have been injured. When we all boarded Noah's boat she was there, and she was fine. Don't get me wrong, she was livid – but she appeared physically okay."

That's a surprise – but there's more to come, I can tell.

"You don't know all of what went wrong, though," she says slowly. "That final day, in the boat… you need to know what *wasn't* there. Firstly, the prize money disappeared, and nobody can prove who took it. But anyone could make an informed guess. Because that was supposed to be the format, wasn't it? That whoever took the money would escape with it in the rowing boat."

"A contestant was missing?" I say breathlessly.

"Not just one. When we all piled onto the boat together, two of the contestants didn't show up. Imogen insisted that somebody'd come back and find them later, but that the most important thing was to take as many people as possible back to the mainland, along with the body of Doc Leaf. For all that we had a fatality on our heads, Imogen seemed totally distracted by the prize money going missing, mainly because the 'winners' weren't caught on camera. She left me to deal with all the contestants' complaints. If you could have been there, if you could have heard the ear-bashing I was getting…"

She rubs the bridge of her nose. "You're going to ask what happened, and I want you to know I'm not being evasive – I don't have a clue where those missing people are now."

I'm so breathless I can only manage a single word. "Who?"

"Dez Votel and Ben Parrish."

Six months earlier

Ben

"You look weird, Ben."

I realise I'm hugging myself tightly. When I was a kid, my foster parents used to worry about me when I did that.

"I was trapped," I say. "And I'm hurt. And I'm shocked."

"Poor Ben."

Subtly, I pull up my T-shirt a little. The graze isn't nearly as bad as it felt at the time. It was more the shock of falling in the darkness.

"How is Ralphie?" the voice asks.

Suddenly, I feel like crying. When the lobby lights were turned on I could see everything: the splintered wooden steps, Ralphie's body sprawled below on a stone floor. I hammered on the door, screaming for help, and then the door opened and I was gabbling madly and then people were pushing past me. I crawled through the doorway into the lobby on my hands and knees.

I think it was Victor who hauled Ralphie out. I was amazed to see that Ralphie was conscious. When I grabbed his hands and apologised, he brushed it off, saying, "Duck and roll, that's all there is to it." But he couldn't disguise the fact that he couldn't put weight on his left leg.

"He keeps telling everyone he's fine," I say. "It's a miracle he didn't hit his head on the way down. I wish he'd agree to be seen by the doctor."

The voice doesn't reply.

I can't decide who's more in the wrong: Imogen's team for allowing an accident to occur, or me for venturing into that under-stairs area, which I now appreciate was clearly out of bounds. I'd hate to be accused of breaking the rules.

Typical Ben, huh? A life-threatening accident, and all I can think about is a game.

"I still don't understand why Dez won," I say, hardly realising I'm speaking aloud.

"You were already caught, sort of. You were the first person I... You were the first person the seeker found."

I think back to when I rushed out of the billiard room when Ruth was shot. "My lights didn't flash."

"Yeah. Odd. But as a gesture, we're adding five thousand to the prize fund because you hid for more than five minutes."

It doesn't add up. But I nod anyway. I've never been good at challenging authority figures.

I turn from the dark window and jut my chin towards the door of the study. "I think you should know it's getting really fractious out there. The drink's already flowing and it's only one PM. Arguments are brewing. I can't imagine what level of carnage there'll be this evening."

There's no reply from behind the blank window.

"The tasks are making the atmosphere worse," I say. "First Mira's injury, then the maze collapsing, now Ralphie being hurt... There's a sense of a loss of control." When there's still no reply, I add, "I mean it seems almost like *you've* lost control."

"I'm in control," the robotic voice says. "Look."

I look at the window. It's still black, with no hint of Imogen on the other side.

"What am I looking at?" I say.

Silence. Then a click and the tail-end of a childish snigger, which sounds really strange through the digital filter. "Ha! I forgot you can't see me. I was waving my arms."

"Okaaay," I say doubtfully. Why is she behaving so oddly?

"What's on your mind, Benedict?" the voice says abruptly.

A shiver runs down my arms.

"Why did you call me that?" I ask.

"It's your name, isn't it? It's in your file."

"Yes, but..." I try to think back. I've never gone by the name Benedict. I refused to let my foster parents call me by that name, and at school I tried to prevent any of my classmates from knowing it in the first place. It sounds old-fashioned and privileged, and I've always felt the pressure of trying to blend in. "Is it really in my file?"

"Must be, or I wouldn't know it. We've got excellent researchers. We're all very caper... cabal... capable."

I narrow my eyes. This conversation is weirding me out.

"But about the games," I say. "They need to run more smoothly. And perhaps it'd help if they weren't a total surprise to all of us. Perhaps it would keep everything on the rails."

There's another sharp laugh. "You mean you want me to tell you what the next task is."

"Yes. But before you protest—"

"Sure, Ben! Let's see... This afternoon you'll all be climbing the east face of the mansion, freestyle, no ropes. Last one clinging to the brickwork wins, but the winner has to bandage up anyone who falls."

"You're messing with me."

"I am."

"You're behaving really strangely."

"You're behaving like a cheat."

I consider this. "But this was your idea, Imogen. *You* emailed *me* about me being here. I thought me being here

267

would be of use. That you'd picked me because you thought I was *good*. I got to the season finale of *Golden Ticket*, didn't I? And you and I, we seemed to understand each other. We seemed to click."

"Did we kiss, Ben? On the lips?"

I stare at the dark surface of the window. "No! And what kind of a question is that?"

"Dunno. My head's all swimmy. Ibuprofen always does that to me."

Suddenly, it all becomes clear to me.

"Oh crap," I say. "You're not Imogen, are you? Were you the seeker in the task? I heard you were hurt."

The story has done the rounds again and again since lunchtime. When I heard Victor repeat it for a third time, he said the seeker had tried to attack him with a roundhouse kick, and when she'd fallen backwards he'd saved her from cracking her head on a metal boot scraper, which would have resulted in certain death. Also, when he unmasked her she was the blondest beauty he'd ever seen. I'm pretty sure none of his story is true.

"I was jabbed in the leg, that's all."

"Shouldn't you be resting?"

"Aw. That's lovely. You've just found out you've been revealing secrets to a total stranger, but here you are, worrying about me. You're a real human being, Benedict."

"Please. Don't call me that."

"It's nice."

"It's not me."

"Are your parents sad that you don't like the name they gave you?"

"I've no idea," I say. "I was taken away from my parents when I was a baby. I don't know anything about them."

"Oh. I'm sorry about that."

We're both silent for a while.

Then the voice says, "I'm going to turn off the filter, all right?"

When the voice speaks again, it's recognisably female, almost musical in comparison to the flattened digital version. "How's that?"

"Much better."

"Good. Anyway, I was going to say that I guess I hate my parents for the name they gave me, too."

I'm grateful for the change of focus, and the presence of a recognisable female voice is calming. "What *is* your name?"

"Dolly."

"It's… cute."

I guess I still have a vague image in my mind of the blonde beauty Victor described. I remind myself I'm single and, as weird as this encounter is, it's still an in-depth conversation with a girl, which are rare these days.

"Sure. But my given name is Dolores."

I can't help snorting with laughter. "Sounds like the name of a madam in an old-time Texas brothel."

"Fuck you."

My eyes go wide in alarm. "Shit. Sorry. I didn't mean that."

"I'm *joking*, Ben."

"Oh." I will my body to relax, but it won't obey me. "So. Dolly. Why is it that you were the seeker in the task, in which you were fairly badly hurt, and yet now you're here conducting interviews?" Then another realisation hits me. "You've *always* been conducting the interviews, haven't you? I've been speaking to you and not Imogen, this whole time."

"Correcto!"

I consider this. "Task 5 didn't go as planned, did it? Even before you were hurt."

"Nope. I wasn't supposed to be 'it'. Another massive

269

fuck-up brought to you by Kestrel and Helmedia."

"Like the fact that Dez was named as the winner of the task."

"That again? I'm not going to give you the key. And I'm not going to give you the answers to the quiz."

"What quiz?"

"Ah. Bugger."

"The sixth task is a quiz?"

"No."

"How does that link to escapism?" I wonder aloud. Then again, barely any of this game-show format is consistent. Even Axel seems to have abandoned his introduction spiels linking to the theme.

I hear a faint click. When the voice speaks again, it's the same robot voice as before.

"Get lost," it says. "I need to lie down."

Aura

I'm basically done with these people. These *children*. Throughout lunch I've had to listen to them sniping at each other and their conspiracy theories about what the hell's going on in this mansion. The fact that they're speaking so earnestly about a game of hide and seek is pretty hilarious, but none of them seem to get the joke. And Ralphie insisting he's not badly injured is literally insane. He's a physical wreck.

When I'm safely alone in my bedroom, I root in my wardrobe for Axel's jacket. When I got back to the mansion just before Task 5, I stashed it away quickly and hurried downstairs. I haven't had a chance to look at what I discovered in its pocket.

I rip open the envelope and pull out the large silver key.

This is my chance to win. Even a quarter of the prize money would be something. Mira was given one key, and she's gone now, which means that this key is one of only four in the possession of contestants.

As I crumple up the envelope, I realise it isn't empty.

I turn it upside down to shake out a second, smaller object. At first I don't recognise what it is: the blunt plastic prong on its underside confuses me. But when I turn it the right way up I see that it's a key, but another kind: a key from a computer keyboard.

I wonder if it's just a joke. Because on the face of the key are written three letters:

esc

Within moments I'm striding down the stairs, through

271

the lobby and out into the open air. The wind snaps at my dress, stinging my skin. I'm carrying Axel's jacket, but I don't put it on. I don't want to draw attention to myself. I make my way around the side of the mansion, heading for the cottage. Last night Axel was depressed and erratic. By now he'll have resumed battling his demons.

I don't know whether I'll confess I took the envelope from his pocket. Probably not, and he can't prove it. What matters is that what happened between us last night means I have a hold over him, and I can use that to my advantage. I need him to tell me what the computer key is for, if I'm going to have a chance of winning this contest. Either that, or I can give up and instead concentrate on establishing myself as a low-rent reality-show celebrity.

I raise my fist to hammer on the door of the cottage, but then I look around, wondering if I'm being watched by other contestants. Then I knock like a normal person.

I can't see through the window, but I can hear sounds from inside the cottage. Is he hiding from me?

I look around for something I can stand on. There's a lean-to at the side of the building, filled with wood and barrels. I ditch Axel's jacket and then, with difficulty, I manage to drag one of the barrels out, then roll it to a position below the window of Axel's bedroom at the rear of the cottage. I take off my heels and scramble onto it.

I'd expected to find Axel hiding in bed, waiting for me to go away. I've made enough noise that he must know I'm out here. But his bedroom is empty. The bed sheets are a tangled knot, and on the bedside table I can make out two squarish bottles, one of them half-full of brown liquid, perhaps whiskey.

Then I see Axel through the doorway. He's in the main room, facing away from me. The light from the windows makes him barely more than a silhouette.

His head looks really weird. Bulky. It takes me a few

seconds to see that he's wearing headphones. I guess he didn't hear me knocking after all. His head bobs, but it's not like he's dancing – it's more like a stagger. He keeps dropping to one side or another and then lurching to correct himself.

He's holding objects in each hand. When he brings up his left hand to his face I see that he's holding a hip flask. He takes a slug, then bobs around again for a bit.

Then he turns to face me. He doesn't seem to see me, though. His eyes are glazed.

He has a stupid grin on his face. He laughs, then nods. It's a strangely theatrical motion, as though he's responding to a compliment. Maybe what he's listening to on the headphones isn't music, but a voice. I can easily imagine him listening to recordings of himself, enjoying his past triumphs on Swedish TV.

He nods again, then throws his head back and laughs. He lifts both of his arms and turns his head from side to side, beaming his movie-star smile as if he's acknowledging an admiring audience. Now I can see both of his hands clearly.

Immediately, I push myself away from the window. The barrel tilts beneath my feet, then gives way entirely. I land on my bum, the impact on the rocky ground sending pain shooting up my spine, but I don't cry out. I don't make a sound.

I can't let Axel know I'm out here.

Because the other thing he's waving around is a gun.

Dez

I've been keeping out of everyone's way since the end of the fifth task. I even missed lunch, because I was certain they'd all be snarky about me winning the game of hide and seek. Or maybe it's more that I'm paranoid that Doc Leaf has told them about the other thing.

It's a problem, this habit of mine. I accept that. But it's a part of me. And once I steal an object from someone, that object becomes a part of me too. I can't explain it any other way.

So I've been lying here in bed these last few hours, trying not to think about my secret being known by another person for the first time ever.

And I've also been studying the contents of the envelope I won by cheating at hide and seek.

It contained two items. The first is a large key. The thought of trying to convince other winners to pool our keys to open the safe exhausts me. All that negotiation, and inevitable backstabbing.

The other item is more interesting, and also more infuriating. It's a laminated square of card, about four centimetres square. On it is printed a simple line drawing. At first I thought it was a sword, or maybe a knife, but it's too narrow to be either of those. Now I notice the sharp object has a small oval-shaped hole at one end, and a wavy line going through the hole, representing a thread.

It's a sewing needle.

I laugh. Big whoop. I've found a needle. And this whole mansion is the haystack.

Dolly

When I enter the production suite, Imogen is crouched at the table, tapping on her laptop. She barely glances up at me.

"How are you feeling now?" she says distractedly.

"My leg's stinging quite badly."

"That's a relief," Imogen says in a dull tone. It's obvious she didn't even listen to my answer.

"I think Ralphie will be okay," I say.

"Mm-hmm."

When I move around the table, Imogen turns the screen of the laptop away from me.

"Are you messaging Helm?" I ask.

"No," she says defensively. Then the air seems to go out of her. "He's not replying, for some reason. And I've been in touch with other Helmedia staff in Sweden, but they all say Helm doesn't want to be disturbed."

"Has he seriously given you no guidance at all, since everything started going wrong?"

"Nothing's gone wrong."

I stare at her. "Imogen, you're a smart, capable woman. I know you can see what's going on, and that you understand how bad it all is."

Imogen's eyes flick back to the screen. "Helm says it's all in hand."

"Meaning he can provide answers?"

"Meaning he thinks everything that's happened is within the tolerance level for a show like this."

I dig my fingernails into my palms.

"But we're beyond that," I say. "What happened to Mira alone should have shut down production. Ralphie could have been paralysed or even killed. And the fact that we effectively don't have a medic means that even much lesser injuries could become really serious. And we'd be liable. Don't you see that?"

Now Imogen's looking up at the ceiling. She seems intent on looking wherever I'm not.

"Seriously, what's in it for you?" I ask.

"Money," Imogen snaps. "Isn't it always about money? This production may be utter chaos, but Helm's certainly making it worth my while."

"How much?" Another good question would be: Why am I being paid my usual pittance?

"A lot."

"Enough to ignore all the threats to life? And does Helm really care enough about this show to ignore the repercussions?"

Imogen is chewing her cheek.

Now I understand. "You haven't told him, have you?"

"Of course I've—"

"Sure. But you've played it down. You want your pay packet, so you need filming to be completed."

Without warning, I reach forward and turn the laptop to read what she's written. Imogen doesn't even try to stop me.

"You've changed, Dolly," she says. "You used to be so much more…"

"Meek?" I mutter.

She doesn't answer.

Maybe she's right. Maybe I *have* changed. Finding myself in the centre of a growing shitstorm could be the cause.

I look over the screen at my boss.

"I can't *believe* you," I say. I'm not holding back now. "I can't believe how callous you are. After everything that's happened, *this* is what you ask for help about?"

276

On the screen, her last three messages read:

We have a problem, Helm. I need your advice about what to do next.

The envelope for the Task 4 winner has gone missing from Axel's room. Ax swears he knows nothing about it.

How important is it to the prize-money puzzle?

Imogen has the good grace to look ashamed of herself.

Then there's a tinny *ting* sound. She moves to look at the screen, to see Helm's reply, which is:

Very very important.

Then:

You'd better fucking find it.

Six months later

Rhea

When Red Cliffs Island finally looms out of the mist, I hear an "Ooh" from behind me. I turn to raise my eyebrows at Ted.

"Sorry," he says. "I got carried away. For a second there I felt like one of the Famous Five, discovering a treasure island in the fog."

"You're past fifty, Ted. Stop acting like a kid."

He looks properly scolded, which makes me feel rotten. He's too easy to embarrass. I glance at Dolly, to see if she thinks I've been cruel. But she's not paying attention to either of us. She's standing next to the captain of the little boat, her hands gripping the console beside the wheel, and her face is all scrunched up. I can't tell whether her expression means she feeling seasick or whether she's dwelling on bad memories. The last time she was on this boat, she was sharing it with Lawrence Bunce's corpse.

I slip my arm around Ted's waist.

"Sorry. I don't know why I was mean. It *is* quite exciting, isn't it? A real adventure. The Famous Three."

He turns to look into the cabin. "Are you sure it was wise to ask Dolly to come along? Isn't there a degree of conflict?"

"You need to think more like a podcast producer, Ted. Let's be honest, whatever we find here is unlikely to add up to much."

"You said it was vital that I take two days off work to

come on this road trip."

I wave a hand. "Sure. But we can't expect to find… I don't know, a dead body slumped on the shore. Any evidence is likely to be subtle. That means we need to amp it up for the podcast. We need Dolly's responses to seeing each part of the mansion if we're going to engage listeners."

Ted nods slowly.

The boat chugs as we approach the coast of the island. The captain – who has the ridiculous name of Noah, which must be a nickname – steers us to a jetty alongside a much bigger, flashier boat already moored there. He helps each of us off one by one, taking longest with Ted, who's such a klutz that he manages to misjudge the tiny gap between boat and boards, and ends up with one sopping wet foot.

"I'll come back two hours from now," Noah says.

Dolly turns sharply. "No," she says. It's the first time she's spoken since we were on the mainland. "You need to wait here for us."

Noah looks at her. Then he *really* looks at her, his eyes widening. Was he operating the crossings six months ago? Does he recognise her?

"We'll pay," Dolly says.

"Another fifty," Noah states firmly.

Dolly looks at me. I look at Ted. Ted sighs and reaches into his back pocket.

*

Before I knock on the door of the mansion, I pull out my handheld sound recorder. Nice and discreet.

The woman who answers is past middle-aged and has kind eyes. Her apron is dusted with flour, which matches the grey in her hair.

"Good afternoon," I say in the politest voice I can

279

muster. "We would like to speak to the owner of the house, if you'd be so kind."

She looks me up and down, then glances at my partners in crime. She frowns at the sight of the big fluffy mic attached to Ted's sound recorder, which he's done nothing to hide. Maybe she thinks it's a sex toy, or some sort of weapon.

Then she looks down at herself and laughs. "Oh! D'you think I'm a housekeeper or something?"

"No?" I say, even though I definitely did think that.

"I'm Margie," the woman says. "I live here. And who are you? You're an odd bunch, if you don't mind my saying."

I stick out my hand. "Rhea Hildred. And these are my assistants. We're from *Rhea View*, a… radio show." My bet is that Margie's not the podcast type.

"And you came all this way for a vox pop?"

"We were hoping to look around your home. It's in relation to something that happened here six months ago, when you leased it out to a production company."

She shakes her head. "Thomas and I didn't live here six months ago. We bought it in September."

Dolly pushes her way in front of me. "Who owned it back then?"

Margie shrugs. "It was an Airbnb, something in that vein." She must clock my nonplussed reaction, because she adds, "I'm told it stands for *airbed and breakfast*. But there were proper beds in all the rooms, so I don't fully understand the 'airbed' part."

She examines me again. I'm not proud of myself, but I bring my walking cane around from my back and lean on it heavily.

The kindness in Margie's eyes multiplies.

"Come on in and have yourself a round of tea and biscuits," she says.

The explanations take a while. Margie knew nothing at all about Kestrel Productions or *Escapism*. By the time she stops force-feeding us Battenberg cake, we've already used up the most of our first hour on the island. Even someone as mild as Ted has his limits, so I'm nervy about asking him to stump up even more cash to make Noah hang around for even longer.

Anyway, after a good deal of head-nodding and charm, Margie's happy to let us roam.

We visit each of the downstairs rooms in turn, and Ted records Dolly's reactions as we enter each one. There's a cosy double sitting room, with sofas in the first part and a big TV in the next – Dolly tells us that it used to be a single big room. Then there's a dining room that appears to be in regular use, and which Dolly says is more or less untouched. Across an echoey flagstoned lobby are two doors, one marked *Billiard Room* but containing only an Ikea table and on it a half-finished jigsaw of puppies, the other leading to a huge hall with a balcony and a high ceiling. It's decked out as a proper medieval banqueting hall, with a long oak table in the middle and candelabra stands dotted all around, and the ceiling is painted with an elaborate design of roses and thorns. It's an absurd space – this building's nothing close to medieval, and what's the use of a room this large in a building with surprisingly few other usable rooms? But maybe Margie and her husband are secret role-play freaks, spending their weekends wearing armour with their mates.

It's all useful data, I suppose. With Dolly's commentary I have a much clearer picture of the activities of the *Escapism* contestants, which will all be helpful as I add meat to the bones of my podcast.

But it's hardly a scoop.

"What about upstairs?" I say.

Dolly shakes her head. "I can't see why that'd be useful. And you've seen what Margie's done to the sitting room. Bedrooms would be even higher on the refurb hitlist."

Instead, she leads us to the right of the foot of the staircase and pushes through a door to what must once have been the servants' quarters. On the right are five identical, plain doors. She opens the second one along. It's filled with cleaning stuff – mops, buckets, a hoover – and heavy-duty shelving containing loads of paint tins with drips on their sides.

"I'm being indulgent," Dolly says apologetically. "This was my room. It's hard to imagine this being a bedroom now, isn't it?"

Without waiting for a response – she really isn't doing much to provide useful audio material – she heads back the way we came. She strides past the farmhouse kitchen, which served as the production suite during filming of *Escapism*. Margie's in there now, baking.

The next room along is an old-fashioned study with wooden panels on all the walls. As soon as she goes inside, Dolly lets out a big sigh.

I recognise this room from the videos I've been sent. This is where the contestants were interviewed.

Dolly doesn't speak, so I'm the one who provides the commentary for Ted's recording. Maybe I'll have to re-record it later because of the bumping noises Dolly makes the whole time, moving furniture around. She shifts an armchair to the centre of the room, then she drags the tall chair from its position before a Victorian writing desk, placing it opposite the armchair, all the way up against the far wall, in front of a door that must lead directly into the kitchen. Then she sits on it.

I describe the setup for the benefit of the recording. Then I say, "So this was where you spent most of your time, Dolly? You sitting over there, the contestant here—" I sit on the armchair to play the part. "With a temporary wall and a one-way window between you, is that right?"

She nods. I make a circling gesture with one hand, encouraging her to speak. Ted hurries forward to point the mic at her.

"That's right," Dolly says. She stretches out her arms, miming touching objects at waist level. "The console was here in front of me, the camera fixed to one side. I'd divide my attention between the levels, and my notes on each contestant, and the contestant themself, sitting exactly where you are."

"How many interviews do you suppose you conducted?"

"Not nearly as many as I was meant to. Most of the contestants gave up coming here. They didn't trust us, I guess. They treated us like parents."

I pause at this odd comment. "Don't children normally trust their parents, or confide in them?"

Dolly's expression darkens. "No idea. I certainly didn't. I hated my parents. My life only really started in my early teens, after they died." Her eyes glaze, and I've no idea what to say in response to a confession like that. Then she shakes off her sombre mood. "Anyway, we couldn't force the contestants to speak to us. Some of them, I never did get an insight into their thoughts. And if you can't achieve that, then what sort of a show have you got, really?"

It occurs to me that the same issues apply to me, to my podcast. Dolly was right – there's nothing to find here on the island. All I've got to work with is Dolly herself.

"How about we play the parts now?" I suggest.

Dolly seems lost in thought. She's looking at me but

not really seeing me.

"What?" she says eventually.

"You be you," I say, "and I'll be the contestant. We can conduct a confessional interview."

Dolly nods slowly.

"How are you feeling today?" she asks in a half-hearted tone. Then she frowns. "My voice doesn't sound right. It was always disguised, and had this weird metallic ring to it, even here in the studio area."

"We can add that effect later," I say. I look at Ted, who nods.

"Okay. How are you feeling today?"

"A bit frustrated," I say, honestly enough. Once again, the similarities between my situation and the contestants' situations seems too great to ignore. "I feel like I'm not getting anywhere, really. It's maddening, the knowledge that there's this big mystery out there somewhere, if I could only piece the clues together..."

"Are you being Rhea now?"

I blink. "No. A contestant."

"Which one?"

These days, there are really only two contestants that occupy my thoughts. Ben and Dez, who either found the prize money and escaped from Red Cliffs Island, or... I don't know. Or they didn't.

I tried to contact their families. Dez's parents claimed they hadn't seen Dez in six months, but that they'd learnt not to fret about them going AWOL for long periods. Ben's ex-wife had no information about his whereabouts, and told me he doesn't have any other family at all.

"Ben Parrish," I say.

Dolly just stares at me for a long while. Then her eyes lift up and she looks around the room. Her hands are like talons gripping the edges of her chair.

Abruptly, she stands, knocking into Ted's mic as she

does. She glares at him as though it was his fault.

"I need some air," she says.

*

Dolly isn't in the courtyard, where I expected her to be.

"Where do you think she went?" Ted asks.

"Dunno. Let's look around." I set off around the side of the building.

Ted walks alongside me. I can sense him glancing at me, at my cane clacking on the cobbles. It's a shock to me too, to realise just how slow I am at getting around on uneven ground.

"I could go on ahead and check things out?" he says. He seems oddly eager. "You can wait here."

I shake my head. "Don't you dare go without me. And keep recording."

As we make our way slowly around the mansion, two buildings come into view. The first is more modern than the mansion, looking very out of place. I figure it must be the poolhouse where Mira Qureshi was injured. Ted makes his way down the grassy slope to its door, then points at the padlock hanging from its handle.

I push on towards a smaller building which must be the groundskeeper's cottage.

I point with my cane. "That's where Axel Griffin was staying," I say. With difficulty, I make it up the three steps to its door. It's locked. I can't see through any of the windows from this position. I look around and see a barrel lying on its side. No chance I'm getting up on that, in my condition.

"Reckon you could get up onto that to see inside?" I ask Ted.

He looks at it doubtfully.

"Go on," I say. "For the podcast."

285

I take his sound recorder and hold the mic in his direction. If he falls off the barrel, we might at least score ourselves a blooper.

Ted's not in great shape himself. He's panting like mad by the time he's pushed the barrel into place and heaved himself up onto it. His arms windmill for balance, then he grips the sill of the nearest window.

"What can you see in there?" I ask.

"It just looks normal."

I grunt in annoyance. "This is *audio*, Ted. Describe it."

"I don't know. A bed. A sofa and coffee table in an adjoining room."

"Is the bed made up, or messy?"

"It's neat."

"Has it been redecorated?"

"How can I possibly know that? I don't know what it looked like back then."

"Does the decor look new?"

He hesitates, then says, "Just clean. *Lagom.*"

"What?"

"It's a Swedish term. Simplicity and balance in the home." When I still look blank, he adds, "A bit like the concept of *hygge*? You must have heard of that."

"Nope. You sure know a lot about Sweden, Ted."

He doesn't reply.

It occurs to me that I know barely anything about Ted's life before he took up teaching at Leeds Beckett uni a handful of months ago. All he's told me is that he's worked on lots of TV shows, and a few indie films, but nothing very high-profile. In that case, why does he warrant the showy title of 'guest lecturer'? And was any of his sound work in Sweden, meaning he might have crossed paths with people who work for Helmedia?

As I lower the mic I hear Ted struggling to get down from the barrel behind me. My attention's fixed on something a hundred metres or so beyond the cottage. There are odd shapes sticking up from the grassland, like spindly standing stones.

As I hobble towards it, I keep looking in all directions, hoping to spot Dolly. But she's nowhere to be seen.

From somewhere behind me, Ted shouts, "Rhea! Wait! Come back!"

What's he so antsy about, all of a sudden?

Despite my slow pace, he takes a while to catch up. We both stare at the dark struts emerging from a heap of blackened timber.

"This must be the barn," Ted says.

I turn to look at him in surprise. He must have been paying more attention to the details of the filming than I'd realised. Dolly told me about the abandoned maze task when she and I met face to face, when Ted wasn't there. I suppose one of us must have referred to it during the slow journey to Red Cliffs in Ted's battered yellow Volvo.

"Why did you try to stop me coming over here?" I ask.

Ted gestures vaguely at my cane. "The ground's really bumpy. I was worried you'd trip."

It's a weak excuse, but I wave it away, no longer interested.

I press the record button of my handheld recorder and speak into it. "It's a dismal sight, here at the northern tip of Red Cliffs Island. The mansion's behind me, and in front of me is only the North Sea, grey and vast and forbidding." I already feel pretty good about my off-the-cuff intro. "That, and the charred remains of a building, which is little more than ashes. The fact that the building materials are all wooden indicate that this was once the barn – the very barn where the *Escapism* contestants conducted their fourth task, in which a complex maze collapsed after Victor Okojie attempted to cheat. But that doesn't explain what happened to the barn itself."

Then, with a gasp of realisation, I say, "In the video of Cécile Guillaume in the interview room, she mentioned a fire. And one side of her face was dark, as if it was covered in soot."

I turn to face Ted.

"I need you to poke around in there," I say, pointing.

He stares at the debris. "It could be dangerous. Anyway, our time's nearly up."

"That's exactly my point," I say, though I only mean the second part of what he said. "This might be the last thing we get to check out. Just a quick look, Ted."

I hold the mic up to record the sounds of him shifting beams aside, along with his piggy grunts of exertion.

"Found anything?" I ask.

He shakes his head.

"Remember this is *audio*, Ted. And keep looking."

He does, though it's pretty half-hearted. After a while, he freezes. For a few seconds, he just stares at the ground.

"What have you found?" I ask eagerly.

He hesitates. In a voice that's probably too quiet for the mic to pick up, he says, "Nothing. Just more wood, and ashes. There's nothing. We should go."

But his face looks even paler than usual. His mouth twitches. He's keeping something from me.

He tries to protest as I pick my way over the uneven beams, holding my cane in both hands like a tightrope walker. The beams rock dangerously as I put my weight on them.

Ted's standing in front of a heap in what must have been more or less the centre of the barn. Before I can begin to describe the sight for the benefit of the podcast, I see what he's been staring at, beneath the biggest beam.

Something beneath it flashes white in the sunlight.

My breath catches.

I remember the sound recorder.

"Beneath the beams of the destroyed barn," I begin, "I can see…" But then I trail off.

It can't be. Can it? I edge closer, peering at the white strut amongst the blackened ones.

Say what you see, Rhea.

"A bone," I manage to say. "And… I think it might be human."

Six months earlier

Ben

The instant I walk into the hall of tasks, it's clear that my insight into the nature of Task 6 is worthless. Anyone can see it's a quiz. There are two long tables for the teams to sit at, and between them a sort of bulky red desk for the quiz show host. Behind it is a tall panel emblazoned with the word *ESCAPISM* in glitzy block capitals, and surrounding the word are images formed out of curved neon tubes. There's a hot air balloon, a mountain peak, a wonky parasol and an odd collection of curly fronds that might be either a cactus or underwater coral.

Axel's missing, and after a quick check I realise that so are Dez, Aura and Doc Leaf. Victor's are skulking around the host's desk, probably searching for question cards, watched on by Ralphie, who's leaning on the table for support. They're not acting as though they've found anything useful.

"What's it all about, do you think?" Sasha asks me.

I shrug. "It's about Imogen having run out of more interesting ideas for tasks."

Sasha laughs. "Agreed. Quizzes are hardly what I thought I'd signed up for when I sent in my application. Still, you'll do all right, won't you?"

I glance warily at her. Is she hinting that she knows I have form as a quiz-show finalist? But nothing in her expression suggests that. She's just making a dig about me being a nerd.

I point at the neon pictures. "My guess is the quiz will be about far-flung destinations where you might do those sorts of activities. You know, holidays as a type of escapism. So I haven't got a chance. I'm not well-travelled."

Sasha nods gravely. "Then maybe I'll get myself on the other team."

Now Victor's approaching contestants in turn, asking a single question before moving on. Behind him, I see Ralphie take something offered to him by Ruth. A compact mirror. Together, Victor and a stumbling Ralphie return to the quizmaster's area, and Victor begins fiddling with one of the neon signs, trying to clamp the mirror beneath one end of it.

Sasha groans.

"What are they playing at?" I ask.

"They're cheating. They're hoping to read Axel's quiz answers in the mirror."

"That won't work. Will it?"

Sasha shrugs. "Dunno. But what's clear to me is that nobody cares. Nobody cares if any of us cheat. If anything, it's encouraged."

"Then what hope do we have?" I say.

What I really mean is, what hope do *I* have? I've basically spent my whole life prepping for game shows. Almost all of my social interactions are defined by *rules*. If there are no rules, I'm lost.

Other contestants have noticed Victor and Ralphie's antics, then they look upwards, as if searching for cameras. They're all be thinking the same thing: isn't anyone going to stop this?

The fact that there are only two tables suggests we'll be split into two teams – a team of four and a team of five, if the remaining contestants actually show up. Putting aside the issue of earning more money for the prize fund – and the additions have been lowering with each successive task – the key that's awarded to the winning team will have to be shared between four or five. Given that everyone knows I've already got a key, there's no chance I'll be trusted to take possession of another one, even if I'm on the winning team.

"Will he even show up?" I say. I hardly notice I'm speaking out loud.

"Axel?" Sasha says. "I doubt it. He looked like he was on the verge of passing out this morning. If he's as wasted as that first thing in the morning, I don't suppose he'll improve throughout the day. He's a troubled guy."

"Then…" I don't finish my thought aloud.

Then this is a waste of time. Suddenly, I can see all the outcomes clearly. If Axel appears and manages to run the quiz – haphazardly, no doubt – then someone will torpedo the task again, voiding the contest. Alternatively, our host will remain absent, in which case nothing will happen at all. And even if all goes to plan, there'll be no key for me.

I'm heading to the door before I even realise I've made up my mind. A few contestants glance my way, but nobody tries to stop me from leaving.

Once I'm out of the room, the wind leaves my sails. I don't know where I ought to go.

I need to clear my head.

I stride to the front door and push my way outside, then gasp as the chill air hits me.

I move around the exterior of the mansion, the opposite direction to the way we were led to the poolhouse. This part of the building is blunter and even less decorative than the rest of it, as though visitors were never intended to come back here. In the distance I can see the groundskeeper's cottage, where I've been told Axel has been staying. I could go and knock on his door, have a man-to-man conversation about his unprofessional behaviour. Yeah, sure, Ben.

I stop when I reach a small archway that leads back into the mansion. This is new.

The door into the main building is locked. Through the small window I can see a blank corridor and a few featureless doors. This entrance must lead to the production area. Imogen and Dolly, the voice of the study, and whoever else works here, must have living quarters of their own, as well as a workspace.

There's another door, just inside the arch. Heavy oak rather than reinforced plastic.

The door clicks open at a push.

The large room is a kitchen. I suppose that in normal circumstances, the reason for the room being accessible from outside the mansion is because it would allow caterers to come back and forth, providing meals for large groups in the banquet hall.

It's clear that only one corner of the room has been in use recently. I see the remains of yesterday's almost inedible spaghetti bolognese in the pots stacked beside the sink. One side of the room is filled with pallets of cereal boxes and tins, along with a far greater number of crates filled with bottles of wine and spirits.

The kitchen island in the centre of the room is oddly empty, given the untidy stacks of dishes and supplies elsewhere. The only thing on it, in its direct centre, is one of those metal cloche domes that are used to keep food warm in fancy restaurants.

It seems significant, so I lift it up.

Beneath the metal dome are two ceramic figures. I've seen them before, or at least ones exactly like them. My ex-wife Carla was given a pair in a secret Santa once. They're salt and pepper shakers in the vague shape of figures, like two ghosts, one black and one white, with dotty eyes and vague stubby arms reaching out. When they're pressed together, they fit together almost seamlessly in a hug.

But these ones aren't pressed together. They're facing each other from either side of a line that spans the diameter of the area that was covered by the metal cloche. The line is made up of both salt and pepper. It's been applied carefully, so that the line of salt on the white ghost's side touches and runs precisely in parallel with the line of pepper on the black ghost's side.

I stare at it for twenty seconds, making sure I've taken in every aspect of the little scene.

Then I pick up both ghosts, hide them on a high shelf, and sweep the salt and pepper off the surface and onto the floor.

I feel ruthless and empowered. Clearly, the ghosts were some sort of clue, and nobody else will be getting it now.

But my sense of achievement fades only moments after I leave the kitchen.

Through the *other* door, the locked one that leads to the production area in the mansion, I see Doc Leaf. What's he doing in there?

I can't hear him, but I can see his lips moving as he walks along the short corridor. Seconds later, I see who he's talking to. I tell myself to duck before I'm seen, but it takes a few seconds for my body to obey the command.

Because it's a total shock to see that Doc Leaf is chatting to the director, Imogen Dorrien-Stewart.

Six months later

Rhea

Since the discovery of the charred bones on Red Cliffs Island, everything has changed. All three of us were silent on the journey to the mainland on Noah's boat, and then on most of the drive back to Leeds. Whenever I asked after her, Dolly only muttered about bad memories and about the whole trip being a bad idea. When I mentioned the burned barn, she stared at me, clearly having no idea what that was all about. I didn't mention it again.

Ted spoke even less than Dolly.

That's the thing that's been bothering me most. What's got into Ted?

The agreement was that he'd drop Dolly off at the train station, then me at my flat. But I got out when Dolly did. Once we were alone, I asked her outright what she thought of Ted.

She didn't answer at first. Then she said she hadn't really got to know him. When I pressed her, she agreed it was strange how much he'd changed on the return journey.

I told her what happened when Ted and I were exploring the island. When I'd headed to the northern tip of the island, and ended up finding the ashes of the barn.

Ted had shouted after me. He'd tried to stop me going there.

But… why? How could he know what we'd find?

Then, once we reached the barn, he tried to stop me from seeing the bones. I can see his panicked expression now, his pale face as he denied there was anything to see in the ashes at all.

It's pretty suspicious behaviour, that's what it is. Then there's the fact that Ted speaks Swedish. He even drives a bloody Volvo, a Swedish make.

There's something not right about Ted.

It's not just the Swedish stuff, and his behaviour on Red Cliffs. I've finally got around to checking his IMDb page, and his list of TV and film credits seems crazily short considering he's supposed to be an industry pro. In my paranoia I half expected to see *Escapism* listed, but it isn't – then again, the UK version doesn't appear on Axel Griffin's IMDb page, either.

But there's more. It was Ted who provided me with the police report about Lawrence Bunce's death, along with that odd claim about knowing somebody high up in the Northumbria Police. Very convenient.

Could he have orchestrated this whole thing? Was he the one sending me videos of footage from *Escapism,* from the off?

So here I am, in my flat, working alone again. I need to get the first episodes of the podcast out into the world, despite the fact that Ted begged me to hold on to them until we have more evidence, for fear of legal trouble.

I know I'm being self-centred, focusing on the podcast. I could call the police today, tell them about the bones in the barn. They'd have to take that seriously. But if I did, I know that nothing would happen. There's already been a cover-up, hasn't there? And the authorities wouldn't have any time for the convoluted backstory I'd provide. I'm aware how conspiratorial parts of my argument will sound.

I may be a nobody, but I have one specialism. I'm the world expert in *Escapism* and what happened on Red Cliffs Island. If anybody can pull together the clues to show what actually went down, it's me. Yes, I want to see justice done. But that means doing it properly. And I'd also quite like to create a hit podcast along the way.

Not having Ted around will make the first episode rougher around the edges. But most of my own segments have already been recorded, so at least I'll be audible. The next task is to capture audio from the video clips I've been sent by INSIDER. Clearly, the opening episode needs to end with Cécile's desperate plea to camera, so I focus on getting audio grabs from it. Then I turn my attention to the promo reel footage.

This was the first video I saw, the first inkling I ever had that *Escapism* existed. So it's strange that I haven't rewatched it since that day. When I set it running again, I'm reminded why I stayed away from it. The fast editing and flickering text makes my brain throb immediately. Forget migraines, the clip might easily provoke a seizure. I set my audio software recording, then I stare at the blank wall as the soundtrack's captured.

But I'll need to describe the visuals for the listeners. To avoid triggering my condition, I work through the footage in slow-mo, making notes about what I see. The overhead shot of the island, the contestants laughing, dancing, arguing, panicking. The footage of the beautiful twentysomethings swimming underwater in their skimpy cossies makes me pause. I think of Mira Qureshi's accident. Surely they wouldn't broadcast any parts of that task?

I scan the faces of the contestants, and to my surprise I don't recognise them.

I remind myself that this is only a promo reel. for the benefit of TV commissioners. When this was created, filming hadn't even begun.

I switch windows and set the audio playing. Without the distraction of the dizzying video clips, I can concentrate on the voices of the contestants as they shout commands at each other during the tasks.

Except I *still* can't understand them.

Because they're not speaking in English.

I'm no language expert, but I enjoy Scandi-noir TV shows as much as anyone. I'm pretty convinced that the contestants are gabbling in Swedish.

OK. Fair enough. These clips could have been taken from an earlier series of *Eskapism*, the Swedish version of the game show.

But that can't be right either.

I pause the video on a frame showing the block-pushing puzzle. The task is taking place in a hall with a high ceiling painted with roses and thorns. It's familiar, because I've seen it before. It's the banquet hall on Red Cliffs Island.

Which means that these can't be the Swedish contestants after all. They must be either actors, or members of the production team, testing the tasks before filming began. A sort of rehearsal.

So that's shock number one.

It's soon eclipsed by shock number two, which I receive when I freeze-frame on a group shot of the so-called 'contestants'.

Even within the big group shot, the expression on his face makes me shudder. His leering smile, like in every photo I've seen of him.

It's unmistakably Doc Leaf.

Six months earlier

Ben

I expect Imogen and Doc Leaf to pass through one of several doors I can see inside the production-team area of the mansion, so it takes me by surprise when I realise they're actually heading directly towards the outer door I'm hiding behind. I let out a little "Eep" sound, then I dart around the stone archway to stand behind it, panting with panic.

I hear the outer door open, then Imogen's and Doc Leaf's voices, mid-conversation.

"—a matter of simple professionalism," Imogen says.

Doc Leaf scoffs. "Professionalism is for the birds. I'm far more than simply professional."

In fact, I only know it's Doc Leaf because I saw him before I hid. From his voice alone, I'd never have been able to identify him. There's no trace of his slurred drawl, no trace of his stoner-lad attitude. His voice has risen almost an octave.

"That's all very well for you to say, but the fact is that your behaviour frequently comes across as threatening," Imogen says. "And with the situation here already so fragile, I'd really appreciate it if—"

"What did your producer request me to do?" Doc Leaf says. "Your man... Helm? Is that the funny name he goes by?"

Imogen hesitates. "I didn't actually participate in your hiring."

"But you know what he wanted of me. What I'm supposed to bring to this shabby production."

There's no reply.

Doc Leaf says, "Destabilisation. That was the word Helm used. My role is to be a destabilising force."

Maybe I'm just slow on the uptake, but it's only now that I really understand what I'm hearing. Doc Leaf is an act. An actor.

"Yes," Imogen says, "but—"

"And am I achieving that, Imogen?"

"Undoubtedly, Lawrence. But…"

"I prefer Mr Bunce."

Imogen pauses. "What I'm saying is that I'm sure Helm wouldn't wish you to turn it up to quite the level you have done."

"Ask him."

"What?"

"I understand he's able to watch all the footage you're creating here, live. Ask him if he's happy with my work so far."

More silence.

"I thought not," Doc Leaf – or rather, Lawrence Bunce – says. "Now, if there's nothing more you require of me, I think I'll take a stroll along the coastal path."

I press myself against the stonework as he ambles past my hiding place, whistling.

Aura

When my hand cramps, I abandon my copying and instead try to memorise the answers. A voice in my head keeps telling me I'm already too late, that the task has already started. Except it can't have, can it? Axel can't begin hosting the quiz without his question cards.

When he staggered out of the cottage, I pictured him going on a rampage, shooting people indiscriminately with the gun he was waving around earlier. But as far as I could see, he wasn't carrying it when he left, and he was jacketless, with nowhere to hide it. I have to believe he's stashed it away somewhere in the cottage.

I'm not proud of the fact that I didn't go into the mansion to check everyone's OK. Instead, I headed straight to the door of the cottage, which was hanging open. On the coffee table, next to a load of empty bottles, was a stack of prompt cards.

I didn't dare stay inside for long. I grabbed the stack of cards, along with a pen and paper. Then I retreated behind the cottage, which is where I am now, glancing up every few seconds to check Axel's not on his way back.

I push the scrap of paper into my pocket – I'm pretty sure I won't be able to read my hurried handwriting anyway – and concentrate on memorising the remaining answers. Machu Pichu, Peru. Benguerra Island, Mozambique. Burj Khalifa, Dubai. Cappadocia, Turkey. I remind myself I don't need to know all of them – in fact, if I did, it would only look suspicious. I just need to do better than the other contestants.

I rush back inside the cottage, plonk the cards back on the coffee table, then get the hell out.

I take the long way around the mansion, and I pass through the front door without meeting Axel. I take a calming, centring breath before I push open the door to the hall of tasks.

Any sense of relief that the task hasn't begun vanishes instantly. It's chaos in here. There's no sign of Axel, and contestants have gathered around Victor and Ralphie, shouting accusations. And there are a bunch of people missing. It's no surprise that Doc Leaf isn't here, but I can't see Ben or Dez either.

At this point, I can't assume the task will even take place. All my hard work learning the answers was for nothing.

What's more urgent is the fact that contestants are roaming around the building, getting up to who knows what. Even though I tell myself that I've got one of the four keys needed to open the vault, I can't shake the idea that they're emptying it right at this moment.

But that's not the only reason I decide to ditch the quiz and stride to the study.

Axel's unpredictable behaviour might easily spoil everything, at any moment. What really pisses me off is that I haven't had a chance to really perform for the cameras yet, to establish myself as the most memorable contestant. To make myself a star.

The study is the one place I can go to make sure I'm on camera.

Dez

I spin around as the door to the study is thrown open. I try to rearrange my features into an innocent expression, but I know I'm failing to disguise my guilt.

"What are you up to?" Aura demands.

I fumble to rehang the painting and climb down from the sideboard. I wrap my arms around myself.

"Nothing," I say.

I wince as Aura's gaze strays to the armchair. Before I can move, she darts forward and snatches up the square card with the picture of the needle and thread on it.

She stares at it, then at me, then up at the framed picture I was messing with when she came in. Her eyes take in the other pictures, which all show more or less the same scene. Medieval peasants with pitchforks, all busy creating enormous piles of hay.

"A needle in a haystack," she says triumphantly.

My head hangs. Nice one, Dez. You get a glimmer of an advantage over the others, and then you squander it immediately. A typical act of self-sabotage.

"Don't tell anyone else," I say as I take the card from her. I hate the pleading tone in my voice.

Aura considers this. "I'm not sure it matters. Things are falling apart out there. I think they'll pull the plug before long."

We both turn to look at the black window.

Aura gestures at it with her thumb. "Is anyone in there?"

I don't reply, and neither does Study.

Aura lets out a long groan. "The moment you *want* to be watched, all the cameras are looking the other way."

303

She seems pretty vulnerable right now. I could try to comfort her. Or, you know, I could use it to my advantage.

"Aura," I say. "I'd really appreciate it if you could keep the clue to yourself. I worked hard for it."

I see her expression harden. Perhaps she's taken it as an insult, a suggestion that she doesn't work hard for things herself. I mean, that's almost certainly true. With a face like that, a body like that, I bet she's had a lifetime of people handing her whatever she wants.

I don't let myself dwell on the fact that Ben should have won the game of hide-and-seek, not me. I shouldn't have the key, or the clue.

"We could form an alliance," I say.

"I'm not going to show you *my* clue," Aura says quickly.

I raise an eyebrow. "You have one too, then? You have a key?" My mind races, recalling the tasks so far. She must have coerced somebody into giving up their prize. My guess is poor innocent Ralphie.

She doesn't reply. But her hand goes to the pocket of her stonewash jeans, which are so tight that I can see a clear outline of a key. Involuntarily, as if we're gunfighters in a western, my right hand goes to my own pocket, but not the one containing my key. Muscle memory makes me pull out Priya's lighter and do what I always do when I'm tense: I flick the spark wheel. To my surprise, a flame licks up from it – I'd forgotten Doc Leaf filled it with lighter fluid.

Aura stares at the lighter, then at me.

The awkward moment is interrupted by the door of the study swinging open again.

Ben looks like a startled rabbit. It doesn't necessarily suggest guilt, though. He's probably just not used to finding himself in a small room with two other people. His sad-sack demeanour always screams *divorced loner dad*.

"Oh," he says, flustered as always. "Sorry."

"Have you come to unburden yourself to our robot overlord?" I ask.

Ben's eyes flick to the dark window, just for a second. His cheeks flush red.

"Yeah. No. I was just..." He turns back to the door.

I remind myself that Ben has a key. Of the three of us, he's the only legitimate task winner.

"You wanted to check out the vault?" I say.

Ben nods eagerly. "Yeah. I know it's daft, without the other three keys."

Perhaps this is my chance to put pressure on Aura.

"For what it's worth," I say, "I'd be interested in teaming up. Our two keys together gets us halfway to the prize."

As I sidle over to the vault, I pull the key from my back pocket. I slip it into the top-left keyhole and turn it. It makes a satisfying click, but I can feel the spring mechanism pushing back. Without keys in the other locks at the same time, the vault can't be opened.

There's a dreamy look in Ben's eyes. He's caught up in the fantasy of opening the safe. He rummages in his pockets, then drifts over to the vault and puts his own key in the top-right keyhole. It's only now that I realise that keyhole has a red outline.

His nose wrinkles. Then he grimaces.

"It won't turn," he says.

He pulls the key out, looks at it, then fits it into the keyhole below the first one. It turns and clicks. He tries the bottom-left keyhole. Turn, click. Then he puts it back into the top-right one. Nothing. He takes the key out again, peering at its serrations.

"Let me try?" Aura says.

Ben jerks away from her. "No. You'll steal it."

Aura lets out a grunt of annoyance. Then she pulls out

the key from her own pocket. Ben watches in amazement as she puts it in the keyhole with the red outline. It won't turn.

Thinking aloud, I say, "But if all the keys that are won in tasks fit in *these* three keyholes, and not *that* one…"

Aura finishes my thought. "Then there must be a different way of getting the fourth key."

We exchange glances. Ben notices.

"Do you guys know something?" he says.

"Do *you* know something?" I counter. "You came in here looking all suspicious."

"What's your clue?" Aura asks him.

Ben's forehead wrinkles. "What do you know about clues, as opposed to keys?" Then he smacks his forehead and groans. "I'm an idiot. There's more than just a key in each envelope, isn't there? Ralphie mentioned something about there being keys, plural – he must have been referring to a clue that is *another* sort of key. And Sasha must have taken the clue we won."

Aura points at me and says, "Dez has one. And a lighter, too, for some reason."

Without thinking, I blurt out, "Aura's got a clue in her pocket."

Then we're all staring at each other in turn. Our gunfight has become a three-way standoff.

And as Hollywood blockbusters have shown us, this sort of situation tends not to end well.

There's only one smart way out.

"We could pool them," I suggest.

Ben raises an eyebrow.

Aura snorts. "It's easy for you to say that. Your clue doesn't tell you anything more than to come in here."

I grimace at her revealing so much, and so clumsily. But I don't look away from Ben. My guess is that his clue hasn't told him any more than that, either. He was eager to get into the study, but he doesn't know what to do now that

306

he's here.

Another thought occurs to me. Another deduction courtesy of my psychology degree.

I say to Aura, "You wouldn't be having this conversation if you knew how to interpret your clue. You've hit a dead end."

She flinches. I've nailed it.

Ben chews his cheek, then says, "I'll share if you will."

Aura nods. "Let's start with Dez, because their clue is basically worthless now."

She's right, so I show Ben my card with the picture of the needle and thread. "Needle goes with haystack. But I've checked behind all the pictures, and there's nothing there." I turn to Aura. "Your turn. What's your clue?"

Aura hesitates for a second or two before reaching into her pocket. She pulls out a tiny squarish object that at first glance looks like a table from a doll's house. Then I see that the letters *esc* are printed on its flat face. Escape.

"It might not even be a clue," Aura says. "It might just be a shit joke."

We both turn to Ben.

"Show us yours," I say. "Remember, we're an alliance now."

"I can't," Ben says. When Aura takes a step towards him, he adds quickly, "Because it's something I saw, and couldn't bring with me."

"Go on," I say.

Ben gestures at the black window. "Do you know if there's anyone in there?"

"Don't think so. Why?"

"Because the clue I found showed two people positioned either side of a wall – one side black, the other white. It can only be the one-way glass, wouldn't you say?"

Aura and I take this in.

Then all three of us turn to stare at the black window.

Dolly

I watched the whole thing. The whole series of deductions. For a while, I almost forgot I was a member of the production team. I felt more like a member of the TV audience, willing Ben, Aura and Dez to interpret their clues. Seeing as nobody's told me the chain of logic that'll lead to the prize money, this is the only way I'm going to find out.

So it's a shock to find all three of them staring at me. I tell myself they can't actually see me. If they're looking at anything, it's their own reflections.

But their stares are only part of what's freaking me out right now.

I can't take my eyes off the little object Aura's holding in her perfectly manicured hand.

The Escape key from a computer keyboard.

I tear my eyes away from the three contestants, and I look down at the computer keyboard on the desk in front of me. The one with the space bar that rocks every time I press it, and which is missing a couple of its keys.

Including the Escape key.

Ben

When I hear the click, at first I don't know what's made it. Then I have the off-putting impression that the dimensions of the room are changing.

Then I realise that the dimensions of the room *have* changed. Part of the false wall next to the black window has swung open. Nothing in this mansion is what is seems. First Doc Leaf, now the architecture.

I hear a gulp, but I can't tell whether it came from Aura or Dez.

"Why do I feel so creeped out?" Aura whispers.

Dez takes each of our hands and we move awkwardly to the new doorway.

The space on its other side is darker than the main part of study. The only light is from a lamp with red cellophane covering its bulb, reminding me of old-fashioned photographic darkrooms.

I'm curious to see behind the scenes of the show. I crane my neck around the door frame to see a desk with camera on a stand, a computer and two monitors. One of them's blank and the other shows a static view of the armchair in the study, a live camera feed.

Dez and Aura seem far less interested in seeing how *Escapism* is produced. They're looking directly at the only other thing of interest in the tiny space. A young woman with messy fair hair and freckles visible even in the red light, or maybe because of it.

"You must be Study," Dez says.

The woman nods. "Yes, but I suppose you might as well call me—"

"Dolly," I say.

Dolly blushes and nods, but doesn't meet my eye. I wonder how much she remembers about our heart-to-heart conversation. Are we friends now? I remind myself she was high on painkillers at the time.

"Why've you let us in here?" Aura asks.

Dolly hesitates. "I think I can help you solve the puzzle."

Perhaps we *are* friends. Even so, it's strange that she seems as much in the dark about the clues as we are.

I say, "But why would you—"

She interrupts me. "I think I'm *supposed* to help you."

Dez folds their arms over their chest. "That doesn't make sense. Now that you've let us in here, this isn't even being recorded. Why would Imogen allow us to solve the puzzle away from the cameras?"

I look at the monitor screen. As far as I can tell, the study camera isn't recording. Does that mean there won't even be footage of us reaching our deductions?

I shake my head. "There's too much riding on this moment. There must be other cameras in the study, not just the one behind the window for interviews. And if being in here is part of the plan…" I trail off.

I reach for the desk lamp, pull away the red cellophane, then turn it to point up at the ceiling. I let out a "Ha!" of satisfaction when I spot a tiny glinting camera lens in the corner of the room, just like the one I found in my bedroom.

Dolly's hand goes to her mouth in shock. She had no idea she's been watched the whole time, just like the rest of us.

Dez reaches out to take her by the hand. "What makes you think you can help us?"

"The computer key."

We all look at the Escape key Aura's holding.

Then, moving as one, we look at the computer

keyboard on the desk. Sure enough, it's missing its Escape key.

Dolly sits at the desk, then wiggles the mouse to wake up the second screen that until now has been blank. A password prompt appears.

I watch carefully as she types in her password: *UNDGA*.

The word is so unusual that I say it out loud: "Undga. What's that?"

Dolly replies casually, "It's Swedish – this whole interface was used on the original version of the show. 'Undga' just means 'escape' or 'evade'. So I've been told, anyway."

On the screen appears a blocky text interface that looks like something from the 1980s.

Dolly takes the Escape key from Aura, then presses it into its correct place on the keyboard.

She lets out a little "Oof" as something juts out from beneath the desk. A drawer has slid open.

It contains only one item. A key. It's identical to ours, except there's a red ring around its middle.

We all rush back into the main part of the study.

In our excitement, it takes a while for us to arrange ourselves so we can each insert our keys. Dolly's standing on the armchair to reach the red keyhole over my head, and she keeps looking down at me with wide eyes.

We all turn our keys. And just like that, the door of the vault opens.

There's no prize money inside. I suppose I should have expected more trickery.

But this doesn't seem like a trick.

It's just… scary.

Because the only thing inside the safe is a pistol.

Six months later

Rhea

Things have been moving fast. Literally.

When I was a kid, I liked nothing more than to move fast. I'd streak around our little cul-de-sac on my skateboard or roller-skates. In the woodland behind my house, I'd bunny hop from one shale hill to another on my BMX. At night I dreamed of bullet trains and bungee jumps.

Since the accident, I haven't been able to handle anything faster than a brisk stroll. It's a curse tailored precisely for me. What did I do to deserve it?

So I'm not handling it well, this frantic dash across the country at top speed. I've had my eyes squeezed tight shut most of the way. The insides of my eyelids have been streaked with fireworks and flailing ghosts.

Even so, each time Ted slows down, I tell him to hit the accelerator. You'd never have thought his rusty old Volvo could move this fast.

Hold on, you're saying. Woah. You're saying: Rhea, what the hell are you doing in a car with Ted? Ted the Mightily Suspicious, as we've come to know him?

I don't have a choice.

At least, that was my kneejerk reaction.

What would you have done?

Usually my life is confined to the four walls of my little flat. Any exciting experience is strictly virtual, taking place in chatrooms or in videogame worlds. If something urgent crops up, I flick to another open window and deal with it.

Meatspace – the real world – isn't like that. You actually have to move around in it. It takes time. And if you never got your license and your punishing migraines mean you never will, you're going to need a driver.

Plus, Ted's the source of this particular lead.

I know, I know. *Veeeery* suspicious, just like the magically appearing police report. All the same, I have to follow any lead right now, because I'm not exactly rolling in them.

What happened is this:

Around lunchtime Ted banged on my door, calling my name.

He said he had information about Axel Griffin. He'd somehow tracked Axel down via a complicated trail of financial records originating in Sweden. Bonds and loans, the sort of thing I've never understood and never will. Ted looked so proud of himself, like he was handing in homework that he already knew would get top marks.

Ted said he hadn't found a phone number, so we couldn't just call Axel.

My choice was straightforward. Follow the lead, or don't.

Of course I did. I'm Rhea Hildred.

Following the lead meant begging Ted to drive us all the way down south to a village called Ashurst, in the New Forest.

Perhaps the fact that Ted was willing to do it, at short notice, should have raised another red flag.

I'll admit it. I don't know anything about Ted, really. I keep replaying his casual use of Swedish words when we were on Red Cliffs together. And I keep thinking about his missing film and TV credits. And him trying to stop me looking at the bones in the ashes of the barn.

313

The fact is that Ted appeared on my radar only a few months ago. Before that, he could have been doing anything at all. For example, he might easily have spent the early part of the summer on a little Northumbrian island called Red Cliffs. And if he was, he was definitely hidden from sight, because Dolly doesn't know Ted from any other guy. And if he was there, then he might have been responsible for all sorts of things.

So yes, I may have made a colossal mistake, getting in a car with him.

I've taken precautions, at least. Or rather, *precaution*, singular. As soon as when we set off, while Ted was busying singing along to 'Mr. Blue Sky' by Electric Light Orchestra, I texted Dolly and told her about everything that's happened today.

She said exactly what you've been saying. *Rhea, you idiot. What the fuck were you thinking?*

But having told her gave me some peace of mind, all the same. If Ted's taking me to some remote corner of the country to murder me, at least I've made sure he won't get away with it.

*

After we arrive in Ashurst, it takes us ages to locate the cottage. Google Maps keeps flaking out, and the houses are spread out, and they just have twee names rather than proper addresses. In the end, the place we want turns out to be way outside the village, away from what passes for civilisation around here.

Farrier Cottage is not only remote, it's almost completely hidden in a dense cluster of trees. It's basically a wreck. Its white-painted walls are pockmarked where the plaster's fallen away. There's scaffolding on one side, but rather than suggesting improvements in progress, it looks as though the scaffolding is stopping the building from collapsing.

After driving along the narrow lane, the only place Ted can stop the car is behind the cottage, beside an outhouse with a big metal garage door. I shudder when I realise that even if somebody thrashed through the undergrowth to find the cottage, they wouldn't spot Ted's Volvo, despite its eye-wateringly bright yellow paint job.

I know, I know. None of this bodes well.

All the same, I'm grateful we've arrived. My head's throbbing, and bright lights are still whooshing in my vision as if we're still hurtling along on the motorway.

"D'you need to take a moment?" Ted asks.

He puts his hand on my arm. I shudder and shake him off.

"I'm fine," I say, opening the door and basically falling out of the car.

I stare up at the treetops swaying above me. I count to ten. Then I nod, telling myself firmly that I'm fine, and I head to the door of the cottage.

I knock.

I wait.

"Doesn't look like he's here," Ted says.

I don't make a snarky response like I would usually. I don't know which Ted I'm dealing with now. Mild-mannered-lecturer Ted, or possibly-just-possibly-a-killer Ted?

At least he doesn't seem to want to hack me to bits just yet.

"Then we wait," I say.

I clamber into the passenger seat of the car, then close my eyes. After zooming along on a motorway for so long my broken brain is exhausted, and I can't help falling—

*

I didn't mean to sleep, but it's done me the power of good. When I open my eyes again, my vision's clear. I can think again.

Ted's not in the car. The sunlight has dimmed a lot – it must be dusk, which means I must have slept for more than an hour. I can make out Ted's silhouette, a few dozen metres away. It keeps bobbing, and one of his arms stretches out like when he's delivering one of his lectures.

I reach over and flick on the car headlights.

Ted turns, shielding his eyes. Now I see he's been talking to somebody, a man.

It's Axel Griffin.

I jump out of the car, leaving the keys in the ignition and my walking cane on the back seat. The headlights pick out the falling leaves and the dust in the air. My body still feels sluggish, like I'm underwater. I think of Mira Qureshi, struggling to breathe. Then I think of Ben Parrish and Dez Votel. One of them might have drowned in the sea, the other burned in the barn.

I should definitely have collected my cane from the car. It takes me an age to hobble over to meet Axel and Ted.

Axel reaches out a hand and I shake it.

He looks different to the pictures I found online. Sure, his jaw is strong and square, and his teeth are good. But his grey hair's sticking up all over, and his forehead's full of creases, and he has a ratty beard struggling to establish itself across all parts of his face equally.

"Your friend has reassured me that you are not from Helmedia," Axel says haltingly, like he's not used to speaking to people, or at least speaking in English. I remind myself he's Swedish. "Perhaps you would like to come inside."

As I nod in agreement, I glimpse what he's holding in his other hand. Swinging loosely from his gloved fingers is the carcass of a squirrel, along with a hangman's noose of thick wire.

316

Six months earlier

Dez

It takes longer than you might expect for the production team to respond to what's happened. I've been trying to imagine the conversation between Dolly and Imogen, and whoever else is hidden behind the locked doors and one-way mirrors. And I've gone through all the permutations about what the gun in the safe might signify. Dolly didn't know what the clues meant, which means she's unlikely to have an inkling about anything even more devious going on.

But I always comes back to the same conclusion: this entire game show is messed up. Everyone seems to be in the dark.

Everyone except the person who took the money, of course. The same person who put a fucking *pistol* in the safe for us to find.

Then there's the issue of the gun itself. It still bugs me that we didn't give it to Dolly, to hand over to someone more senior.

But seniority means nothing any more.

All the same, if I can't trust anybody here, why should I trust Ben? Sure, he was pretty convincing. First he clicked open the chamber of the pistol and showed us that there were no bullets inside. Then he insisted that he could be trusted to hide it away. I mean, fair enough, I can't imagine anyone less dangerous than nerdy Ben. But there's still a gun in this building, and I don't have my eyes on it.

317

And a knife, too. We never did find Doc Leaf's knife.

An hour after our shenanigans in the study, Imogen summons all the contestants to the sitting room. Some of the contestants have been in the hall of tasks this whole time, waiting patiently for Task 6 to begin.

In general, we're an unhappy lot right now. We all jostle each other on the sofas. After four days in close proximity, we're all craving personal space. Only Victor and Ruth look content to squeeze up together.

One person is getting their personal space, though. Doc Leaf is sprawled out, eyes fluttering closed every so often. He looks utterly wasted. Here's hoping it means he won't tell everyone about my magpie tendencies.

Me and Ben keep exchanging nervous glances. How much is Imogen going to confess to?

"Where is Axel?" Cécile asks in an innocent tone. "And Aura?"

"Indisposed," Imogen says. It's unclear whether she means just one of them, or both. Hurriedly, she goes on, "Thank you all for coming here at short notice." She sounds as though she's running a village-hall meeting, not a game show. "Now, I'm sure it can't have escaped your attention—" she winces, probably due to her accidental use of the word 'escape' "—that things haven't quite been going according to plan today."

"You mean the whole bloody time we've been here," Victor says.

Imogen hesitates, probably searching for the right phrase to avoid blame. "What I'd say is—"

Doc Leaf's eyes are still closed, but that doesn't mean he's not paying attention. He says, "Don't you dare pull the plug." His tone is firm and surprisingly coherent.

Imogen doesn't have a chance to respond. Ralphie wails, "I used up all my holiday allocation to come here!" It's hard to believe that *that's* his complaint, as opposed to the fact that he's fucked up the entire left side of his body falling into a cellar, but there you go.

"I quit my job at the Co-op," Ruth says.

Imogen presses on. "What I'd say is that we've all had a lot of fun, and—"

"I wouldn't call it fun," I say, interrupting her.

Imogen won't even look at me. She must be terrified I'll bring up what happened to Mira.

"Are the cameras still on?" Cécile asks.

"Filming has been paused," Imogen says. Her eyes flick to Doc Leaf, who's still lolling with his eyes closed.

"Paused, meaning it might restart?" Ben asks.

Imogen shakes her head. "I should say stopped. Filming has stopped. We're done here."

Groans come from all around. Not all of them sound bad-tempered, though. Clearly, some of us relish the idea of getting off this stupid island.

"So will we just pack up and go?" Ruth asks, her eyes flicking to Victor.

"Sorry," Imogen says. "You can't leave immediately. The next boat won't arrive until the morning, at dawn."

For some reason, *this* is what seems to break everyone. We've all been tolerating each other's company for the sake of the game, in the knowledge that cameras have been trained on us the whole time. Without either of those things, what's the point?

Within seconds, Imogen is swallowed by a tide of angry contestants rising from their seats, shouting their demands.

Six months later

Rhea

"How come you retreated here, of all places, after *Escapism* tanked?" I ask.

Axel shakes his head. He looks like a sad old bloodhound. "I should have returned to Sweden. But my pride and my shame did not allow it."

"Your shame at failing to break into British primetime TV?"

He hesitates. "Yes, of course."

"And nothing else?"

He stops munching his piece of toast. When he offered Ted and I a snack to go with our weak tea, the only thing he could find in the kitchen cupboards was stale bread. Even the tea was a stretch, though he could have offered us any number of spirits and liqueurs. The fact that he's living like a vagrant makes me wonder if he's even renting this cottage, or whether he's just squatting here.

"What are you insinuating?" he asks. The final word seems to cause him difficulty, and I wonder whether it's due to the language barrier or whether he's drunk right now.

He glances nervously at the boom mic, then at Ted's sound recorder.

"I'm not insinuating anything," I say. "I'm just trying to establish the facts."

Whenever Axel's not speaking, I've been soaking up our surroundings. Later, I'll record a description of the interior of the cottage, with its rusty horse brasses on the wall, the table propped up with a warped telephone book that itself must be an antique, the gaps under the door where dry leaves keep blowing in from outside.

"The facts?" he repeats. "The facts are that I was contracted to appear on a television show, and it was a terrible television show. It did me no favours."

"But it was never broadcast," I say. "Hardly anybody even knows about it. There was no black mark on your CV."

Axel considers this. He shrugs.

"Unless there was another reason it 'did you no favours'," I suggest. I weigh up whether to say more, then add, "Axel, we know about the death of Lawrence Bunce, otherwise known as Doc Leaf."

"That's nothing to do with me."

But it is. It must be.

"Do you know why Doc Leaf would have taken part in rehearsals for *Escapism*?" I ask. "He was in the promo video, which was made before filming began."

Axel sighs. "Lawrence Bunce was an actor. A fake contestant. All Imogen was told he was chosen by Helm, and that his job was to rile people up, to create good TV. But he…"

"Went rogue?"

"Maybe he just lost control."

"What about the various accidents? Might he have lost control to the degree of causing them? If nothing else, we know he was carrying a knife."

Suddenly, Axel stands up, knocking his plate onto the stone floor. Gnawed stale crusts scatter in all directions.

I sense Ted's posture stiffen, too. But I don't think Axel will do anything rash. For one thing, he surprised us by allowing us to record this conversation.

When Axel first led us to the door of the cottage, I

321

noticed he was limping. Even now, his weight is all on his right leg.

"Were *you* involved in an accident, Axel?" I ask.

He lets out a hollow laugh. "Not on Red Cliffs Island. It was long before that. A car accident. My greatest shame."

He doesn't volunteer any more information, and I'm reluctant to ask. Getting him to open up about his distant past might be at the expense of learning anything new about *Escapism*.

So I say, "We're beginning to understand what happened during the week of filming on Red Cliffs."

"How it ruined what's left of my reputation."

"But Lawrence Bunce's death is recorded as suicide. Do you mean the confusion surrounding Dez Votel and Ben Parrish going missing?"

Axel just stares at me.

Finally, he shakes off his daze. "I was talking about my honorary role as executive producer of *Escapism*. I am partially liable for the failure of filming to be completed. What's this about missing contestants? I was told—"

I bite my tongue. Keep talking, Axel.

He does. "I was told the boat returned to the island and collected the remaining people, after most of us were taken to the mainland. Are you saying that didn't happen?"

"It seems not," I say. "But that doesn't necessarily mean anything bad happened to them."

I glance at Ted. He's frowning, watching Axel intently.

I go on, "Maybe Ben and Dez actually won the game show. Found the prize money and escaped in the rowing boat."

Axel sits down heavily. His face crumples. I'm tempted to describe his deflated appearance for the benefit of listeners of the podcast, but that would definitely interrupt his flow.

"Knull, knull, knull," he mutters.

When he looks up, he appears far older than before.

"Do you know what happened to them?" he asks.

The longer I look into those teary sad-puppy eyes, the more I'm convinced he doesn't have an inkling about any of it.

"We think one of them is dead," I say. "Maybe both."

Axel shakes his head slowly. "The rowing boat was missing, on the morning we all left the island..." He shakes his head again, more decisively. "No. No. It cannot be." But it's not a real denial. His tone is pleading.

His head snaps up. "Do you have proof somebody died?"

I reach for my phone, which has the photos of the human bones in the wreckage of the barn. But my phone isn't in my pocket. I must have left it on the dashboard of the car.

I'm an idiot. I don't dare pause the interview now, just as Axel's beginning to open up.

I turn to Ted. "Can you get my phone from the car? Won't take you a moment."

Ted looks warily at Axel, then nods and leaves.

Ted's sound recorder is perched on the sofa. Shouldn't there be a light flashing, to show it's recording?

My heart races. Either Ted turned off the recording just now, when he stood up to leave... or he hasn't been capturing any of this conversation at all.

Maybe he doesn't want a trail of evidence.

I can't reach over and fiddle with the controls of the sound recorder now. It'd draw Axel's attention to it, and he might easily change his mind about going on record, now that it's clear we're discussing a murder.

But – yes, of course! I'd forgotten about the handheld sound recorder in my jacket pocket.

I perform a pantomime of a yawn, stretching my arms.

I slip one hand into my inside pocket and set the handheld device recording.

Something's nagging at the back of my mind. It takes me a moment to pin it down. Axel said the rowing boat went missing, but he still seemed certain Ben and Dez didn't win the game the conventional way. And that can only be because…

"They didn't take the money, did they?" I say.

Axel's posture immediately becomes defensive. "I do not think so."

"And those NDAs the contestants were made to sign," I say, thinking aloud. "They came with big payments. Who was it who paid those bribes to the contestants? Kestrel, or Helmedia, or… the executive producer?"

With a sigh, Axel says, "Helmedia."

I look around at the shabby interior of the cottage. There goes one theory, then. For a moment I'd assumed Axel had paid for the NDAs out of the prize money.

Axel looks around too, as if seeing his home for the first time. He laughs, but there's no humour in it. He stands and begins to pace up and down, making the loose flagstones clack underfoot.

"Me, I was already ruined," he says. "I was relying upon my payment for Escapism, and the wealth that would have come with fame in the UK. Helm knew this. He knew about my many debts."

"Then you're hiding here from the people you owe money to?"

"In a sense."

The first thing Axel said to me when I arrived was that he'd been reassured I wasn't from Helmedia.

Quietly, I say, "No. You paid off your debts. And now you're hiding from the people you stole money from in order to pay the loans back."

I yelp as Axel stamps his foot, making the flagstone

under his feet rattle. He stamps again, pressing more forcefully on one corner of the stone. Then he reaches down to prise it away entirely. He sticks his hand into the hole and pulls out a sheaf of notes. Cash.

It's not much, though. Even if the notes are twenties, there's only a few hundred quid there. If that's all that's left after he repaid his loan, he's in serious trouble.

"I took the money from the safe," Axel says. "I told myself that it was mine already, that I was supposed to be a winner of the show."

He drops backwards to sit on the cold floor. He couldn't look more like a scolded child if he tried.

I'm experiencing a mixture of emotions right now. Triumph, because this is new information, and it'll make for a twist in an episode of the podcast. Disappointment, because it looks like Axel really doesn't know anything about what happened to Dez and Ben. And confusion, because...

"Axel," I say slowly. "Why are you even telling me all this?"

Axel glances at Ted's sound recorder, obviously unaware that it's not turned on and I'm now capturing this conversation on my little handheld device. He sighs. "Because I have nothing left. Because before long—"

He's interrupted by a choking, growling sound from outside. It takes me a second to identify it as the engine of Ted's knackered old Volvo.

Axel and I look at each other in confusion.

I jump up and lurch to the door. Axel does too, his limp making him almost as slow as me.

When I burst out of the cottage, the only thing I can see is a cloud of exhaust fumes hanging in the cold night air.

Ted's gone.

325

Six months earlier

Aura

In response to the sound of hammering fists on the door, I pull the sheets around my naked body. I hear raised voices, but I can't make out the words. They sound ghostly because of the wind that's been picking up in volume throughout the evening, making everything I've done here in the groundskeeper's cottage seem both dramatic and somehow doomed.

"Don't answer it," I say.

"I've no intention of doing that," Axel says wearily. He throws his legs over the side of the bed, revealing the old scar tissue I've seen before. He reaches for his hip flask and takes a swig. During our sex, his breath reeked of alcohol, and eventually I stopped letting him kiss me. It made the whole thing even less tender than it was already.

The banging continues. So does the moan of the wind and so do the shouted voices. Lots of them.

"I guess it's all over," I say.

Axel only grunts.

I can't really understand how I ended up back here in the cottage. Probably, my subconscious just assumed I'd seduce Axel again. That I'd fall into bad habits. Finding the pistol in the safe was the clincher, I suppose. The gun was the only reason I had to fear Axel, and now it's safely in Ben's possession.

It's crazy to think that as recently as this morning I'd imagined that my seduction of Axel would be a way to become famous. But filming has stopped now, and Axel won't conquer the UK primetime media after all. Nobody will care that I've slept with an old Swedish guy. On the other hand, I'd hoped I might get away with it without further embarrassment.

The hammering carries on. They're not giving up.

I let out an undignified squeal as the door slams open and people stream into the cottage. The gaggle of contestants look around at the unfamiliar space. The second somebody looks into the adjoining room and spots me and Axel in bed, they're *all* looking.

My heart's in my mouth. It's just like the school disco with Mr Berry, all over again –complete with Sasha bloody Shiel, her hand pressed on her mouth in shock.

What will my mum say when she hears about this? Because there's no chance she won't hear about this.

I was right when I said it was all over.

I'll never leave the village again. I may be an adult now, but I have no formal skills, so any means of escape relies on my parents backing me financially. And they won't, of course. I'll be working in the farm shop for the rest of my life, with a smile pasted onto my face even as red-faced retired farmers peer down my top.

Everyone's shouting. Mostly, they're shouting at me.

Seriously, is my behaviour really the most alarming thing that's happened recently?

"Hey Axel, we want a word with you!" Victor says. "Is it true that we won't get paid if the show isn't completed?"

Axel replies, "You should ask Imogen, the director."

"She's locked in the staff-only area!" Ruth says.

Axel nods slowly. He mumbles, "Then speak to Helm, if you can find him."

When the shouting begins again, Axel holds up both his hands and says in a louder voice, "I cannot help you! My executive producer title is purely honorary. I have no knowledge of the workings of this production. And I can assure you that I'm as horrified as you are at what's been happening. The Swedish version of Escapism was professionally operated and was a great success. This..." He makes a sweeping gesture of an arm as if to indicate the whole island. "This has been hell on earth."

After that, he falls silent, ignoring the shouts. Victor and Cécile have switched from questions to insults. It's becoming clear that what the contestants really want is a punchbag. They don't really expect Axel to know anything. He's just the talent, the frontman.

I don't know why, but I feel protective towards Axel. There's a hint of nobility in his posture, despite the fact he's only wearing his boxer shorts, revealing his saggy pecs as he faces the horde.

There are people here who are far more deserving of people's anger.

I yank the entire bedsheet free and pull it tight around me. Then I get out of the bed and approach Doc Leaf, who's been hiding amongst the mass of people.

"Has anybody figured out what *his* game is?" I shout.

Everybody turns to look at me.

"There's something really weird about Doc Leaf," I say. "We've all noticed it. It's time to have it out."

I could hug Ben when he adds, "Yeah, I saw Doc Leaf with Imogen, in the locked area for production staff. She called him Lawrence Bunce. And he's an actor, put here by this producer guy, Helm, just to rile everyone up."

Gasps come from all around. I swear, to some of these people this whole thing is basically a soap opera.

Doc Leaf seems more alert than usual. But not alert enough to stop me from shoving my hand into the pocket of his ugly fleece, then pulling out the phone I saw him using after the maze task.

"Why's he got his phone back already?" someone

shouts. "Imogen said we'd get them in the morning!"

"He's had his phone this whole time!" I reply.

Doc Leaf's hand snaps out to grab the phone, but he misses and then tries again. I palm the phone and slip it to Dez.

Its screen lights up.

Doc Leaf manages to grab the phone finally, but not before Dez and I have read the text message that's popped up on its screen. The sender is Imogen Dorrien-Stewart, and the message reads:

I need to speak to you NOW.

Ben

I can't handle this any more.

I bailed early this evening. After Doc Leaf fled from the groundskeeper's cottage, some of the contestants followed, but they soon lost him. Given that he has access to the locked areas of the mansion, they didn't stand a chance. After that, the contestants gave up roaming the grounds in a halfhearted witch hunt, partly because the wind was getting even stronger and icy cold. Their only ambition seemed to be to drink the mansion dry. Most of them were blind drunk before dusk fell.

I retreated to my room. At first I tried reading one of my books on game theory, but I ended up tossing it to one side. What's the point, now? There'll be no more games here on Red Cliffs. At least, if there *are* games, I can't even begin to figure out the rules.

I managed to sleep, for a bit, despite the wind rattling the windows.

I woke just after 3 AM, coated in sweat. Another bad dream. Carla was in it, and the girls. I wish I could believe that when I leave this island, I'll see them all. But instead I'll just trek back to my flat and be as alone as I am right now.

The bird of prey in the glass case leers at me. I imagine it's laughing. Ben Parrish, chucked out by his parents as a toddler, then chucked out by his wife and kids as an adult. Ha bloody ha.

"Shut up," I mutter.

I find myself fully dressed and sitting on the floor beside my bed, spinning the pistol we found in the safe. I make bets against myself: will the barrel come to rest pointing at me, or not? I suppose it's a game of sorts.

It's a good thing there's no ammunition in the gun. I'm depressed enough that it'd be a temptation.

Is that true, or am I just being maudlin because I'm worn out?

I tell myself I'm not suicidal. When I get home, I'll find a new game to play, a different group to play it with, and that'll keep me occupied for a while. You can fill a life like that, more or less.

The howl of the wind has become almost soothing. When I hear a jarring sound from the corridor outside my room, my head jerks up in surprise.

It's almost 4 AM. Who could be prowling around at this time of the night?

I'm on my feet before I know it. It's only when I'm outside my room that I realise I'm still holding the gun. It's comforting, even though it's useless. I'm keeping it for now.

The door to Doc Leaf's room is wide open. I peer inside. The lights are on but nobody's home.

I head along the corridor. Halfway down the staircase, I hear the sharp click of a door opening, then the whistle of wind. It stops as the front door closes again.

If anyone deserves a scare, it's Doc Leaf. He's the one who's been laughing at us all, this whole time. And worse still, he hasn't been playing by the rules.

So outside I go, gun in hand.

The air outside is bitingly cold, and the wind knifes through my thick fleece. It's black dark.

I listen. I hear a sound to my right. I slip along the side of the building.

Moonlight illuminates the area between the main building and the groundkeeper's cottage. I wonder if Aura's decided to stay in there, now that we all know she's been sleeping with Axel. Nobody has anything to lose now that the cameras have stopped recording.

I see the silhouette of someone standing beside the cottage. Short. It must be Doc Leaf.

Is he about to go into the cottage? As executive producer, it would make sense that Axel knew all along that Doc Leaf was an actor.

But then the silhouette moves past the cottage.

I follow slowly, keeping my distance.

By the time I reach the cottage, I can't see Doc Leaf anywhere.

But there's nowhere for him to hide either, is there? The only thing out here is the barn where we did the maze task.

I should call it a night. Finding out the truth about Doc Leaf led me to believe there's mystery in progress, and I could be the one to solve it. But once again, I was wrong.

But I find I'm still moving towards the barn. On instinct, I raise the heavy pistol as I walk. I'm grimacing, partly because of the sting of the wind, partly because it's the expression I imagine someone having as they track somebody with their pistol drawn.

The double doors of the barn are closed. I pull at one of them, and it rattles, but it's too heavy for me to open with one hand. There's no padlock. I'll be able to open it if I use enough force.

I try to slip the gun into my belt, but then I realise my jeans are elasticated and don't have a belt. I don't fancy tucking the gun in, pointing the barrel at my genitals, even if it can't actually be fired.

So I put the pistol down on a flat stone beside the barn doors.

I put all my effort into opening the right-hand door. As I'm doing it, I remember that Doc Leaf's shorter than I am, and probably no stronger than I am. Why have I assumed he's gone into the barn?

Things move too fast for me to dwell on that thought.

The barn door swings open, wrenching my arms, and then it flaps madly in the wind.

Amid deafening slaps as the door hits the flat stone, I hear another sound. A distinctive series of clicks that remind me of action films, for some reason.

I look down at the flat stone.

No pistol.

Smack. Smack. The door keeps hitting the stone. Perhaps the gun was just knocked onto the grass?

But I know that's not right.

Because I've registered what that series of clicking sounds was. A sound effect from a million mindless Hollywood blockbusters. A chamber being opened, bullets being pressed into place. Then a gun being cocked.

I turn around. My eyes take a second to adjust.

All the air leaves my lungs.

I hold up my hands. Somewhere in the back of my mind is the realisation that I'm pleading for my life.

But then there's a sudden, shocking sound far louder than the barn door hitting the stone, perhaps the loudest sound I've ever heard in my life.

Then heat bursts from the centre of my chest.

Aura

I sit up sharply in bed, gasping for breath.

A loud cracking sound echoes from my dreams. Now I can only hear the moan of the wind outside.

The clock reads 4.20 AM.

I look at the window. The curtains are moving with the breeze. So are the wooden shutters. There must be so many air gaps in this old place that the wind has sneaked in and made the shutters rattle.

I calm my heart rate and try to settle myself.

But I can't sleep.

Dolly

The wind keeps screaming.

"I need you to calm down," I tell Axel in my firmest voice.

His eyes are staring wildly. I hadn't really taken stock of just how much he'd had to drink. Has he been drunk this whole time?

To think I once found him attractive.

"I have to get off this island," he mutters.

"And you will. In the morning. Right now, you need to sleep."

He stares at me. "Sleep? I can't sleep!"

Suddenly, I can't be bothered with this any more. Since when have I been Axel's PA, or his carer? He may be the 'talent', but filming has been abandoned. There is no *Escapism*. Which means I'm no longer being paid for my time here. I'm no longer on the clock.

"Don't sleep, then," I say wearily. "Just stay in your cottage and then slink away when the time comes."

As I back away, his hands grasp after me.

Once upon a time, I wanted those hands on my body.

Tonight, not so much.

Six months later

Rhea

I've been ignoring Axel as he drinks himself into oblivion beside the fire. Instead I'm worrying about Ted.

Ted, who speaks Swedish, and who drives a Swedish car, and who pretends to have friends in the police force, and who abruptly quit the TV industry within the last six months, and who's been behaving really oddly, and who abandoned me here.

It's only now it's occurred to me to ask myself *why*.

"Oh shit," I say aloud.

Axel looks up groggily.

"Axel, have you ever actually spoken to Helm?" I ask.

"Not exactly."

"What does that mean? You must have dealt with him in Sweden."

He shrugs. "He was only an investor back then, not a producer."

"Did you ever speak to him on video call? Phone call? What was his voice like?"

"We emailed. Always emails."

When I don't speak for a few seconds, Axel takes another gulp of whiskey. Then his head lolls.

I stare at the fire. I'm certain I've cracked it.

Ted.

Ted is Helm.

It's the only answer that makes sense.

Ted was Helm all along.

He created *Escapism*, back when he still worked in the industry, before he became a lecturer in Leeds. Maybe he was on the island, maybe not. But he was ultimately responsible for the failure to complete filming. The accidents. The disappearances. The death of the actor he himself hired, Lawrence Bunce.

And he sent me the videos which made me start this investigation.

Ted is Helm is INSIDER.

The only reason I can think of is that he counted on me being a shoddy journalist. Why else would the videos be sent to a podcaster with no track record and no discipline?

He's been using me this whole time, with the aim of shifting blame for Escapism from him and onto someone else. It probably didn't even matter who I concluded was responsible for the death of Lawrence Bunce, and maybe the deaths of Ben Parrish and Dez Votel too. All that mattered was that anyone but him was blamed.

Dez

I feel like Batman, striding around in the dark, my jacket billowing out behind me like a cape.

I left my suitcase in the lobby before I went down to the shore, to the jetty. I'd hoped the boat would already be there. No such luck.

I tell myself I'm not weird just because I'm outside at 4.30 AM. I was like a caged animal inside my bedroom. Walking helps me think. And it's way weirder that other people are somehow managing to sleep through this storm.

Or at least some of them are.

There's somebody standing on the edge of the cliff in front of the mansion. I hesitate, then head in that direction.

It's Doc Leaf. Or rather... what did Ben call him? Lawrence Bunce. I can't decide which name sounds more ridiculous.

He's just staring out to sea. When he turns to look at me, he shows no surprise at all. His smile is wry. He's like an entirely different person to the idiot we've all come to know. And of course, that's the truth of it.

"What's up, Doc?" I say.

"Got things on my mind. You?"

"Same."

And it's true, I do have things on my mind. Thoughts of getting off this island, and what that actually means. I've learned nothing about myself on Red Cliffs Island. I've kept on with the same old mistakes. When I get on the mainland, my situation with Priya remains the same as always. That is, she'll have nothing to do with me. I stole from her, and if she let me back into her life, I'd do it again.

It's what I do. I steal bits of other people to fill the gaps

338

in me.

After all my years of hiding, I don't know how to allow myself to be found. To be seen.

"It must have been weird for you, experiencing everything from the outside," I say.

"I suppose that's true."

"I presume you wouldn't have been allowed to win."

A wry smile. "Certainly not."

"Was it fun, being Doc Leaf?"

He considers this for a while. "It was freeing."

"I should have known that nobody could be as repellent as that."

He chuckles. "I apologise for targeting you, Dez. You know what they say. I was just following orders."

"It hardly matters. I don't know what I was doing here in this human zoo, myself."

"Then your own role wasn't freeing?"

I'm tempted to retort that I wasn't playing a role. But I was. All of us have been, the whole time.

"Not a bit of it," I say.

I think of the game of hide and seek, which was the most alive I've felt while I've been on the island. Why is it that I acknowledged that I always loved hiding, since I was a child, and yet I've been telling myself to do the exact opposite? To get out there, present myself to the world. Not everyone has to do that. And people like me who aren't good at it... well, they end up stealing bits of other people's identities, trying to cobble together one for themself.

"Maybe I'll pick a different role next time," I say quietly.

When I reach out to pat him on the back, Doc Leaf doesn't respond.

339

Six months earlier

Aura

I look at the clock again. It's now 4.45 AM.

I feel wide awake.

I drop down from the bed. The cracking sound I heard seems to echo in my mind. What could have made such a loud noise? I imagine ships striking the coast, splintering. I shudder at the thought of being stranded on Red Cliffs even longer than I have been already.

I yank open the curtains, then open the shutters. My room's at the front of the building, but I can't see all the way down to the jetty, because of the slope that descends from the mansion. The courtyard is dimly visible, and beyond that an expanse of black rock – the cliffs that overhang the shore. Only its tip is picked out by the moonlight. On the other side of that black horizon is the sea.

At first I think the rock formations are more spindly than I'd noticed before. But then I realise that the two shapes I can make out aren't actually rocks.

It's two people, facing one another in conversation. From this distance, there's no way of telling who they are.

When one of them moves closer to the other, I wonder if it's Ruth and Victor. But I'd notice their size difference, and why would they meet up on the cliffs?

Anyway, the movement doesn't look like an embrace.

I squint, trying to make out what's happening.

The person who stepped forward backs away again.

It's like a magic trick.

The other figure has disappeared.

Six months later

Rhea

Dinner is more toast. Axel roasted the squirrel over the fire, then offered some of the meat to me. I told him I was vegetarian, even though I'm not. I just don't eat rodents.

As he sits chewing flesh, he seems calmer. His eyes glaze as he talks about hunting and trapping in Sweden during his childhood. When I ask whether he still has family there, he stops and puts the squirrel carcass onto the saucer he's been using to catch the drips of fat.

"Not any more," he says in a thick voice. "My mother... she died suddenly, last year, in her rest home. I didn't know she was so ill."

He turns to the fire, taking sips from a hip flask.

When there's a knock at the door, he barely seems to notice it.

Seriously, Axel? You're really going to make me answer the door? Even though it's probably Ted, determined to finish me off?

I glare at Axel's back. He doesn't move.

So I go and open the door.

"Huh?" I say. I actually say that. *Huh?* Like in a cartoon.

Because it's not Ted.

It's Dolly.

"Same to you," Dolly says breathlessly. She cranes her neck to look past me, then mouths the words, "Is he in there?"

"Ted's done a bunk," I say. "And... I'm pretty sure he's actually Helm, your mysterious producer."

She blinks rapidly, processing this. Then she puts her hands on her hips and leans forward, getting her breath back. "Fuck. But he's gone, right? That's good. Isn't it?"

"Except I don't know where he is now." I point over her shoulder, at the dark forest. "He could be out there somewhere."

"Ah, okay. Out here, where I am. Any chance I could, you know, come inside?"

I stand back, still confused that she's here at all.

Dolly reads my thoughts. "I set off like five seconds after you sent your text. It's not an easy matter getting here, you know. There's no direct train to Nowhere-in-the-New-Forest. And I've spent a pretty penny too."

Once she's properly inside the cottage, she notices Axel sitting by the fire. "Oh. Hiya, Mr Griffin."

Axel turns sluggishly to look at her. He's drunker than I realised. He blinks slowly as if his eyelids are heavy. There's meat juice in his grey beard.

"I don't know if you remember me," Dolly says to him. "I was the production assistant on—"

His laugh becomes a sort of choked cough. He stares at her for a few seconds before saying in a croaky voice, "I remember you."

Dolly nods uncertainly. After I close the door, she and I both look at it, then at each other. Somehow, the situation seems more dangerous now than when it was just me.

"Thanks for coming," I say.

Dolly grins. "I'm never one to miss a party."

Axel grunts and returns to watching the fire.

Dolly flops onto the saggy sofa, then notices Ted's recording equipment. She gestures at it and mouths, "Get anything good?"

I shrug. I still don't know whether Ted actually recorded anything at all before he left.

Dolly picks up the bulky device, fiddling with its controls.

343

Six months earlier

Dez

I stride away from where I left Doc Leaf, continuing my rounds.

But the island is tiny, of course, so I shouldn't be as surprised as I am when I realise I've reached its southern tip. I've ended up facing the mansion and the barn again.

Something about the barn catches my eye. Movement. One of its doors is flapping open.

As I head towards it, the wind keeps pushing me off to the left, to the west, as if it doesn't want me to go that way.

Why do I feel so anxious all of a sudden?

I resort to my old tic. I pull Priya's lighter from my pocket, and thumb the spark wheel, and it produces a flame. I keep forgetting that since Doc Leaf filled it with lighter fluid yesterday, I've been carrying a contraband item. Not that it matters now.

I keep flicking the spark wheel of the lighter as I peer at the flapping door of the barn.

The wind dies down suddenly, and for a moment the stillness feels like death.

DAY 5

Aura

When I finally make it downstairs, I'm greeted by what my mum would call pandemonium. Everybody's stumbling over the luggage that they've stupidly left in the middle of the hall, and banging into each other like wound-up clockwork toys. I know it's only 5.30 AM, but it's a ridiculous caricature of people who are up too early and haven't been fed coffee.

Cécile hurries down the stairs, pushing past me, and addresses the contestants in the lobby.

"Has anyone seen Dez, or Ben, or Doc Leaf?" she demands.

There are a few head shakes. Nobody seems to care about anyone else at this point.

"The doors to all their rooms are open," Cécile says to me. "All their luggage is still in their bedrooms. Where can they have gone?"

The mayhem in the lobby continues until Sasha takes charge. She hurries everyone out of the building efficiently, marshalling them like a military commander. They trundle their luggage out of the door in turn.

Making my way down the rocky slope to the shore is no problem at all, now that I'm wearing comfy trainers. There's no reason to dress up any more.

I'm ahead of the pack. Which means I'm the first to realise our hurry has been for nothing.

"Where's the boat?" I say.

The jetty's empty. In fact—

"Where's the *other* boat?" Victor shouts.

The only trace of the rowing boat is a rope coiled at the end of the jetty.

"If the rowing boat is missing…" Ruth says, cottoning on as slowly as ever, "does that mean somebody's actually won the game?"

My whole body goes cold. It can only be Ben and Dez. During the night, they must have figured out where the prize money was really hidden. The gun in the safe must have been part of the puzzle, somehow.

Some alliance that turned out to be. They must have calculated that I'd be weak enough to return to Axel. Then they worked together, found the money, then sneaked away in the rowing boat.

I stare unfocused at the empty jetty. No prize, and still no escape.

Then I snap out of it.

There's a dark shape on the jetty. It looks like a heap of clothes.

Did Ben and Dez strip off before they left?

I move away from the pack of contestants to approach it.

I already know what it is.

I replay the vision I saw last night from my bedroom window. It has the quality of a dream, but I know I didn't imagine it.

Two people standing on the cliff above the shore. Then one of them reaching forward. And the other disappearing.

I stand before the heap. I crouch beside it.

I stare into the lifeless eyes of Doc Leaf.

Six months later

Rhea

I'll be honest, it doesn't feel great, the idea of sleeping at Axel's house. But it's night, and the opportunity to venture out and search for a B&B has been and gone. Anyway, Dolly's here with me now, and that gives me strength. We'll huddle up on the saggy sofa together, for warmth and safety.

As soon as we can get rid of Axel, that is.

He's been drinking all evening, taking slugs from his hip flask when he thought we weren't looking, then retreating to the kitchen and clanking around clumsily to refill it. He's barely spoken. But I don't like the way he's been looking at me. Even more, I don't like the way he's been looking at Dolly.

Me and Dolly have been talking in quiet voices while Axel's stared into the fire. She's told me all about her aggravating housemates, her ambitions to work on a genuinely good TV programme one day, or even better, to direct one herself. She's told me how much she hated her parents, who were cruel and abusive, and how conflicted she feels that she was delighted when they died in a car crash when she was a teenager.

In turn, I've spilled out my life story, warts and all. Dolly lapped up all the details about my childhood, the foster kids who paraded through my house and who, at times, made me feel unsure about my status in my own family. And my injury, the treatments I've been enduring my whole life, all the things my condition has stopped me doing. Her lip trembled throughout my sob story. She's a kind soul.

And I need kindness right now. My head's been hurting more and more all evening. The smoke of the fire has made the air thick, but Axel refuses to douse it, and it's too cold to go outside or even open a window.

"But you're really *doing* something," Dolly says encouragingly. "You're making this podcast, and it'll be a hit, and it'll catapult you to great things."

I laugh bitterly. "You think? There's a good reason I haven't put out the first episode yet. It's all speculation. No real facts."

"But that's what it's *for*. Your job is to sift through the evidence. To sort the truth from the lies."

We both squeak as Axel lurches up from his little tree-trunk stool before the fire.

"Lies," he repeats. "So many lies."

I honestly didn't think he was listening to our conversation. He seemed in his own world, just him and his whiskey.

"What lies, Axel?" I say. It occurs to me that the sound recorder in my jacket pocket must still be recording. It'll be muffled, but there might be something usable.

I open my jacket in anticipation as Axel begins to speak. But it sounds garbled, and I can't make out the words. Then I realise the problem. He's speaking in Swedish.

A thought flits through my mind: where's Ted when you need him? But no, having him here wouldn't be a good thing.

Axel's eyes roll. Now that he's on his feet, he seems to be struggling to stay conscious.

"He's making no sense," Dolly whispers. "We should get him up to bed."

She gets up from the sofa. Axel flinches away from her, then reaches out to the mantelpiece for support, and misses. He sways wildly, trying to stay upright.

He's still speaking in Swedish. The only things I can make out are names. Doc Leaf. Lawrence Bunce. Helm.

"Alright mister," Dolly says as she gets up from the sofa. "I think it's teeth-brushing and bed for you."

"Wait!" I say. "Axel. Are you saying what I think you're saying?"

Axel's face contorts. It's as if he forcing his mind to recalibrate to English.

Simpler, Rhea.

"Are you saying that Doc Leaf – Lawrence Bunce – was Helm?"

An idiotic grin spreads across Axel's face. "You win!" He performs a clumsy dance – an echo of one of his past performances as a TV host, perhaps. "A key for the winner! A key and two hundred and fifty thousand pounds, plus my career and my dignity!"

Doc Leaf.

Not Ted.

I've got it all wrong.

"But why?" I say, hardly noticing I'm speaking aloud.

"Because he was rich, and bored, and a junkie, and a…" Axel pauses, concentrating on his pronunciation. To be honest, I'm amazed he's found the power of speech at all. "He was a *nihilist*. He was nothing to do with *Eskapism*, in Sweden. He was just an investor who got lucky. But he took the credit and then decided to run the UK version himself. He designed the whole thing and then he decided to put himself in the middle of it, to watch. Even Imogen didn't know who he was. She thought he was an actor installed as a contestant by Helm."

"Did he ever believe it would be broadcast? It was so shoddily designed that it's hard to believe it would ever

350

have been completed and broadcast."

My eyes flick to Dolly. I wonder if she's offended by that comment. She tried her best in impossible circumstances. But she doesn't react at all. She's just staring up at Axel, still gripping his arm.

Axel sways silently for several seconds.

"You're right," he says. "Helm built a toy, and he stuck around to watch people play with it. And he was the only one with access to the footage, for him to gloat over later." He slaps his forehead in a caricature of dismay. "There was no fucking TV show. I lost my career for nothing. Literally nothing." His eyes glaze over and his head hangs.

So Helm was a rich kid playing God. Too much money, and a messed-up idea of what constitutes entertainment.

But solving the mystery of who was behind *Escapism* doesn't explain how I came to be involved in this whole thing. If Lawrence Bunce was Helm, then Helm is dead.

I'm about to ask Axel another question when Dolly yelps and lunges after him as he drops to the floor, narrowly missing striking his head on the hearth.

Six months earlier

Aura

Eventually, Lonnie – the member of the production team with bad tattoos who we last saw putting people in straitjackets in the third task – lumbers down to the jetty carrying a tarpaulin. He mutters some words over the body of Doc Leaf before covering it, and then he stands guard beside it, completely motionless like an overweight Beefeater at Buckingham Palace.

I look up at the cliff above the shore. The angles are all wrong. I can't be sure where Doc Leaf was standing when I saw him fall, during the night. But there's no possible position that would end up with him lying spreadeagled on the jetty.

It's too much to process. My head hurts. Even though I now know that Doc Leaf was an actor named Lawrence Bunce, I can't help but think of his behaviour over the last few days – not just his drunkenness, which could have been a sham, but he *did* steal Ben's EpiPen, for example – and a voice in the back of my head whispers: *He had it coming to him.*

The contestants soon tire of watching Lonnie, and the volume of conversation rises again. Most of them aren't even talking about Doc Leaf. They all have the same mindset now. Getting off the island is the top priority.

I move away from the group and sit on my suitcase, not caring whether I'm ruining the outfits inside it. When I get back to the village, I'll have no use for them any more. I'll be wearing Arran jumpers and leggings and wellies for the rest of my life.

I feel more trapped than I've ever been. I never really had a shot at becoming a TV personality. *Escapism* was as cursed as I've been my whole life.

When Sasha strolls over to me, it's all I can do not to hiss at her.

She hasn't looked directly at me this morning. I wonder if she really is disappointed at my behaviour with Axel – or whether she's just biding her time, looking forward to blabbing to my mum.

"How are you?" she asks me. That's all.

I burst into tears.

"Amie... Oh, Amie," she says quietly. She spreads her arms, inviting me in for a hug.

I rub my eyes with the back of my arm. My nose is streaming with mucus.

I see myself lashing out at her again. The image in my mind is so vivid I believe I've actually done it.

But no. I'm just standing there, my whole body trembling with sobs. I need a hug more than anything. From anyone in the world except Sasha Shiel.

I stagger away, up the slope. To my relief, Sasha doesn't follow me.

"Are you unwell?" a voice says.

I hadn't realised Cécile was at the top of the slope, staring up the black face of the mansion. The wind's died down, and the sun's trying to come out from behind the clouds, shining directly behind her head. It makes her look like an angel.

She really is beautiful. And it's actual beauty, not a triumph of makeup and fast fashion, like me.

"Fuck this place, huh?" she says. Her pretty French accent makes even her swearing sound sophisticated.

"Yeah," I say in a thick voice.

Without knowing I'm about to do it, I throw myself at

353

her, squeezing her in a bear hug. Her bones are as thin as a bird's.

I feel her twist in my arms. Is she trying to get away?

When I back off, I realise that she's been trying to look behind her. Not at the mansion, exactly, but above it. Grey smoke is rising to meet the grey cloud. A fire.

Cécile looks at me with one eyebrow raised.

We abandon our luggage and start running.

*

The barn is burning.

Like, *really* burning.

We keep heading towards it, for some reason. There's something magical about the sun penetrating the clouds and making slanting god rays, and the air that's suddenly still, and us being out of bed so early. I have the strange idea we're taking part in some sort of pagan solstice tradition.

It's the rear of the barn that's blazing most furiously, and in places the roof has already fallen in. The front of the building is still more or less intact, though it's clear it'll be swallowed by the fire soon enough. The inferno is making horrible deep belching noises. I imagine the fire eating its way through the toppled walls of the maze.

Me and Cécile just stand and stare, like we're hypnotised.

I think I know who did this. When we were in the study together, I saw that Dez has a lighter. But I've no idea why they'd want to burn a barn. Maybe it's just a different sort of expression of anger and frustration.

That idea leads to another one, a worse one. Now I'm thinking of what I saw during the night. The person who disappeared was obviously Doc Leaf, pushed from the cliff to his death. The other person – his murderer – was around the same height as him.

Dez killed Doc Leaf.

I don't know how much time has passed before Cécile says, "What is that?"

She's pointing at one of the barn doors. It's only now that I notice the dark stain on it. Whenever the fire flickers, the stain glistens.

I hang back as Cécile walks towards the barn.

When she reaches the door, she reaches out her right hand. Then she stands very still for a few moments. I watch her tiny silhouette against the orange of the fire.

Get away from there, I think, but I don't manage to say it out loud.

Finally, Cécile turns around.

She holds out her hand. It's dark now, and dripping with something sticky.

Blood.

As she makes her way back towards me, I see that one side of her face is covered with soot. I don't know what to say, so I just point at her face. Cécile frowns and touches her forehead, and in doing so she smears her face with blood.

She grimaces, realising her mistake.

It's only now that she begins to cry. Within seconds, she's totally breathless. It's as if she's been bottling up her emotions for so long that now she's finally letting them out, they're overwhelming.

"Fuck this place," she says again.

I can't take my eyes off the smear of blood on her forehead. "What shall we do?" I ask.

When Cécile speaks again, I'm impressed at how hard and steady her voice is. "I'm going back in there." She points at the mansion. "I am going to give the director of *Escapism* a… What's the phrase?" She makes an impatient gesture with her hand, sending droplets of blood flying. "A piece of my mind."

A horrible image comes to my mind: Cécile's head collapsing like a burning building, then her reaching inside to pluck out a bloody part of her brain.

I hurry away to the jetty.

*

The boat is here, and it's full to bursting. It was only meant to carry half of the contestants at a time.

I scan the faces. There are still a handful of people missing. Cécile, of course. Imogen, the director. And Ben and Dez, those traitors. Murderous traitors, it seems. Could it really be the case that within a single night they found and stole the prize money, killed Doc Leaf, set a fire in the barn and then escaped the island?

Axel's on board, looking massively uncomfortable to be crammed in alongside ordinary people. And I see Dolly, the woman from behind the one-way glass in the study, who's glaring at Axel across the crowd of complaining contestants. Lonnie is still standing sentry beside the body of Doc Leaf under the tarpaulin, and the need to give the corpse space is making the conditions even more cramped.

I push my way over to stand beside Axel. As soon as he sees me, he backs away.

"It's too late to be coy," I say. "They all saw us in bed together, remember?" Then I wonder if he *can* remember, or if he was drunk enough to have wiped it from his memory.

"I know that," he whispers. "I know you're angry and ashamed. But you came to me, not the other way around. So why punish me?"

"What are you talking about?"

His eyes search my face. "Then it wasn't you?"

"*What* wasn't me?"

"Who tied me up. When I was… sleeping." His eyes dart, which I assume means he was actually blind drunk at the time.

He keeps examining my face, looking for a response. I guess I must look innocent enough, because he says, "I woke up this morning in a... a jacket."

"That doesn't sound like a punishment."

"No." He seems to be searching for the right word. "A *strait*jacket. One of the ones from the underwater task. I couldn't move my arms."

I don't know what to say to that. So I don't say anything.

My eyes drop down to look at something bulky nestled at Axel's feet. A sports holdall. Since when does somebody like Axel travel with a holdall?

When I reach down, Axel makes a sort of strangled sound. But he doesn't stop me as I pull at the zip of the bag.

Inside the bag is money. Cash. A *lot* of cash.

It means Ben and Dez didn't get the prize money after all. So there's that. I wonder where they are now, and what was so important that Doc Leaf had to die.

It doesn't really matter to me.

I draw myself up to my full height, glaring at Axel. He looks like a school kid expecting to be put on detention.

I think of Cécile, who's currently inside the mansion, hunting for Imogen. Trying to make somebody accountable for everything that's happened here.

I can do my bit, too.

Sure, I'm also thinking of the farm shop, and my imprisonment with my family. Perhaps I can escape the village, even if my dreams of starting again as a TV personality have been shot down.

I realise something else: I'm not going to tell the tabloids about my liaison with Axel. I've been there before. That's not how I'm going to effect my escape.

"You can't expect this whole thing to just go away," I say. I point at the money, then gesture at the huddle of contestants, then at the covered body of Doc Leaf. "That

357

money was supposed to be leaving the island in our hands, not yours."

Axel blinks. After several seconds, he nods.

"I'm the executive producer," he says. "I'll make sure everybody receives payments. Large payments. Okay?"

He's still staring at me. There's pleading in his eyes.

I realise what it means. He's not trying to con me about the payouts for contestants. But that money won't be coming from him directly.

"Helmedia will pay, won't they?" I say.

Axel gives the faintest of nods.

"And this isn't your money, it's theirs."

His eyes are glistening now. I remember that he told me about his debts. This is his means of escape from them.

"Please," Axel says in a choked voice. He reaches into the holdall and pulls out a roll of notes. His turns so that his back hides the roll from the other occupants of the boat, and offers it to me with shaking hands.

"Please," he says again.

I take the money. I suppose I ought to feel sick about receiving stolen cash, and extorting a man on the brink. But I don't. I shove the roll of notes into the pocket of sweater, and that's that.

I turn to see Cécile arrive and board the boat. To my surprise, her face is scrubbed clean. Then Imogen jogs down the slope after her. In one hand she's carrying a small travel suitcase, and in the other the black canvas bag that contains all our phones. A few contestants whoop at the sight of it.

Imogen pauses on the jetty for a moment, hands on hips, staring at the loose rope that was once tied to the missing rowing boat.

"Let's get going," she says to the captain of the boat. When Dolly protests, she says, "If there's anyone else on the island, we'll come back for them. I promise."

358

Dez

I'm crouched in an awkward position, holding both sides of the rowing boat, the oars across my knees. The wake from the supply boat has produced bigger waves that keep bumping the rowing boat against the rocks of the cliff, but I'm pretty sure it won't be audible over the chug of the engine.

Plenty of the contestants are standing at the rails of the boat, looking out to sea. But they're either staring at the mainland, or up at the mansion. As a psychologist, I suppose the direction they're facing could tell you a lot about each of their outlooks.

Nobody looks towards me, only a hundred metres away, hugging the shoreline of the island behind an outcrop.

I don't know if I did the right thing.

After I loosened the ropes to free the rowing boat, I set off to the south. On my walk around the periphery of the island in the early hours of the morning I'd noticed the outcrops and proved to myself I could hide out easily rather than risk being spotted if I headed out before the supply boat.

I'd only rowed a handful of strokes when I saw the bundle of clothes on the shore.

I steered to the shore.

Is it bad that I wasn't surprised to find it was Doc Leaf, and that he wasn't breathing? Events on Red Cliffs Island have become so surreal, it just seemed to fit. The last I saw him, he was looking out to sea from the clifftop. I was so wrapped up in my own thoughts that I didn't consider that he's been on a journey of his own, these last few days. The fact that I don't know anything about Lawrence Bunce means I have no insight at all into whether he might have been suicidal.

I could have left him on the shore below the cliff. But if I had, he mightn't have been found at all. I'm not so callous to ignore a corpse.

I'd already touched his clothes, so I didn't concern myself about leaving fingerprints as I hauled him into the boat, then pushed back to the jetty and dragged him onto its wooden boards.

And that was that.

I'd already abandoned my possessions in my bedroom in the mansion. Plus the *other* collection of possessions, which were never mine. My hope is that somebody will recognise their missing stuff and restore it all to their rightful owners. Or perhaps they won't and it doesn't matter. Perhaps those objects aren't actually meaningful to the people I stole them from.

It was always about me. It was about the need to piece together an identity from other people's identities.

I'm tired of all that.

I know who I am. I'm the same person I've always been, deep down.

If anything, the threat of having Doc Leaf's death pinned on me is kind of useful. It means there can be no going back.

At the very least, everybody will know I'm a thief, and that I can't be trusted.

I'm going to have to use my famous skill of hiding. I'll be quiet and I'll take my time. I'll let myself be myself, rather than a patchwork of other people's characteristics.

The supply boat is tiny now. Before long it'll dock on the mainland, and the contestants and production staff will spill off it. They'll hover uncertainly because the spell will have been broken, because nothing physical will hold them together any more.

And my guess is that each person's instinct will tell them to get away, as fast as possible.

Me, I have all the time in the world. I know where I'm going. When the mood takes me, I'll pick up the oars, slide them into the water, make my way to a part of the mainland coast far from the supply boat.

At which point, I'll become somebody unrecognisable, simply by shedding all the act and by being myself. It's the only escape.

I reach into the pocket of my jeans and take out two objects. One stolen, one a gift.

Sure, I promised Priya I'd given up smoking. But I'll never see Priya again. And what I've been through this week would make anyone feel tense.

I wonder how Priya will react when she receives her lighter in the post after so long, sent anonymously. My guess is that she always knew I took it.

Fuck 'em, the lighter says.

The cigarette is bent but still usable. I salute the boat on the horizon and murmur, "Cheers, Doc."

Then I flick the spark wheel of the lighter.

Six months later

Rhea

The dreams are worse than usual. This time, the flailing bodies with spindly limbs are the contestants of *Escapism*. The faces of their Facebook and Twitter profiles are pasted onto the shadows, grinning as their arms flap madly in the wind.

I wake up retching.

The air in Axel's sitting room is still thick with smoke, even though the fire's died down to embers.

I sit up, then moan. My head's pounding.

At first I think the sound I can hear isn't real, that it's just my brain pulsing.

Then I realise it's coming from outside. Outside my head, and outside the cottage.

It's the chug of an engine.

A car.

Ted?

I look behind me. When we fell asleep, Dolly was the big spoon. Now she's gone.

Oh fuck oh fuck.

I roll off the sofa. My mind keeps rolling even after I drop to the floor.

My chest feels stiff. I reach up to unbutton my cardi, and find something flat tucked into the pocket, beside my handheld sound recorder. The flat object drops out. An envelope. Unmarked.

I feel like I'm still in a dream. I can't work out what

order to do things. My hands are shaking as I open the envelope.

It's written in Sharpie, in shaky capital letters. My vision swims as I try to read it.

I DID'NT KILL BEN PARISH.
BUT I AM ~~RESB~~ RESPONSBLE FOR MY ACTIONS.
SMITOLYCKA
IM SORRY

Axel wrote this. From the mistakes and the handwriting, he was almost paralytic at the time.

I can't think. The pain in my head and the constant chugging of the engine make it impossible to order my thoughts.

The engine.

It's not the wheezing sound of Ted's Volvo. It's much deeper than that.

Why has an engine been running this whole time?

Oh.

Oh no.

Bile rises in my throat as I throw open the door of the cottage. It's black dark outside, so my attention is caught immediately by the halo of light around the edges of the metal door of the outbuilding, which must actually be a garage. There's something odd about the light, too. It looks wispy, like tendrils. I realise that's because it's not just light that's leaking out. It's smoke too, or fumes.

The engine keeps chugging.

Finally, I realise what's happening.

I fumble with the handle of the garage door, then manage to wrench it. The door swings up on its creaky mechanism.

I splutter immediately as a cloud of fumes hits me. It's so dense I can't see a thing.

"Axel!" I shout. I wave my arms like crazy, trying to fan away the exhaust fumes.

It's already triggered one of my migraines. I think I might black out. I'm literally seeing stars.

All the same, I edge into the garage like a hero. Somehow, I manage to find the car, then its driver's-side door. When I pull it open, a body drops into my outstretched arms. I scream.

I still don't know if Axel's alive as I drag him out of the garage. And I don't know how I manage to drag his heavy bulk, either. I just do.

The engine's still chugging away, polluting the air.

I can't drag him any further than the concrete edge of the garage. I drop to my hands and knees. I take a second to let my brain catch up and unleash fresh waves of agony, then I start shaking Axel's body.

He groans. He's still alive.

Dimly, I realise somebody's standing in front of me. They look like one of the spindly figures I often see in my migraine visions. Their legs are lit by the light from inside the garage, but the exhaust fumes make it hazy, like in a club at the end of a Friday night.

It's Dolly.

She's not looking at me. She's not even looking at Axel.

She's looking into the garage, at the car.

"Is this the same car?" she says in a tone that sounds like… I don't know. Awe. "Did you keep it, all this time?"

Axel's too far gone to reply.

"What are you talking about?" I ask her.

When she doesn't answer, I turn to look into the garage too. The car's a big black 4x4, clearly expensive. The registration plate looks wrong. On the back window is an oval sticker with an S in it. It must be Swedish.

Why would that mean anything to Dolly?

Dolly drops to her haunches before me, with Axel's body between us. She reaches out and pushes him onto his back. She's stronger than I'd have thought.

Something's not right. I mean, *obviously*. This whole situation is insanely messed up. But there's something particularly not right about Dolly's behaviour right now.

She stares down at Axel, muttering something. Even though the words are audible, I can't understand them. And it's nothing to do with the shooting pain in my head.

There's an odd rise and fall to her words. I recognise the intonation, from the Scandi-noir shows I love so much. She's speaking in Swedish.

"Who *are* you?" I manage to say.

"Dolly."

I shake my head, then I wish I hadn't, because it makes everything blurry. "Not really, though. You and Axel know each other... from way back. You're..." I trail off, trying to remember the wording in Axel's note. "You're *Smitolycka*."

Her head jerks up. "What?"

"Axel wrote it in his suicide note."

She stares at me with wide eyes. Then she cackles with laughter.

"No," she says once she's composed herself. "I really am Dolly Nyman." After a pause, she adds, "Though of course Nyman is a Swedish surname, so you're on the right lines."

An odd detail comes to my mind, something that bothered me long ago, but only subconsciously. When Dolly mentioned a school trip to the Leeds medical museum, she said she returned home by plane. It was a slip, and I didn't catch it.

"Then who's Smitolycka?" I say stupidly.

"It's not a name," Dolly replies. "It means 'hit and run'. A car accident caused by a coward."

I lurch backwards in alarm as she leaps to her feet to kick Axel in the stomach, hard. Then she drops to her haunches again and strokes his face as he moans in pain.

"My love," she murmurs. "Min kärlek."

I know I should get up. I should get the hell away from here, even if I can't save Axel. But I can barely breathe, let alone move.

"The car crash," I say. "You're talking about the accident that killed your parents."

"It was fate," Dolly says dreamily, still stroking Axel's face. "He came from nowhere. Smitolycka. Hit and run. Axel's car – *that* car in there – hit my family's car. He killed my parents. He saved me."

My mouth's hanging open. Why is she grinning?

"I was in the car too," she says, "but I was spared." It's only now that she notices my amazed expression. "I told you I hated my parents. They were evil, Rhea. They wanted rid of me but they couldn't manage it. They made damn sure I understood how much they hated me."

I try to process it all. The flailing ghosts in my head won't stop screaming at me.

"I'm very sorry you had a bad childhood," I say. "And I'm sorry you lost your parents when you were so—"

"I was fourteen years old. My life after they were killed, it was what I wanted. The children's homes, the institutions… they were what I wanted, instead of living with my parents who beat me." She falls silent for a few seconds. "When I learned that this man was responsible, I worshipped him. I thanked Axel Griffin every night."

She's mad. But that knowledge doesn't help me a bit, right now.

"You make it sound like Axel meant to do it," I say. "But it was just an accident, an awful coincidence."

Dolly stops stroking Axel's face. Abruptly, she pinches the skin of his cheek, hard. He spasms but doesn't wake.

"You're right," she says. "I came to terms with that fact only recently. After believing for so long that Axel Griffin worked very hard to deliver me from evil, it was… upsetting. So I decided that I would be the one to bind us together."

My mind races. "You found a way to get yourself on the production team working on *Escapism*, so you could meet him face to face."

Dolly grins again. "More than that. I had to make sure Axel would be the host of the UK version in the first place. The anchor that kept him in Sweden had to be removed. His mother. She was perfectly well when I first began work at her care home. Then not so much, after I started serving her drinks."

So she's not just a lunatic. She's officially a murdering lunatic. Okay then.

"Anyway," Dolly goes on, as if we're just chatting about weekend activities, "I wanted to do more than meet Axel."

"You wanted to kill him?"

Dolly laughs. "That's a recent development, since he failed me."

"Then you…" I try to follow the breadcrumb trail of her story, insane as it is. "You wanted him to do something for you."

She nods enthusiastically. "I wanted him to perform the same service he did once before. Axel the avenging angel. But this time his actions would be deliberate, not coincidence. Only that could bind us together fully."

"You wanted him to kill for you."

"That's right."

"To kill the family you hated."

"Yes."

"But your parents were already dead."

Dolly shows her teeth. "Yes, but my brother wasn't. My

367

brother who escaped all that pain. My brother who my parents *did* get rid of, when he was tiny. My brother who lived a normal life, and who never once wondered if he'd left anyone behind to face our parents alone."

Ah.

Now I see.

"Ben Parrish," I say.

"Formerly known as Benedict Nyman. Yes. I arranged for him to be selected as a contestant on *Escapism*. Just a little nudge, a file inserted among other files. When I found out that he loved games, I decided to make his death a game too."

I try to shuffle away from her. But I'm too weak – and even if I could do it, I'd only end up trapped in a garage full of exhaust fumes. I slump to the ground again.

"Are you telling me you and Axel killed Ben together?" I say.

"I *wish*. Despite my encouragements, he chickened out." Dolly slaps Axel's face, producing no more than a murmur of complaint. "But when he failed me, I was still able to use Axel's pistol, rather than stabbing Ben as I'd planned. At least Axel and I have that small connection. We *are* bound together, after all."

There it is. A confession. I look around, half-expecting something to happen. Roll credits, please. But there's nothing. And Dolly's confession of murder doesn't seem nearly complete.

Despite everything, I still want answers.

"Are you telling me you arranged all that chaos on Red Cliffs Island," I say, "just to kill your brother?"

Dolly rocks back on her heels. "I'm not capable of quite so much as that, Rhea. The chaos was just a bonus, a handy smokescreen. I can't describe my glee when I saw how Helm, in his role as Doc Leaf, was behaving on that first day. That first inkling that the whole week was going to be an absolute mess. I played my part diligently, of course. The show had to go on... until I had a chance to kill Benedict, with Axel present."

"All those accidents..."

"Not all of them were my handiwork. Victor smashing the maze, that was unforeseen. And I had no particular desire to endanger other contestants. I'd arranged the teams for the underwater task, and I was certain Ben would end up in the cage with the tampered lock. He was surprisingly evasive at becoming a murder victim. In the hide and seek task, I guided him towards the cellar steps that I'd half sawn through using Lonnie's tools. I laced his crisps with peanut oil, too. But in the end I'm glad he was facing me as I killed him. Even if he never understood who I was. He didn't even recognise my name."

My brain literally aches. But still it's pulling at threads, trying to tie them together.

"What about Lawrence Bunce?" I say. "His death wasn't suicide, was it?"

Dolly shrugs. "Like I say, I enjoyed the chaos he provided. The whole show was for his entertainment alone – I knew the footage would never be broadcast. But it existed, and there was already a chance that it would implicate me if he ever shared it. And my attitude towards him hardened when I realised he'd rigged up way more cameras than he admitted to. Cameras in the bedrooms, in the production suite, in my cubbyhole in the study... everywhere. The moment I'd dealt with Ben and got cowardly Axel tucked up tight in his cottage, I had one job left. Helm had to die." She mimes stabbing the palm of her left hand with the index finger of her right. Then her 'stabbed' hand sails down and she splays her fingers: *splat*.

There it is, then. Mystery solved.

But instead of the madness on Red Cliffs, my thoughts keep coming back to something closer to home.

I think of Ted, abandoning me in his car.

Except he didn't.

He wouldn't.

"And you killed Ted too," I say tonelessly.

Dolly clucks her tongue, then checks her watch. "Yeah. I suppose he's probably dead by now. He'll have bled out."

She produces something from her pocket and examines it proudly. A gun.

The gun that killed Ben Parrish. And Ted Monhegan.

I suppose my lack of reaction might be a defensive measure. I won't survive this, and even if I did, the idea of a lifetime spent blaming myself for getting faithful, idiotic Ted killed isn't something I relish.

I'm still staring at the gun. My mind's still reeling, still latching onto the wrong details.

"Why me?" I say.

Dolly grins. "I suppose you should know. You should know that you're not the hotshot journo. That you weren't picked because of your *potential*."

I stay silent. It's clear she can't wait to tell me.

"I needed to locate Axel, and I couldn't risk being noticed. So I needed to set someone else on the case, someone to use as a shield if the authorities were alerted."

That doesn't explain it, though. "Why *me*?"

Dolly waves the gun. "There were just a few loose ends. Trailing threads." She waves the blade, as if snipping the imaginary threads. "Axel had to be shut up for good, of course. And after we're done here, I'll need to pay your parents a visit."

What?

"My… parents?" I say in a hoarse voice.

"Your angelic parents, who took in a confused young boy who'd bounced from home to home, and gave him a fresh start after a bad beginning. The same beginning I had."

370

My body goes cold all over.

"My parents fostered Ben Parrish?" I say. I will an image of his younger face to come to mind, but instead there's the usual fog that clouds all my childhood memories. All the same, I believe Dolly. One of the parade of foster children in our household might easily have been Ben, and I'd have known nothing about it.

I laugh. It sounds pretty weird. My vision's all blurry. I wonder if my brain has been permanently damaged by the exhaust fumes still pumping out around me. Not that it matters.

I've always been a straight shooter. So I just come out and say it.

"You're going to kill me, aren't you?"

"Yes. And your parents too. I'd have done them first, but I didn't want to put you off your investigation."

I refuse to let an image of my parents come into my mind. Saving them means saving myself first.

"How will you do it?" I say. "A gun wound's going to look suspicious."

She gestures with her thumb at the garage. "Maybe chuck you in there, along with my true love."

"People will think me and Axel made a suicide pact," I point out.

This makes her pause. The idea of connecting anybody else to Axel must be distasteful.

"True," she says thoughtfully. "Axel can go back in his car to choke to death. You'll be in the cottage. I'll burn it down. It'll make for a nice callback to Red Cliffs."

To think I once enjoyed her company. What does that say about my judgement of character? Despite my inability to get up off the floor and do a single thing to prevent my fate, it's my idiocy that's really pissing me off.

I tell myself to get a grip. This is the moment of your death, Rhea. Behave accordingly.

371

I manage to push myself up from the ground. I'm still kneeling, but it seems a more noble posture, somehow.

I look up at Dolly.

Then I smile.

It throws her off completely. She frowns in confusion.

Her being preoccupied with me means she doesn't see the figure lumbering behind her. She doesn't see the walking cane – *my* walking cane – raised above her head.

Even if he wasn't bleeding so freely from a gross-looking slash in his neck, I would never have thought Ted would have so much strength in him.

The cane comes down, hard.

And then so does Dolly. She lands on the concrete right next to Axel, so that they're facing each other in their upside-down positions like a human ying and yang, like she always wanted.

Ted drops to his knees, too. His head rises slowly.

"It's okay," he says in a croaky voice.

I nod.

"Yes, it's okay," I repeat.

I reach up to pat the pocket of my jacket, where my handheld sound recorder is tucked away.

I grin sleepily and say, "I reckon I got the whole thing."

Printed in Dunstable, United Kingdom